JOURNEY

THROUGH THE

MIRROR

Also by T.R. Williams

Journey into the Flame

www.satraya.com

JOURNEY
THROUGH THE
MIRROR

BOOK TWO OF THE
RISING WORLD TRILOGY

T. R. WILLIAMS

ATRIA PAPERBACK
NEW YORK   LONDON   TORONTO   SYDNEY   NEW DELHI

ATRIA PAPERBACK
A Division of Simon & Schuster, Inc.
1230 Avenue of the Americas
New York, NY 10020

First Atria Paperback edition December 2014

ATRIA PAPERBACK and colophon are trademarks of Simon & Schuster, Inc.

For information about special discounts for bulk purchases, please contact Simon & Schuster Special Sales at 1-866-506-1949 or business@simonandschuster.com.

The Simon & Schuster Speakers Bureau can bring authors to your live event. For more information or to book an event, contact the Simon & Schuster Speakers Bureau at 1-866-248-3049 or visit our website at www.simonspeakers.com.

Manufactured in the United States of America

10 9 8 7 6 5 4 3 2 1

Library of Congress Cataloging-in-Publication Data

Williams, T. R. (Tyler Ronald)
Journey through the mirror / T. R. Williams. — First Atria Paperback edition.
    pages cm. — (Rising world trilogy ; book 2)
1. End of the world—Fiction. 2. Survival—Fiction. 3. Rare books—Fiction.
4. Conspiracies—Fiction. 5. Quests (Expeditions)—Fiction. 6. Magic—Fiction. I. Title.
PS3623.I5646J685 2015
813'.6—dc23

                          2014023015

ISBN 978-1-4767-1341-0
ISBN 978-1-4767-1342-7 (ebook)

To the magnificent reflection we behold when we look into the mirror.

JOURNEY
THROUGH THE
MIRROR

PROLOGUE

Cassandra sat still in a red cedar tree as she waited for a rabbit or a mouse or any small animal to wander by. The food was running out, and her clan badly needed new provisions. No one had eaten meat in two weeks. Over the last twelve months, hunting had become more and more difficult. The Great Disruption of 2027 had forced most of the wildlife in the Ozark National Forest to migrate south for water and a more hospitable climate. What animals remained had largely perished from lack of water and the influx of people who had taken refuge in the forest, desperate for food.

Although the leafy branches of the trees provided some protection from the noon sun, it was a hot summer day, and Cassandra could feel the sweat on her brow. She reached into the satchel she wore looped over her shoulder and across her chest and pulled out a cloth to wipe her face. Then she froze, hearing the sound of cracking twigs.

"Do you hear that, Cassie?" a deep voice asked quietly from another branch, a few feet above Cassandra.

"Yes, RJ," Cassandra whispered back as she readied her rifle. This was what they'd been waiting for all morning. The sounds of crackling brush and breaking branches indicated something was approaching from the west. The noise was loud enough to suggest multiple targets and enough meat for most of their clan. Cassandra repositioned herself to get a better look at their prey.

A man was coming in their direction; Cassandra's heart fell at the sight of him. Large, long-haired, and bearded. Cassandra slowly leaned back, pressing her shoulders against the trunk of the tree, gladly giving up her view for better cover. She took a deep breath. She'd thought her clan had moved a safe distance from the Bateriman clan, whose reputation for viciousness was well-known. They weren't hunters, they were killers.

"RJ," she whispered. "Don't move. Don't make a sound."

"What do you see? Is it a deer? How many?"

"Forgotten Ones. From the Bariman clan. Quiet."

RJ gritted his teeth in silence, narrowing his eyes. As much as he might have wanted to take down a member or two of the Barimans, he knew this wasn't the right time and place. Not with Cassie here.

Cassandra's heart beat faster. The heat from the sun seemed to become more intense, as sweat on her forehead began to roll down her face. She did not dare wipe it off with the rag in her hand.

Cassandra hated what the Great Disruption had done to people. Turned them into savages who stole or killed to get what they needed, brutes who would do anything to survive. Cassandra didn't judge them, though; in her heart, she knew she was not far away from becoming another casualty of the times. She'd found a group of survivors who still valued the rules of a civil society. But with their food supply dwindling each day, she wondered how much longer they would be able to maintain that sense of community.

The Great Disruption had thrown the world into chaos. It began when the decades-long financial turmoil and political unrest became much more widespread and turned more violent. The first effective worldwide civil war had begun. Then a Carrington-class solar storm struck the earth, knocking satellites out of their orbits and taking down electrical grids, power stations, and communication systems. It seemed as if the Mayan gods had played a dirty trick on humanity, delaying the end of the world, which they had predicted for 2012, by fifteen years. Then, on December 21, 2027, as in the final scene of a Shakespearean tragedy, the earth shifted four degrees south on its axis. Over the next three months, weather and temperature patterns across the globe changed. The once-lush Ozark National Forest turned sere. Wildlife fled the arid landscape, and wildfires became constant. Earthquakes shook all seven continents, causing tsunamis that depopulated islands and ravaged coastlines.

In less than one year, the world lost almost half of its population, and the survivors, many of whom did not consider themselves the lucky ones, lost their way. The lives that people had once complained about seemed idyllic compared with this new world.

"Here they come," Cassandra whispered.

She and RJ watched as ten men and three women walked in single file along the dirt path below them. They all wore necklaces made of small animal bones, which clanked as they walked, and black bandanas tied around their right thighs. The men's and women's heads were shaved except for a double trail of hair along the right and left sides. The clansmen had rifles slung over their shoulders and flare guns clipped to their belts. They used the flares to signal others that a target was nearby and being pursued.

Cassandra saw that most of the men were carrying government-issued ration boxes. The spoils of a raid, she knew. How many had died for that? Cassandra noticed something fall from the belt of the last man in the troop, but she was too far away to see exactly what it was. She and RJ remained still for several minutes after the Bearimans passed.

When Cassandra could no longer hear their steps in the brush, she secured her rifle around her shoulder and climbed down the tree, jumping the last five feet to the ground.

RJ followed her. "That was close," he said.

"*Too* close," Cassandra said, picking up a small black pouch that one of the Beariman men had dropped. "It's one of their flare pistols. And two cartridges."

"Little good that's gonna do us. We can't eat it," RJ said. "Besides, we're trying to keep away from them, not draw their attention."

Still, Cassandra put the black pouch into her satchel. "Another empty-handed day," she said, looking around. "We need to get to the rendezvous stump so we don't miss our ride. It's a long walk home." She adjusted the piece of rope that tied back her long blond hair.

"We can't go back yet," RJ said. "We haven't eaten anything substantial in a week."

"I know, RJ. But maybe the others found something. Maybe a freshwater lake and some fish. You never know."

RJ shook his head. "What are the odds of that? The streams are down to a trickle, and the lakes barely sustain the algae. We need to keep hunting."

"But not here, not with the Beariman clan wandering around." Cassandra sighed. She looked at the slowly decaying forest around them. "Maybe we have to seriously consider moving on. I know you don't want to hear this, but it might be time to make our way to Dallas."

"No!" RJ glared at her. "The cities are still filled with fascist pigs. People who once lived in the lap of luxury while the rest of us got our hands dirty so they could buy their pricey shoes and drink their thousand-dollar bottles of wine. Do you think anything has changed?" Cassandra didn't answer. "Those people still think they're better than everyone else. I guarantee you they'll still be trying to figure out how to have more than everyone else."

"You can't know that," Cassandra countered.

"Greed is greed," said RJ, "and those people ain't gonna change. We need to let them kill each other off before we go back to the cities. Until then, we take our chances out here where the rules are clear. You know the others agree with me."

A rustling sound came from their right. Cassandra and RJ turned; a jackrabbit was darting out from under a pile of broken branches. RJ ran after it, and Cassandra started to follow before deciding not to waste her energy. RJ didn't need her help to catch a rabbit, and they had to stay on the trail to get to the rendezvous point. She sat down on a large fallen tree limb. She placed her rifle next to her and took the black pouch she had found out of her satchel. She let out her breath lightly, and then it caught, as the blade of a knife was suddenly pressed to her throat.

"Hey, girl," said a hoarse male voice behind her. The large blade of the hunting knife pressed against the bottom of her chin, indicating that she should stand up. "I see you found my pouch." He slipped a muscular arm around Cassandra's waist and held her tightly against him, his foul odor threatening to overwhelm her. He reached into her satchel and groped around. "Now, what's a pretty thing like you doing out here all alone . . . ?"

Cassandra stiffened.

"She ain't alone."

Cassandra heard RJ's voice. The knife retreated from her throat, and she pulled away from the man. Turning, she saw RJ standing with his own knife pressed to the clansman's throat. "Let's get out of here," she said, her voice still trembling.

RJ didn't budge. "Apologize to her," he said, pressing the knife harder on the man's throat. "Apologize, and maybe I'll let you go."

"Sorry," the man said quickly.

"I don't think you really mean that," RJ said, tightening his grip. "I hope your sins don't keep you from heaven's gates."

"RJ! No!" Cassandra yelled.

But it was too late. RJ slid his blade across the man's throat. Blood spurted from the man's neck, and then it gushed, streaming down his chest and shoulders. RJ released his grip, and the man fell to the ground, gurgling. Then RJ kneeled at the man's side, wiping the blood from his knife onto his shirt. "You shouldn't have touched her," he said. He put the knife back into the sheath he wore on his ankle, then looked up at Cassandra, who was still stunned. "Don't worry, Cassie. I'll never let anything bad happen to you." RJ yanked the necklace of bones from the man's neck and put it in his pocket. "*Now* let's get out of here," he said with a smile, holding up a dead jackrabbit.

They walked in silence. Cassandra still couldn't say a word to RJ, and she kept ahead of him so as not to have to look at his bloodstained shirt.

After a half hour, they reached the rendezvous stump. Cassandra, RJ, and four other hunters jumped into the bed of a silver pickup while two others got into the cab. They drove six miles down a dirt road until they arrived at the encampment.

"Looks like it's going to be another night of root vegetables and berries," said Allen, the leader of the group meeting the truck. He looked at RJ's meager snag and the empty hands of the other hunters.

"Slim pickings out there," RJ said, handing the dead rabbit to Allen's wife, Mary, who was in charge of provisions.

"Doesn't look like this rabbit ate any better in the last few months than we did," she said. "Well, we'll do what we can to get everyone fed tonight."

Allen looked at RJ's shirt. "A lot of blood for such a skinny rabbit," he said.

RJ smiled, launching into an account of their encounter with the Beariman clan and boastfully displaying the necklace of bones. Cassandra walked away without adding a word.

The encampment included about three hundred people. Some lived in teepees, and most lived in tents. A few of the less fortunate occupied pieced-together plywood and tin-roof shelters. Such a scene was not uncommon after the Great Disruption. In the spring of 2028, a year after the devastation started, rumors circulated that what few government institutions remained were organizing reconstruction efforts. But as time passed, their priorities became clearer. Resources were being directed to the big cities that hadn't been altogether wiped out, and the people in rural areas were left to fend for themselves. They called themselves the Forgotten Ones, because they believed their government had forgotten them.

Discouraged and tired, Cassandra entered her tent, which was pitched under the canopy of a white oak tree. She ate the last of her fireweed, a wild plant that had some nutrients and could be easily digested, and then lay down on her bedroll. A green and yellow checkered blanket had been folded up for use as a pillow. She closed her eyes and drifted off into a disturbed sleep, haunted by RJ's deed. She saw a row of shrouded bodies lying on the forest floor and a man walking from body to body, peeking under each shroud, saying, "Cassandra? Cassandra?" It was her father; he was searching for her.

"Daddy!" she called, but he didn't seem to hear her. "Daddy! *Daddy!*"

"Over here, Mel," a female voice said. "I found him."

Cassandra looked to her left and saw her mother kneeling next to the dead body of Cassandra's younger brother, Tony. A bloody sheet had been pulled back from his face. Cassandra's father walked over and knelt down next to his wife, his face overcome with grief.

"We need to find Cass," Cassandra's mother said. "We need to find her before it's too late."

Suddenly, Cassandra saw four members of the Beariman clan approaching her parents from behind, their knives out and readied. "Mom! Dad!" Cassandra screamed, but she couldn't move. She screamed again, this time loudly enough to wake from her nightmare. She sat upright, gasping for air. She covered her face with her hands, wishing she were back in her old life, with her parents, her brother, and her friends. She didn't know how much longer she could stand to live in this brutal new world.

She got up and opened a waterproof box containing her few possessions. She took out a voice recorder she had found in an abandoned electronics store in her hometown of Vickery Meadow, a suburb of Little Rock, and a stash of AA batteries, which she kept hidden from the others—they were a valuable commodity these days. Every evening,

Cassandra recorded what had happened that day; it was the closest thing she had to a journal.

I know RJ saved my life today, and I'm grateful. But even after everything I've witnessed, it was still horrible to see the blood pouring out of that man, to see him collapse gurgling on the ground. I've never seen eyes as cold as RJ's when he said that thing about sins and heaven's gates before killing the man. There was no remorse in them, no sorrow. I hope I never see those eyes again.

What is happening to us? We have to get back to civilization. I only hope I can convince the others tonight that it's time for us to move to a city. We're running out of time.

Cassandra turned off her recorder, and her thoughts returned to her parents and brother. She hadn't seen them in close to three years. She didn't know if they were dead or alive. As in her dream, they could still be looking for her, still trying to make their way back from New York, where they had been when the solar storm started, changing the world forever. Cassandra knew part of the reason she was so anxious to get to a city was that she believed she stood a better chance of finding them if she did.

She heard the familiar sound of fiddle music. It never failed to raise her spirits. Hank, the fiddler, was a white-haired, apple-cheeked man in his eighties who had been a famous bluegrass musician before the Great Disruption. Every evening, he played a lively little tune to let people know when supper was ready. Cassandra grabbed her wooden bowl and silver spoon and left her tent. She was joined immediately by RJ, who always seemed to be waiting by her tent to escort her to supper. He had changed his shirt and was wearing a bright red bandana on his head. The sun was setting, and a welcome breeze was chasing away the heat of the day.

As Cassandra and RJ waited in the food line, he looked annoyed. "This line gets longer every week."

"People all over are hungry," Cassandra said.

"Yeah, well, we can't take care of everyone. We need to start turning them away."

"Turning them away? To what? Death? We're all in this together. Why, I don't know, but we are."

"It's either us or them," RJ said.

Cassandra did not reply. She knew that there was some truth to what RJ was saying. Each week, more and more Forgotten Ones joined their clan, known as the Osagy, named after the original Indian tribe that inhabited the Ozark forest. Unlike the Beariman clan, the Osagy never turned anyone away. But each additional person meant more strain on their already limited resources. Pretty soon the system was going to break, and people would begin to starve.

Cassandra put on a smile as she accepted her paltry meal. It was a broth made from root vegetables spiced with seasonings pillaged from abandoned supermarkets. The mood at the encampment was grim. It had been that way for some time. This was the seventh day without anything substantial to eat, and there was little hope for more anytime soon.

Cassandra and RJ took their usual seats with the leaders of the clan, four men and four women.

"We need to pick up camp and find another spot," Allen said.

"Agreed," said Mary, who was sitting next to him. "After RJ and Cassandra's Beariman encounter this morning, I'd say that they're getting too close for comfort."

This was the opportunity that Cassandra was hoping for. "Where will we go?" she asked.

"South," a man at the table answered. "Follow the animals. They are moving south, and so should we."

"What about going west to Dallas or north to St. Louis or Chicago?" Cassandra suggested. "Maybe it's time to see if the government—" She was interrupted by protests from the other people at the table.

"Don't talk about the government," a woman named Beth said. "They helped get us into this mess."

Others at the table nodded their agreement, including RJ. "Maybe we need to take matters into our own hands," RJ said in a voice that quieted the others. "Maybe the Beariman clan has it right. We're seeing more and more armed government transports traveling up and down Route Forty. Instead of letting them take over again, let's stake our claim."

"We don't know that they're taking over," Cassandra said. "They could simply be transporting supplies to people in need."

RJ shook his head. "The Bearimans take what they need, is all I'm saying. Maybe we need to do the same." RJ grabbed the barrel of his shotgun, hinting at what he meant. "It was the sins of the government that put us here. Time for us to collect," he added with a smile.

No one at the table refuted him.

"I can't believe any of you are listening to him!" Cassandra said in disbelief. "What about the miracle you all said you wanted? You plan to ambush trucks and kill innocent people while you wait for God's sign? Tell me again why we shouldn't have been forgotten!"

Before Cassandra could continue, everyone's attention turned to a flare rising high in the twilight sky. A moment later, another flare appeared, then another.

"Looks like the Beariman clan is tracking something," RJ said, intrigued.

"Or someone," Allen added. "And they're not far away. The flares look like they're coming from Route Forty. Alert everyone, just in case we have to deal with the Bearimans tonight."

Two more flares shot up, this time east of where the others had appeared.

"You're right, they're too close," Cassandra said, rising to her feet. "We need to find out what's going on. Otherwise, we'll be sitting like turtles in a tub." That was a phrase Cassandra's father used to say to her and her older brother during their vacations. Holidays were more like survival adventures as they explored some of the more exotic places around the world. Just prior to the Great Disruption, Cassandra and her family had returned from a two-week exploration of jungles surrounding Angkor Wat.

They agreed and rose. RJ gave his shotgun a quick pump.

Cassandra retrieved her rifle and satchel from her tent, then returned to lead a group of twenty men and women into the forest toward the last set of flares. Some people held crossbows, others carried rifles, but most could muster only clubs and long sticks. Night had fallen, but the moon provided enough light for them to see the way.

Suddenly, Cassandra motioned for them to stop.

"What?" RJ asked.

"I hear something. It sounds like a car engine."

Allen nodded, confirming that he heard it, too, and they continued in the direction from which the sound was coming. Moments later, Cassandra halted the group again. The sound had stopped. They waited silently, looking for more flares. The sound of a car door opening and closing broke the silence. Someone was up ahead, very close. Cassandra led the group forward until she saw a clearing about twenty feet away. They had come to the edge of a campsite. At the center was a circle of large rocks that formed a fire pit, a stack of logs nearby. Cassandra motioned for everyone to be quiet, and they watched from the forest as one man helped another lie down on the ground.

"Who are they?" RJ asked, maneuvering for a better view and stepping on a twig that snapped loudly. Cassandra pressed a finger to her lips.

"Hello!" the man standing in the campsite called out, still just a silhouette in the darkness. "Is anyone here?"

Everyone remained silent, watching. The man threw the beam of his flashlight around the campsite. It landed on a nearby tree trunk. The man drew closer and picked up something that looked like a small bag. *What did he find?* Cassandra wondered. *How did this man know about this campsite? And why haven't we come across it before?*

The man returned to the fire pit, sat down on a rock close to where he'd set the other man, took something out of the bag he'd found, and used his flashlight to inspect it.

RJ tried again to get a better view, this time setting loose a stone that bounced along the ground. The man heard the sound and reached for something next to him. In a moment, he was pointing a small gun in their direction.

Cassandra grabbed RJ by the arm, imploring him to be still. She took the flare gun along with the two cartridges she had found that morning from her satchel and handed them to Beth, who stood close by. "I want you to make your way to Route Forty and walk west for five minutes or so. Then stop and fire one flare; wait thirty seconds, and then fire another. We need to throw the Beariman clan off this trail." Beth left, taking two other members of their group with her.

Cassandra turned back to the man at the campsite. He had lowered his gun and returned his attention to what he was holding in his hand. Cassandra still could not make out what it was, her view further compromised by the sudden emergence of a brilliant blue light emitted by whatever the man was holding. Soon the glow of the blue light encompassed the entire campsite. *Who is this man?* Cassandra asked herself, awestruck. *And what strange magic does he possess?*

RJ readied his gun, but both Cassandra and Allen grabbed the barrel and pushed it toward the ground. They dared not disturb what was happening at the campsite. The light seemed to be coming from a kind of supernatural ball floating in front of the man's face. Incredibly, after a moment, the man also began to float, rising off the ground and drifting around the campsite. Cassandra gazed on in disbelief. In a fleeting moment, she realized that the blue was somehow warm and comforting. The light intensified almost to the point of being blinding before fading. When the man returned to the ground and the blue light disappeared, Cassandra could not hold the group back any longer. Almost hypnotized, the Forgotten Ones walked out of the woods into the campsite. The man grabbed his gun and thrust it out in defense.

Cassandra saw a red flare shoot into the sky, then another. Beth had successfully fired the decoy flares, or so she hoped.

"Go away! I don't have anything you want!" the man yelled as he waved his gun at them.

Whoever this man was, Cassandra could tell that he was scared. With her rifle slung over her shoulder, she pushed her way to the front of the crowd. She saw that he was younger than she'd first thought, perhaps even her age. She walked slowly, not sure what she was dealing with. Noticing a book of matches lying on a large stone, she picked it up.

"Nice campsite," she said, in a tone she hoped would hide her own fear. The young man remained silent. Cassandra struck a match and threw it into the fire pit, where logs and kindling had been meticulously arranged. "I'm surprised we didn't come across it before."

The campfire roared to life, illuminating the site. Now that she could see him better, Cassandra was sure that he was her age. Just over six feet tall, he had short brown hair and matching brown eyes. And fear was clearly evident on his face.

"This isn't my campsite," the young man said. "I thought it was yours. I don't have anything you want."

"I heard you the first time," Cassandra said, as she walked around him. He was holding the gun in his right hand and something else in his left. "Are you a magician?" she asked, as she took what he was holding in his left hand. It turned out to be a book.

"Me? No," he replied. "I don't know what that blue orb was. I just opened that book, and all of a sudden, I was floating around."

Cassandra looked at the cover. There was only a title and a symbol, both embossed in gold leaf:

The Chronicles of Satraya

(•)

She opened the book and began to read the first page.

"You can read?" the young man asked, sounding surprised. Cassandra looked up at him, annoyed by his assumption. "Sorry. I've just heard some things about you people."

"Us people?" she retorted. "Not all of us are what you think we are. If we were, you and your friend wouldn't be alive." She looked over at the man who lay asleep or unconscious on the ground.

There was a commotion in the crowd. Cassandra saw RJ emerge from behind the young man, pressing the end of his shotgun into his back.

"Don't move. Drop your gun," RJ ordered, and the young man's small .38 handgun fell to the ground. "Now, turn around." The young man did as he was told. "Come on, Cassie," RJ said. "We got better things to do than mess around with these *cared-for* folks. Let's empty their pockets, grab their food, and go home." Cassandra watched as RJ cocked his shotgun and sneered at the man. "I hope your sins don't keep you from heaven's gates."

"Put the gun down," Cassandra told RJ. "Put it down right now, or I'll shoot you instead of him."

RJ glared at her but did not move. Cassandra walked over and pushed the barrel of his shotgun toward the ground. A moment passed, and the two continued staring at each other. Then RJ ripped off his red bandana and threw it to the ground. He stepped back.

Over RJ's shoulder, Cassandra could see more Forgotten Ones arriving at the campsite after seeing the dazzling light from the encampment. Two more red flares shot into the sky, this time farther away. The Bearimans were off the trail.

Cassandra looked into the forlorn faces of her Forgotten brothers and sisters, the clan she had come to love over the last three years. "We have wanted a miracle for a long time," she said loudly so everyone could hear her. "Some sign that we will be all right. Something, anything, to let us know that we have not been forgotten . . ." She paused a moment, taking in the crowd. "You all saw the blue orb and the light.

You all saw him lifted off the ground. Maybe that is the miracle we have been waiting for. Not him," she said, pointing to the young man, "but this." She held up the book in her hand. Then she opened it and read the first page aloud.

In a time of great need, we are with you.

As it has always been.

Contained in the pages of these books are the answers to your deepest questions. They are questions that have been asked by many who have come before you. Now, in this time of great despair, these words will provide you with resolution. Within each of you is a secret. If it is uncovered, something will be triggered in you, something that has not been activated in a long while. You have been asleep. Now it is time for you to wake up and claim your freedom. The rising of mankind is upon the land.

In a time of great need, we are with you.

As it has always been.

Cassandra paused and looked at the faces of her Forgotten Ones. For the first time in as long as she could remember, she saw a glimmer of hope in their eyes.

"Read on!" Allen shouted.

Cassandra walked back to the young man and stood beside him.

"Yes, read on!" yelled another, and soon there was a chorus of voices urging her to continue reading.

"See?" Cassandra said, smiling at the young man. "You do have something we need. *Hope.*"

1

A civilization can construct monuments to the
gods and learn nothing.
A man can build a fire to keep himself warm
and learn everything.

—THE CHRONICLES OF SATRAYA

MEXICO CITY, 10:20 A.M. LOCAL TIME, MARCH 20, 2070

A high-pitched scream jolted Logan awake. He sat up in the beach chair and looked around for his son and daughter. This wasn't the first time he had heard his daughter's distress call. He spotted a group of teenagers standing at the shoreline, pointing at something. He raised his hand to shield his eyes from the blazing Mexican sun and saw his daughter, Jamie, frantically wading through the chest-high water toward the shore. Logan sprang up and jogged toward the ocean, looking for his son, Jordan, who was supposed to be keeping an eye on his younger sister. He was nowhere in sight. People walking on the beach paused and pointed at Jamie. Someone yelled, "Shark!"

As Logan's jog turned into a sprint, spraying sand on other vacationers, he spotted the fin near Jamie. More people were yelling, "Shark! Shark!" Logan veered around a group of onlookers and grabbed a boat paddle, which was stuck in the sand next to an upside-down kayak.

He held it above his head as he ran full-force into the water toward his panicked daughter. Jamie let out another shriek as she splashed toward Logan and wrapped her arms around his waist when she reached him.

"Get behind me," Logan said, as he eyed the fin moving slowly through the water. Logan felt Jamie squeeze him tightly as the shark moved closer. He placed both of his hands on the paddle and raised it above his head with both arms. A few more feet, and the shark would be close enough for Logan to drive it off with a single well-aimed blow. At least, that's what he hoped. Suddenly, Logan's mind blanked, and the sound of Jamie's screaming became muffled. Logan's view of the advancing shark blurred, and somehow another perspective was overlaid on top. Logan could see someone's legs and feet walking along the floor of the ocean. The flash lasted but a moment before the overlay disappeared. He found himself now only a meter or so away from the shark. The fin stopped its advance. Logan bent his legs to better support himself as he prepared to strike.

The fin popped out of the water. It was affixed to the top of a young man's head, held there by a strap that ran under his chin. He removed a scuba mask from his face and took the snorkel out of his mouth. "Hey, Dad," he said. "What's the paddle for? Are we going kayaking?"

Logan lowered the paddle. "Jordan, what are you doing?" he said. "You're supposed to be watching your sister, not scaring her and the other people on the beach half to death!"

Jamie waded out from behind Logan. "Yeah!" she yelled, agreeing with her father. "Stop scaring me!" She skimmed the surface with her hand and splashed water into her brother's face.

Jordan looked at his sister and his father, then noticed the crowd on the shore looking at them. Two lifeguards had left their stations and were heading toward them. "Sorry, Dad," he said, realizing that what he had done was not very amusing. "Sorry, Jamie."

Logan looked at his daughter, who seemed to have recovered from her brother's prank. "Both of you have twenty more minutes in the water before we have to leave," Logan said sternly. He held his hand out to Jordan, who sheepishly waded over and handed him the goggles, snorkel, and artificial fin.

"Where did you get this thing, anyway?" Logan asked, shaking his head and heading back to shore without waiting for an answer. Logan handed one of the lifeguards the fin and apologized for the commotion. He stuck the paddle into the sand next to the kayak and made his way back to the lounge chair, where his girlfriend, Valerie, was waiting.

"What happened?" she asked. She was dressed in a red bikini top and a rainbow-colored cover-up, a long way from looking like the senior agent of the World Crime Federation that she was. She had just returned from the beach bar and was carrying two tropical drinks, complete with slices of pineapple and strawberries. "You don't look very happy."

"Jordan being Jordan," Logan answered, as he straightened out the towel on his chair. "One day, his little sister's going to roar back, and Jordan's not going to like it." He went quiet, his stare lingering on the ocean.

"What is it?" Valerie asked.

"You know that thing I've been telling you that's been happening to me lately, where I'm suddenly looking at something different? Well, it happened again."

"Really?" Valerie set the drinks down on the small wooden table between them.

"I was standing in the water, and all of a sudden, I caught a glimpse under the water. Like my perspective shifted for a second. I saw a set of legs walking on the ocean floor."

"It sounds a bit like what happens to you when you stare into a candle flame. But you probably should get it checked out to be safe. It could also be related to all the stress you've been under for the last year." Valerie stretched out in her chair and adjusted the brim of her sombrero. She held up her new PCD. "What do you think? It's the latest in personal communication devices, with a few government enhancements."

"Is it integrated with your thoughts?" Logan asked facetiously.

"Almost," Valerie said. With a few taps on the screen, a book was projected in front of her. "I want to get through this chapter before we have to leave for the Institute."

"That actually looks like a real book and not a projection," Logan said incredulously, reaching over and passing his hand through the book.

"And check this out. It tracks with my eyes, so when I get to the end of the page, it automatically turns to the next."

"What are you reading?" asked Logan.

"The *Chronicles*. I figure it's about time I read the books that saved humanity forty years ago and then wreaked such havoc in our lives this past year. It doesn't seem possible that books that have brought so much good to the world also provoked so much evil."

"The books didn't provoke evil," Logan said. "People did. History is filled with instances of people committing terrible deeds in the name of a philosophy, religion, or political system that they have distorted to suit their own selfish purposes. There is a thin line between the justification of good versus the rationale of evil."

Valerie gave Logan a questioning look, as the projected book in front of her disappeared. "In law enforcement, the line between good and evil is pretty clear."

"In terms of the law, I agree," Logan said. "But in terms of people . . ."

"I can't believe that you, of all people, would believe that. After what Simon and Andrea did?"

"Keep reading," Logan urged. "And let me know if there's anything in the books you need me to explain."

Valerie made the sound of a roaring lioness, putting a grin on Logan's face. She looked back down at her PCD, causing the first volume of the *Chronicles* to reappear. The pages flipped to where she had left off.

Logan, his children, and Valerie had flown down from New Chicago yesterday at the invitation of Juan Montez of the National Institute of Anthropology and History, who had hired Logan to restore a piece of pre-Columbian statuary. The Institute had put them up at the luxurious Orilla de Joyas, a newly constructed beach resort, located a few kilometers west of Mexico City. During the Great Disruption of 2027, a massive earthquake sank a large portion of Mexico's west coast, from Guadalajara to Salina Cruz, into the Pacific Ocean. Only a ten-kilometer area surrounding Nevado de Toluca, the largest stratovolcano in central Mexico, remained above sea level. The eight-kilometer-wide gulf between the new island and the shore of Mexico City had become a getaway for vacationers from all over the North American Federation, which was made up of Canada, the United States of America, and Mexico. While hotels and resorts had been constructed up and down the Mexico City shoreline, development on the island was forbidden. During the reconstruction efforts that followed the Great Disruption, a period known as the Rising, the NAF's flag was placed at Pico del Fraile, the highest point on the island. It could be seen from the shore of Mexico City and came to represent the perseverance of mankind. It was rumored that a fifth original copy of *The Chronicles of Satraya* was hidden somewhere on the peak, but that claim had yet to be proven. Daily excursions to the island afforded visitors the opportunity to search for it themselves, one of the area's major tourist attractions.

While Logan's children had spent the last two days frolicking in the ocean, Logan and Valerie had lounged on the beach. Logan badly needed a break. Only nine months ago, he had been a relatively poor artist, living a solitary life, burdened by increasing debts and decreasing confidence. His ex-wife had taken custody of the children, and he'd still been coping with the emotional fallout of his parents' brutal murder three year earlier. To make ends meet, he'd auctioned off the original copy of *The Chronicles of Satraya* that he'd inherited from them. The subsequent revelation that his father was actually Camden Ford, one of the four people in the world who had found an original copy of *The Chronicles of Satraya* during the chaotic aftermath of the Great Disruption, and his mother, Cassandra, who had witnessed Camden's discovery in the Ozark forest, had forced Logan into battle with a group that was plotting to seize control of the world. With the help of Valerie and her father, Alain Perrot, who had been with Camden in the forest, Logan had succeeded in foiling them. He found some satisfaction in knowing that the group's leader, Simon Hitchlords, and his accomplice, Andrea Montavon, were now both dead, but he still didn't know the identities of the others who may have been working with them. There were still many unanswered questions.

"A picture, *señor*?" asked a male voice with a strong Mexican accent. Logan opened his eyes and saw a tall, well-built, dark-skinned man standing in front of him and Valerie, holding a camera. "A picture, for you and your beautiful wife?"

"No," Logan said abruptly. "No pictures." The man frowned before he walked away.

"He's only trying to make a living," Valerie said. "You should be nicer."

"I know." Logan sat up. "I can't seem to clear my head."

"You have too much going on." Valerie shut down her PCD, and the projection of the book disappeared. "The children, the art studio, your parents' commemoration, not to mention your responsibilities as a new member of the Council of Satraya—it can all wait. You're on vacation this week. Remember, as a wise book you once read and I'm reading now said, 'Every choice is yours. You and you alone bear the responsibility of your decisions. No matter how great or small they may be.'" Valerie smiled, taking a sip of her drink.

"Listen to you," Logan said, smiling in turn and picking up his own glass. "You sound like a Satrayian scholar."

"I'm just sayin' . . ." Valerie's PCD rang. "It's the office," she said, as she rose from her chair and walked off to take the call.

"What about being on vacation?" Logan yelled after her. He saw that Jamie and Jordan had made their way out of the water and were now building an elaborate sand castle together. The photographer whom Logan had abruptly dismissed was standing near them and taking a picture of it. He also seemed to be giving the kids some building tips. Valerie was right, Logan thought. It is all choice.

He checked his PCD. It was almost 11:00 A.M. He rose and called the children, spinning his finger in the air to indicate that it was time to wrap things up. Logan had started to place his belongings in his well-worn backpack when Valerie returned with a stressed look on her face.

"Everything all right?" he asked.

"Potential new case," Valerie said. "We're being asked to look into the destruction of a well at a natural gas plant in the African Union, actually in the North African Commonwealth. Some are saying that the Republic of South Africa is involved. But I'm not going to deal with it; I'm *choosing* to let Sylvia and Chetan handle it until I get back."

Logan chuckled.

"Dad," Jordan said excitedly, "let's get a picture taken of all of us." Logan saw that the man with the camera had returned with the children.

"Yeah, let's get one," Jamie said.

Logan nodded. He was not about to shoo the photographer away again.

"OK, come together," the man said, and they did, bunching closely. "Smile for the world. No, big, big, big smiles." The camera clicked a few times, and the man projected a 3-D image for everyone to see. "Beau-ti-ful," he said.

"Thank you," Logan said, holding out a few universal credits as a tip, while Valerie helped the children stuff their belongings into their bags.

"Thank you very much, sir," the photographer said, as he accepted the money. "I like to make people happy. Show me your PCD, and I'll transfer the photos." Logan pulled out his PCD and placed it against the back of the man's camera to allow the transfer. "There you go," the man said, before giving a slight bow and walking away. "Your smiles are captured forever."

"'Bye," Jamie said, waving to him. "Thanks for helping us with the castle."

The man waved back.

"See, he just wanted to make people happy," Valerie said.

Logan nodded. "Everyone ready?" he asked, swinging his backpack

over his shoulder. The kids kicked around in the sand, looking for anything they might have forgotten, before leading the way back to the
hotel. "We're off to the pyramid."

The man with the camera walked along the shore, incoming waves
sliding over his bare feet and ankles. He put his camera into a small gray
shoulder bag and placed a call on his PCD. "Yes, they're here," he said,
now speaking without the Mexican accent. He stopped and gazed at
the island in the distance, where he could see the flag flying on the peak
of Nevado de Toluca. "I will," he said. "You should receive the photos
shortly." He ended the call and kept walking.

2

*Perfection is a dangerous thing. For how then does one evolve
and journey forward after it is achieved?*

—THE CHRONICLES OF SATRAYA

MEXICO CITY, 11:30 A.M. LOCAL TIME, MARCH 20, 2070

After changing, Logan, Valerie, and the children met their guide, Carlos, in front of the hotel and set off for the National Institute of Anthropology and History, which was in one of the most impressive pyramid cities in the world, Teotihuacán. "We should be there in an hour," said Carlos, who was seated in the front of the van next to the driver. "The city, which is located approximately fifty kilometers northeast of Mexico City, is believed to have been established in 100 B.C. and grew to become the sixth-largest city of the world by A.D. 600. Historians tell us that as many as one hundred twenty-five thousand people lived at Teotihuacán."

"Are you getting all this down?" Logan asked Jordan, before turning back to Carlos. "My son decided to do his school report on ancient pyramids around the world."

"Wonderful," Carlos said, while Jordan pulled out his PCD to take notes. "I will make sure to tell you everything I know. But new discoveries are being made there every day. While Teotihuacán was an important trading city and a spiritual and cultural center for Mesoamerica in the first half of the first millennium, it is still a place of great mystery today."

"Why?" Jordan asked, typing feverishly.

"Well . . ." Carlos paused for dramatic effect. "It was built by an advanced civilization that disappeared as mysteriously as it arrived. No one knows who built the city, no one knows why it was razed by fire and then abandoned in the year A.D. 650, and no one knows its original name."

"But wait," Jamie broke in. "You said the name. You said we're going to Teo-something."

"Teotihuacán," Jordan said.

"Yeah, that name."

"Very good," Carlos said. "Teotihuacán is what the Aztecs called it when they found the ruins beneath lots of dirt and vegetation in the fourteenth century. They were so amazed by the city's well-organized geometric layout and monumental structures that they named it Teotihuacán, which means 'the place where men become gods.'"

The van jolted, causing Jamie to grab her father's arm.

"As you can see," Carlos explained, "the roads outside of Mexico City are still in poor condition."

Logan looked out the window, noticing a change in the landscape. The arid landscape contrasted sharply with the tropical and well-manicured suburbs of Mexico City. "Didn't the World Federation of Reconstruction allocate money to this part of Mexico?" he asked.

"Certainly doesn't look like it," Valerie said. "Look at all the crumbling homes out here."

Carlos nodded. "The homes have been abandoned since the Great Disruption. During those terrible times, most of the people left the countryside and moved closer to the city."

"And this part of Mexico was never cleaned up," Logan inferred, eliciting another nod from their guide.

"Ancient sites like Teotihuacán did not seem essential after the devastation. The whole central plateau was hit hard by the earthquakes." The van swerved right and then left as it maneuvered around potholes on Route 132D leading out of Mexico City. "Even though the WFR was recently defunded, we have strong hopes that with a native Mexican like President Salize now in office, the government will allocate monies to this region of the North American Federation. If resources were made available, I'm certain this area would flourish once again. The people here work hard. This area has a rich tribal heritage. Farming is in their *sangre*."

Jamie looked at her older brother quizzically. "*Sangre* means 'blood,'" he told her.

Carlos turned and smiled at both children, then pointed to a dilapidated farmhouse in the distance. In a field nearby, a man was steering a plow pulled by a large animal. "Even without electricity or running water, some people stayed, continuing to work the land, because they heard about the terrible violence and lawlessness in the city. There was no better place to go, so they struggled to survive here, growing mostly wheat and corn. Then *Las Crónicas de Satraya* arrived. The books gave people hope."

"Did you grow up out here?" Valerie asked. "You speak of the countryside with great affection."

"Yes," Carlos said. "I grew up north of here. In a town called San Isidro. My parents spoke of the books until the day they passed." He turned to Logan. "Your parents were great people. They helped many by giving them the books."

"Yes, they accomplished a lot in those difficult times," Logan said, wishing yet again that he had known his parents' true identities when they were still alive. The vast majority of what he knew of his parents' past came from Mr. Perrot, Valerie's father and his father's best friend,

who had shown him photographs of their time in Washington organizing the remnants of the government and the dissemination of the books
throughout the world. Mr. Perrot and Logan's parents had formed the
Council of Satraya for that purpose. Made up of them and the other
three people who had discovered original sets of the *Chronicles* along
with a few of their family members, for seven years the Council had
worked relentlessly to deliver copies to those who needed them. It had
been an idyllic, productive time, until the group's leadership splintered
at the hands of Fendral Hitchlords, who attempted to commandeer the
organization for his own political purposes.

"Dad, check out those bridges!" Jamie called, breaking Logan's reverie. "Are they strong enough to hold a car? There's nothing supporting
them."

"Those bridges are made from hydrodized metal," Carlos said. "The
really strong stuff you might have learned about in science class. They
discovered it when they mined the Themis Four asteroid ten years ago.
The bridges are one of the few projects the WFR was able to help us
with. Fissures in the earth opened up during the earthquakes. Without
the bridges, the residents of these outlying areas would not be able to
commute to the city to work."

"How deep are the cracks?" Jordan asked, while taking pictures.

"No one knows," Carlos said. "Some say they lead to the center
of the earth." There was an awed silence as Jamie moved closer to her
brother to get a better look out the window.

"Look at those mountains," Jordan said then, pointing at a craggy
purple triad in the distance that rose into the blue sky.

Carlos laughed. "They're not all mountains. Do you see the massive
gray shape in front of the purple one? That is the Pyramid of the Sun."

Jordan pressed his face against the window to get a better look.
"That thing's huge!"

"It sure is," Valerie said, also laughing.

Carlos nodded. "It is sixty-five meters high, about half as tall as the

Great Pyramid of Egypt, but just as broad at its base. It is the largest pyramid at Teotihuacán."

"There's more than one?" Jordan asked.

"There are three major pyramids: the Pyramid of the Sun; the Pyramid of the Moon, which is the second largest; and the Feathered Serpent Pyramid, which partially covers a temple dedicated to its namesake god."

Some twenty minutes later, the van slowed down. Through the front window, they could see security personnel controlling the flow of traffic into the ancient city.

"Teotihuacán is very crowded today," Carlos explained. "People come from all over the world to celebrate the spring equinox."

"I know what that is," Jamie said. "That's when the day is as long as the night."

"Today we celebrate the end of winter and the beginning of spring. Many people, including pilgrims dressed all in white, climb to the top of the Pyramid of the Sun when the sun is directly overhead at noon and hold their arms up high to receive the sun's blessing and the special energy coming from the heavens." Carlos turned and handed a printout to each of them. "I know you all have PCDs," he said, "but I find people enjoy looking at an old-fashioned map of Teotihuacán when exploring the ancient city."

"What are these little triangles? More pyramids?" Jordan pointed to marks along the ancient city's main road.

"The Aztecs assumed they were burial tombs, but archaeologists discovered they were apartment houses. It turns out the Teotihuacános were not so different from us."

Carlos told to the driver to turn off the main road and into the VIP lane. He displayed his credentials to the security guards, and their van was allowed to bypass the mile-long traffic jam, making its way to the entrance of the ancient city, where it stopped.

"Stay close," Logan said to his children as he swung his backpack over his shoulder and they all got out of the van. "And put your caps on so we can keep an eye on the two of you."

Jordan and Jamie took bright red baseball caps out of their backpacks and put them on.

"This place is amazing," Logan said, taking in the eight square kilometers of the geometrically laid-out ancient city. At the end of a long road, directly north, he could see one of the stone pyramids. Halfway down the road and to the right stood a much larger one. Many other, smaller pyramids, with flat tops, could also be seen throughout the complex. Tourists moved from monument to monument, some in open-top vehicles that resembled golf carts, others on foot. People of all ages were climbing up the steep stairways of the ancient structures.

"We are at the southernmost point of the city," Carlos said. "The road we are standing on is known as *La Calzada de los Muertos*, the Avenue of the Dead. Two kilometers long and more than forty meters wide, it was the main transit road at the peak of the city's development from A.D. 300 to 600."

"Why do they call it the Avenue of the Dead?" Jordan asked.

"You see all those *talud-tablero* structures on both sides of the road? Those are the structures I mentioned earlier. The Aztecs believed they were tombs, so that is why they named the road as they did." Carlos pointed north to the farthest of the pyramids. "At the end of the avenue stands the Pyramid of the Moon. The smaller structure with the ornate carvings directly to our right is the Feathered Serpent Pyramid. This is where much of the celebration will be held tonight."

"What about that gigantic pyramid in the middle that all those people are climbing? Is that the Pyramid of the Sun?"

"Yes, that is the one we saw from the van. Even though it is one of the largest in the world, I think the Moon Pyramid is the most interesting. They recently discovered a tunnel there that led to a chamber filled with treasures." Carlos paused for a second, then added with spooky effect, "And a few skeletons."

Jamie gasped, and her eyes opened wide.

"That's so cool!" Jordan said, turning to his father. "Can we go see that?"

"I want to go, too," Jamie added, with less enthusiasm.

"I'm not sure we are going to have time," Logan said, checking his PCD. "We have to meet Mr. Montez." He paused, seeing a Jeep approach; a man with a straw cowboy hat, a khaki shirt, and a neatly trimmed gray mustache was in the driver's seat. "That could be him there."

The Jeep pulled to a stop, and the driver leaped out. "You must be Logan," he called. "Welcome to Teotihuacán! I am Juan Montez, special advocate of the National Institute of Anthropology and History." He shook Logan's hand vigorously and then greeted Valerie and the children. "I hope you enjoyed the drive from Mexico City."

"Yes, we did," Logan said. "Carlos has been a wonderfully informative guide."

"I'm glad," Mr. Montez said, and smiled. "Come. I am anxious for you to see our special statue."

"Would you like me to show the children around?" Carlos asked. "We can join in some of the celebrations, get some ice cream, perhaps climb the steps to the moon. We can meet back here in a couple of hours, if that is enough time for your business at the museum." He looked questioningly at Logan.

Valerie tugged on his arm. "Why don't you let them explore with Carlos? They'll enjoy that more than being indoors with us."

Logan looked at Jamie and Jordan and then at Carlos. "Would you mind?" he asked.

"Not at all," Carlos said. "I will get us a touring cart so we can travel around Teotihuacán in luxury. There may be more treasure to be found!"

"And maybe even a mummy or two," Jordan added.

"I want to stay with Dad," Jamie said. "This place is spooky."

Jordan shook his head at his younger sister. "Come on," he said, grabbing her by the shoulder.

"You stay close to Carlos," Logan added as a final reminder. "Valerie and I will see you back here in two hours."

He watched his children walk down the Avenue of the Dead with Carlos, before they disappeared into the growing crowd.

3

Be wary of the prophet who attempts to peddle you truth;
instead, listen to the one who endeavors to teach so that you
can learn to convince yourself.

—THE CHRONICLES OF SATRAYA

MEXICO CITY, 12:35 P.M. LOCAL TIME, MARCH 20, 2070

Mr. Montez, Logan, and Valerie climbed into the Jeep. "The museum is near the Pyramid of the Sun," Mr. Montez said. "We will take an ancillary route to avoid the crowds."

As Mr. Montez turned the Jeep and headed toward a peripheral road on the east side of the city, Logan gazed back at the Avenue of the Dead. "This place is truly impressive. It looks as if modern-day city planners laid it out."

"Eight square kilometers of urban planning," Mr. Montez said. "The original inhabitants were skillful builders and also proficient astrologers and scientists. This ancient city's grid is oriented fifteen degrees twenty-five minutes east of true north."

"What is the significance of that?" Valerie asked.

"It is perfectly aligned with the setting of the sun on two days of the year," Mr. Montez said. "August 12 and April 29. On those days, the Pyramid of the Sun, the setting sun, and the Pleiadian star system are in perfect alignment. At least, they were before the Great Disruption and the four-degree shift in the rotation of the earth. But that is the theory held by those of us who believe that the city was positioned that way intentionally."

"Yes," said Logan. "There are some who believe that pyramidal sites such as this one could not have been built by humans alone." He pointed to the sky. "They had some help."

Valerie gave Logan a skeptical look.

The Jeep made its way north, and Mr. Montez slowed down when they came to a small bridge that crossed a dried-up riverbed. "Interesting," Logan said. "Did a river run through the middle of the city?"

"A man-made river, we believe," Mr. Montez said. "The Teotihuacános rerouted many small streams outside the city to create it. Water was very important to their civilization for more than the obvious reasons, as you will soon see."

The Jeep sped up, and Logan and Valerie gazed in awe at the enormous Pyramid of the Sun, which loomed ever larger as they approached it. The stairs on the west façade were filled with people climbing to the top, while many more waited at the base. Within minutes, Mr. Montez pulled into the parking lot and led them under a walkway partially covered by scaffolding instead of to the main exhibition hall. "We are putting the final touches on our new research center," he explained. Inside, workers were busily cleaning and tagging hundreds of relics. "These artifacts are from the tunnels that we recently discovered under the Pyramid of the Moon."

"I hope you're not expecting me to restore all these pieces," Logan said in jest, as he surveyed at least ten tables covered with artifacts.

"No, no." Mr. Montez laughed. "While I wish we could use you for all our restorations, we have only the one job for you to do."

"Juan!" a female voice called. "You should see what they discovered in the tunnels today."

Mr. Montez led Logan and Valerie to a table where a woman was organizing dirty bits of broken pottery. "This is Elvia," he said, introducing them to an attractive middle-aged woman, who smiled at them. He picked up one of the pieces and examined it. "It resembles a water jug that was found in the initial excavation. I will examine them more closely after I show Logan and Valerie our prize discovery."

Mr. Montez led them to a door at the other end of the room, which he opened with a beep as the lock disengaged. Logan and Valerie followed him into a stunning room that consisted of four triangular walls made of brown-tinted glass, each approximately twenty meters long at the base, sloping up and in, with their tips converging at a single point. Together they shielded the interior from the sun's rays yet provided an excellent view of the Pyramid of the Sun. "Welcome to Teotihuacán's newest pyramid."

Valerie and Logan looked around at several small statues and something larger at the center of the room that was covered with a white sheet, then up at the apex of the room, which was easily fifteen meters above their heads.

"Extraordinary," Valerie said. "But I have to ask, how were you able to build all this? Carlos indicated that not much money had been allocated to nonessential construction efforts. I didn't think any of the museums in the state of Mexico were this well funded."

"Nonessential to politicians, perhaps," Mr. Montez said with a smile. "But you are correct, the North American Federation provides very little financial support to cultural institutions. Our discoveries at Teotihuacán have captured the interest of a research consortium. Have you heard of the Tripod Group?"

"I have," Valerie answered. "But I didn't realize they were interested in archaeology."

"They funded the construction of this room," Mr. Montez said. "And found my efforts and theories most fascinating."

"What theories are those?"

Mr. Montez took out a pair of eyeglasses and began to clean the lenses with a handkerchief. "Tell me, what do you know about the pyramids? Do you know why they were constructed in the first place?"

"They were used as tombs for the pharaohs and kings and as places for ritual activities," Valerie answered.

"Yes," Mr. Montez said as he put his glasses back on. "That is the general understanding."

"But I sense you have another explanation," Logan offered.

"Power," Mr. Montez said. "I believe that the Pyramid of the Moon and possibly the other two large pyramids at Teotihuacán were used to generate, collect, and transmit copious amounts of energy." Valerie and Logan looked at him skeptically. "And not just the pyramids here at Teotihuacán. Of the thousands of pyramids around the world, I believe that many were used for the same purpose. Obviously, the most famous pyramids are here and in Egypt, but I believe those in China, Spain, and Greece may have also been used to induct power."

"*Induct* power?" Logan said. "An interesting choice of words."

"A precise and accurate choice of words," Mr. Montez said. "Electricity is an integral part of all biological life. Everything has a spark of electricity in it, even the air we breathe. Between the core of the earth and the atmosphere above is an abundant supply of energy. More energy than the world could possibly dream of using. And I am close to solving a puzzle that has baffled mankind for generations." He walked over to the covered object at the center of the room. "I believe this holds the key." He gave the sheet a good tug, and it snapped in the air before floating to the ground and revealing what was underneath.

Logan's eye's widened. "Where in the world did you find that?" he asked, setting down his backpack and walking over to a two-meter-high, pure white statue of a man kneeling on the ground, holding his hands up near his mouth and nose.

"We found it in a secret chamber beneath the Pyramid of the Moon," Mr. Montez explained. "Based on our carbon dating, I place the statue at around A.D. 550. It coincides with the time when Teotihuacán was flourishing." Logan ran his fingers over portions that had been chipped off. "As you can see, this statue is very different from traditional Toltec sculptures. It is much more lifelike."

Logan's PCD made a strange noise, half chirping and half squeaking; he pulled it out of his pocket and inspected it. "Sorry, not sure what that sound is," he said, pressing buttons until it went away. "Might be time for a new device." He gave his PCD an annoyed look before putting it back into his pocket.

Valerie joined Logan near the statue. "It looks like he's praying," she observed.

"Yes," Mr. Montez said. "Worship and rituals were important aspects of the Teotihuacán culture."

"Where did they get such a large block of Slyacauga?" Logan asked. "The only place I know of in the world where this stone is found is in the southern part of the former United States."

"I see you know your marble," Mr. Montez said. "I can only assume it was transported here at some point."

"Has this level of detail been found in other statues or works of art here at Teotihuacán?"

"Neither here nor anywhere else in this entire region," Mr. Montez replied. "Toltec art has mostly depicted skulls and snakes etched and carved into walls. The images of Chac-mool, also known as the Leaning Man, were their primary sculpting expression. The era to which we have dated this piece was dominated by statues of the Atlantes."

"What are Atlantes?" Valerie asked.

"They are the rough figures of men carved into tall, free-standing columns of stone," Mr. Montez said. "You should visit Tula, the most important Toltec site in Mexico, and see them. It's only about an hour's car ride from here."

"They're similar in style to the facial sculptures found on Easter Island," Logan added, "but the Atlantes depict entire bodies."

"That is why this particular statue is so intriguing. The finely chiseled facial features and body parts are not typical of Mesoamerican sculpture in the first half of the first millennium, when Teotihuacán was a thriving civilization."

"This type of statuary belongs in Greece or Rome," Logan suggested.

"The figure's hands appear to be raised in prayer, and his lips are slightly puckered, as if he is reciting something."

Valerie knelt down and looked at the statue's black stone platform.

"The platform is made of mica," Mr. Montez explained. "Mica has been found throughout Teotihuacán—under the Pyramid of the Sun, in many tunnels and chambers. We even have a place here known as the Mica Temple. More important, we recently found a large amount under the Pyramid of the Moon. I and other archeologists believe that it was transported here, probably from northern Brazil, which is more than three thousand kilometers away."

"How could people in the first century do that? And why?" Valerie asked.

"The mica wouldn't enhance the structural integrity of the pyramids, but it has great electrical and thermal insulating properties," Logan answered for Montez. "Mica is used by the electronics industry. It's in all of our PCDs."

"That is correct," Mr. Montez replied eagerly. "I believe that these pyramids not only could generate immense amounts of power but also could transmit and store the energy. Mica is not indigenous to this area."

Valerie bent way down, placing her head a few centimeters off the floor. "It looks like there is something written on the platform. Not sure what language this is."

"It is Nahuatl," said Mr. Montez. "The phrase reads *Tlamatini tetlax-intli quitzitzquia canahuac itapazol.* Translated, it means, 'The wise man of stone holds the nest of the snake.' You'll notice that there is an image of a coiled serpent on the surface of the platform."

Logan's PCD vibrated; a new message had arrived. "Carlos, Jamie, and Jordan are exploring one of the caves under the Moon Pyramid as we speak."

"Wonderful," Mr. Montez said. "Carlos is very well acquainted with that structure and the tunnels underneath it."

"Assuming that the pyramids were energy-generating devices," Valerie resumed, "how did they turn them on?"

"My theory proposes the existence of a radioactive device," Mr. Montez said.

"Radioactive?" Logan asked, astonished.

"Yes. I believe that radioactivity was used to activate the pyramids."

"How could they harness radiation back then?" Valerie asked.

"Did you know that certain gems and precious stones give off radiation?" Mr. Montez said. "Gems such as autunite and coffinite actually give off a great deal."

"So what did they use the energy for?" Valerie asked doubtfully. "Toasting bread? I don't recall learning about microwave ovens or electric chariots existing two thousand years ago."

Mr. Montez laughed. "That's right. We have not unearthed any electrical appliances from that era. But are you familiar with the term *electroculture*?" Logan and Valerie shook their heads. "It is the postulate that if you can introduce electrical current into plant cells, the plant will grow rapidly. There is also something called *electrotherapy*, the healing of wounds through the introduction of electrical charges. I believe that the people of Teotihuacán also created arc lamps."

"Arc lamps?" Logan said. "Now that I think about it, I remember hearing rumors about those existing in Egypt during the time of the pharaohs."

Mr. Montez nodded.

"What's an arc lamp?" Valerie asked.

"A type of lamp that produces light by sending an electrical current between two conductive points," Mr. Montez explained. "I believe that there were once people, here at Teotihuacán and at other pyramid sites around the world, who knew how to harvest electricity."

"Now I see why the Tripod Group is interested in your work," Valerie said. "There are a lot of people who would be willing to pay handsomely to become energy sovereign."

Logan turned and looked up at the face of the statue. "Any man who knew how to produce electricity out of nothing would be considered a god."

Mr. Montez nodded. "*Teotihuacán* means 'place where men become gods.'"

Logan's gaze lingered. The eyes of the statue were closed, and a gentle calm was chiseled on its face. Logan wondered about the artist who had sculpted it and the secret he may have possessed. He turned to Mr. Montez. "Is this the artifact you want restored? It seems to be in pretty good condition already."

"I will get to that in a moment," Mr. Montez said, "but there is something else I would like you to look at first. Come here." Logan and Valerie followed him around to the back of the statue. "Look at the back of the figure's headband. The five symbols carved into it . . ."

"They're from the *Chronicles*," Valerie said in surprise. She turned to Logan. "Peace, Joy, Love, and Freedom. I just read about them."

Logan remained silent. He, too, was surprised to see the Satraya symbols on the ancient statue.

"Yes," Mr. Montez said, with deep reverence. "And the last is the enigmatic and unmistakable emblem that appears on the cover of the books."

"What's that other symbol that looks like a flower or a snowflake?" asked Valerie.

"I doubt it's a symbol at all," answered Mr. Montez. "Just a bit of artistic flare, I suspect."

"How can this be?" Logan asked. "The *Chronicles* were found in 2027, and you said this statue has been buried for more than fifteen hundred years."

"That is why I contacted the Council of Satraya," Mr. Montez said. "As I mentioned in our phone conversation, Adisa Kayin said that if anyone could solve this mystery, it would be you."

"Have any of these symbols been found anywhere else at Teotihuacán?" Logan asked, with great curiosity.

"No. But much about this civilization is shrouded in mystery; so much must have been lost in the fire that destroyed the city in the seventh century. I believe that this atypical lifelike sculpture and the Satraya symbols indicate that the ancient people of Teotihuacán were far more advanced than historians and archaeologists realize." Mr. Montez walked over to a work table that held an array of stone artifacts. "These pieces were scattered on the ground in the same chamber where the statue was found." He picked one up and handed it to Logan. "We would like you to reconstruct whatever this is and provide any insights you might have about the symbols on the—"

A loud rumbling suddenly interrupted them. The pieces of broken stone slid across the smooth surface of the table. Alarmed voices could be heard in the work room. The floor began to shake.

"I think it's an earthquake," Logan said.

"We need to get out of here," Valerie said.

Logan grabbed his backpack and hooked it over his shoulder. The three of them quickly walked back to the large work room. The shaking intensified, and a part of the scaffolding buckled, crashing down on one of the fleeing workers. Mr. Montez rushed over to help lift the scaffolding off the worker's legs.

"Let's go! We need to get out of here!" Valerie yelled, as she pushed people toward the exit.

Mr. Montez grabbed Elvia by the arm and escorted her to the door.

The hysteria and pandemonium were no different outside the museum. People screamed and ran as stones tumbled down the sides of the pyramid onto the visitors below.

"The kids!" Logan shouted. "We have to find them—they were at the Pyramid of the Moon!"

Valerie nodded, and they ran north along the Avenue of the Dead. Hordes of panicked, screaming people were running in the opposite direction toward the exit and the parking lot. As Valerie and Logan navigated through the rampaging crowd, Logan heard a loud hum coming from the Moon Pyramid. The hum got louder, and suddenly, an arc of light shot out of the Moon Pyramid, hurling hundreds of its stones and bricks. Logan and Valerie stopped in their tracks. The exploding stones flew high into the air and dispersed in all directions, landing on men, women, and children indiscriminately as they attempted to flee.

"Jordan! Jamie!" Logan yelled, as he started running again.

May the answers you receive be as great as
the questions you ask.

—THE CHRONICLES OF SATRAYA

Every stroke of the bow on the finely tuned strings of the violin reverberated through the courtyard that lay between the roofless ruins of the Cathedral of St. Germaine and the main grounds of Peel Castle. The sun, which had not graced the Isle of Man for many days, had reappeared that morning and was now setting in the west. The shadow cast by the castle spire had reached across the courtyard's immaculately manicured lawn and was now creeping up the weathered stone wall of the cathedral. The violin player's black dress and long blond hair fluttered in a strong and sometimes gusty wind as she played on. Her bow transitioned from the slow *louré* stroke to *legato*, then from the haunting sound of the *col legno* back to *louré*. Flawlessly, she spun her tale. Two men sat on a stone bench in the adjacent courtyard, listening. The piece she'd composed told the story of a captive's despair and the arrival of a savior who provided hope.

"This piece is about you, my friend," Sebastian said to Lawrence, the steward of his home, Peel Castle. "We would not be enjoying her music at this moment had you not taken action years ago."

"You played a part in that liberation, too," Lawrence answered, his eyes resting on his adopted daughter, Anita, who was still lost in her music. "Those were terrible times. We were all required to act after the Great Disruption and the Rising. Your parents would be very proud of you, Sebastian. Even today, you continue with your work. The son of Camden and Cassandra would not have made his way and escorted the world to safety had you not helped to lift the veil from his eyes." Sebastian did not immediately answer, and a pause ensued before Lawrence spoke again. "You think there is more to this, don't you?"

"Others are moving into place," Sebastian said. "There is one whose full intent has not yet been made clear." Sebastian bowed his head in contemplation. His parents had bought the grounds of Peel Castle from the Manx National Heritage Foundation in 2034. It was here that they constructed their new residence, which provided not only a place to house their art collection and extensive library but also a place where they could carry out the duties of their lineage. Their passing ten years ago left Sebastian as the last genetic descendant of a group known as the *Tutela de Luminis*, the Guardians of Light.

At length, Sebastian looked up and fixed his eyes back on Anita. "The arrival of the *Chronicles* forty years ago set in motion a series of intricately woven events. A great gamble was taken with the release of that knowledge." Concern was clear in his voice. "The ebbs and flows of that gamble have yet to be completely realized. The Rising is over. Now we must see if the wager on mankind was well placed."

Sebastian and Lawrence noticed that Anita had stopped playing. She adjusted the tuning pegs on her violin and then once again began to play.

"We gamble every day," Lawrence said. "Even the simple act of loving someone is risky, as we hope that our love is returned in kind. Your mother and father's faith in mankind brought the books to the world; I have no doubt of that." The wind returned exuberantly, providing a howling overtone as it passed through the ruins of the cathedral, heightening the drama of the evening. Lawrence filled their glasses with more wine. "Not long after you were born, your parents asked me if I regretted not having a family of my own. They knew that my choice to live a life of service came with sacrifices. I casually answered no. I didn't realize at the time how much of an untruth that was." A serious look came to Lawrence's face as he watched Anita perform. "What the Pottman family did is hard to fathom. I wonder often what possesses people to do such horrific things."

"Anita was fortunate you turned up at their infamous dinner party," Sebastian said. "The lives of many people changed that evening, including yours."

"Especially mine," Lawrence said. "I know now that I would have answered your parents very differently if they asked me their question again."

"Life would not be so grand if our answers today were the same as they were yesterday or the answers we provide tomorrow were duplicates of what we uttered today." Sebastian touched his glass of wine to Lawrence's and took a sip. "To wisdom."

"You sound like Razia when you say things like that," Lawrence said. Sebastian smiled. "There are parts of the grounds that I believe still hold her energy. I regret that you had to let her go. It would have been pleasant to have her with us. I'm certain Anita would have enjoyed it. But we all had choices to make, lives to live, and journeys to take."

Sebastian nodded, his attention suddenly drawn away from Anita. "And it would seem that my current journey is not very dissimilar to yours." He looked over at eleven-year-old Halima as she quickly made her way across the courtyard to them. Bukya, a large German shepherd, followed close behind, his muddy paws indicating that the two of them had gone on an adventure. "Here comes the newest member of our ever-growing family."

"You look like you have been digging for buried treasure," Lawrence said to them, as he took the serviette that was wrapped around the neck of the wine bottle and used it to wipe the dirt from Halima's face and hands. "I am at a loss to say who did more digging, you or Bukya."

"Mr. Sebastian," Halima said, slightly out of breath, "who is Sumsari Baltik?"

Sebastian thought for a moment. "I have no recollection of that name. Lawrence?"

"Nor do I," Lawrence answered, as he finished wiping Halima's hands.

Halima pulled something out of her pocket and handed it to Sebastian. It was a silver neck chain with a silver tag attached to it. "I found that. Actually, Bukya found it."

"It appears to be a dog tag, a type of identification worn by members of the old U.S. military," Sebastian said, and then read the engraving: *Sumsari Baltik, ID #2974630*. "It must have been lost before the Great Disruption. Perhaps when the grounds of Peel Castle were a tourist attraction." Sebastian handed the necklace to Lawrence. "Where did you say you found it?"

"In one of the tunnels under the old armory," Halima said. Lawrence gave her a stern look. "I know, but my little brothers weren't with me. And Bukya won't let anything bad happen to me." Halima turned toward the cathedral. "Maybe Anita will help me figure out who Sumsari Baltik was."

Lawrence cleaned off the chain and the dog tag and placed them around Halima's neck. "Every great mystery needs a great detective to solve it."

Halima's face brightened, and she went to sit beside Bukya on the grass.

Anita continued her violin solo. She had been playing for a couple of hours now. The castle's groundskeepers were lighting the torches in the courtyard. If the past was an indicator, Anita would remain lost in her melodies and continue playing well into the night of the spring equinox without stopping for rest.

"How is she able to play so long?" Halima asked.

"She has trained herself," Sebastian said. "When one learns the art of singularity of mind, one loses all sense of time." At his words, Anita stopped playing again. She was adjusting the tuning pegs again. Sebastian looked at a fiery blend of orange and red in the sky as the setting sun kissed the horizon. He rose to his feet, his fists clenched.

"What is it?" Lawrence asked.

Sebastian closed his eyes. As if sensing his master's consternation, Bukya stood and let out a strong bark, casting aside Halima, who was leaning against him. "The voice of the earth has been disturbed," Sebastian said, when he reopened his eyes.

A scream ripped through the darkening evening. It was Anita. Her violin and bow had fallen to the ground, and she was clutching her head. Bukya darted over to her, and the others quickly followed.

"What's wrong, dear?" Lawrence asked.

"I don't know." Anita struggled to reply. She rubbed her temples, grimacing. "My violin keeps going out of tune, and now I have this terrible headache."

Sebastian squatted next to her and placed his thumb on her forehead, gently massaging it for a few seconds. Then he said, "It is not your violin that is out of harmony. It is you who are out of tune." Sebastian paused and glanced up at Lawrence. "I think it is time for one of our masterpieces to find a new home."

5

Desire is the voice of an immortal soul.

—THE CHRONICLES OF SATRAYA

MEXICO CITY, 2:46 P.M. LOCAL TIME, MARCH 20, 2070

Logan and Valerie hurried down the long, darkened tunnel. They held their PCDs out like flashlights in front of them. Mr. Montez followed. The earthquake was over, and the shaking had stopped, but outside, many visitors lay wounded or dead, crushed by falling rocks along the aptly named Avenue of the Dead. Logan tried calling his son's PCD, but there was no answer.

They navigated down one of the newly discovered tunnels that Carlos had mentioned earlier. The strung lights attached to the ceiling had been knocked out. The ground was lined with uneven bricks, and the walls and ceiling were reinforced with metal bracing. As they made their way deeper inside, they passed several anterooms where they saw frightened people huddled in the dark. Valerie quickly instructed them on how to get out of the pyramid safely.

They continued forward, maneuvering around the fallen beams and damaged bracing material, looking for any sign of the children and Carlos. Then they came to a gaping hole in the ground, where they had to stop. "The earthquake ripped up part of the floor," Logan said, eyeing the three-meter gap. "Should we jump?"

"Too far," Valerie said. She grabbed Logan by the arm, leading him back to where some bracing had fallen off the tunnel wall. "We might be able to use this," she said, bending to pick up one end of a beam.

"Good idea." Logan grabbed the other end. Together they carried the heavy beam to the breach in the floor, and with the help of Mr. Montez, they were able to slide it across the gap.

"How are your gymnastic skills?" Valerie asked, as she stepped onto the beam and began to walk across, raising her arms to balance herself.

Logan bent down and held the beam steady, and once she was across, Valerie did the same from the other side, letting Logan and Mr. Montez follow. They continued, and the farther they walked, the worse was the destruction they saw. More bodies littered their path, and more of the tunnel's bracing had given way. They instructed the survivors to wait by the opening in the floor until help arrived. Some did as they were told, but others took their chances and made their way over the beam.

Logan looked through the doorway of a chamber and spotted something on the ground: a red cap. "It belongs to one of the kids," he said, running toward it. There was a large pile of stones that had fallen from the ceiling at one corner of the room, and Logan noticed the pieces of Jordan's crushed PCD under one of them.

Mr. Montez was lifting stones from a pile of rubble. "Oh, no," he said.

Logan and Valerie saw an arm extending from the bottom of the heap. They rushed over to help. The face was badly bruised but recognizable. Carlos. He was dead. In silence, they quickly removed more stones from the pile.

"The kids aren't under here," Valerie said with relief.

Logan surveyed the chamber more carefully. In the far corner, he spotted a one-meter-round hole in the floor. There were no ceiling blocks near it. "Looks like part of the floor collapsed here," he said, walking over. He shone the light from his PCD down the hole. "I think there is another chamber down there." He called out for his children, his voice echoing.

Valerie and Mr. Montez hurried to his side, and they all peered down, waiting.

"Dad!" a voice answered from below. It was Jordan.

"Jordan!" Logan yelled back. "We're here, we're coming to get you!"

"You have to hurry!" Jordan said, his face barely illuminated by the light from Logan's PCD. "Jamie's hurt."

Logan took off his shirt and wrapped it around his PCD. It glowed like a small lightbulb. "I'm going to toss my PCD down to you!" he yelled. "Move your sister, and move away from the opening."

A rustling sound could be heard below. "OK," Jordan said. "Go ahead." Logan tossed his bundled shirt into the opening and a few seconds later the glowing ball hit the ground. "It's down here now," Jordan announced. He walked over and unwrapped the PCD from the shirt.

"Turn up the intensity!" Logan called.

"Is there another way down?" Valerie asked Mr. Montez.

"I don't know," he answered. "It seems the earthquake has exposed another secret chamber."

Valerie nodded. "I'll get some help," she said to Logan. "Hold tight. I'll be right back."

Logan leaned over the hole. "Jordan, we're getting help."

"Hurry up! Jamie says her head hurts really bad!"

Mr. Montez examined the edges of the opening. "This floor is made of mica," he said quietly. He raised his voice as he called down to Jordan. "Can you see a door or an opening of any kind?"

Logan could see the moving glow of the PCD as Jordan walked around. "There's a lot of strange stuff down here." The boy's voice echoed upward. The light moved farther away from the opening. Jordan screamed.

"What is it?" Logan shouted. There was no answer. "Jordan! Jordan, answer me! Are you all right?"

A moment passed. Then Jordan's illuminated face reappeared under the hole. "There are two skeletons over there," he said, his voice filled with horror. He pointed to his right. "They're leaning against some kind of big archway. I don't see any kind of door."

"It might be a burial chamber or a place for sacrificial rituals," Mr. Montez said.

"Go over and wait with Jamie," Logan told his son. "Valerie should be right back with some help."

Mr. Montez rose and took a seat on a large, flat stone. "It's very strange, this earthquake," he said. "They're not common in this region. One of this magnitude has not occurred since the Great Disruption."

The strung lights on the ceiling suddenly came on. "Looks like they restored power," Logan said, looking through the doorway. Frightened people were running toward the tunnel's exit. To Logan's relief, he heard Valerie who returned with a rescue team carrying lanterns, equipment bags, and medical kits.

The four men threw a rope ladder down the hole. Logan grabbed a lantern from one of their bags, turned it on, and set off downward, Valerie's warning to take it slow falling on deaf ears. He climbed about six meters down the ladder, with Valerie behind him, and the two of them reached the lower chamber.

"Dad," Jordan said, hugging his father. "Jamie's over here."

She was sitting against a wall with Logan's shirt wrapped around her head. "Jamie, honey, are you OK?" Logan asked.

"My head hurts," she said.

Logan examined his daughter's head. "I don't see any scrapes or bruises," he said.

"I don't see any blood, either," Valerie added. "Did you hit your head when you fell?"

"I don't remember."

"You're going to be fine," Logan reassured her, but she did not seem convinced.

Logan and Valerie stepped back as the rescue team arrived and began attending to Jamie.

Logan turned his attention to Jordan, who looked to be in good shape, considering. Logan pulled out the red hat, dusted it off, and put it on his son's head. "So what happened?" he asked.

"We were on the floor up there, when all of a sudden, the ground started to shake and shake. People in the tunnel started screaming. Jamie lost her balance and fell to the ground, and I went over to help her." His voice began to quiver. "Carlos was at the other end of the room when a bunch of rocks fell on him. Jamie and I tried to pull the rocks off, but they were too heavy. We tried, Dad, we really tried . . ." He was struggling not to cry, but tears filled his eyes nonetheless.

"It's all right, Jordan," Logan said. "It's not your fault."

Jordan nodded. "Jamie and I were still trying to get the rocks off of Carlos. Through the doorway, we could see people running down the tunnel. They were yelling and screaming, and a lot of them were hurt. The shaking kept going, and all of a sudden, we heard a big bang. The hair on our heads stood straight up, and then all the lights went out."

"I wonder if that was the arc of light we saw," Valerie said.

"You say the hair on your heads stood up?" asked Mr. Montez, who had been standing nearby. "Did you feel little shocks on your fingertips or your head?"

"Yes," Jordan said. "My hands felt funny."

Mr. Montez nodded, turning to Logan and Valerie. "Static electricity," he said, before walking off as something caught his eye.

"Then what happened?" Logan asked.

"Jamie said her head started hurting. I grabbed her, and we tried to get out of the room and follow the people out of the tunnel."

"Wait," Valerie interrupted. "Jamie told you her head hurt before you fell down here?"

"Yeah," Jordan replied. "Then all of a sudden, more rocks fell from the ceiling. That's when I dropped my PCD, I think. We moved over to the corner of the room, and that's when the floor broke apart, and we both fell through it." Jordan wiped the last remaining tears away. "And then you and Valerie showed up."

"Well, at least the two of you are safe," Logan said.

A rescue worker approached them. "Aside from her headache, your daughter appears to be fine," he said. "I suspect she might have a small concussion. We'll get her ready to transfer up. It will be a few more minutes."

"Thank you," Logan said. He could see them lowering a small gurney via the hoist that had been set up above. Logan looked back at his son. "After all this, you're going to be able to write one heck of a report."

"Logan." Mr. Montez's voice called out from the opposite end of the room. "You must see this."

Logan hesitated to leave Jamie, who was being readied for transport.

"Go," Valerie said. "I'll watch her."

"You stay here with Valerie, too," Logan told Jordan. "This chamber might not be structurally sound."

Jordan shook his head, picking up a lantern. "I'm going with you," he insisted.

Logan and Jordan joined Mr. Montez in front of a wall of murals depicting six marching men in colorful regalia. "They look very similar to the statue you found," Logan observed.

Mr. Montez pointed to the head of one of the figures. "Look at their headbands."

"The symbols of Satraya," Logan said, startled to see the symbols in another ancient work of art. "And there's that snowflake again. Similar to what we saw on the statue."

Mr. Montez nodded his head.

"What is that smoke coming from their mouths?" Jordan asked.

"I do not believe that is smoke," Mr. Montez said. "I think these men are priests, and the wavy lines represent the prayers they are reciting. This mural is similar to others found in the compound of Tepantitla here at Teotihuacán. But none of the other murals includes the depiction of the symbols."

Mr. Montez held his lantern above his head and moved to the center of the room, pointing to a number of small, half-meter-square openings in the rounded ceiling. Jordan started to count them. "Twenty-one of them," he reported.

"They're way too small for anyone to climb through," Logan said, "and definitely too high for anyone to get to without some kind of ladder."

"They seem to dart off in every direction," Mr. Montez observed. "Very interesting."

Logan and Jordan walked over to another section of the chamber, and on their way, Jordan tripped over something on the floor. Logan caught him by the arm before he fell. Looking down, he saw a dark circular platform on the ground. He called to Mr. Montez, "Isn't this similar to the base of the kneeling man statue in the research center?"

Jordan bent down and brushed the dust off the surface, revealing a carved image of a coiled serpent at its center. A small red stone served as one of the serpent's eyes.

Mr. Montez walked over and examined the platform, which rose to ankle height off the ground. "Yes!" he said excitedly, running his fingers over the etching. "It is made out of mica, like the one I showed you. And with another coiled serpent," he added softly.

As Jordan continued to clean the surface, he inadvertently dislodged the red stone. "Sorry!" he said, trying to put it back into place. "I didn't mean to."

Mr. Montez gently grabbed Jordan's arm, and before the boy could replace the stone, he bent down and placed his ear over the hole where it had been set. He smiled and looked at Logan. "You must hear this."

Logan joined him and listened. "It sounds like trickling water."

"Yes. Because of the volcanic activity that once occurred here, there are many deep lava tunnels below Teotihuacán. At one time, water flowed through them, a natural irrigation system."

"I wonder if this tunnel is linked to the river we crossed over earlier."

"Perhaps. Do you remember what I said about electrical transmission and conductivity?"

Logan's eyebrows rose. "Water is an excellent conductor of electricity."

Mr. Montez nodded thoughtfully.

"What are these things?" Jordan asked, squatting next to seven small, oddly formed ceramic objects. "It looks like a different animal is painted on each one." Jordan held one up to show Logan.

Mr. Montez turned to see what he had found. "Those are whistling vessels. You can tell by the double-chambered barrels. They are similar to ones found in Peru." Mr. Montez picked one up and dusted it off with a handkerchief. "These were used by shamans and priests. You blow into the shaft attached to the back chamber. It is said that their sound produced miraculous healing and visions for those who knew how to play them properly." He placed his lips around the end of the shaft and attempted to demonstrate, but he was only able to manage a few broken sounds. "Well, something like that."

"The skeletons are over here by the archway," Jordan said, grabbing Logan's arm and leading him under an archway that was almost twice as tall as Logan and wider than his outward reach. On the ground leaning against each side were the skeletal remains of a body. In the corner near the archway was a small wooden cart with a single wheel. It looked like a wheelbarrow.

Logan squatted down, his lantern casting an eerie shadow on the skeletons. He blew the dust off something resting on the nasal bone of the skull. It appeared to be a headband made from a narrow strip of copper. "It's similar to what the figures in the murals are wearing." Logan looked around, trying to spot anything that resembled a door. "How could they have gotten down here?"

Mr. Montez inspected the wall set into the inner portion of the arch behind the skeletons. He ran his hands along the smooth surface. "A façade of some kind. This is the only portion of the walls that doesn't have any paintings on it. I wonder if this used to be a doorway."

"Are you saying that someone entombed these men in here?" Logan asked.

Mr. Montez shook his head. "If this was truly the only door to this chamber, then its smooth-finished surface suggests that these two entombed themselves."

"Why would they do that?"

Even if Mr. Montez had an answer to Logan's question, he didn't have a chance to offer it. Valerie was calling out to Logan. He turned and saw her kneeling next to Jamie with a concerned look on her face. He rushed over and realized why: Jamie had fallen unconscious.

6

It may take but a second to change, but it will
take a life time to prove it.

—THE CHRONICLES OF SATRAYA

NEW CHICAGO, 5:05 P.M. LOCAL TIME, MARCH 20, 2070

The sound of crumpling packing paper filled the northeast work room of the Camden and Cassandra Ford Studio of Art in New Chicago, which Logan had established in honor of his parents. Valerie's father, Mr. Perrot, and the studio's gallery manager, Jasper Jones, were busy preparing items for shipment for the upcoming commemoration of the founding members of the Council of Satraya in Washington, D.C. Logan had decided to show some of his mother's artwork at the commemoration and to donate one or two pieces for permanent display at the Council headquarters as a tribute to his parents.

Logan had recently hired Jasper to assist him in managing the gallery. An extremely energetic twenty-four-year-old, Jasper spoke in short bursts of sentences and rarely stood still. He was thin, stood more than two meters tall, and always wore colorful clothing and high-top black canvas shoes with bright white laces. No one ever knew what color his hair would be on a given day. Over the past three months, Logan had been pleased to see that Jasper's eccentricity was matched by his extreme efficiency.

Mr. Perrot, himself a founding member of the Council of Satraya, was delighted to have just learned that the wooden box in which the late Deya Sarin had found her set of the *Chronicles*, known as the River Set, had arrived at the Council headquarters the day before. Deya's husband, Babu Sarin, had sent it from his home in Banaras, India. The Council's attempts to locate Madu Shata, the finder of the Pyramid Set, had been unsuccessful, which surprised no one, since Madu hadn't been seen in close to forty years. Even though Mr. Perrot was one of the few people in the world who knew the true account of the discovery of the fourth set of the *Chronicles*, known as the Train Set, he reluctantly supported the Council's attempts to contact the executor of the Hitchlords estate. As it turned out, the estate would contribute nothing to the commemoration, because the World Crime Federation had seized all of Simon Hitchlords's assets.

"It is going to be a fabulous event!" Jasper said excitedly, handing a shipping label to Mr. Perrot. "The Council is lucky to be getting a few of Cassandra's mosaics for the exhibit and all those photographs from your album."

Mr. Perrot secured the label to a shipping box. "All of these photographs certainly bring back some good memories," he said with a smile. Alain Perrot had been Camden Ford's closest friend. Camden had rescued him from marauders at a safe house near the Ozark forest forty years ago, when he was still known as Robert Tilbo. He changed his name when he, Camden, and Cassandra fled from Washington, D.C., with their children for New Chicago after the splintering of the original Council. To this day, the circumstances surrounding the Splintering had never been fully revealed to the public.

Mr. Perrot looked at a few of the photos they had decided not to send. There was one of him holding his baby daughter, standing next to Camden and Cassandra at the hospital just after Valerie was born. Logan, almost a year old at the time, was sitting in a stroller. Valerie's mother, Andrea Montavon, was still in the intensive-care unit, recovering from the complications of her long and arduous labor. Mr. Perrot took a deep breath and slowly shook his head. "Beauty can truly have thorny origins," he whispered.

"What was that?" Jasper asked.

"Nothing," Mr. Perrot replied. "Just some old memories."

Jasper gave Mr. Perrot a curious look but did not press. "Have you heard from our world travelers today?"

"No, not yet. They must be having too much fun in Mexico. But come now, we still have more of Cassandra's things to rummage through." Mr. Perrot felt his PCD vibrating and quickly checked his pockets. "Where did I put that thing?" He reached inside his tweed jacket and, fumbling, located his PCD and took it out. "This might be them," he said, as he looked at the PCD number, and then he thought otherwise. "Actually, I'm not sure who this number belongs to." The main line to the studio had started ringing, and Jasper ran to the front to answer it, as Mr. Perrot tried to project a 3-D image of the caller. He didn't recognize the face of the well-groomed man with graying hair and sad eyes that was finally projected. "This is Alain Perrot," he said.

"I am looking for a Robert Tilbo," the man answered. "I was told he could be reached at this number."

Mr. Perrot's heart began to beat faster. While his true identity had recently been made public, he was hesitant to speak with an unknown man calling from an unknown number. "Who should I say is calling?" Mr. Perrot asked.

The man didn't immediately answer, adding to Mr. Perrot's tension. "Tell him that his past has finally caught up with him. Tell him that I am the man who taught Camden Ford the King's Gambit and the one no one could take in a chess match."

Mr. Perrot thought for a moment and then squinted, trying harder to recognize the man in the projection. "Madu?" he finally asked in a low voice.

The man began to laugh heartily. "Yes, Robert. It is me," Madu confirmed. "You were always so easy to play with." His laughter continued.

"Where . . . What have you . . ." Mr. Perrot stammered, his heart still racing, now with excitement. "I am at a loss for words."

"What, Robert Tilbo at a loss for words? How can that be? You could never stop talking when we were together on the Council."

Mr. Perrot joined in his laughter. "I am not sure what my first question should be. I have so many to ask."

"I am certain we both have many stories to share and questions to pose," Madu replied.

"Yes," Mr. Perrot said. "To begin with, how did you find me?"

"Not very difficult after you and Logan emerged from hiding," Madu said. "That was a great surprise to both my wife and me."

"How is Nadine?" Mr. Perrot asked.

"Well, very well," Madu said. Then he continued in a more serious tone, "Robert, is it true that Camden and Cassandra were murdered? It was reported that the killer was never caught. We wondered if their deaths had anything to do with their past dealings with Fendral and Andrea."

"Yes, Camden and Cassandra were killed, by whom we do not know." Mr. Perrot sighed. "Much has happened over the last few years, in particular the last nine months. Simon and Andrea returned and attempted to pick up where Fendral had left off. It forced Logan and me to come forward."

"Yes, Simon and Andrea. Is the news of their demise accurate? It was reported they died in an accident along the Ganges River?"

"The story spun by the authorities conceals most of the facts. But yes, they are both gone," Mr. Perrot said. "My daughter and Logan witnessed the death of Andrea, and all three of us watched Simon die."

"And does your daughter know the truth? That Andrea was her mother?"

Mr. Perrot sighed deeply. "She knows the complete story now."

Madu took that in before asking, "What happened to Fendral's set of the *Chronicles*? Have they been bequeathed to anyone?"

"No," Mr. Perrot answered. "In fact, before he died, Simon possessed three of the sets."

"*Three?*" Madu seemed stunned at the news.

"Yes," said Mr. Perrot. "The Train Set, left to him by his father; the Forest Set, which Logan unwittingly auctioned off; and . . ."

"My set," Madu said regretfully. "It was Simon who stole it from the Cairo Museum, wasn't it?"

"Yes."

"What has happened to the River Set? Does Babu still possess it?"

"No," Mr. Perrot answered. "Logan has Deya's books under lock and key."

"Good," Madu said. Both men were quiet for a moment. "Camden once told me that all four sets of the books should never be possessed by one individual. He never elaborated. Neither did Deya when I asked her. She only confirmed what Camden had told me." Mr. Perrot knew the reason behind Camden's warning, but he remained silent. "I see now that I was wrong in thinking that donating my books to the Cairo Museum would keep them safe."

There was another pause, and then Mr. Perrot continued. "Madu, why have you come forward? Why now?"

"I have only come forward to you, Robert," Madu replied, "and I would appreciate it if we kept it that way for now. My story is a long one, and I will need a good deal of time to relate it to you accurately. Unfortunately, I can't do it now. But I will call you again soon."

"When?" Mr. Perrot asked. "There is a commemoration in honor of the original members of the Council. You must attend! Come to Washington with Nadine, and make a grand entrance. People will be shocked by your emergence."

"That may not be possible," Madu said. "My work requires me to travel the world. But we will consider it. Until then—"

"Journey with care, Madu," Mr. Perrot said.

The call ended, and the image of Madu disappeared. Mr. Perrot stared into space. He wasn't sure what to think about the sudden reappearance of Madu Shata after forty years. "Is it really so shocking?" he whispered to himself. "You, too, had to disappear for that long."

"Mr. Perrot!" Jasper called, running into the work room. "That was Logan on the phone. There was a terrible earthquake in Mexico."

"What?" Mr. Perrot's thoughts immediately turned to his daughter, Logan, and the children. "Is everyone all right?"

"Logan said that Jamie fell and may have hit her head inside a pyramid at Teoti—" Jasper had trouble pronouncing the name. "Wherever they are. Jamie's in serious condition; they are at the hospital now. Logan said that Mexico City is a mess. The earthquake caused a ton of damage to the outskirts of the city. The hospitals are flooded with wounded people. They're going to get back as soon as they can once Jamie's condition is stabilized." Jasper pulled out his own PCD and brought up and projected a news report.

"Reports of earthquakes are still coming in from around the world," the news anchor said. "Thus far, twelve reports have crossed our desk here at the studio. Scientists are baffled by the sudden quakes and are unable to identify their magnitudes and the locations of their epicenters. An inside source is telling us that the E-QON II system, which was put in place after the Great Disruption to predict seismic activity, appears to have failed. President Salize of the NAF urges people to remain calm, despite speculation among local authorities in the hardest-hit areas that these quakes are a precursor to another Great Disruption–class event."

Mr. Perrot watched the report in disbelief. He was well aware of the events leading up to the Great Disruption and the enormous pain and suffering it had imposed on the world. *It can't be happening again . . .*

7

Believers are in a perpetual state of anticipation.
Stop believing, and know.

—THE CHRONICLES OF SATRAYA

CHÂTEAU DUGAN, SWISS ALPS, 1:08 A.M. LOCAL TIME, MARCH 21, 2070

"Any word on how much longer we need to stay here?" said a young WCF agent, as he zipped up his jacket. "This is not what I expected on my first assignment."

"Don't complain," an older agent advised. "At least you're not sitting behind a desk. This is how many of our assignments go. You've been watching too many HoloPad dramas."

The younger agent looked out over the large lake, which bordered the north side of Château Dugan. He and his partner stood on a wooden dock that stretched twenty meters into the water. A thick, chilly fog hovered over the surface of the lake. Their only companions were a band of coyotes howling in a dense forest to the west and an owl that hooted occasionally as it searched for a midnight meal. The young agent turned and gazed at the grand stone stairway that traversed four terraces and led to the main house at the top of a hill. "How does someone get so rich?" he asked, as he adjusted the rifle slung over his shoulder.

"It's all family money," the other agent replied. "The Hitchlordses were rich before the Great Disruption, and somehow they stayed that way."

"I heard Simon Hitchlords gave a lot of money to charities and foundations."

"Yeah, that's the story."

"You don't believe it?"

"If he was such a good guy, why are we guarding his estate? I heard that members of our NAF team were after him in India, and before they could arrest him, he fell into some kind of fire pit." The agent shook his head. "I think he committed suicide."

"Now, see," the young agent said, "that's a good assignment. Why can't we do something like that instead of standing out here?"

"You can take it up with Colette in the morning," the older agent said. Then something caught his ear. He walked to the end of the dock, drawing his weapon. The younger agent followed him. "Do you hear that? Sounds like a boat motor."

Following his partner's lead, the younger agent readied his rifle. "I can't see a thing through this fog."

The two of them listened to the sound as it grew louder. The boat emerging out of the fog was smaller than they had expected. "Stop!" the older agent shouted. "Stop, or we'll shoot." The boat was close enough now for them to see that it was empty. They both lowered their weapons, confounded. It bumped into the dock, its motor still running. "That's weird. Call it in," the older agent said.

As the younger agent took out his PCD and started walking back to shore, he heard a muffled thump. Turning, he saw his partner lunge forward and fall into the lake. The young agent rushed to help him but was stopped by a sharp pain in his side. The last thing he saw was someone in a black diving suit.

The howling of the coyotes grew louder as the intruder pulled himself out of the water. With his gun still drawn, he walked to the end of the dock and made sure that the young agent was dead. He rolled the body off the deck and into the water, next to the floating body of his partner. Then he pulled his PCD from the water-tight compartment of his wetsuit and pressed a few buttons, and the boat's motor stopped running. After replacing his PCD in the pocket of his wetsuit, the man lowered himself into the water, grabbed each of the WCF agents by an arm, and, staying close to the dock, waded closer to shore. The dock led to a utility house adjacent to the steps leading to the Château's lakeside entrance. But that was not going to be his means of entry. There was another way into the dungeons of Château Dugan.

A few meters before he reached the shore, he ducked under the dock and maneuvered himself through the support beams, struggling at times to maintain control of the agents' bodies. He came to a steel-barred door, similar to those found in old-fashioned jail cells. The cold lake water flowed freely through the iron bars. He pulled from the pocket of his wetsuit a brass key. But when he pressed on the door's handle, he found it unlocked. Returning the key to his chest pocket, he opened the door and pushed the bodies through the doorway before entering the dark tunnel himself. He took out his PCD and attached it to his left wrist, pressing buttons until the body suit he was wearing began to glow, providing ample light. He pressed more buttons on his PCD, and the image of a hand-drawn map was displayed. He'd been warned that the secret tunnels under the estate were like a rat's maze, where a person could easily get lost. He shut the iron door and proceeded.

After a series of left and right turns, the man stood in front of a brick wall spanning the width of the narrow tunnel. The man reached down and ran his hands along the lower portion of the wall below the water line. He took a deep breath and submerged himself. A moment later, he popped out of the water on the other side of the wall. He cleared his eyes and saw that he was at the bottom of the Château's well. He intensified the light from his suit until he could see the top, which he ascertained was twenty meters above him. A narrow spiral staircase ran up the interior. Using the wall as a support, he carefully climbed the slippery, mold-covered steps. After about three minutes, he reached the top of the well and slung himself over the edge. He had made it unnoticed into the dungeons.

The luminosity from his suit filled the large circular area, where eight iron doors lined its circumference; the handles of each door had been removed. There was security tape across each doorway, indicating that the WCF had searched them all.

The man projected another hand-drawn map from his PCD. He zoomed in on the configuration of the eight doors and the nearby staircase. A red marker indicated that the room he was interested in was three doors to the right of the staircase. He walked over and ripped off the security tape. He pushed the door open, its hinges squeaking as he entered. There was a musky, damp smell in the air.

The man walked across the stone floor, past a couple of metal buckets and a metal chair, toward the northeast corner of the room. Once there, he took a magnet out of his pocket. Starting at the floor, he slowly ran it up the corner of the wall until it was drawn to a particular spot one meter off the ground. He pulled back the magnet, and the stone it attracted slid from the wall, causing a hidden door to his left to open. The man left the magnet in place and walked through the doorway, causing lights to come on. A table was at the center of the room, and the walls were lined with stainless-steel shelves and boxes and other items. The man grabbed a Gore-Tex bag from beneath the table and squatted down in front of one of the shelves. On the lower shelf, he saw ten stacks of electronic bearer bonds, EBBs. One by one, he placed each stack of forty in the bag. After the Great Disruption, paper money became less popular, but everyone agreed on the need for some form of currency that could not be manipulated by unscrupulous governments. The result: EBBs, palm-sized pieces of glass that could be micro-encoded with any desired amount of Universal Credits by sanctioned central banking authorities. The EBBs could not be tracked, and whoever possessed them held claim to them without question.

After the man had put all of them into the bag, he went over to another shelf, where he found a large silver case with a security keypad attached to it. He grabbed the case and placed it on the ground. The man typed a series of numbers on the keypad, and the case opened. Inside was the prize he was looking for: nine leather-bound books and a blue journal. Satisfied, he closed the lid, put the case into the bag alongside the EBBs, and zipped it closed. He pulled from his chest pocket a small aerosol can and sprayed it all over the bag, paying special attention to its zipper. The green foam quickly dried into a rubber-like coating, making the bag waterproof. He returned the can to his chest pocket, swung the bag over his shoulder, and left the hidden room. He pushed the dislodged stone back into place, watching as the door to the hidden room closed. Then he removed the magnet from the wall.

The man made his way back to the well and down the slippery stone stairway. Once again, he ducked through the opening in the well wall to the other side. The waterproof bag floated alongside him as he backtracked through the tunnels and returned to the iron-barred door. He pushed aside the bodies of the two dead agents, then closed the barred door and this time locked it with the brass key. He quickly waded to the end of the dock and swung the large bag into the boat before climbing in himself. He started the motor and sped onto the lake, disappearing into the thickening fog. He heard coyotes howling in the distance.

8

You will never be bigger or smaller than what you do.

—THE CHRONICLES OF SATRAYA

NEW CHICAGO, 6:10 P.M. LOCAL TIME, MARCH 20, 2070

Mr. Perrot waited anxiously for an update on Jamie's condition, but neither he nor Jasper had heard from Logan or Valerie in the last hour, and his PCD calls to them hadn't gone through because of a disruption of the communication network in Mexico's Central Plateau. All they could do was wait and continue diligently to prepare for the commemoration to keep their minds occupied, something Mr. Perrot was clearly still struggling with. The news of Jamie's injury, the rash of earthquakes, the unexpected emergence of Madu Shata—it seemed strange, if not ominous, for them all to happen at once.

"Jamie will be fine," Jasper said, alert to Mr. Perrot's consternation. "No sense worrying about something we can't control."

"Agreed," Mr. Perrot replied. He put the lid back on a box that he'd been rummaging through. "I haven't found anything in these boxes that is worth sending to the commemoration. Does Logan have any more of Cassandra's possessions here?"

"Yes, there's much more in the vault, along with his mom's mosaics."

Jasper walked to a solid metal door near the corner of the work room, typed a series of numbers onto a keypad, and then placed his eye in front of the retina scanner. An extended beep sounded, and the lock on the door disengaged. Mr. Perrot followed Jasper into a neatly organized cement-fortified vault, which was half the size of the work room.

"We moved all of Mrs. Ford's stuff from Logan's house a few weeks ago. Art stuff in front of us. Files, books, and other office stuff over to the left. Jewelry, trinkets, and other valuables are in the secondary safe to the right. But you'll need Logan to get into that. He is the only one with access."

Mr. Perrot walked straight ahead. A smile came to his face. "These are Cassandra's mosaics. It's been a while since I've seen them."

"Aren't they gorgeous?" Jasper said. "Three of them are headed to the commemoration. It's going to be a mosaic extravaganza! Logan plans to display the rest here at the studio."

Mr. Perrot chuckled at Jasper's exuberance, then turned to the mosaics, set up on eight easels. One depicted three dolphins swimming in the ocean. Another showed a woman gazing into a mirror. Mr. Perrot moved closer to a third mosaic, which was roughly half a meter tall and the same wide. "This one is my favorite. It took Cassandra more than a year to make it." Two trees stood on top of a hill in some far-off imaginary land. One was tall, the other much smaller and situated in the foreground. "I just love how majestic these trees look," Mr. Perrot said, running his fingers over the many small, multicolored tiles. "This scene is from one of the *Chronicles* stories, you know."

Jasper shook his head. "Which story is that?"

Mr. Perrot turned to Jasper with an incredulous look. "You young people really need to bone up on your history. The world rose from the ashes of the Great Disruption because of the *Chronicles* and all the wonderful stories in the books." Mr. Perrot turned back to the mosaic, shaking his head in mock disgust. "Everyone should read the fable of the Golden Acorn. What are they teaching you in school these days, if not that?"

Jasper walked over and stood in front of the seventh and most abstract mosaic of the group, which was just more than half a meter tall and approximately three times as wide. "Logan told me that his mother never explained to him what this mosaic depicted," Jasper said, tilting his head from side to side and stepping back to try to figure it out. "It looks like a broken dish or something."

Mr. Perrot looked at the mosaic. "Yes, that one is a real head scratcher. Cassandra always taunted me for not being able to discern its meaning. As far as I know, she never told anyone, except perhaps Camden."

Jasper shrugged, giving up on interpreting the mosaic. "So what are we looking for?"

"Ideally, items from the days of the first Council," Mr. Perrot said. "Anything that might shed new light on the experiences or accomplishments of the original Council members. We can start with those," he added, motioning to a set of boxes stacked against the wall.

They were filled with file folders, books, art supplies, and other knickknacks. Jasper started rummaging through plastic containers that held an endless supply of arts-and-crafts materials. Mr. Perrot uncovered a sturdy, heavy metal box that contained a trove of mosaic tiles of all shapes, sizes, and colors. Jasper found a box with some thin circular objects that shone when they caught the light. "What are these?" he asked, holding one up.

"Those are DVDs," Mr. Perrot answered with a chuckle. "That is how the world once distributed its music and movie entertainment."

Jasper gave the disk a quizzical look and tossed it back into the box.

"Here we go," Mr. Perrot said, pulling out a box of newspaper articles. "These are from the *New Chicago Broadcaster*, dated May 15, 2037, a few months after we came to Chicago." He leafed through a stack of clippings. "After the Great Disruption, paper publishing was the only way to disseminate information. All the years of converting paper to digital went out the door in ten short months. It looks like Cassandra kept everything she could find on the activities of the Council." Mr. Perrot looked at the dates on another set of clippings. "These are more recent, from August 2052."

"That's about the time the *Broadcaster* went back to an all-digital format and the Akasha Vault came online," Jasper said, then gave Mr. Perrot a big grin. "See, I know *some* history."

While Mr. Perrot began to read some of the articles, Jasper struggled to drag something that looked like an old sea chest away from the wall. Mr. Perrot stopped to assist him. The chest was made of wood that looked distressed from age. There were two leather handles on each side and another attached to the lid. Together they moved it to the middle of the room. There was no lock on its tarnished brass latch. Jasper eagerly raised the lid, and the two of them peered inside with the anticipation of pirates who had just opened a long-lost treasure chest. Jasper removed a green and yellow checked blanket that covered the chest's contents.

"That was Cassandra's blanket when she lived in the forest with the Forgotten Ones," Mr. Perrot said. "Logan made use of it when he was a baby. Even my Valerie used it for a time." Jasper set the blanket aside and removed an old oil lamp, along with a bundle of pens and pencils bound with a rubber band. Then Jasper removed something that brought a reminiscing smile to Mr. Perrot's face. "That's Cassandra's satchel. When we all were on the Council and lived in Washington, she used to carry this with her wherever she went."

Jasper laughed. "So that's why Logan carries his backpack all over creation. It's a genetic trait!" Mr. Perrot chuckled in agreement. Jasper opened the satchel's flap and pulled out an old wooden bowl and a tarnished silver spoon. "Why would she keep these?"

"For remembrance," said Mr. Perrot, taking them from Jasper. "This was the bowl and spoon that Cassandra used when she lived with the Forgotten Ones." He rubbed the tip of the spoon with his thumb to see if any of the tarnish would come off. "She kept them because they reminded her of how precious and fragile life could be. The bowl and spoon reminded her not to take for granted even one day or a single meal."

Jasper ran his fingers along a series of small nicks on the bowl's side. "Looks like it's been through a war."

"In a way, it has," Mr. Perrot said. "Cassandra put those marks there purposefully. Each one represented a day without food. "

"Sir," Jasper said then, looking at Mr. Perrot respectfully, "you need to write down all these stories. They're a lot more interesting than the bland history lessons they give us in school. Maybe more young people would be inspired by history if they heard the more human side of it."

Mr. Perrot smiled. "Let's see what else is in this satchel."

"I'm serious," Jasper said, setting the bowl and the spoon on the floor. He reached back in and took out a rectangular silver device, which easily fit into his hand. He also removed a handful of small tube-like objects. "These look interesting," he said, holding them out to show Mr. Perrot.

"I can't believe she kept it," Mr. Perrot said, astonished, taking the silver device from Jasper. "This is Cassandra's voice recorder. While Logan's father kept a written journal, his mother kept an oral one."

Jasper held up a fistful of the small copper and black tubes. "What are these things?"

"Those are the batteries for this recorder," Mr. Perrot said.

"I wonder if it still works." Jasper inspected it. He pressed the Play button, but nothing happened.

"After all this time, the batteries must be dead," Mr. Perrot said. Jasper opened a small slot on the side of the recorder and pulled out a thin piece of black plastic about two centimeters wide and a little longer. "That's the old-style memory card where the recordings were stored. Are there any more in Cassandra's satchel?" Mr. Perrot was pensive for a moment. Jasper turned the bag upside down and shook it. Two more batteries fell to the ground. "With all the recordings I saw Cassandra make, she must have had a whole slew of these memory chips. I wonder if they stole them when they—" Mr. Perrot caught himself before saying any more.

"Who stole what?" Jasper asked.

Mr. Perrot didn't have time to answer the question. "We need to find a way to listen to the contents of this chip," he said. "If we can get it working, this is sure to provide an important historical account of life right after the Great Disruption."

Jasper thought for a moment, then rose to his feet and walked over to a shelf. "We could try the Uni-P," Jasper said, connecting the leads of the Universal Power Device, known as a Uni-P, to the recorder's battery compartment. Jasper took the memory chip back from Mr. Perrot and inserted it into the recorder. "Here goes nothing," he said, as he pressed the power button. Mr. Perrot waited in anticipation. Suddenly, the recorder activated. "*Magnifico!*" Jasper said, looking at the recorder's LCD display. "Looks like there are two entries. One from December 2037 and the other recorded much later, in February 2064." He selected the first entry and hit the Play button.

"It is December 1, 2037," a woman's voice said, faint and raspy, mixed with static. Still, Mr. Perrot smiled. He knew that voice—it was one he had not heard in almost three years. Jasper turned up the volume, and Mr. Perrot listened to Cassandra speak across the years.

. . . and this is going to be my last recording. We've made it to New Chicago to start our new lives. Logan is too young to understand what is happening. As we feared, the Council of Satraya has splintered. Camden tried to reason with Fendral, and Robert pleaded with Andrea, but to no avail. Robert has joined us here with his beautiful little girl. I'm so sad that she won't have a mother in her life. But it had to be done. Andrea is as cruelly ambitious as Fendral. I feel so sorry for Simon—he is such an intelligent boy. If his mother were here, I would have a thing or two to say to her. Camden has left the leadership of the Council in the hands of Cynthia Brown. I hope she is able to accomplish what we couldn't. One thing is clear: there is no telling what Fendral and Andrea will do to advance their agendas.

Jasper paused the playback. "Is that the same Cynthia Brown who was murdered last year along with those other Council members?" he asked.

"The one and the same," Mr. Perrot answered.

Jasper considered asking Mr. Perrot about Valerie's mother but thought better of it. Instead, he resumed the playback with a more serious expression on his face. He was beginning to grasp just how much history he had never been taught.

We all agree that for our own safety, our past must be forgotten. We are all changing our names. Even Robert's daughter's name will change, just to be safe. I like Valerie much better than Tabatha, which I think was more Andrea's idea than Robert's, anyway. Tomorrow will be my first day as Alexandra Cutler.

For our new identities to work, we need to let go of everything—family, friends, loved ones. It's so hard not being able to tell anyone where we are going.

As a precaution to safeguard our identities, I've decided to stop using my recorder. It's going to be so difficult to discard all these old memory chips. So much of my life is on them. But I need to let the past go.

This is my final entry as Cassandra Toliver Ford.

Mr. Perrot and Jasper heard a soft gasp and stifled sobbing before the recording ended.

"It must have been so hard for all of you," Jasper said reflectively. "Giving up your lives and all that you worked so hard to accomplish . . ."

Mr. Perrot nodded, moved. "You mentioned that there was one more recording."

"Yes." Jasper looked at the recorder's display and pressed the Play button. "It's from February 2064, twenty-seven years after the one we just heard."

I'm breaking my long-standing promise about making my last recording. Camden . . . I mean, Henry—after all these years, I still can't get used to our new names. Henry came across an article in the January 15th edition of the Swiss Times *reporting that Alfred Benson was found dead in his home, cause unknown. Accompanying the report was a photo of Andrea. Henry and I debated if we should tell Alain, and we decided not to. Why stir up the past when he and Valerie are so happy now? Simon Hitchlords was also in the photograph, standing next to Andrea. Looks like Andrea had another child. Her son, Lucius Benson, is also shown and identified. Simon has grown up to look just like his father, Fendral. A slight man in a wheelchair was in the background. He's the same man we used to see from time to time in Washington visiting Fendral and Andrea.*

Mr. Perrot gestured for Jasper to pause the recording. "Would it be possible for you to find that article?"

Jasper whipped out his PCD. "Searching for *Swiss Times*, January 15, 2064 . . . What was the man's name?"

"Alfred Benson," Mr. Perrot said.

After another moment, Jasper projected the article and the photo from his PCD.

Mr. Perrot studied the photo. "This is Simon, Andrea, and Lucius," he said, pointing them out to Jasper. "And this man in the wheelchair, I do remember seeing him, but I never spoke to him or caught his name." Mr. Perrot took one last look, and Jasper pressed the Play button again.

I didn't think much of the photo at first, but then Camden noticed the black roses. Andrea is carrying one in her hand, and Simon, Lucius, and the man in the wheelchair have them in their lapels. I can't help but remember the black roses that were found in Deya's car and Madu's home after their lives were threatened when the Council was splintering. Camden and I had the same thought. Was Andrea's husband, Alfred Benson, murdered? Are Simon and Andrea up to something? And is that man in the wheelchair somehow involved?

Camden wants to investigate, but I won't let him risk his life and the life of our son by getting involved again, even covertly, with these dangerous people. After all, we only have suspicions, no proof of wrongdoing or any clue to their motives. It would be foolish to stir the hornet's nest.

We have been anonymously writing to Cynthia Brown over the past year, offering advice. The Council seems to be faltering. Camden wants to send Cynthia this article, but I'm not so sure it's a good idea.

I also saw a photo of RJ in the paper today. Camden doesn't think it is him. But I know it is. His eyes had that same cold expression I'll never forget. I can't believe what he's become.

There was an extended pause in the recording. Mr. Perrot and Jasper could hear some shuffling and the sound of book pages being turned. A few moments later, Cassandra spoke again.

When it unfurled, it was filled with golden acorns. Hundreds and hundreds of them. A bright and intoxicating gold light glistened from each as the acorns seemed to be gently nestled among leaf-filled branches. The man understood in that moment that what is given in unconditional love is never truly lost.

That was the end of the recording. Jasper looked at Mr. Perrot. "Interesting last entry."

"Interesting indeed," Mr. Perrot agreed. "Why would she read from the Golden Acorn story in the *Chronicles*? While it's a wonderful tale, with many lessons for us all, why make it your last entry? It doesn't make sense. We must find out what she did with the other memory chips. I certainly hope she didn't destroy them."

Jasper set the recorder down, pointing to the mosaic with the trees. "Isn't the Golden Acorn the same story that inspired Cassandra to create that?"

Mr. Perrot turned and looked at it. Then he walked over and examined the back of it. "I wonder if Cassandra might have hidden something behind the matting."

"Mr. Perrot, I like the way you think." Jasper went to take hold of one end of the mosaic as Mr. Perrot grabbed the other, and together they lifted it from the easel and attempted to set it facedown on a nearby table. As they did so, the frame slipped from Mr. Perrot's hand,

and his end of the mosaic hit the table. He cringed at his clumsiness. Jasper set his end down more cautiously.

Mr. Perrot ran his hand over the matting. He grabbed a pair of scissors off the table and pierced the black cardboard. He proceeded to cut the backing along all four sides.

With great anticipation, Jasper removed the black cardboard. The two of them inspected the mosaic for anything that looked like recording chips. Mr. Perrot set the scissors down in disappointment. "I thought we had it."

"So did I," Jasper said.

After replacing the backing, Jasper helped Mr. Perrot move the mosaic back to the easel. When they returned to the table to clean up the scraps of cardboard that had been cut away, Mr. Perrot was alarmed to see that two tiles had been dislodged when he'd dropped the mosaic. "I'll get some glue," Jasper said, and walked over to the supply shelf.

Mr. Perrot carefully picked up the two small tiles. One was green and rounded at the corners, the other square-shaped and painted gold. He walked back over to the mosaic and easily found where they needed to be glued.

"Don't worry, sir," Jasper said. "We'll get them reset in no time." Jasper placed a dab of glue on the green tile and put it back into position. He held it in place for a moment. He was ready for the second tile, but Mr. Perrot was still examining the back of it. "What are you looking at?" Jasper asked.

Mr. Perrot scratched the tile with his fingernail, and tiny flakes of gold paint floated off of it. "It seems I may be vindicated for my blunder." After scratching the rest of the paint off, he held up the title. "Now, doesn't that look exactly like one of Cassandra's recording chips?"

Jasper looked at the mosaic and counted about twenty similar gold tiles in it. "I think you may have found Cassandra's missing memories."

9

Do you really believe that it takes a lifetime to
know what a master knows?
Everyone who has reached the pinnacle of his
enlightenment will say to you, it took a lifetime to
realize that it didn't need to take a lifetime.

—THE CHRONICLES OF SATRAYA

OVER THE PACIFIC OCEAN, 7:40 P.M. LOCAL TIME, MARCH 20, 2070

Madu Shata looked out the airplane window at the Pacific Ocean far
below him. The sun was setting, and the brightest of the stars were
beginning to appear in the dusky sky. The cabin lights had been
dimmed, and his attention was drawn to his reflection in the window.
He thought about the puzzle whose solution had eluded him since the
day he'd found an original set of *The Chronicles of Satraya*. Even though
so much time had passed, he was still obsessed with learning the secret
of the pyramids. He had hoped that the emergence of Logan Ford and
his old friend Robert Tilbo would shed some light or offer a fruitful
new direction for his search. Destiny, he thought, had forsaken him; it
seemed to be the principle that ruled his existence. He leaned back in
his seat and thought about that pivotal day, forty years ago, that had
determined the course of his life and about the events leading up to it.

The Great Disruption ravaged northern Egypt. Earthquakes turned
the famously picturesque Mediterranean Sea into a raging cauldron of

water that flooded the coast as far south as Banha. People fortunate enough to survive the flooding, the earthquakes, their aftershocks, and tsunamis migrated south to Cairo, their last bastion of hope. While the city might have been spared the flooding, it was not spared the earthquakes or the climate changes that came with the earth's shifting four degree on its axis. Now there was rain in the deserts and drought in the rain forests.

As refugees from the north arrived in Cairo, they found a city riven by civil war. Within six months, Cairo had been divided into twelve sections called nomes, each run by its own ruthless Khufu. These twelve tyrants and their militias fought one another house to house and street to street, staking out their territory. With the city's police force disbanded and the Egyptian military in disarray, the Khufus were left unchecked, and their bloody battles continued.

By the spring of 2028, a tentative and fragile peace accord was forged among the twelve leaders, more out of necessity than desire. None of them wanted to rule an empty kingdom. More people had died in Cairo at the hands of the Khufus than in the natural disasters. Stone walls and fences were erected around each of the twelve nomes of Cairo, which were named after regions of post-Ptolemaic Egypt: Khent-abt, Kha, Ahment, Ati, Tehut, Am-Pehu, Sopdu, Khensu, Ka-khem, Theb-ka, Semabehdet, and Sap-Meh. Armed guards stood at the gates of the adjoining nomes. Without the proper paperwork, citizens of one nome could not pass into another. Once a person was branded on his right arm with the insignia of the nome in which he lived, that was where he stayed. If a person was caught trying to jump the borders, he was taken to the local Khufu to face justice. The penalty for most crimes and violations was public execution.

The edicts of the Khufus were carried out by their armed guards, the Medjay, who drove around Cairo in Jeeps, the only motor vehicles permitted in the city. Many of the Medjay had broken out of the Tora Mazraa prison and were more than happy to support the Khufus, who provided them with food and shelter that was not only better than what they'd had in prison but far superior to what the people of Cairo subsisted on.

A meager amount of food and other essential supplies were dispensed to Cairenes each day at a central location in every nome. People were not permitted to cultivate their own gardens or raise livestock.

One hour of electricity was provided each day by the nome of Ati, which was ruled by Khufu Kesi Sefu Khalfani. How Khufu Khalfani came to possess the large generators and the fuel to power them was unknown, but his possession of them made him the most powerful of all the Khufus.

Water was the only resource the Khufus did not completely control. Even after the Great Disruption, the northern-flowing Nile River's two major sources, the Blue Nile and the White Nile, continued to bring fresh water to the nomes. People could have as much as they were willing to carry home. But most preferred to use the dispensing stations, where, during the one hour of daily electric service, water was pumped into numerous reservoir pools located throughout the nomes. Citizens also created cisterns to collect the runoff water from rainstorms, which were frequent now because of the change in climate.

The only relief the Cairenes had from their hard, dreary lives was the Summer Jubilee, a seven-day celebration of the twelve Khufus' leadership. During the Jubilee, the guards at the gates of the nomes left their posts, and citizens could move freely throughout the city. Extended families separated all year were reunited for one precious week. But even during the Summer Jubilee celebrations, the Khufus kept close watch. The Medjay would discard their uniforms and dress as ordinary people so they could more easily blend into the crowds, where they would listen for any criticism of the Khufus. All Cairenes were required to attend the Jubilee's organized events at the stadium and the fairgrounds near the three Giza pyramids on the outskirts of Cairo. Failure to attend was punishable by death.

Madu recalled the soccer match of the 2029 Jubilee, when his life changed forever. He sat next to his grandfather and cheered for their home team from Tehut, which was playing the team from Ati, the most hated of the nomes because it controlled the city's electrical grid. His childhood friend Amun, whom he was only able to see during the yearly celebration, sat on his other side. Before the Great Disruption, both Madu and Amun attended the engineering school at Cairo University. Madu studied electrical engineering, while Amun pursued a degree in mechanical design. Both had recently celebrated their twenty-fourth birthdays, milestones that, before the rise of the Khufus, they had always celebrated together with their families and friends.

"Who are you looking at?" Amun asked.

"Does that girl look familiar to you?" Madu whispered. "A row ahead of us and a little to the left. She is wearing a gold dress with a wesekh necklace." Amun looked closer and shook his head. Madu asked his grandfather the same question, but he didn't recognize her, either. "I'm certain I've seen her before," Madu said, frustrated that he couldn't place where.

"She is pretty," Amun said. "And you are ugly. Therefore, I should be the one who speaks to her."

"I need to get a better look at her face," Madu said, losing interest in the soccer match. "There is something about her."

Madu decided to catch the girl's attention by letting out an excruciatingly loud cheer anytime his team advanced on the field or scored. But that didn't work. Then he decided to heckle even more loudly anytime the team from Ati fumbled. That worked better, anyway, as the young woman and her friends would turn from time to time to see where the ruckus was coming from. Madu acted as if he was intently focused on the match, but he was actually stealing glances at the girl, trying to figure out where he had seen her before.

"I don't think that girl and her friends are very happy with you," Amun said. "I think you're beginning to annoy them. Probably best to stop now."

"It is Jubilee, and I am only voicing support for our team," Madu answered. "I have to find out who she is." He leaned far to his left to get a better view of the girl. Amun grabbed him by the collar of his shirt and pulled him upright.

"Listen to Amun," Madu's grandfather said, giving his grandson a look of warning. "Mind her tattoos." They were on the girl's right arm. Unlike the rest of the citizenry, who were branded with the insignia of their nomes, members of the Khufus' families or those under their protection received customized ink tattoos. "She is from Ati and bears the mark of Khufu Khalfani. Stay clear of her, Madu. She is the Khufu's property or a member of his family. She has the authority to bring the wrath of the Khufus upon us."

Amun hit Madu in the arm and gestured for him to look at the two men flanking the young woman. They were unusually muscular and had the bearing of Medjay guards. Madu's grandfather was correct; the girl was someone of importance. Madu had no desire to draw the attention of any of the Khufus—that would be asking for it. It had happened before, and Madu was not going to repeat that experience. He remained quiet for the rest of match, which ended with the team from Ati taking the day.

Madu stood, and as he helped his grandfather to his feet, Amun urgently whispered, "She's looking at you!"

Madu turned. The young girl was indeed looking at him. Her expression indicated that he looked familiar to her, too, though she couldn't place him. They stared at each other some moments, and then Madu saw the young woman's eyes widen as if she had solved the mystery. Her eyes darted to Madu's grandfather and then back to Madu. She pointed to her right arm, signaling that she wanted to know which nome Madu was from. Without hesitating, Madu raised his arm to show her. He immediately saw an expression of dread come over her face. She broke eye contact and hurried away with her escort, leaving Madu to wonder where a member of Khufu Khalfani's circle and he would have crossed paths.

The firing of a shell from an Abram tank announced the final event of the Summer Jubilee, an event that no one but the Khufus enjoyed.

Armed Medjay began herding the crowd out of the soccer stadium toward the Menkaure Pyramid. The Khufus and their advisers were seated on a podium fifty meters away from the base of the ancient structure. The next and last event served as a warning to the people of Cairo: *This is what will happen to you if you challenge our authority.*

"Let us leave," Madu's grandfather said, as they exited the stands. "I will not watch another one of these abominable shows."

"They will not let us leave," Amun said. Everyone was required to watch the Pyramid Run. "The guards will force us to stay and watch."

"I know a way." Madu's grandfather pulled a package of cigarettes from his pocket and flashed it at Madu and Amun. "Follow me."

Another shell was fired, and Medjay guards fanned out at the base of the Menkaure Pyramid, while Madu, his grandfather, and Amun made their way to the southernmost gate. When Madu's grandfather presented two packages of cigarettes to the guard stationed there, the three of them were allowed to pass from the Giza Plateau and walk north to Al Ahram Road.

"I must leave you," Amun said sadly.

"Until next year, my friend." Madu hugged him, and Amun headed down another road to the nome of Semabehdet.

"Life cannot continue this way," Madu's grandfather said, shaking his head defiantly. "What kind of life is it to have seven days of freedom for each year of captivity? Something must be done."

A series of gunshots rang out from the direction of the pyramids. "You mustn't say things like that in public," Madu said, looking around to see if anyone might have heard him. "Don't you remember what happened?"

"Of course, I remember," Madu's grandfather said solemnly, looking down as he and Madu walked home. "They tried to do what needed to be done for the people. For Egypt!"

"Yes, but they failed and lost their lives because of it." Madu put his arm around his grandfather's shoulders. "I told them it was too soon. The day I learned of their plan, I told them to wait; the Khufus had just brokered the peace agreement. In time, that accord will weaken and fall apart. That will be a more opportune moment to strike. But as it was, they should have known. They even chose to strike the most heavily guarded of targets, the power plant. Khalfani guards it with eighteen of his best Medjay. It was not the right time or place."

"But how long will the people have to wait before they reclaim their freedom?" Madu's grandfather asked. "I do not believe that the Great Disruption removed us from the clutches of one group of tyrants only to land us with worse. Why would Neter do that?"

"Grandfather," Madu said, "you might be the only man on earth who believes that the Great Disruption was brought on by the hand of God."

"Who else could it have been?" his grandfather asked. "Who would have provided the world with such a golden opportunity to start over? No, it was Neter, acting out of compassion, who provided that opportunity. And look how we have squandered it! Our people, who fought hard to claim their freedom before the Great Disruption, turned weak when the Khufus arrived. They didn't fight."

The two men made the rest of their two-mile trek home to Tehut in silence. By the time they entered their small house, the sun had set. There would be no electricity until sometime the next day. They went to their beds knowing that when the sun rose, the struggle of life would start again. As on countless other nights over the past two years, Madu had trouble falling asleep. But this time, it wasn't because of his thin, well-worn mattress or the clamoring of noisy neighbors. Tonight his mind was racing with thoughts of the young woman he had seen at the soccer match. *Who was she, and why did she seem to recognize me?*

Madu was awakened the next morning by the grinding sound of the water pumps. He dressed quickly and grabbed two pails. He needed to get to the dispensing station while the water was still flowing. Otherwise, he would have to risk walking to the river to get their supply of water. Bored teens congregated on the river road and amused themselves by throwing rocks at people carrying water back from the river, trying to make them spill it. When Madu arrived at the station, the line was long, and fights had already broken out. Two Medjay guards stood nearby, doing nothing to restore order. Madu could see he would get no water from the station today. His only choice was the river.

As he approached the Nile, he saw the banks were relatively empty. Only a few other people were filling pails. He took off his shoes, rolled up his pants, and walked into the water, holding his dented pails. The Medjay were patrolling the river in boats, looking for anyone who might be trying to move illegally between the nomes. Madu stood for a moment, enjoying the sensation of the cool water on his legs. A kilometer to the south, he could see the electrical generators of Ati. His parents had died because of those generators. He wondered for a moment what life would have been like if they had succeeded in carrying out their plan.

Last year, Madu's parents and five other brave souls had attempted to overthrow Khufu Khalfani by taking control of the power plant for the people. If they had succeeded, they might have been able to muster the resources to take down the remaining eleven Khufus. Instead, everyone involved in the plot had been rounded up by masked Medjay guards the night before the attack was to take place. One of the collaborators had been loyal to the Khufu. Madu and his grandfather had barely escaped that night, fleeing and taking up residence where they lived today.

"You could drown," a voice said, interrupting Madu's thoughts. He turned around, still holding the empty pails, and saw a familiar face. It was the young woman from the Jubilee, seated on a brown Arabian horse with two mounted guards behind her. "I thought it was you," she said, hopping down to him. She motioned to her Medjay guards to continue riding, which they did with some hesitation. "You don't remember me, do you?"

Madu remained silent, looking intently at the young woman's face. She stood only a few meters away from him on the riverbank.

"Well, I remember you," she said, taking the scarf from around her waist and wrapping it around her face, revealing only her forehead and eyes. "Maybe this will help."

Madu dropped his empty pails into the river. He recognized her now, to his horror. "You were part of the group that came and arrested my parents!"

"Quiet," the young woman said, as she looked over her shoulder to make sure that the guards had ridden away. She removed the scarf from her face and tied it back around her waist. "Things are not what they seem. I was helping your parents. I was providing them with information about the layout of my father's power station and the fuel supply. Like them, I wanted to see a free Egypt. But we were betrayed."

"Your father?" Madu asked.

"Yes. My father is Khufu Khalfani," the woman replied. "Though I am not proud of that fact."

"Why would you take down your own father?" Madu asked doubtfully.

"Leave him in error who loves his error," the young woman answered. "No, my father is an evil man to be certain. The life I was born into is not the one I choose to live. One must be prepared to do what is needed in order to be liberated from the ill-conceived notions of others. Be they good men or bad."

"You are a philosopher?" Madu asked sarcastically. "Your words cannot wash the blood from your hands."

"Perhaps not. But I work every day to rid my hands of those stains."

Madu didn't answer. He just stared at her, fists clenched.

"I came that night to warn your parents," the young woman said. "I thought I could reach them before the guards arrived." She walked into the water and picked up Madu's pails, which were floating away. She was only an arm's length from him. "But do you think I didn't see you and your grandfather flee through the back door the moment the guards seized your parents? I would have done anything to see all of you escape."

She handed the pails to Madu, who still remained silent. She walked out of the river and back to her horse. In the distance, the Medjay were motioning for her to hurry and join them.

"Your father and mother were heroic people," she said to him before parting. "There are those of us who still believe in a life without the Khufus. If you want to avenge your family, come back here tomorrow at this same time. Tell no one, not your grandfather or that friend of yours."

"What is your name?" Madu asked, still unsure if he could trust her but certain that he wanted to see her again. "I am Madu."

The young woman smiled. "Nadine," she answered. "My name is Nadine."

Then she adjusted the reins and rode off.

10

Everything that takes place in your universe is from the
result of a series of quantum events.
The question is, what meaning have you assigned to the
events that you witness?

—THE CHRONICLES OF SATRAYA

OVER THE PACIFIC OCEAN, 8:16 P.M. LOCAL TIME, MARCH 20, 2070

Madu had indeed shown up the next day at the same spot on the bank
of the Nile. Nadine again arrived on horseback, the Medjay guards
replaced by an older man and woman who turned out to be her uncle
and aunt. The three of them were part of a growing group of Cairenes
determined to end the Khufus' reign by commandeering not only the
large electrical generator and petroleum supply in the nome of Ati but
also the large weapons cache in Sap-Meh. While Madu knew he was engaged in a plot that could get him killed, he had come to trust Nadine.
Or had he simply fallen in love with her?

She repeatedly assured him that they could trust her aunt and uncle,
who abhorred her father's treatment of the people of Cairo as much
as they did. In commandeering the power station, they would take advantage of the timing of the guards' shift changes and use a large store
of automatic weapons her uncle had secreted in the cellar of his house
during the Great Disruption. And this time, the details of the plot

would be known in full only to a handful of the twenty-six conspirators. It was an ambitious, dangerous plan, and over the next ten months, Madu found himself walking in his mother and father's footsteps. Even to the point where he was betrayed as they were.

Once again, a traitor had given up the plot to Khufu Khalfani. The conspirators, including Madu, Nadine, her aunt, and her uncle, were rounded up. Khufu Khalfani did not attend the circus of a trial, claiming it was because he was so disgusted with the actions of his third wife's eldest daughter. The collaborators were summarily judged by another Khufu and sentenced to death. But unlike his parents, Madu would not be executed in Tahrir Square. The entire group of twenty-six conspirators would have the opportunity to fight for their lives in the Pyramid Run during the upcoming Summer Jubilee . . .

"Sir, would you like chicken or falafel?" a woman's voice asked.

Startled out of his reverie, Madu looked up at the pretty flight attendant. "Falafel, please." He eyed the meal that was set in front of him. A serving of falafel with some dolma. It reminded him of his final meal before the race to the top of the Menkaure Pyramid. The goal of the Pyramid Run was simple: make it to the top of the Menkaure Pyramid before getting shot and killed by the Medjay, who were below showing off their marksmanship as they picked off the climbers one by one. If a climber somehow managed to reach the top of the pyramid, not only would his life be spared, but so would the life of another person of his choosing. Provided, of course, that that person was still alive.

A rifle shot struck a limestone block just above Madu's right shoulder. He looked down and saw four of the elite Medjay guards aiming their guns at him. A chorus of cheers and horrified screams came from the thousands watching the spectacle unfold. Madu turned upward. He had only made it halfway to the top, and the most harrowing part of the climb was yet to come. If he and Nadine were to survive, he had to push on.

Another shot rang out. Madu ducked, not seeing where the errant bullet went. The roar of the crowd grew louder. Madu's hands were getting sore. His knees and feet were bloodied from more than an hour of climbing. He wondered how the others were faring and, more important, how Nadine was. A loud scream sounded, curdling the blood in his veins. Madu turned and saw another of his fellow conspirators tumble down the side of the pyramid. The Medjay down below were celebrating the kill. Madu had counted twenty-one such screams. There were only five climbers left. He made his way across a ledge and swung himself around the corner of a jetty block, which provided some cover. From there, he could see Nadine lying on a ledge just below him. "Grab my hand," he said, reaching out to her.

"No," she called back, out of breath. "What are you doing? You must keep going. It is better for us to stay apart. One of us must make it to the top if we are to survive."

"Survive? No one has ever survived the run. Our lives are not our own. They never were in this new Egypt." Madu suddenly felt very weary and helpless. "Your father will not let us go."

"We cannot give up! We must go on!" Nadine insisted. "Go!" She sprang to her feet and ran along the narrow edge of the limestone blocks away from Madu. Flecks of stone burst in all directions as bullets struck around her.

Madu watched Nadine disappear around the western side of the pyramid. He looked down and watched two guards run around the base, tracking her. The other two were watching him, waiting for Madu to continue. It began to rain, making his climb even more perilous. But at the same time, it also made it more difficult for the guards to aim their rifles accurately. Block by block, level by level, Madu made his way up the Menkaure Pyramid. From time to time, he would hear gunfire and a reaction from the crowd. Two more screams, two more deaths. Now there were only three climbers left. Madu had to navigate over the putrid, vulture-ravaged remains of past traitors who had not fared well during their Pyramid Runs. More shots rang out, and Madu saw the burst of limestone nearby. The guards were focusing on him, yelling frantically below. He looked up. He was close to the top.

The rain poured down, and the cheers from the crowd reached a feverish pitch as Madu arrived at the block of stone just below the apex of the pyramid. It was the farthest any climber in the Pyramid Runs had gotten. The Medjay fired more rapidly now, because if any climber succeeded in reaching the top, the guards would lose their own lives. Amid bits and pieces of stone flying in all directions, Madu looked down. He couldn't see Nadine anywhere on his side of the pyramid. He called out her name, but there was no answer. He yelled louder, but still there was no response. Madu looked up. One last block left to climb. He leaped up through a barrage of gunfire and grabbed hold of the ledge. More bullets landed near his right hand. With all his remaining strength, Madu pulled himself up, falling exhausted onto the set of blocks that had once supported the capstone of the ancient structure.

The crowd went wild. The gunshots ceased. Madu had made it.

But what about Nadine? He rose to his feet and looked down all four sides of the pyramid. She lay motionless on the eastern face, on a ledge about fifteen meters below him. His heart sank. He could see blood on her right hip.

"Nadine!" Madu yelled. She didn't move. He yelled her name again. *She's dead*, he thought, covering his face with his hands. *I have survived, but for what? For whom?* No one had ever succeeded in the Pyramid Run. Would the Khufus really keep their promise and let him go?

Madu heard an angry roar from the crowd. He moved to the edge and saw four Medjay climbing toward him. His question was answered: neither he nor any other climber would be allowed to live. It was a competition only the Khufus could win. Madu dropped back down to the ground.

As he sat stoically at the top of the pyramid, waiting for the Medjay to reach him, something caught his eye. A brown object tucked into a large crack between two of the limestone blocks. He crawled over to it, ignoring the jeers of the crowd, and put his hand inside. He pulled out a small brown leather bag with a brass buckle. Inside he found three leather-bound books. *Who put these here?* he wondered. Madu took the books out, setting two of them down. On the cover of each book was the title, *The Chronicles of Satraya*, and below it a symbol embossed in gold leaf.

(•)

Madu noticed that as the rain fell on the books, the leather covers didn't seem to get wet. And for some reason, as dire as Madu's circumstances were, he felt compelled to open the book in his hand. When he did so, a blue orb emerged from the pages and hovered before him. A brilliant blue light emanated from it. The rain striking the blue orb vaporized with a sizzling sound. At first, it was the size of an orange, but it slowly grew larger. Madu stood and stepped away from the glowing orb, but it followed him, and within moments, the light engulfed the entire apex of the pyramid.

A single phrase sounded repeatedly in Madu's head: *In a time of great need, we are with you.* Madu was mesmerized. He was surrounded by a warming blue light, the likes of which he had never seen or felt before. He lost all awareness of the crowd below, the Medjay climbing up the pyramid, Nadine lying unconscious a few meters below him. He could only focus on the blue orb and the light it was emitting.

Subtle electrical charges touched Madu's body from head to toe. As the charges grew stronger, he felt his body vibrating and heard a ringing in his ears. The sound grew louder and louder, and the waves of vibration flowing through his body intensified. Then Madu heard a loud bang, like the sound of a firecracker. Instinctively, he cringed and shut his eyes, believing he'd taken his last breath.

When he opened his eyes a moment later, he found himself in a large square chamber with hieroglyphics on the walls. Tall granite pillars at each corner of the room supported the ceiling. He looked for a door but couldn't find one. How had he gotten into the room? At the center of the ceiling was a large opening. Had he fallen through it? The light of the large blue orb continued to engulf Madu's body, and as he moved, the blue light moved with him. He looked at the hieroglyphics etched on the walls. The same series of symbols was repeated over and over again.

What did it mean? At the center of the room was a round platform that stood about a half step off the ground. Madu walked over to it. An image of two flute players was carved into the surface.

When Madu stepped onto the platform, the air around him seemed to shimmer, as he had seen it do many times above the hot desert sand. He felt heat rising and heard a whistling sound like wind passing through a slightly opened window. He looked around but felt no air current or breeze. Then he felt a rumbling beneath his feet, but it only lasted a second or two. The granite pillars at the corners of the chamber were now glowing with a bright white light.

Madu felt more rumbling beneath his feet, and then there was silence. The electrical charge once again touched his body, and in the blink of an eye, he was back on top of the Menkaure Pyramid. The orb of blue light that had engulfed him began to shrink, until it was once again the size of an orange. After hovering before his eyes for a moment, it sank back into the pages of the book that he was still holding.

There was a great commotion below. *Nadine!* Madu thought, putting the book down next to the others. He quickly moved to the edge of the pyramid, looking for her, but he could only see the stain of her blood on the ledge. Madu saw that hordes of people had overrun the podium where the Khufus were sitting, and others had overwhelmed the Medjay guards, who were now held at gunpoint. He heard a voice calling him from the base of the pyramid. It was his friend Amun, who was standing next to Madu's grandfather. Amun raised both his arms into the air and began to yell Madu's name. The people standing near Amun followed his lead. *What happened?* Madu wondered, as he looked at the books lying on the limestone block next to the leather bag. *What power do these books possess?*

Madu heard the sound of someone approaching from the eastern façade of the pyramid. He rapidly picked up a loose stone from the ground and readied to throw it in case it was a Medjay guard. He turned around. It was Nadine.

Filled with relief, he dropped the stone and ran over to her. She had tied a scarf around her wounded hip. "I feared you were dead," Madu said, putting his arms around her.

"How did you do that?" Nadine asked, astonished, as Madu helped her sit on the ground. "The blue ball of light, the illumination of the entire city. You seemed to disappear for a moment."

Madu looked to the east and saw that it was as she said: all the lights in the city of Cairo were turned on. He shook his head at her. "I don't know. Whatever it was, it was done to me, not by me."

Nadine pointed at the brown leather bag. "What's in there?"

He picked up the three books. "I found them inside. They seem to possess a power I cannot begin to describe or understand. All I did was open the cover of one of them." He opened the cover of the first book and then the covers of the other two to demonstrate, but this time, no orb appeared.

Nadine pointed to her ear. "Listen," she said. They both heard the crowd below chanting Madu's name. "Whatever has taken place, whatever divine hand has moved here, it has inspired the people to take back Cairo and reclaim their Egypt."

11

What listens to you when you pray? Is it an old man or
woman high in the heavens? Or perhaps a wise sage atop a
mountain? Or a holy man in a church or temple?
When you realize the answer to this question, you
will realize yourself.

—THE CHRONICLES OF SATRAYA

ISLE OF MAN, 2:10 P.M. LOCAL TIME, MARCH 21, 2070

Anita grabbed a couple of books off the shelf and stacked them on
top of the others on the cart. She continued to peruse the art history section of the Isle of Man University library. While the contents
of all books published after the Great Disruption were stored in the
electronic library at the Akasha Vault, books and periodicals that had
survived the Great Disruption could only be found in university libraries or private collections. Anita grabbed one more book and rolled the
cart to a study table, where her friend Britney was flipping through a
holographic book projected in front of her.

"I should be the one getting the books, and you should be sitting
down," Britney said. "We still don't know why you almost fainted the
other day."

"I'm fine," Anita said. "Whatever it was didn't last very long."

"Uh-huh," Britney said. "Tell me again what we're looking for?"

Anita took a seat across from her. "We're looking for a painting of
a person in distress. A man, I think, although I'm not sure. It looks as

if he is in a great deal of pain. Also, I'd guess it's from the Modernist period, early twentieth century."

Anita and Britney were in their final year of medical school at the Isle of Man University. The campus was at the northern end of the city of Douglas. Construction had begun twenty years earlier, when a large endowment was made anonymously to the island nation for its creation. It was the only university in the world established during the Rising. Situated along the coastline, overlooking the Irish Sea, the university offered degrees in business, medicine, engineering, and the arts. And even though it was relatively new, it had already attracted fifteen thousand students from around the world.

There was a great deal of speculation about who had provided such a substantial endowment, especially at a time when the world was still recovering from unprecedented destruction and loss. The predominant theory was that it came from the mysterious Quinn family, who had moved to the island in 2034 after purchasing Peel Castle from the Manx National Heritage Foundation. Felix and Maria Quinn, along with their son, Sebastian, had restored the grounds and built a spectacular home overlooking the western shore. Rumors about the family and the origins of their seemingly endless wealth abounded.

Anita frowned. "When I went into the Tapestry Room this morning, I noticed that the painting I just described was no longer hanging there."

"Sounds like a rather unpleasant image. Maybe Mr. Quinn just got tired of looking at it." Britney swiped her hand to turn the page of the holographic book.

"I vaguely remember Mr. Quinn's saying something about art when that awful headache hit me last night. Then this morning, I noticed a painting missing. I'm pretty sure the two things are related."

"Why don't you just ask him what he did with it?"

"I can't. He left on a trip."

Britney groaned. "He's always traveling. This would be a lot easier if you knew the name of the painting or even the artist who did it."

"I know. It wasn't one of my favorites, so I never bothered to learn anything about it." Anita looked up from the book she was flipping through. "There was something about the painting that bothered me. One thing I do remember is that it had a plaque mounted on the lower part of its frame, but the words were in German—or some other foreign language, I'm not sure. Either way, I couldn't read them."

"Well, that should narrow it down," Britney said sarcastically. "Paintings by German artists."

"I think you saw it once," Anita continued. "Do you remember when we were in Mr. Quinn's study at my birthday party a few months ago?"

"Are you kidding?" Britney said. "Every time I go over to your place, I'm afraid I'm going to run into that man. He's spooky. If you ask me, that castle you live in is haunted."

"The castle is not haunted; you've slept over enough times to know that," Anita said. "And what are you talking about? Mr. Quinn is a peach."

"Really?" Britney stopped browsing in her book and gave Anita an incredulous look. "Last time I visited, Mr. Quinn asked me how Biscuit's bad leg was doing. I didn't know what he was talking about. Two days later, we found white line disease in Biscuit's right hind hoof." Britney waited for Anita to say something, but she didn't. "First of all, how did he know I had a horse? And how did he know my horse's name?"

"I probably told him," Anita answered, opening another art history book.

"All right, then how did he know Biscuit was sick? No one knew about that. Not even me. Listen, I think your father's great, but that Mr. Quinn, well, he's a little weird."

"We all can know things," Anita said, looking across the table at her friend. "Mr. Quinn says everyone has that ability. They just have to learn to utilize it."

"Don't start with me about all that *Chronicles* stuff," Britney said. "I know those books helped the world, but some of that stuff is just plain hocus-pocus." Anita continued to gaze intently at her friend, her mouth set in a mischievous grin, and Britney grew uncomfortable under it. "Are you reading my mind right now? Did Mr. Quinn teach you how to do that?" Her voice grew louder, eliciting a look of admonishment from the librarian. In a more hushed voice, Britney said, "Stop looking at me like that, you're freaking me out!"

Anita laughed. "You're such a goof," she said, as she started paging through her book again. "Just keep looking for that painting."

Britney shook her head. "One day, you're going to tell me the whole story about that man your father works for, and while you're at it, I want the real story about your life before you were adopted. I still don't believe that you grew up in a foster home."

"Now look who's claiming to be psychic," Anita said, still laughing.

Britney had been Anita's best friend ever since Anita had come to the island with her adoptive father, Lawrence Kinelot. Britney was right; Anita had made up a story about her early life. Someday, maybe, Anita would tell her about the events that took place thirteen years ago, when Lawrence, the Quinn family's steward, liberated her from dire circumstances and brought her to Peel Castle. But at the center of that story was a scandal and a town's secret, which were best left buried.

Suddenly, they were interrupted by two young men walking past their table. "Hey, Brit, a bunch of us are getting together at the tavern tonight. You should come."

Britney smiled and nodded as the young men walked out of the library. "We should go," she said to Anita. "Michael's a good guy, and so is his friend Barrett. And they're not bad-looking, either."

"If they wanted me there, they would have told me to come, too," Anita said.

"You know," Britney countered, "if you paid more attention to the guys, they would pay more attention to you. And you could doll yourself up more if you wanted. Do you remember when we dressed you up for the spring concert and everyone saw you play?"

"I remember." Anita blushed a bit.

"You looked so beautiful standing on the stage as you played your violin solo. Your hair was down, and that white gown fit you perfectly." She playfully imitated her playing the violin. "If you looked like that more often, you'd have plenty of guys asking you out. You'd just have to make sure they don't meet Mr. Quinn."

Anita chuckled at that, but after a moment, she broke off, wincing in pain.

"What's wrong?" Britney asked. "It's that headache again, isn't it? I'm telling you, you need to see a doctor."

Anita rubbed her temples. "I'll be all right. It won't last long."

Britney shrugged off her friend's obstinacy. "Hey," she said, "is this the painting? It says it's the work of some Norwegian named Munch."

Anita looked up at the page of the book Britney was showing her and immediately stopped rubbing her temples. "That's the one," she said. "That's the screaming man."

12

Can you articulate the difference between your
personality and your consciousness?
Now, who just made that articulation?
Your personality? Or your consciousness?

——THE CHRONICLES OF SATRAYA

ZURICH, 3:30 P.M. LOCAL TIME, MARCH 21, 2070

A man walked through the enormous main hall of the abandoned Zurich train station. The clicking of his cane as it touched the ground
was followed by the slight dragging sound of his right shoe. He looked
around keenly at the remains of the old homeless encampment that had
been built in the station immediately after the Great Disruption. Old
cooking stoves, cobbled-together furniture, and scraps of wood littered
the ground. The iconic station had not been restored after the Great
Disruption, nor had it been repaired. Its fate was now in the hands of a
Zurich-based company that had purchased it after the city could come
up with no way to repair it or make use of it.

The man paused for a moment and looked up at a sign dangling at
the end of a frayed cable: *Track 7*. He pushed a lock of his shoulder-
length gray hair off his face and behind his ear and continued, tapping
his cane on the ground with a bit more force. He looked down the
platform, lit eerily by beams of dust-ridden sunlight passing through

holes in the roof. The flapping wings of pigeons could be heard as they wandered the station in which they made their home.

The man looked around before making his way down the platform adjacent to a dilapidated commuter train. As he approached, a memory came to him, frozen in time. He gazed down at the tracks under the train as he stopped in front of the number fourteen car. Its doors were open.

The man sighed deeply before stepping inside the place he had once called home. The car had certainly changed; it had been pillaged and ransacked. The thin mattress he had slept on had been pushed into the corner, its bedding stripped. He reached up and grabbed a short pole he had suspended from the car's ceiling to hang and dry his clothing. Now only a single wire hanger remained. He walked over to the toppled nightstand and set it back on all fours. He smiled slightly as he ran his fingers over some candle wax stuck to the surface. He looked for a candle holder but didn't see it. Instead, he saw a shattered picture frame on the floor with a photo still inside. It was of a woman with a teenage boy and two young girls.

"Caroline, my love," he whispered, as he picked up the picture frame. "George, Sophie, Nicole." His voice cracked as he called out the names of the children.

Gathering himself, the man pulled the photo from the frame and tucked it in the inside pocket of his jacket. He turned and glanced up at the overhead baggage shelf. "I wonder if it is still there," he whispered to himself, taking a quick step forward and reaching up. He felt around anxiously, shuffling as best he could, using his cane to support him. But what he was searching for had probably been taken long ago.

"Hey!" a voice called out to him. "You shouldn't be in here. Don't you know we're getting ready to demolish this place?" The man turned to see someone in overalls and a hard hat standing on the platform outside the door. "Oh, sorry, it's you," the construction worker said, realizing whom he was talking to. "Take your time, sir. Just let us know when you leave." The worker walked away.

The man fiddled with a gold button on his knee-length jacket as he took one last look around car number fourteen before exiting and making his way back up the platform. He could hear the hustling and bustling of the crew, which he had hired to demolish the train station he had purchased from the city.

Then the expression on his face turned wary. Standing under the dangling sign was someone he was not expecting to see, with a dog sitting at his side. "Why have you come?" the man asked as he limped forward, pausing and resting both his hands on the silver handle of his cane. "I thought we said everything that needed to be said, Sebastian."

"No, Giovanni," Sebastian answered. "There is always more to say."

13

If you do not wish to climb the mountain to the east, then look
to the west. Perhaps there you will find one more to your liking.

—THE CHRONICLES OF SATRAYA

NEW CHICAGO, 1:11 P.M. LOCAL TIME, MARCH 21, 2070

"Welcome back!" Jasper said, jumping out of his chair as Logan walked
into the art studio. "How is everyone? Is Jamie all right? We were worried."

Logan smiled and set his backpack and a large tin box down on the
desk, as Jasper took a deep breath. "She's still experiencing severe headaches, but after Mr. Perrot picked us up at the airport, we took her to
a neurologist her pediatrician recommended. The doctor said she must
have hit her head, even though she doesn't remember it, because she has
a slight concussion. The good news is that they did a brain scan and
didn't find any serious injuries. She's resting at home now with Jordan
and Ms. Sally, our housekeeper."

"That's a relief," Jasper said.

Logan nodded. "Both kids had a hard time down there. The earthquake was really frightening. Mexico City was mostly spared, but the
highways and the airport got ripped up pretty badly. If Valerie hadn't

gotten us on a WCF transport plane heading to New Chicago while she was arranging her flight back to Washington, we'd still be stuck down there."

"Well, it's good to have you back," Jasper said. "The studio missed you."

The studio was on the northwest corner of Franklin and Hubbard Streets, a prime location only a few blocks from the Merchandise Mart and the heart of New Chicago. After the Great Disruption, the surrounding area had remained in a state of disrepair for twenty years. As intrastate and global commerce grew during the Rising, New Chicago's mayor, Tim Malak, pushed to reestablish the iconic Mart's reputation as the premier bastion of design and architectural innovation. The success of the initiative earned him nationwide recognition. The city's airport, which had been named for a previous Chicago mayor, was renamed Malak International.

"I expected blue today," Logan remarked, gesturing at Jasper's currently orange-colored hair.

"Stay tuned," Jasper said. "Next Wednesday is turquoise day. What's in the box?" He nodded at it. "Did you bring me a gift?"

Logan chuckled, placing his hand on the tin box. "No, it's the reason we went to Mexico in the first place. It contains the artifact I've been hired to restore." He gave Jasper a long look. "Mr. Perrot told me the two of you had a very interesting day yesterday."

"Understatement," Jasper replied, as he sat back down. "Did he tell you everything that happened?"

Before he could answer, the front door opened, and Mr. Perrot came in. "Traffic is getting worse around here every day," he said, hanging his floppy hat on the coat rack.

Logan glanced at Mr. Perrot. "No, he didn't give me any details."

"Then follow me," Jasper said, leading everyone to the work room, where a large wooden crate in its center caught both Logan's and Mr. Perrot's attention.

"What's in the crate?" Mr. Perrot asked.

Logan gave him a questioning look. "I assumed that was part of your *interesting day.*"

Mr. Perrot raised his eyebrows and shook his head.

"It came this morning, without any return address," Jasper said. "The delivery man didn't know anything more, either. Do you have any ideas?"

Logan shook his head. He placed his backpack on the floor and grabbed a toolbox from the shelf. He took out a pair of snipping shears and cut the metal bindings around the crate.

Following Logan's lead, Jasper grabbed a power screwdriver and began to remove the numerous screws securing the lid in place. "This is better than Christmas!"

Logan used the claw side of a hammer to remove some reinforcing nails, while Mr. Perrot watched. Soon the three of them were able to get the lid off.

Jasper removed a layer of packing foam, revealing a framed work of art below. "Oh," he said, startled by what he saw. "That's not a happy piece of art at all."

"It's not supposed to be," Logan said, recognizing it. "This is one of the most famous paintings in the world, 'The Scream.'"

"Done by Edvard Munch, if I remember correctly," Mr. Perrot said, as he picked up a small white envelope lying on top of the masterpiece. "It is addressed to you." He handed the envelope to Logan.

Logan broke the formal blue wax seal and pulled out a piece of beige parchment paper. He recognized the exquisite penmanship. "It's from Mr. Quinn," he said, looking at Mr. Perrot, who slowly nodded, not surprised.

Logan read the note out loud.

Salutations,

Many have claimed to understand the meaning of this work of art. Some suspect it was inspired by a slaughterhouse located near the artist's home. Others believe it represents the artist's reaction to his sister's incarceration in an insane asylum. Some believe it represents how the artist felt when he was going through his own nervous breakdown. I will say to you that these, and the many other theories put forth, are erroneous. This picture is linked with something far more profound. It is related to the activities of another man who was diligently work- ing halfway around the world at the same time. The secret of this picture lies in what caused the artist to make it.

All is never what it seems. As in the Michelangelo, which you now proudly and deservedly possess, science and allegory have wonderfully collided yet again.

Is it not amazing to see how the choices and decisions we make can have profound and lasting effect on those we have never met nor ever will?

For the moment,
Sebastian Quinn

"It appears that Mr. Quinn is not done with you," Mr. Perrot said. "He has presented another riddle for you to solve."

Logan turned his gaze to the Munch, which still lay flat in the crate. "It seems so," he said softly.

"Someone needs to roll the truck backward here," Jasper said. "First of all, who is Sebastian Quinn?"

Logan glanced at Mr. Perrot before turning to Jasper. "I'm not sure that there's anyone in the world who can really answer that question," he said. The events that led to Logan's first encounter with the enigmatic man could easily be summed up in a sentence or two. But Jasper's ques- tion, *Who is Sebastian Quinn?*, was one that Logan had contemplated many times over the last nine months, coming up with no good answer.

"He is the gentleman who donated the *Creation of Adam* fresco to the studio," Mr. Perrot said. "He is a good friend."

Before Jasper could ask another question, a crash sounded in the front of the studio.

"What was that?" Logan asked.

Jasper darted off to find out, and his departure provided space for Logan and Mr. Perrot to speak more freely.

"The last piece of art that Mr. Quinn presented to you turned out to be at the center of a deadly series of events," Mr. Perrot said. "The anguish portrayed in this painting foretells an even greater threat."

"I know," Logan said, frowning. "As little as I know of Mr. Quinn, I'm certain he doesn't do things idly."

They carefully lifted the artwork out of the shipping crate and set it on an empty easel, admiring it. It portrayed a person screaming as he stood by the railing of a bridge over a waterway. An expression of agony and terror was on the person's face as his hands clutched his distorted, ghost-like head. Two men were in the background, one looking over the railing at something in the water, the other looking at a boat in the harbor or a building in the distance. The sky was filled with angry red and orange whorls, seemingly reflecting the intense anguish of the main subject.

Logan moved closer to the artwork. "This is not the oil version of the painting. If I remember correctly, Munch did four versions of this picture. This is the pastel version." He shook his head. "Amazing what he was able to convey with just a few colors. His style was so different from that of most other late-nineteenth-century artists. This is one of the most polarizing pictures in history; people have always either loved it or hated it."

"I would venture to say that those who dislike it do so because on some inner level, they feel what this man feels." Mr. Perrot walked closer to the pastel drawing and looked at the lower part of the frame, where a message had been inscribed on a small plaque. "I can't make out what it says. This is not a language I understand."

Logan pulled out his PCD and within seconds an image of the work was displayed, along with a description. "This is the pastel version, which he did in 1895. It was the only one of the four iterations of "The Scream" that had a plaque with words inscribed on it. The message is written in Norwegian." Logan brought up an English translation on his PCD and read:

I was walking along the road with two friends—the sun was setting—suddenly the sky turned blood red—I paused, feeling exhausted, and leaned on the fence—there was blood and tongues of fire above the blue-black fjord and the city—my friends walked on, and I stood there trembling with anxiety—and I sensed an infinite scream passing through nature.

"Pretty apt," said Mr. Perrot.

Logan nodded. "Assuming that this was a sort of self-portrait, what could have possibly taken place halfway around the world that would have made Munch feel this way?"

"May I see the note?" Mr. Perrot requested. Logan handed it to him.

As Mr. Perrot read, Logan put his PCD away and examined the drawing more closely. He wondered if it was the original. Logan remembered the moment he had learned that the *Creation of Adam* fresco, which he had believed was an excellent replica while restoring it, was actually the very fresco that once graced the ceiling of the Sistine Chapel. Mr. Quinn had somehow salvaged it from the Vatican after the Great Disruption had left the papal city in ruins. Had Mr. Quinn once again acquired another priceless work of art?

"There is some intriguing information in Mr. Quinn's letter to you," Mr. Perrot said. "When did you say that Munch did this drawing?"

Logan tore his gaze away from the picture. "In 1895."

"Mr. Quinn says that this picture is somehow linked to another man halfway around the world. He also notes that science and allegory are combined in it."

Logan ran his hand across the top of the frame, still wondering if the pastel was the original. "If we assume that the *allegory* portion of this work was provided by Munch . . ."

"Then we might assume that the *science* was provided by a scientist. So we might start by looking for a scientist who was alive in 1895."

Logan nodded. "It's a place to start, anyway."

Mr. Perrot folded the note and put it back in the envelope. "I doubt Mr. Quinn expected you to figure it out within moments of receiving the drawing, but based on the relevance of Michelangelo's message to events that were taking place in the real world nine months ago, it seems prudent for you to figure out the secrets of this work of art sooner rather than later." He handed the note back to Logan.

"That's what I am afraid of," Logan said. "What truth is going to be revealed by a picture of pain and agony?"

14

How many battles will you fight for someone else's cause before
you take up the armaments for your own?

—THE CHRONICLES OF SATRAYA

MONTEPULCIANO, ITALY, 8:20 P.M. LOCAL TIME, MARCH 21, 2070

"Long live Reges Hominum!" said Dario Magnor, his voice raspy. He
stood before his guests, holding up a glass of wine for a toast.

"Long live Reges Hominum," repeated the seven people sitting in
the solarium of the thousand-acre vineyard known as the Magnor Es-
tates, as they drank from their goblets.

"Simon Hitchlords is dead," said a sharp-chinned blond woman
named Catherine, emphasizing the last word. "And so is Andrea Montavon. According to tradition, should the Dux Ducis suddenly pass, the
leadership of our group will pass to its most senior member."

Catherine gestured toward Dario, who walked over to a plush high-
back chair, making a soft humming noise as he walked. When he sat
down, the hem of his trousers rose, exposing metal prosthetics. "We
have no grand bell to call our meeting to order as we did at Château
Dugan," he said, pouring himself a glass of water and taking a sip. "We
will not wear masks or inhale the smoke of incense to bind us. No, we
will hold off on those rituals until we have ennobled ourselves with

at least one noteworthy accomplishment. The epic failure of Simon Hitchlords and Andrea Montavon not only brought about the death of my dear friend Victor Ramplet, but it cast a great shadow of ineptitude upon our order. And I mean to restore our dignity."

"I did not expect us to continue after Simon's death," said a German man named Klaus. "I am glad to know that you will not let Simon's failure thwart our advance."

"I, too, was happy to hear from Dario," said Yinsir, a Japanese man with a shiny bald head. He placed his PCD on the table in front of him. "But I fear our path has been made more difficult. The appearance of the blue light caused by Simon's failure to perform the Purging has only emboldened the Satrayians. They believe it is the same blue light experienced by the finders of the *Chronicles*."

"That light had nothing to do with the books," Catherine snapped. She sat up straighter in her chair, perturbed. "The light was simply a side effect of the Akasha Vault satellites."

"Nonetheless, people believe what they want to believe," said Yinsir. "I am only restating what has already been reported."

Steeped in traditions that dated back to the time of the first pope, Reges Hominum was made up of members of the twelve wealthiest and most influential families in the world. For more than two millennia, the group had manipulated mankind from the shadows. While the accumulation of great wealth was a very welcome by-product of their machinations, power and control were the group's primary goals. While the Great Disruption of 2027 loosened their grip on humanity by diminishing their wealth and wrecking many of their mechanisms of power, *The Chronicles of Satraya* made them irrelevant, and the group disbanded. For more than forty years, Reges Hominum was inactive, until Simon Hitchlords took up his father's cause and brought the group together again.

"Before we continue, there are some questions that must be answered," said a woman named Ilia with jet-black hair and dazzling eyes, which had once been dark but had been surgically altered with a deep blue pigment. "There are many rumors concerning Simon's passing. It is my understanding that the son of Camden and Cassandra Ford was instrumental in foiling his plan."

"A plan that we all sanctioned," Yinsir added. "And I am told that the WCF has seized the Château along with all the other Hitchlords assets."

"How can we be certain that our involvement will not be exposed?" Ilia asked. "My family, the Miltuns, has a great deal to lose."

"As do the Letuhs and everyone else here," Klaus said to her. "You are not alone in your concern."

Dario shook his head and spoke casually. "Do not agonize. They will not find anything at the Château that links us to the Hitchlordses. Fendral was too cagey to keep anything of import there."

"I'm not concerned about what Fendral may have hidden there," Catherine said. "But I do worry about what Simon might have entrusted to the secret rooms of the Château. I pray that you are correct and there are no vestiges of our gathering."

"I have been assured that the WCF was not able to find anything significant at the Château," Dario said.

"Who assured you?" Ilia asked.

Dario smiled. "I have been assured, as I said, that there is no evidence that points in our direction. Are you not impressed by how quickly and efficiently the mishap last Freedom Day was explained away?"

"What was Simon doing in India?" Klaus asked, annoyed. "I am told he fell to his death in a pyre along the Ganges. Shouldn't he have been helping Andrea?"

"Simon was distracted," Catherine said. "His personal vendetta against Logan Ford clouded his judgment and tripped up his execution of our plans. I knew when we met at Château Dugan and Simon displayed the *Chronicles* on the meeting table that he was as obsessed with the books as his father. Who I still don't believe had this group's best interest at heart."

"I assure you that he did," Dario countered. "I visited Fendral often in Washington during his time on the Council of Satraya. He was quite close to molding the original Council to our liking."

"What happened, then?" Ilia asked.

"Camden Ford happened," Dario answered. "He discovered Fendral's secret."

"And what secret was that?" Catherine asked with keen interest.

Dario hesitated. "I suppose now that Simon is dead and the Hitchlordses are no more, little harm will come from telling you that Fendral did not actually find his copy of the *Chronicles* as he reported," he said. "He stole them from a man named Giovanni Rast. Camden somehow came across this fact and used it to force Fendral off the Council and return to Europe."

"So that is what instigated the splintering of the first Council of Satraya," Ilia said, before the rest of the members of Reges Hominum went silent.

History had placed Fendral Hitchlords in the same company as Camden Ford, Deya Sarin, and Madu Shata. They were the four original finders of the *Chronicles*, which were all discovered on the same day, July 21, 2030, in different parts of the world. The revelation that Fendral actually stole his copy of the books would not only have been shocking, but shameful. The entire Hitchlords family would have been disgraced.

"Did Muriel know this?" Ilia asked.

"Fendral's wife was a fool," Catherine said. "She cared only to find new ways to spend the Hitchlords fortune. The real question is what became of this Giovanni Rast?"

"Dead, I'm certain," Yinsir said. "Fendral was not one to let loose ends linger."

"Enough about history," Dario said. "We will not find our future in the past."

"Agreed," Ilia said.

Dario adjusted himself in his chair. "There was a time, before the

Great Disruption, when we and our families controlled a very valuable resource." He motioned to Catherine. "We controlled the world's oil supply."

At the center of the solarium, a holographic map of the world appeared, projected from Catherine's PCD. Various parts of Canada, Argentina, the Gulf of Mexico, and the Middle East were marked with green indicators.

"More important," Catherine added, "we ensured that oil was the most affordable source of energy available. Do you remember the American people's fascination with renewable energy before the Great Disruption? Start-ups spent billions researching solar, wind, and other clean energy sources."

Dario chuckled. "A few corporate acquisitions and mergers later, Americans realized it would take the average family twenty-five years to recoup the cost of equipping their homes with solar panels. And how much money could you really save with an electric car when you had to purchase a new battery for it every six years?"

"People never understood that a free market doesn't mean a free existence," Klaus said.

The group laughed.

"Even though the world now runs entirely on electricity," Dario said, "the puzzle of how to produce sufficient electricity without the use of combustion still eludes us. There is still reliance on what is below the surface of the earth."

"Natural gas," Catherine said.

"You intend to seize control of the gas fields," Yinsir said. "That will not be easy to accomplish. My family has tried for years, with no success, to influence the Jabarl family of the North African Commonwealth, first the mother before her death and now the daughter."

"No, Yinsir," Dario said. "I do not propose to take control of the world's natural gas supply. I intend to destroy it."

"That seems a bit rash," Ilia said, leaning forward in her chair. "If you somehow expunge the gas supply, we all will suffer."

"How would the destruction of the world's primary energy source help anyone?" Klaus asked. "Do you expect us to live without electricity?"

"We will provide a new source of electricity," Catherine answered.

"How?" Klaus sounded impatient. "With what?"

Dario smiled. "Rashidi!" he called out.

A tall man with dreadlocks and an intimidating bearing entered the solarium. He had a massive physique and a well-sculpted jaw line and chin. His light-colored eyes, which lacked eyelashes and eyebrows, were a stark contrast to his dark skin. Rashidi walked around the solarium, handing an envelope to each guest.

Dario rose, setting off a soft humming sound. He looked at Yinsir. "Your recommendation of Rashidi was a good one. He is a man worth his weight in gold."

Rashidi finished his task and came back to stand next to Dario as he addressed the group.

"Inside, you will find two items: first, directions to the location where I would like all of us to meet in two days, and second, a thin gold bracelet with a distinctive letter N molded onto it. Please be sure to wear the security bracelet when you arrive. Once there, Catherine and I will show you our little project and answer all of your questions."

"Until then," Catherine added, "I would advise you and your families to stay away from Western Australia."

There was a short burst of laughter.

"You will also meet the newest members of our order," Dario said. "Long live Reges Hominum!"

"Long live Reges Hominum!" the others replied.

15

It is true that the Kingdom of Heaven has many mansions,
But we assure you that none is reserved for the privileged.

—THE CHRONICLES OF SATRAYA

NEW CHICAGO, 3:30 P.M. LOCAL TIME, MARCH 21, 2070

"What was that noise?" Logan asked Jasper when he returned.

"The Sentinel Coterie again," Jasper replied. "They smashed a few
bottles on the sidewalk out front. I swept up the broken glass. You
know, a bunch of them showed up the other day while you were in
Mexico. They chanted, 'Shut down the studio,' and 'Death to the Ford.'
I thought we'd seen the last of them a couple of months ago when I
called the police and they broke up their demonstration. Those people
need to find something better to do with their time and energy than
complain about the government and cultural institutions every waking
moment of their day. Why do they keep picking on the studio?"

"They're concerned with far more than the government," Mr. Perrot
said. "Like their leader, Randolph Fenquist, the members of the Coterie are anarchists. They want to bring down all kinds of authority—
businesses, religions, philosophies. They even believe that the *Chronicles*
pose a threat to their freedom. After Logan revealed his true identity as

the son of Camden and Cassandra Ford last year, I'm afraid he and his studio landed on their radar."

"No one has seen hide nor hair of Randolph since the disaster at Compass Park," Logan said. "I wonder what that weasel is up to. He has a strange way of showing up when you least expect it."

"Anyway," Jasper said, "while I was in the front, some gentleman called and said he's interested in purchasing one of your mother's mosaics."

"How does he know about my mother's mosaics?" Logan asked.

"Probably because the Council has been promoting the upcoming commemoration," Jasper replied. "He wants to meet you and purchase the dolphin one. He says he's willing to pay handsomely for it."

Both Logan and Mr. Perrot had distrustful looks on their faces. "How did he know about the dolphin mosaic?" Mr. Perrot asked. "We never told the Council which mosaics we were sending over."

"Did he give his name or contact information?" Logan asked.

Jasper first looked at Mr. Perrot and answered, "Don't know." Then he turned to Logan. "Didn't say, and no. He only told me that he would talk to you at the commemoration. If I had to guess, he was from the South, had a bit of a drawl." Jasper walked over and took a closer look at the Munch pastel. "This thing is hideous. You should sell it and keep the mosaic." Jasper spun around and looked at Mr. Perrot. "Did you tell Logan about the recorder and the memory chips yet?"

"What recorder and memory chips?" Logan asked.

"I was just about to," Mr. Perrot said. "Let's go into the vault."

Jasper glanced at his PCD. "Oh, it's getting late. I need to get a few things done. I need to leave at five today. The Ming Peera concert is tonight. A bunch of us are meeting up over at O'Tool's before heading over." And he dashed out of the room.

"He is just a big bundle of energy," Mr. Perrot said, as he led Logan out of the work room.

"But he gets the job done," Logan said, as they went to the vault.

He put in the security code and looked into the retina scanner.

When the door opened, Mr. Perrot walked over to the large stainless-steel table where he'd left Cassandra's recorder and one of the memory chips.

Logan picked up the recorder. "Looks like you found an old toy."

"This is your mother's voice recorder," Mr. Perrot said. "Because of the circumstances surrounding the splintering of the first Council, she probably never told you much about her time with the Forgotten Ones in the Ozark forest."

"No, I only know what you've recently told me."

"Until we all fled here to New Chicago, your mother used this voice recorder as a diary of sorts. She recorded her most intimate and private thoughts on memory chips."

"Like my father's journal."

"Yes, very much like that," Mr. Perrot said, picking up the memory chip. "This is the chip that Jasper and I found in the recorder. You only need to insert this and press the Play button."

Logan took the chip from Mr. Perrot and did just that. His face lit up with a smile when he heard his mother's voice for the first time in almost three years.

"That was my reaction, too," Mr. Perrot said.

*   *   *

The recorder clicked off as the second of the two recordings ended. Logan was no longer smiling. "My parents knew," he said. "They suspected six years ago that Simon and Andrea were up to something."

Mr. Perrot nodded. "And they never said anything to me about their suspicions."

"I wish they had." Logan sighed. "You might have been able to get them to take the threat of Andrea and Simon more seriously. Maybe they'd still be alive today if they did. I know Simon denied it," he continued, "but I still think he had something to do with their murders. I guess we'll never know for sure now." He saw a strange look come over Mr. Perrot's face. "What is it?"

"I still worry about the others who might have been helping him," Mr. Perrot said. "We always suspected that Simon and Andrea could not have done that alone. When Victor Ramplet was exposed, our concerns were justified. We also heard Simon say at Ramnagar Fort that he intended to parlay with a man named Dario. Nine months have gone by, and no additional evidence of co-conspirators has surfaced, but this still weighs on my mind." As much as Logan wanted to put the Freedom Day plot behind him, it still weighed on him, too. "Your mother's mention of the man in a wheelchair also troubles me somehow."

"Did you know him?"

"I only saw him on rare occasions, cavorting with Simon and Andrea," Mr. Perrot said. "I would say four or five times in the years that I was on the Council. But that doesn't mean he didn't visit them more often. He was always very well dressed, and we all assumed he came from means, just like Fendral."

"You told me that my father was communicating with Cynthia Brown as Henry Cutler," Logan said. "Why would my parents speak to Cynthia about their suspicions and not you?"

"I don't think they ever fully relinquished their desire to help guide the organization they were instrumental in establishing. I can understand that. Besides," he added, smiling, "they were probably trying to protect me. Camden always did, you know, ever since he first found me."

Logan took that in appreciatively before changing tacks. "My mother mentioned someone named RJ. Sounds like he gained some notoriety or at least got his face in the paper. Do you know who he was?"

"I remember him as one of the Forgotten Ones who returned with us to Washington, D.C., after your father found the books," Mr. Perrot said. "He seemed to be very fond of your mother, but he didn't take to Camden or me. He would leave anytime we approached. He was younger than all of us and actually spent most of his time with Simon. I only knew him as RJ. He didn't stay in Washington long; he left soon after your mother and father announced that they were getting married."

Logan nodded. "My mother talked about her other recording chips. I wonder if they can shed some light on the man in the wheelchair."

Mr. Perrot smiled. "Yes, the missing chips." He walked around the table and over to the Golden Acorn mosaic. He motioned for Logan to join him and took the recording chip that he and Jasper had discovered the day before out from the easel tray.

"Where did you find this?" Logan asked, as Mr. Perrot handed it to him.

"Right here." Mr. Perrot pointed to the empty spot in the array of gold tiles on the mosaic where the chip had been. "All of these are the same shape and size as the recording chip you are holding in your hand."

"So that's why she read the passage from the story of the Golden Acorn."

"Exactly," Mr. Perrot confirmed.

"Have you listened to it yet?" Logan asked, holding up the chip that Mr. Perrot had given him.

Mr. Perrot shook his head.

Logan walked back over to the table and placed the chip from the mosaic in the recorder. Then he hit the Play button.

16

*The reason something happens is as important as
the reason other things do not.*

—THE CHRONICLES OF SATRAYA

After landing at Dulles International Airport, Valerie made a quick stop at her apartment in Washington, D.C.'s Glover Park district and then went directly to the World Crime Federation's headquarters. She was sitting alone in a conference room waiting for Director Sully, the newly installed director of the WCF, who was late for the meeting she herself had urgently requested. Waiting for a meeting to begin was not Valerie's idea of productivity. She wanted to get down to the lab and join her team so they could start strategizing about their investigation into the gas-processing plant disaster in the North African Commonwealth. Valerie glanced at the time on her PCD and checked for any more messages from Logan about Jamie's condition.

She looked around the large conference room. This was the first time she had set foot in it since the infamous WCF and WSA meeting nine months ago. The then head of joint operations, Samuel Covington, had made the blunder of his career by assigning Victor Ramplet, the head of the World Security Agency, to take command of the worldwide mission to stop the Freedom Day plot. The traumatic events immediately following were still fresh in her mind. Victor Ramplet turned out to be a traitor, and that meeting was the last time she'd seen her old boss, Dominic Burke, alive. The gag order suppressing the existence of the Freedom Day plot along with the involvement of Simon Hitchlords and Andrea Montavon in the killing of tens of thousands of people along the east coast of the North American Federation was still in place. People had been told that a satellite had malfunctioned, emitting a radiation pulse that was lethal to certain susceptible individuals. No less alarming, world leaders hadn't even revealed that 99 percent of the world's population was still walking around with altered DNA because of a serum Simon and Andrea had covertly dispensed via the worldwide MedicalPod System. NAF president Enrique Salize had convinced his counterparts around the globe that panic and insurrection would ensue if people learned that the entire world had been seconds away from experiencing the same carnage that had taken place on the NAF's east coast. Samuel Covington had to take the blame for the entire fiasco so that politicians could escape accountability, and Valerie felt sorry for him. In order to keep Covington from talking, President Salize had appointed him to the position of budget attaché, which added up to nothing more than a glorified accountant.

The doors to the conference room swung open. Director Sully entered, followed by two men wearing dark blue suits and deep-burgundy-colored kufis. Bridget Sully was tall and slender, with green eyes and brown hair in a chic bob. She wore a designer pantsuit and high heels that brought her height to just less than two meters. One of the men was carrying a shoebox-size gray plastic container with a biohazard emblem on it. Valerie stood and greeted them.

"This is Senior Agent Valerie Perrot," Director Sully said. "Agent Perrot and her team have been assigned to investigate the processing plant implosion."

"Nice to meet you, Agent Perrot," said the taller of the two agents. "We have heard many good things about you. We are from the WCF field office in the North African Commonwealth and are leading the investigation there. I am Senior Agent Duna, and this is Agent Ayalla." The second man nodded.

"I've just returned from a trip and will be catching up with my team as soon as we are finished here," Valerie said. "They've already started their investigation."

"With the cause of the explosion still unknown," Agent Duna said, "we have had to shut down the other three drilling platforms as a precaution."

"Are there any theories?" Valerie asked.

"Yes, which is why we have come in person." Agent Duna set the box down on the table in front of Valerie. "These are samples of a foreign residue we found in the pump chamber of the well that imploded."

"We sent a video probe into the well," Agent Ayalla said. "We estimate that there are more than two tons of this material under the collapsed well site."

"Two tons?" Valerie asked.

"Yes. We have no idea how so much foreign material could have gotten into the well cavity."

"What about the other wells? Do they contain whatever this is?"

"The foreign substance has been discovered in all four wells. We believe that it was only a matter of time before all the platforms imploded."

"What kept the other three wells from imploding?"

"We don't know," Agent Duna said.

Valerie placed her hand on the box. "I've already dispatched one of my agents," she said. "Alex Daniels should be arriving in the Commonwealth in less than four hours. Let's see what my team can find out."

"What Agent Perrot means," Director Sully interjected, "is that she and her team will figure this out."

Valerie kept silent, uncomfortable with the possible overstatement.

"Our new facilities here are state-of-the-art and well equipped to handle this type of investigation. Valerie will have the sample analyzed before any of her team members leave tonight."

"We arrived with President Jabarl earlier today," Agent Duna said, rejoining Agent Ayalla. "She is planning to meet with your President Salize to discuss the energy supply problem. She and the business leaders of North Africa are gravely concerned that if the natural-gas issue is not addressed promptly, the NAF will turn to other gas suppliers."

"The Commonwealth has worked long and hard to establish the strong economic development of Africa," Agent Ayalla said. "I would hate to see our efforts over the last decade go to waste."

The Commonwealth's current president, Sanura Jabarl, took over when her mother, Dalia Jabarl, was assassinated in 2049. Dalia had organized one of the largest grass-roots movements in the history of Africa when, in 2040, she led the effort to bring the message of *The Chronicles of Satraya* to every corner of the African continent. She traveled from cities to suburbs to farmlands to the most remote pockets of civilization on the vast continent, offering people hope and a new way of thinking. They instantly threw their support behind her unorthodox approach. She did not tell them what they wanted to hear; she expressed in no uncertain terms what they *needed* to hear. She challenged them to grow their own food, to start businesses based on barter, to band together in communities to provide services for the common good instead of waiting for the world to come and save them.

Her assassination in 2049 divided Africa into two nations, the North African Commonwealth, of which Dalia's daughter Sanura was elected president, and the Republic of South Africa. Dalia Jabarl's assassin was never identified.

Director Sully turned to Agents Duna and Ayalla. "Would you gentlemen mind waiting in the hallway a moment? I need to speak with Agent Perrot privately. Then I will escort you to your meeting with President Salize." They nodded and left, and Sully turned to Valerie. "Agent Perrot, this is your top and only priority. Director Burke might have accepted words like *try* and *see*, but I don't. Your team *will* figure this out, or I'll find another unit to handle this investigation. I don't have to tell you the implications of one of our energy trading partners being crippled. I assured the president we would get to the bottom of this promptly."

Valerie knew it would be more politically expedient to nod her head and not bristle at her supervisor's tone, but she said, "With all due respect, Director, if you have a problem with something that I or my team has done or is doing, no problem. Tell me about it. But do not think, imply, or suggest that my unit isn't giving one hundred percent every day they come to work at the WCF. If you want to assign another team to this case, do it now, and tell the president you pulled us off. I have no problem with that. But I can assure you, my unit *is* the best the WCF has."

"Good to know, Agent," the director said, seemingly unruffled by the rebuke. She walked to the door and said over her shoulder before leaving, "You've confirmed my suspicions about you."

Valerie watched her go, unsure of what she meant. Choosing not to dwell on it, she grabbed the biohazard box and left the conference room through another set of doors.

After the defunct WSA had been absorbed into the WCF, a larger and more advanced research facility was required to accommodate the additional personnel and added responsibilities. Crates and boxes lined the corridors and hallways leading to the new lab, which was known as the Cube. Valerie used her badge to open a set of doors leading to the large warehouse-like room whose dimensions made it a perfect square. Electricians and computer technicians were still working to get everything fully operational.

"There you are," Valerie said, finding her team, Sylvia and Chetan, and walking over to where they were sitting.

"We're so relieved that you're OK," Sylvia said. "You had us all worried after the earthquake."

"How are Logan and his children?" Chetan asked.

"Everyone is basically OK. His daughter hit her head when she fell, but the doctors said she'll be fine once she gets some rest." Valerie paused and looked around. "This place is a mess."

"It looks worse than it is," Sylvia said. "They have all the critical systems up. They're spending most of their time now getting the global monitoring system up and running." She gestured to the north side of the Cube, where a huge three-dimensional image of a rotating globe was projected.

"They say it's better than the one at the Akasha Vault," Chetan said, then added more skeptically, "but I am not sure I believe that . . . yet."

"How was your trip from Nepal?" Valerie asked him.

"Fine, very fine," he said. "I'm staying in the WCF lodgings at the moment. I'll start looking for a permanent place this weekend."

After Chetan's help at the Akasha Vault with the Freedom Day plot, Valerie didn't have to pull many strings to secure a position for him on her team. He was their new forensic specialist.

"How did the meeting go with the new director?" Sylvia asked.

"Peachy," Valerie answered. "Just peachy."

Sylvia and Chetan both laughed.

"This is for the two of you. It just arrived from the Common-wealth." Valerie set the box that Agent Duna had given her on a lab table. "It contains samples of a foreign residue found in the remains of the gas well that imploded and the other three wells, too."

"We've been waiting for these," Sylvia said, opening the box to find eight glass vials, each of which had been dipped in a semiclear green liquid sealant. A handwritten label was affixed to each one. "It looks like they sent us two samples from each of the three wells."

Chetan came over and picked up a vial, holding it to the light and shaking it gently. "Looks like fine powder of some kind."

"The agents told me that whatever this is, it was found in the pump chamber," Valerie said. "They're estimating that there are two tons of it in the well that imploded."

"That's considerable," Chetan said.

"That's what I said." Valerie grinned.

"How did it get down there?" Sylvia asked.

"That's what we need to find out." Valerie looked around. "By the way, where's Goshi? We're going to need his bio expertise here."

"He's dealing with an issue over at forensic entomology," Chetan answered, typing a message into his PCD. "A few of their culture incubation chambers are malfunctioning. I'll let him know we need him."

"While we wait, I can show you what we have so far." Sylvia returned to her desk and brought up an aerial image of the North African gas processing plant on the HoloPad. Valerie watched from the seat across from her. "This is what the location looked like before the explosion. The site sits nine hundred fifty miles due east of Marrakesh. Smack dab in the middle of the Algerian desert." Four towers, standing more than two hundred fifty meters in height, were positioned in a straight line. Large silver pipes connected the towers and ran along the ground toward the main processing plant half a kilometer to the north. To the east of the processing plant was a large area filled with saucer-shaped devices. "This is the site just after the explosion. As you can see, tower two is now a heap of rubble." Sylvia zoomed in on the new image and what remained of the second well. "At last count, more than three hundred people are confirmed dead and fifty still missing."

"More than one hundred civilians," Chetan said, shaking his head. "These are four of the largest gas wells in the world. All built in the last ten years after large deposits of natural gas were discovered under the bedrock of the Commonwealth."

"Chetan and I have combed through the operation logs," Sylvia said. "Approximately ten minutes before the explosion, tower two reported a problem with its pressure induction columns. A sensor started reporting an unknown substance in its polymeric-membrane chambers."

"Probably the stuff in the vials," Valerie said.

"Two minutes later, the well platform collapsed," Chetan said. "At the same moment, the other three wells also began to report traces of a foreign substance. The operation centers at each of those wells shut their systems down immediately."

"One of the strange things in the logs is that they reported a drop in pressure coming from subterranean fissures," Sylvia said. "That lasted for another twenty-one seconds before stabilizing."

"Stop." Valerie held her palm up in the air. "Induction columns, poly-something or other, fissures—I don't get any of that. What I really want to know is whether this substance is naturally occurring. Is it the side effect of something they're doing? Or did someone put it there?"

"I have my doubts about its occurring naturally. Here's how this whole thing works." Sylvia cleared the picture of the natural-gas plant from the display and brought up another image. It was a cross section of the earth's crust. "About eight thousand feet underground, natural gas is trapped in the shale and the rock. It was created, over thousands of years, by the decomposition of organic matter such as plants and animals. Before the Great Disruption, a process known as fracturing was used. It involved drilling down into the rock and setting off small explosions that caused the surrounding rock to break, crack, and fracture. After you create large enough cracks in the rocks, you inject chemically treated water into the cracks. That water displaces the gas and forces it to come to the surface. Some believed it led to an increase in seismic activity and had an adverse effect on the water tables. But nothing was ever proved definitively."

"The Commonwealth is using a similar concept," Chetan added. "However, sound waves instead of explosives are used to cause cracks in the surrounding rock. Once the gas has been extracted, they pump an additive into the treated water that creates a solid formation, resealing the fractures. This way, theoretically, the ground will not be susceptible to seismic movement."

"That theory might be up for some debate now," Valerie said. "Could this new procedure be causing the earthquakes we've been having?"

"That's a good question," Sylvia said. "There are other major gas plants around the world using the same method. But I'm not sure how to connect those dots. Once the gas is extracted, it goes through the polymeric-membrane chambers to filter out any acidic and toxic gases. If everything goes well, the gas then gets further refined into elemental sulfur, ethane, butane, propane, and pentanes."

"I take it that's where things broke down?" Valerie said.

"Yep," Sylvia said. "Whatever this foreign substance is, the polymeric membrane couldn't handle it."

"So a membrane of some kind has a problem, and an entire well tower implodes?" Valerie leaned back in her chair. "How does something like this suddenly happen? These wells have been in operation for years. Alex is going to the Commonwealth to interview the workers and managers and find out if there has been any recent suspicious activity or security breaches at the facilities."

Suddenly, a loud alarm came from the north end of the Cube, where the rotating globe was located. Valerie jumped to her feet as agents scrambled to their monitoring stations. Red spots appeared on the surface of the large 3-D map of the world.

"More earthquakes." Sylvia groaned. "As you know, it's been a very seismic few days."

When the alarms stopped, Valerie returned to the vials. "What's the next step here? This is a political time bomb that is counting down quickly. If we don't come up with some answers, the energy markets are going to be in chaos. The higher-ups want to know what we are dealing with."

"It's going to take Goshi some time to quarantine these vials," Chetan said, referring to the third member of their team.

"How long?" Valerie asked.

"At least thirty-six hours to do a full light-spectrum analysis before we know it's safe to crack the seal and take a look under the microscope. After that, I don't know—we have no idea what we're dealing with."

"Do what you have to do," Valerie said. "If this *is* sabotage, then we need to understand who benefits from it." She was interrupted by the arrival of a message on her PCD. The grave expression on her face as she read the alert did not go unnoticed.

"What's wrong?" Chetan asked.

"It's an alert from Switzerland," she said. "Château Dugan was broken into last night. Two agents are dead."

"Wasn't that Simon Hitchlords's home?" Sylvia asked.

Valerie remained silent.

17

You are already an immortal being.
The problem is acting as if you are not.

—THE CHRONICLES OF SATRAYA

NEW CHICAGO, 7:34 P.M. LOCAL TIME, MARCH 21, 2070

Logan and Mr. Perrot were listening to the memory chip dislodged from Cassandra's Golden Acorn mosaic. It was dated July 21, 2033, at 9:15 A.M.

> Today is the big day. Camden and I are getting married. Our friends are calling it the wedding of the Magician and the Scholar. I understand why they'd refer to Camden as a magician, but I'm not so sure why I'm the scholar, although that's what the Forgotten Ones started calling me after we first encountered Camden and he was shocked that I could read. I still haven't let him forget about that.

Logan and Mr. Perrot heard Cassandra giggle.

> The wedding is going to take place early, at ten in the morning, because we don't want to detract in any way from the first annual Freedom Day rally. Deya came up with a great idea to add a Liberty Moment to the Freedom Day celebration. At 6:00 p.m., everyone will light a candle and focus on love, compassion,

freedom, and joy—the four fundamental precepts of the Chronicles. *We had two thousand T-shirts made, with one of the four fundamental symbols on the front and the symbol of Satraya on the back. People can choose which symbol they want to wear when they come to the rally in the park. We've received word that people in London, Deya's hometown of Banaras, and Madu's home city of Cairo will be holding their own celebrations! We hope that this Freedom Day rally will catch on and become an annual worldwide celebration. It's going to be beautiful seeing so many people in unity.*

There was a slight pause in the recording, and Logan and Mr. Perrot could hear the rustling of paper in the background before Cassandra continued.

I received a letter from RJ today, declining my invitation to the wedding. He congratulated me, but I don't think he was sincere about it. He left so abruptly after we arrived in Washington. I wish he would have made an effort to get to know Camden, but then I think Camden may have been right. RJ was more infatuated with me than I realized. I've read his letter a couple of times and honestly, it strikes me more as a good-bye than a note of congratulations. I can't help him anymore. He is a good soul beneath all his emotional difficulties and rough edges. I wish him all the best.

A doorbell chimed on the recording.

I have to go. Deya is here. Time to get ready!

The recording ended. "Who is RJ?" Logan asked.

Mr. Perrot shook his head. "As I said, no one knew much about him. He was a Forgotten One and didn't stay in Washington long."

"My mother seemed to know him well," Logan said. "Even to care about him. They exchanged letters after he left, she said. I wonder if she kept any."

"Your parents' wedding was very enjoyable," Mr. Perrot said, changing the topic. "As I was rummaging through those old storage boxes, I came across one of the T-shirts your mother spoke about."

"I remember seeing them in some of the photos you showed me," Logan said. "But I don't recall which one you chose."

Mr. Perrot smiled. "The one with the symbol of Love on the front."

Logan looked at the recorder. "This next message is from 11:34 A.M. the next day." He pressed the Play button.

The wedding was incredible. Everything was perfect. It took place at the north end of the park under the magnificent oak, one of the few centuries-old trees in Washington that survived the Great Disruption. The provisional government has designated it as the new national Christmas tree. Camden received permission to set up large screens similar to those used as theatrical backdrops so that we didn't have to look at the crumbled remains of the old White House in the background. In front of the dais, we set up fifty or so chairs, figuring that would be enough. But many more people showed up and had to stand during the ceremony. Most of them we didn't know. I think they arrived early for the Freedom Day celebration and decided to watch. We didn't mind. Hank walked around playing his fiddle, entertaining the guests as they arrived. Camden and I stood in front of the minister, with Robert next to Camden and Deya next to me.

There was a pause, before Cassandra continued.

Something strange happened then. As we listened to the minister read passages from the Chronicles, *I swore I saw the face of a young man peer out from behind him. I blinked my eyes a few times, and the face suddenly disappeared. I looked at Camden, who didn't seem to notice anything. I'm not sure who or what I saw, but there was something familiar about his face. I guess I'll just have to take it as a good omen that angels are watching over us.*

Logan pressed the Pause button and stared at Mr. Perrot, astonished. "Do you remember when I told you last July about my candle vision and finding myself at my parents' wedding, standing behind a minister?"

Mr. Perrot nodded, a look of amazement on his face, too.

"I wonder," Logan mused, resuming the recording.

After the minister spoke, both Deya and Robert said a few words. I think Robert was a little nervous about having to follow Deya, who recited from memory a wonderful passage from the Chronicles, *but he was just as moving. Then Camden and I made our vows, which we wrote ourselves, I'm proud to say. It was one of the few times I saw Camden nervous. But I have to admit that I was a little nervous, too. And then, in unison, we said, "I do."*

Mr. Perrot pressed pause. "It's true," he said. "I was so humbled by Deya's recital. She spoke those words as if she lived them. I was so inspired by her that I began to study the *Chronicles* much more earnestly."

"I recall seeing a man do the same thing the day we revealed our true identities to the Council of Satraya nine months ago," Logan said with a wink. "When you spoke, you had the same effect on everyone in the room that Deya had on you." He pressed the Play button.

I had a wonderful time at the Freedom Day celebration last night. People came from all over the country. I was even surprised to see some of my clan from the forest; they decided that coming back to civilization would not be so bad after all. Camden and I had changed out of our wedding clothes. Camden decided to wear the peace T-shirt, and I wore the one with the symbol of Joy. Robert and Cynthia came to the rally together. I think the two of them would be perfect for each other, but I think Robert is more tempted by someone he can't have.

As usual, Fendral and Andrea were reserved during the celebration. I've known them for almost a year and a half, and they haven't shared much about their personal lives. I remember Andrea and her fashion empire before the Great Disruption, but I know nothing about Fendral, except that he comes from one of the wealthiest families in Switzerland. His son Simon seems so lonely. I wonder why his mother isn't here to care for him. The only person I noticed Fendral speaking to was a handsomely dressed man in a wheelchair. I've never seen him before. He must be a friend of Fendral's from out of town.

Camden and I went for a walk and eventually found a bench where we sat, holding hands and looking at the stars in the clear night sky. People wearing their new Satraya T-shirts would meander by from time to time, congratulating us on our marriage. One man stopped by for an extended conversation. He introduced himself as Sumsari Baltik—I just love that name. Maybe we'll name our first child Sumsari.

Logan and Mr. Perrot could hear Cassandra giggling. "Good thing she didn't carry out that threat," Logan said, also laughing.

He is a charming, cultured, middle-aged gentleman who has traveled all over the world. He said that he recently arrived from someplace in England called the Isle of Man. I've never heard of it, but Camden has. Sumsari is short and stocky, with long brown hair and the sweetest of smiles. He has a tattoo on his arm. Camden recognized it as the emblem of the old Navy SEALs. But what I found most exciting about him was that he is a music teacher! Just what I've been looking for. Robert came by, asking Camden to help him with something, so after they went off, I told Sumsari about my days in the forest with the Forgotten Ones and how Hank, a fiddler, brought a great deal of cheer to us in those trying times. I told him that I wanted to learn to play the violin and what a difficult time I was having trying to find one in good condition. Sumsari said that I could use one of his and that he would be happy to teach me how to play. I'm so excited! I'm going to have my first lesson in a few days.

Oh, I have to leave now. I promised Mrs. Wonderful that I would meet her for lunch. I want to hear what she thought of the wedding and the first Freedom Day celebration.

The recording clicked off. "I don't remember my mother playing the violin very often while I was growing up," Logan said to Mr. Perrot. "Maybe once every few months."

"After we fled from Washington, the frequency of her playing diminished. But prior to that, she played every day. She even serenaded you when you couldn't fall asleep. You were just too young to remember.

We were all amazed by how quickly she picked up the instrument. And we said her teacher, Sumsari, must truly work wonders."

"Why the curious face?" Logan asked.

Mr. Perrot looked at Logan. "She didn't just become *good* over the four years of training; she became *great*. I see that same thing in your daughter, Jamie, when she plays. I wonder if your mother passed along some of Sumsari's training."

Logan nodded. "It didn't take Jamie long at all to learn. When she was only four, my mother started to give her lessons. Jamie used to love standing in front of a mirror and pretending she was performing a concert in front of a packed house." Logan paused for a moment allowing his thoughts to linger before selecting the next voice entry on the recorder. "This next one is from 8:40 P.M., July 22, 2033. Same day as the one we just heard."

I love Deya. She is so sweet and sincere. We went for lunch at the new Indian restaurant that just opened a few blocks north of the council offices on Eighteenth Street. I think it will be her and Babu's favorite place for a while. They miss Indian food. We were seated at a table by the window, and we saw Fendral, Simon, and that man in the wheelchair. Simon was sitting on a sidewalk bench eating an ice cream cone while his father talked to the other man. We didn't see Andrea anywhere. I told Deya that Camden and I had seen the man in the wheelchair at the Freedom Day celebration. I asked her if she knew who he was; she said no but expressed concern about Simon, who looked so unhappy even while he was eating his ice cream. She doesn't like the way Fendral treats his son, either.

Babu and Deya's sister Joyti joined us for a short time, and then we all headed back to the Council offices.

It's getting dark, I'm going to light some candles . . .

Logan and Mr. Perrot could hear movement in the background, then the striking of a match. "Seems like my mother had a soft spot for Simon," Logan said. "If she only knew what a monster he would become."

"Your mother had a great deal of compassion for everyone," Mr. Perrot said. "Perhaps if someone like her had taken more interest in Simon, he would have turned out differently."

As we walked back to Council headquarters, Babu and Joyti engaged in a spirited debate about the reconstruction effort. Deya and I trailed behind them, and I confided to her that something has been bothering me. I told her that I wasn't having as much success with the Satraya flame technique described in the Chronicles *as Camden was. Deya reminded me of what the books suggested, that no one technique would resonate with every individual. That's why many were offered. Each person had to choose his own path and forge his own way. Deya told me that she, too, struggles with the candle. Her favorite technique is Reflecting. She told me that once she put the flame aside and started to practice Reflecting, she found some success. As she progressed in her Reflecting work, her focus on the flame suddenly improved. She told me, "Mind is mind, it doesn't matter what you choose. Mind is mind."*

I'm going to her house tomorrow, and she's going to show me what she has learned.

The recording ended. "There's one more on this chip," Logan said. "It's dated 9:10 P.M., July 23, 2033."

We went into the basement of Deya's house, where there is no natural light. Deya showed me the spot in a corner where she meditates. Babu and Joyti have their own corners. In Deya's spot, a large mirror was leaning against a wall. A small cushion and a box of candles lay on the floor in front of it. Her copy of the Chronicles *was also there. I found it strange that one of the books was opened to a blank page. I wanted to ask her about it, but I didn't.*

Logan pressed the Pause button on the recorder. "Deya must have known about the hidden symbols."

Mr. Perrot nodded. "I wonder how far she was able to progress. I also wonder if she and Camden ever discussed them."

"Mr. Quinn said that the first hidden symbol in Deya's set of the books was called the A-Tee-Na," Logan said.

"Is that the symbol that you saw when you first looked at the pages? Have you been able to see it more clearly?"

"I have. I've even been able to see portions of the next symbol on the second blank page. Mr. Quinn explained to me that it was a progression. He told me that first I would see the symbols and then I would experience them. Not really knowing what the symbols mean, I can't say if I've experienced their power or not."

"What about the third page?" Mr. Perrot asked. "Have you been able to see what your father and Mr. Quinn said was the most powerful symbol of all?"

Logan shook his head. Then he pressed play again.

Deya walked over to Babu's area, picked up his pillow, and set it down a few feet from hers. She asked me to sit down and slid her mirror in front of me. She adjusted it so that I could see the reflection of my face and upper body. Then Deya lit a few oil lamps and turned off the overhead lights. The reflection of my face in the mirror looked shadowed, ghostly. Deya took a seat on her cushion beside me.

Deya told me that the technique of Reflecting described in the Chronicles *was very similar to the ancient practice of scrying. People once used crystal balls, reflecting pools, bowls of liquid, almost anything that could reflect an image. She said that over the ages, dogma set in, and people forgot the true purpose of scrying, and it ended up becoming a technique associated with witches, magicians, and warlocks. She told me that the* Chronicles *present the technique in a fresh way, which, if done correctly, will yield interesting results to the devoted practitioner. Deya then recited a familiar nursery rhyme:*

> *Looking glass, Looking glass, on the wall,*
> *Who in this land is the fairest of all?*
> *Thou art fairer than all who are here, Lady Queen,*
> *But more beautiful still is Snow White, as I ween.*

I told her I'd heard it before. It was from the story of Snow White. She said many people were familiar with that more modern version of the tale but that it had actually been adapted from a much older folk tale the Brothers Grimm had set down in writing. The mirror in the tale conveys an essential point about scrying, one that the Chronicles also teaches. The mirror never lies. It does not judge good or bad, right or wrong. It has no heart and does not care about how one feels. It is only a tool.

First, Deya instructed me to close my eyes and slow down my breathing. Slower, she told me, slow and relaxed. Then she told me to open my eyes and look directly at my reflection in the mirror. In particular, at my forehead. She placed a red bindi on the middle of my forehead. She joked that now that I was married, I needed to start wearing it as she does. Deya told me not to lose sight of that particular spot—it was the key to mastering the technique of Reflecting. She told me to pretend I was looking through that spot to the other side, as if looking through the dirty window of a house to see inside.

I did as she instructed. After what seemed to be a half hour, nothing happened. I felt frustrated, just as I had with the Satraya flame. My body language must have conveyed my feelings, because Deya encouraged me not to give up. She suggested I close my eyes again and take a few more deep, slow, relaxing breaths. When I opened my eyes and looked at my reflection, it was different. My eyes were more relaxed, and I appeared to be smiling, even though I knew I wasn't actually smiling. Deya told me to keep focusing on the bindi on my forehead. I did. She told me that if I started to feel frustrated, I should close my eyes and breathe deeply until my frustration dissipated. Deya was very patient with me.

I don't know how long I sat there, but there was a moment after I opened my eyes when my straight hair looked curly. I blinked a few times until it looked normal again. Deya told me not to be so anxious to readjust my gaze. She told me to allow my reflection to morph without my conscious mind's interference. It was as if Deya knew what I was seeing. Over and over, I repeated the processes of closing my eyes and reopening them.

Then the moment came when I was suddenly looking at something I didn't expect to see. My heart raced as I gazed into the mirror. My face had been replaced with my mother's. I was looking at her curly brown hair, her magical smile. Her blue eyes were looking back at me. I couldn't help but try to figure out *what was taking place, and the moment I did, her image vanished, and I saw my own reflection once again. Deya could tell that something had occurred. She told me to close my eyes. I expected her to tell me again to take four deep breaths, but instead, she told me to focus on what I had seen—not to analyze it but simply and gently to ponder it until the answer came. I wasn't even sure that I had asked a question, but I did as she instructed.*

There was an extended pause in the recording. Logan and Mr. Perrot could hear something being poured into a glass.

What happened to me next I can't talk about right now. All I can say is that it was so real that I was inconsolable. Deya was hugging me. She told me that my first journey through the mirror had taken place. The answer to a question that I have been asking for five years was given to me: Flight 1849.

The recording stopped. "That was the last recording on this chip," Logan said. "What is Flight 1849?"

"I don't know," Mr. Perrot said. "But perhaps the answer lies somewhere in the mosaic." He and Logan looked at the Golden Acorn mosaic; it was time to dislodge more of Cassandra's memory chips.

18

Making a choice from the past is impossible. All
choices are made from the present. So you have no
excuse not to make a different choice.

—THE CHRONICLES OF SATRAYA

BIJAURA, UTTAR PRADESH, INDIA, 10:18 A.M. LOCAL TIME, MARCH 22, 2070

The waters of the river flowed by as they had for a thousand years. The
Ganesh Ashram, which was located in the forest along the Ganges River,
had been constructed twelve years after the Great Disruption. Known
for its ayurvedic healing methodologies, the ashram never turned away
anyone in need. It was funded by the government and also relied on
donations from its former patients and devotees. The river provided
the only access to the ashram, and just a few meters downstream of the
southernmost hut, a group of people were being led through their daily
yoga practices. The sun had risen many hours earlier, and the river was
bustling with activity. Boats filled with fruits and vegetables were making
their way to the marketplaces near the holy ghats a few miles to the north.

An old woman wearing a green sari entered one of the ashram's
eighteen huts. She was carrying a tray of food and had a brown cloth
bag slung over her shoulder. "Glorious morning to you, sir," she said
cheerfully as she set the tray down on a small table. "You are looking
better and stronger each day."

The man, in his bamboo and wicker chair, said nothing as the old woman opened the curtain, letting some light into the room.

"Perhaps this is the day you will begin to remember who you are. The doctor communicated that he will come by this afternoon to remove the last of the bandages from your face."

The man squinted as the sunlight hit his face. He remained silent as he began to eat his meal and drink his tea.

"The doctor is very optimistic that the facial repair will turn out well for you. You go through more candles than anyone else at the ashram," the old woman said, reaching into her bag and taking out new candles to replace the ones that had burned down. She tossed the remaining stumps into her bag.

The man struggled as he ate to get the food and drink around the bandage that ran across the right side of his face and the edge of his mouth.

"Any dreams or memories that might help us in locating your family?"

"No," the man replied softly. "I remember today as much as I remembered when I first arrived, whenever that was."

"You were brought to us on July 22 of last year," the old woman said, continuing to straighten up the room. "I remember, because it was the day after the wonderful blue light appeared on Freedom Day. Maybe you remember seeing that light? Everybody remembers the light."

The man paused for a moment. "No," he said, with a hint of annoyance, as he sipped his tea. "I don't remember such a light."

"That is all right. Life is a series of fantastical events," the old woman said, as she made the bed. "After the Great Disruption, all hope was lost. In many ways, the world was like you—it seemed to have forgotten its identity. Then the *Chronicles* miraculously arrived, and people began to remember their purpose and place. Have you ever read the books?"

The man did not answer and continued to eat.

"Don't remember that, either, do you? Well, Deya Sarin found her books just north of here. That is one of those fantastical events that will never be forgotten. I wish I could have met her before she died." As the old woman picked up the pillow to fluff it, a piece of paper tucked under it flew out.

The man caught a glimpse of the paper as it fell to the ground. The old woman picked it up and noticed what had been drawn on it. "Hand that here," the man said, agitated. "Quickly."

The old woman did as requested. "I see you're a bit of an artist." She handed the pencil sketch to the man, who only took the paper and set it facedown next to his food. The old woman resumed her activities. "Your memories will return, I am certain of it. We once took care of a woman who spent three years here before she remembered who she was. Keep the faith."

"What is the limit to your faith?" the man asked suddenly. "Isn't that the question that we are all supposed to ask ourselves?"

"So you have read the books," the old woman said.

"It's been a while."

"I can get you a copy if you want. We have many of them at the ashram. Maybe they will help you remember something."

"No," the man said. "I don't feel much like reading them."

The old woman stuffed the used bed sheets and towels into her cloth bag and headed out the door. She stopped for a moment. "You should take a walk today along the river." She took a deep breath of fresh air. "It's a good day to be alive!"

The man pushed his tray aside and walked over to the HoloPad set up at the corner of his room. He wore a loose-fitting light tan kurta over a pair of thin cotton pants. He brought up videos of various news feeds, learning what was happening around the world. One segment in particular captured his attention. He watched the political ramblings of Enrique Salize and his counterparts around the world. They were locked in a debate on energy and the crisis created by the explosion of a natural gas well in the North African Commonwealth. The man smiled. "What are you up to, my old friends?" he whispered.

With a motion of his hand, he cleared away the news feeds and placed a call. The image of a dark-skinned bald man wearing a black, red, and gold dashiki appeared before him. "Kashta, my friend," the man said, "it is time."

The brief HoloPad call ended. The man brought up a news report that he had read every day since he had found it, five months ago. It reported the opening of the Camden and Cassandra Ford Studio of Art in New Chicago. A blue dot flashed in the corner, indicating that there was a new article related to the one he was reading. The man waved his hand over it and brought up the linked article. It announced that a commemoration was going to be held at the Council of Satraya offices in Washington, D.C. The event was in honor of the members of the original Council of Satraya. It stated that Logan Ford, the son of Camden and Cassandra Ford, would attend and that Mr. Alain Perrot would be appointed to one of the vacant council seats. The man looked at the photograph of Logan Ford and Mr. Perrot, which ran alongside the article. With a hand gesture, the man brought up a recent photo of Logan and Valerie and Logan's children enjoying a day at the beach. He zoomed in on Logan's face and stared at it coldly.

The man, who had spent the last nine months recovering at the ashram, did indeed know his own identity. His denial to the old woman and the rest of the people who tended to him was part of a game he was playing. He walked over to the small mirror that hung over the sink. He had suffered devastating burns to his face, neck, and shoulders. While his memory loss was a ruse, the pain he was experiencing was very real. He looked at his reflection, wondering what he would find under the bandages. He winced as he ripped off the pieces of tape holding the bindings in place. He then removed the layers of gauze that had kept his identity a secret.

The man was not pleased with what he saw in the mirror. He did not recognize his own face. The doctors and the old woman were wrong. The facial repairs did not turn out splendidly. The skin grafts on his neck and shoulders were hideous. The right side of his face was red and riddled with scars. The skin sagged over a protruding cheekbone. He stared intently at the face in front of him. His left eye blinked, while his right could not. In the mirror, he saw the smiling faces of Logan Ford and Alain Perrot. The man punched it, shattering the glass to pieces.

He tossed the gauze into a small trash can and looked around the room. He grabbed a sack and threw into it the remnants of the clothes he had been wearing when he was found. He lifted the mattress off his bed and pulled out a few papers with scribbled notes. He grabbed the paper with the sketch he had drawn and put it into his pocket. He could hear the sound of a boat's motor outside. When he went to the door, he saw Kashta approaching along the river.

Simon Hitchlords took one more look around the hut. His prolonged stay at the ashram was over. It was now time to deal with those who had put him there.

19

Everyone has something to say. Don't cut short their
articulation, lest your own words be dismissed one day.

——THE CHRONICLES OF SATRAYA

NEW CHICAGO, 11:20 P.M. LOCAL TIME, MARCH 21, 2070

Logan sat on the floor at the center of his meditation room in his
house. A single candle burned, illuminating the blank pages of an open
book lying in front of him. He needed to settle down and focus, but
he couldn't stop thinking about the news that Valerie had relayed when
she'd called earlier that evening: two WCF agents had been killed at
Château Dugan. The disaster in Mexico, Jamie's headaches, the discovery of his mother's recordings, and the mystery of Flight 1849 only
added to his anxiety.

He looked at the plastic container of his mother's chips resting on top
of his backpack. Next to it was Deya's Destiny Box. Logan and Mr. Perrot had found it during their cat-and-mouse game with Simon along the
Ganges last July. The box had contained her copy of the *Chronicles*, known
as the River Set, along with a small mirror and the mysterious blue Manas
Mantr candle, which they knew was somehow linked to Sebastian Quinn.

Logan took a deep breath and focused his gaze on the candle flame.
Soft music was playing in the background. Like his father, Logan

had progressed in honing the Satraya Flame technique described in the *Chronicles*. His father had indirectly introduced him to the Satraya Flame via the pages of his journal, which Logan had found along with the Manas Mantr candle buried in the basement of the Council of Satraya building last July. While Logan hadn't yet fully mastered the technique, he could not deny that the experiences he'd had over the last nine months focusing on flame had led to some of the most intriguing and meaningful revelations of his life.

Logan had also learned from his father's writings that the blank pages in the third book of the *Chronicles* held veiled images and that if one entered a deeper state of mind while looking at the pages, the images would reveal themselves. The third blank page, he also knew, held only a partial symbol. Logan's father had suspected that it was the symbol of immortality, but Sebastian Quinn had hinted that it might be something even greater. The only way to see the complete final mark was to possess all four original sets of the *Chronicles*.

After many months of diligent work, Logan was finally able to see two of the veiled symbols. Under each one was a word, which Logan surmised was the symbol's ancient name. The first symbol Logan saw was the A-Tee-Na, and the second was the Sin-Ka-Ta. Sebastian had told Logan that seeing the symbols was only the first step in a progression. He needed to experience them to truly gain their wisdom. What exactly he meant by that, however, Logan didn't know.

Logan gently shifted his gaze from the candle to the blank page. Gray-blue distortions appeared, floating like ghosts above the blank page. The cloudy hue was a signpost that indicated that he was entering a deeper state of mind focus. It was usually at this moment that the broken fragments of the symbols appeared. And eventually, after more diligent concentration, the full symbol emerged. But tonight all he could see were the cloudy gray-blue distortions. Frustrated, he broke what focus he had and stretched his legs. His mind was too scattered. Impulsively, he leaned over and grabbed the memory chips and his mother's recorder. Maybe he could answer at least one of his questions:

what did she see in the mirror concerning Flight 1849? Logan inserted the chips into the recorder until he found the one he was interested in. It was time-stamped 6:01 P.M., July 24, 2033, the closest date to the last recording he and Mr. Perrot had listened to at the studio. Logan pressed the Play button.

These last twenty-four hours after my experience in Deya's mirror have been the saddest of my life.

I don't know how I ended up on that flight. All I remember was that after I closed my eyes, as Deya told me to do, I was suddenly sitting on a plane. The flight attendants were walking up and down the aisle, serving drinks. I looked out the window. We were flying above a thick layer of clouds, and the light from an oddly bright sun was streaming through the windows on the right side of the plane. No one was sitting next to me. The top portion of a boarding pass was sticking out of the seatback in front of me. I removed it and read that I was on Flight 1849. I stood and made my way into the center aisle. The light from the sun coming through the windows seemed to be getting brighter. I was at the back of the plane and began to walk toward the front. People were talking with one another, some were reading, children were watching movies. A few of the passengers were complaining to the flight attendants that the inside of the plane was getting too warm and asked if the air-conditioning could be turned up. I continued to make my way up the aisle, and two hands reached out and grabbed mine. One grabbed my left and the other my right. I looked down to my left and saw my father. Seated next to him was my brother. I turned to my right and saw my mother. They were sitting across the aisle from each other. Before I could say anything to them, the plane jolted, and then it jolted again more wildly. The intensity of the sun through the windows caused me to squint, and I was sweating from the heat. It was easily more than one hundred degrees in the cabin. I heard the voice of a distraught captain come over the intercom, but I couldn't make out his words. The lights in the plane flickered and went out, and suddenly, the sound of the engines stopped. The plane banked sharply to the right and then nosedived. Passengers were screaming. I looked at each of my parents and then my brother. I yelled out, "I love you!"

The next thing I knew, I was crying, and Deya was hugging me.

I didn't get any sleep last night. This morning, I finally told Camden what I had experienced in the mirror at Deya's house. I told him about Flight 1849. He didn't doubt me for one second. He grabbed my hand, and we drove to the central rebuilding offices, which are housed at the old Pentagon. We found Camden's mother, who was helping to salvage data from various computer systems all around the country. She took us to the archive and helped us comb through various air traffic logs from the day the solar storm hit, August 18, 2027. It took a while, but we found the log entry. It was for Centennial Flight 1849 from New York's JFK to Little Rock.

Logan could hear his mother crying. He heard what sounded like tissues being pulled from a box.

The log confirmed that Flight 1849 had gone down in the solar storm during the Great Disruption. The plane had crashed near Louisville. My mother, father, and brother were all on the manifest. Their seats were listed as 14C and 14D, two seats across the aisle from each other, and my brother sat in 14B.

Somehow the mirror had transported me to the moment right before the plane went down. The mirror answered the question of what happened to my family, which has haunted me for nine years. Until now, I had hoped that they were still alive somewhere. I would have given anything to see them again. My first journey into the mirror has taken place, but it was not a joyful one.

Logan heard more crying. His mother's words struck his heart. He understood how she felt. He would give anything to see her and his father again.

Deya wasn't kidding when she said the mirror had no heart and didn't care about our feelings. As hard as this experience was, I'm glad I had it. I needed to know the truth, and now I can move on. I do have a question about my experience in the mirror, though. Did my parents hear me say I loved them? Are their spirits alive somehow, somewhere, with the ability to interact with me? Is that what immortality really is? I remember reading something about this in the Chronicles.

Now Logan heard the flipping of pages in a book.

Here it is. It's the parable entitled Desire, the voice of Immortality.

Logan knew the parable that his mother was referring to. There was a long pause before Logan's mother's voice came back.

What if the Chronicles *are right? I can't deny that I saw my mother's face in the mirror. And I saw both of my parents and my brother on the plane. What if a person's consciousness is eternal? Could I actually send my parents a message? Is that possible? I have to speak with Deya—maybe she knows more about this and if there's any merit to the outlandish thing I'm suggesting. I'm going over to see her right now.*

The recording clicked off, but there was one more on the chip. It was made at 11:12 P.M. the same night. Logan selected it and pressed play.

I spoke to Deya tonight and told her what Camden and I learned about Flight 1849. While saddened by the news, she was not surprised by it. She gave me advice: "Do not become enamored with the faces or places you see in the mirror. They must remain secondary to the information you receive. If you get consumed by what is presented, you will lose sight of why you see it." She was right. While seeing my mother and father was both wonderful and heartbreaking, the information obtained from the vision about Flight 1849 is what is important. While it is hard to accept, I have to admit that it is liberating.

Logan thought about his many candle visions. He could see how Deya's advice about the mirror also applied to the Satraya Flame. The information he had received in the flame was indeed more important than the images that had delivered it. Every component of a vision conveyed an essential piece of information. The voice of Logan's mother continued.

> *Deya then asked me a very provocative question: Where had the information that my parents were on Flight 1849 come from? Had it already been in my mind when the Reflecting process brought it forward?*
>
> *I had no idea how to answer. Deya asked me another question: How did the looking glass know that the queen was the fairest of them all at one moment and, later, that Snow White had replaced the queen as the fairest of them all?*
>
> *Once again, I didn't have an answer. But I feel that the mirror and the Reflecting process do, that maybe there is not a single question they can't answer.*
>
> *I wonder how far Deya has taken this.*

Logan looked at Deya's Destiny Box and the mirror she had hidden in it, and he recalled the strange experience he'd had when he first glanced into it. He'd never told anyone that he had seen, as clear as day, the face of his mother looking back at him. At the time, he'd doubted that he'd really seen it at all. But now, having heard his mother's account and Deya's explanation, Logan wondered what his doubt had caused him to miss. He leaned over and picked up the mirror. It was time to look into it again.

20

One day, you will learn that the distance between your discernment
and your judgment is equal to your own desire to change.

——THE CHRONICLES OF SATRAYA

Logan sat in the half lotus position. He straightened his back and closed
his eyes. He took a few deep breaths, inhaling and exhaling slowly. He
tapped the index finger of his right hand on his forehead, just above
the bridge of his nose. In his left hand, he held Deya's mirror. He took
another deep breath and opened his eyes. He adjusted the angle of the
mirror slightly, so that he could see the reflection of his entire face.
Logan directed his gaze to the spot on his forehead that Deya had told
his mother was important. His eyes did not waver. The music continued to play in the background, and the candlelight cast an eerie shadow
on Logan's face in the mirror. From time to time, he would close his
eyes and take a deep breath, slowly exhaling each one. Then he opened
his eyes and continued looking at his reflection, resting his gaze on the
spot on his forehead that he had tapped with his finger.

Logan began to see a gray-blue fog, similar to what appeared when
he stared at the blank pages in the *Chronicles*. The cloud-like forms
floated in front of him, interfering with his efforts to focus on his re-

flection. He tried to blink away the distractions, but the fog persisted. He noticed that the edges of the mirror were blurring and that a blackness was encroaching on his peripheral vision. As Logan had learned to do with the Satraya Flame, he pressed on, not allowing himself to question what was taking place.

Soon his reflection in the mirror became distorted, as if waves of heat on a hot desert road were rising before it. For a fleeting instant, Logan thought he saw himself with a beard and a mustache and long blond hair. His eyes, however, remained the same. The morphing of his face in the mirror continued more rapidly, and soon he was looking at a procession of faces he did not recognize. He forced the image of his mother into his mind. The flow of faces halted, his peripheral vision returned, and the blackness vanished. Logan saw his own face in the mirror. The moment had ended.

"You know better," Logan whispered to himself. "Do not get distracted." He had learned in working with the Satraya Flame that the instant *thinking* occurs one loses the *singularity of mind* discussed in the *Chronicles*. Logan readjusted his body and said with conviction, "Let's try that again." He recentered his thoughts and looked into Deya's mirror.

✻   ✻   ✻

The procession of faces was as rapid as before. This time, Logan did not allow his judgments to interfere; he simply observed. The faces transitioned, from smiles to frowns, from blue eyes to black, from straight hair to curly and pointed noses to flat ones. Then, without warning, the procession stopped, and a single face presented itself. Logan was looking into the gray-blue eyes of a man who appeared to be in his mid- to late thirties. He had neatly combed jet-black hair and a thick black mustache, a pointy nose, and a firm, distinguished chin. As Logan gazed upon him, he could feel the man's determined and steadfast bearing; he could sense that this man was searching for something. Logan recalled the instruction that Deya had given to his mother and closed his eyes. The face of the man was the only thing he held in his mind.

Logan ducked as a series of ultraviolet blue lights passed over his head, making a crackling sound. He was in a dimly lit room, where a man was rocking back and forth in an antique chair in front of a desk, writing feverishly in a book. The man wore a white collared shirt under a dark gray tweed suit. He was slender and about two meters tall. Logan walked over to him. It was the man whose face he had seen in the mirror. Logan could not help noticing his thin fingers and unusually long thumbs. Books were scattered on the floor around his chair. Logan squatted down and read the title of one of the larger, thicker ones: *Theoria Philosphiae Naturalis* by Boskovich. A book Logan was more familiar with lay next to it, *A Connecticut Yankee in King Arthur's Court* by Mark Twain. There was a third by an author named Vivekananda. After a moment, Logan looked up at the man and said, "Hello." There was no response. "Hello," he said again. The man remained engrossed in his writing, unaware of Logan's presence.

Logan gazed around the room. Metal cages, long glass tubes, and copper balls of all sizes were scattered around it. This was clearly a laboratory of some kind. He walked over to what looked like a group of large batteries connected by thick black wires. Near them was a wheel about three meters in diameter, made of coiled copper. When Logan touched it, he received a shock. He looked at the table in the center of the room, where an illuminated lightbulb lay. The large bulb was not attached to any wires, but somehow it gave off light. Logan looked back over at the man in the chair, who was still writing, undisturbed by Logan's exploration. Logan looked over the man's shoulder to see what he was writing.

The idea gradually took hold of me that the earth might be used in place of the wire, thus dispensing with artificial conductors altogether. The immensity of the globe seemed an insurmountable obstacle, but after a prolonged study of the subject, I became satisfied that the undertaking was rational.

Farther down the page, Logan read:

Like a flash of lightning, the truth was revealed. I drew with a stick on the sand the diagrams of my motor. A thousand secrets of nature which I might have stumbled upon accidentally I would have given for that one which I had wrestled from her against all odds at the peril of my existence.

The man stopped writing and looked around, as if sensing that he was not alone. Then he looked back down and began to doodle something in the margin of the page. Logan looked at what the man was sketching. A cross, it seemed, but within each quadrant, the man drew an elliptical shape; then darkened the lines. When satisfied, he drew a circle around his sketch.

The image looked familiar, but Logan couldn't place it. The man turned to a blank page.

The lightbulb on the table at the center of the room began to flicker. Logan looked past it and noticed something in the far corner of the laboratory. A cloth was draped over an easel. He walked over and removed the cloth, tossing it onto the floor. He couldn't believe his eyes. He was looking at *The Scream* by Edvard Munch. He turned back to stare at the man, recalling Mr. Quinn's note. Was this the one whose diligent work halfway around the world was related to Munch's picture?

Logan turned back to the Munch with a start; the images had become animated. The red sky was swirling, and the water in the harbor was cresting into waves. The two people in the background were walking forward toward the person in agony, who still stood motionless on the bridge. As the people approached, their faces became clearer. While Logan had never seen one of them before, he did recognize the other. It was his daughter, Jamie.

The lightbulb in the center of the room flickered more rapidly and caught the attention of the man sitting at the desk. Logan watched as the man walked over to the table and picked up the flickering bulb. Holding it in his hand, he looked perplexed. Logan turned back to the picture and saw that the face of the screaming man was now a blur, because it was shaking so rapidly. A terrifying scream rent the air. The image of Jamie continued to move forward, until it horrifically merged into the countenance of the screaming man. The light in the room flickered faster and faster. The screaming became so loud that it was unbearable. Logan put his hands on the sides of his face, mimicking the man in the picture. *What's happening? Why is my daughter in this painting?* The scream hit a feverish pitch, and suddenly the image of his daughter exploded into a morbid convulsion of colors. Logan screamed himself. He turned away and looked at the man standing at the lab table. The lightbulb fell from his hand and crashed onto the floor. Everything went dark and silent.

Logan's singularity of mind was gone. He became aware of his surroundings—the feel of the cushion beneath him, the soft music, the wavering light of the candle. Deya's mirror was slowly coming into view, and the blackness in his peripheral vision was receding. Logan heard someone coming up the stairs. He rose and walked out of his meditation room. It was Ms. Sally and Logan's daughter, Jamie.

"She had a terrible nightmare," Ms. Sally said. "She started screaming in her sleep."

Jamie ran over to her father and hugged him around the waist. "My head hurts again," she said.

21

If you know what to do but do not do it, does it
matter that you know what to do?

—THE CHRONICLES OF SATRAYA

"It's down here," Anita said, as she descended the spiral staircase.

Britney followed. "You have the wickedest home. And I mean that in a good way. Where are we going?"

"To the Alexandria Room."

"See, that's what I mean. Who names the rooms in their house? Or should I say their castle?" Britney laughed.

They reached the bottom and stepped onto the marble floor of Peel Castle's master library.

"Are you kidding me?" Britney said in astonishment.

Anita laughed at her reaction. The Alexandria Room was named after the library of Alexandria, of course, one of the largest and most significant libraries of the ancient world until Julius Caesar burned it down. The twenty-five-square-meter room boasted a translucent white marble table below an illuminated domed ceiling. Lighting installed underneath caused its surface to glow, and thirty high-back chairs with blue velvet cushions were placed around it. The room's walls were lined, floor to ceiling, with bookshelves. Multiple rolling ladders were mounted on each of the four walls. At the north end of the room were rows of glass cases containing precious documents dating back to the Middle Ages.

"How do you find anything in here?" Britney asked.

"Hypatia can help us," said Halima, popping up from one of the thirty armchairs that faced away from the library's entrance.

"What are you doing here?" Anita asked, walking over to her.

"My homework," the younger girl replied. "Mr. Quinn gave me a few things to read before he left on his trip. What does *benediction* mean?"

"It means blessing," Anita answered, glancing at the book. It was titled *Enuntiatio de Tutela.*

"Who is Hypatia?" Britney asked.

"She's the librarian down here," Halima said.

Britney spun around, looking for her.

Anita laughed. Halima jumped out of the chair and walked over to a nearby control pad. "You can type in what you're looking for, or you can just say it. Find *A Christmas Carol.*"

A soothing female voice seemed to come out of nowhere. "Searching for *A Christmas Carol.*" One of the ladders along the west wall began to move. A red laser originating from the domed ceiling pointed to a particular book on the fourth shelf from the bottom. "*A Christmas Carol,* written by Charles Dickens in 1843."

"Hypatia can find almost anything you are looking for," Halima said. "Simple."

"What if you want information about horses?" Britney asked.

"Find *horses,*" Halima said into the control panel.

"Searching for *horses,*" Hypatia said. All twelve ladders began to move. A hundred laser lights activated and pointed to a hundred books on the shelves. "Multiple results," the voice said.

"You have a lot of climbing to do," Halima said with a giggle.

"You get back to work," Anita said. "Britney and I have to look for something."

"What? Maybe I can help. I'm really good with Hypatia."

"No," Anita said. "You keep reading those assignments Mr. Quinn gave you."

Disappointed, Halima walked back to the armchair with her book.

Anita stood at the control panel, with Britney beside her. "We need to figure out what's so important about that painting Mr. Quinn sent off to someone," she said, as she typed in *"The Scream,* Edvard Munch." Ladders on all four walls moved; forty-four laser lights activated and pointed to books scattered throughout the library. "Too many."

"Did Mr. Quinn say anything else about your headaches before he left?" Britney asked.

"No." Anita tried to recall exactly what had happened the night of the vernal equinox. "I remember Bukya rubbing his ears, and I remember telling Mr. Quinn and my father that my violin was out of tune. Mr. Quinn told me that it was actually me that was out of tune. He turned to my father and said something about a masterpiece."

"He said that a masterpiece needed to find a new home," Halima said, poking her head around the side of her chair. "And he said something else, too. But since I'm not helping . . ."

Anita sighed. "OK, you can help us."

Halima gave them a big smile. "He said that the voice of the earth was disturbed."

"What does that mean?" Britney asked.

Anita worked the control panel and brought up a projected image of the picture by Edvard Munch.

Halima jumped out of the chair and joined them. "Is that the picture you were looking for? That man doesn't look happy."

"Let's see if we can translate the writing on the black plaque on the frame," Anita said. She pressed a few buttons and read it out loud.

I was walking along the road with two friends—the sun was setting—suddenly the sky turned blood red—I paused, feeling exhausted, and leaned on the fence—there was blood and tongues of fire above the blue-black fjord and the

city—my friends walked on, and I stood there trembling with anxiety—and I
sensed an infinite scream passing through nature.

"Well, that just brightens your day, doesn't it?" Britney said. "Makes me want to rush out and run through Farmer Bigelow's field of daisies."

"An infinite scream passing through nature, the earth's voice being disturbed," Anita repeated. "That can't be a coincidence. Whatever Mr. Quinn sensed that evening prompted him to send this picture somewhere."

"How can nature scream?" Britney asked. "I've never heard it say a word."

"It is speaking to us all the time," Anita said.

Halima's eyes widened. "Sarvagita!" she hollered, rushing back to the armchair. Anita followed her.

"Sarva . . . what?" Britney stammered.

Halima flipped through the book she was reading. "Here it is, Sarvagita," she said, showing a page of the *Enuntiatio de Tutela* to Anita. "Do you remember reading about the Song of the Universe?"

"I do," Anita said. "But it's been a long time since I read it."

"You'll remember once you hear it again," said Halima. She read a passage out loud.

Sarvagita is the voice of the universe. It is a vibration that passes through all things great and small, all things high and low, all thing moving and still. It is the voice that urges you to wake up early and gaze upon the rising of Ra. It is the voice that puts you to sleep, urging forth your dreams and gently asking you to forget the worries of the day. It is the voice that promises a tomorrow.

Be still and listen, can you hear its call? Can you feel something familiar whispering in your ears?

In a realm where nothing stirred, came a voice that nothing heard.

Behold, it said, I have arrived. I have a call so all will thrive.

Hear my name and speak it well,

For in my rhyme all can dwell.

My voice will echo to and fro,
Through all of life it will flow.
Look high and low, and you will see
My greatest song in your story.
Sarvagita will usher in,
A new world for all my kin.

"That's beautiful," Britney said. "Not that I understood a word of it. What's the book?"

"It is called the *Enuntiatio de Tutela.*" A male voice suddenly echoed through the Alexandria Room.

The three girls turned and saw Lawrence coming down the spiral staircase, carrying a tray. "It's a very rare book. In fact, that might be the only original copy in existence." Halima took a cookie off the tray as Lawrence approached and set the tray on the table. He looked at the image of the picture that was projected. "Now, what are the three of you doing down here? And why the sudden interest in Munch's masterpiece?"

"We're solving a mystery," Halima said, as she chewed a cookie. A stern look from Lawrence reminded her of her manners, and she swallowed instead of continuing to speak.

"Do you know what happened to Mr. Quinn's version of this picture?" Anita asked, deciding to take a direct approach. "It used to be hanging in the Tapestry Room."

"He sent it to Logan Ford," Lawrence answered, matching his daughter's directness.

"There you have it," Britney proclaimed. "Mystery solved, next topic."

Anita put her hand over Britney's mouth, silencing her. Halima giggled. "Why?" Anita asked. "Why Logan Ford? And what does it have to do with Sarvagita and my sudden struggles with my violin?"

"Those are questions that only Mr. Quinn can answer," Lawrence said.

"Did Mr. Quinn say that the voice of the earth has been disturbed?" Anita asked, persisting with her questioning.

"Yes," Lawrence said.

"Told you," Halima said, as she grabbed another cookie.

"A proper discussion of Sarvagita can run deep and long," Lawrence said. "The poem that Halima just read points out that everything in the universe has a sound, a song, a frequency."

"A voice," Anita said, and then she recited: "'My voice will echo to and fro, through all of life it will flow.'"

"Exactly," Lawrence said. "Everything, from a grain of sand on the beach to an eagle soaring high in the sky, has a vibration or a voice."

"We just learned that in my physics class," Britney said. "A scientist by the name of Max Planck said that all physical matter is composed of vibrations." Anita looked at her, impressed. Britney grinned. "I pay attention . . . occasionally."

Lawrence nodded. "At about the same time as Planck, the scientist Nikola Tesla also identified that phenomenon. But it wasn't until the early 1950s that Winfried Otto Schumann postulated mathematically that the earth emitted a vibration that the human ear could not hear. Schumann's theory was later confirmed in the 1960s, when the vibration was actually measured. That is why the frequency of the earth's vibration came to be known as the Schumann resonance."

"The voice of the earth," Anita said in a low voice.

"So the Schumann resonance is what Mr. Quinn said was disturbed?" Britney asked.

"Yes," Lawrence said. "And if you read further into *Enuntiatio de Tutela*, you will learn that the individual vibration of every living thing on this planet combines to form the voice of the earth. Now, imagine if the vibration of every star, planet, asteroid, and dust particle in the universe were combined. What would that voice sound like?"

"Sarvagita," Halima answered. "The Song of the Universe."

Even Britney was captivated. "What more can you tell us?"

"As I said before, one could become immersed in the study of Sarvagita for a long period of time," Lawrence said. "How the Schumann resonance relates to that work of art and its relationship to Anita's violin are beyond my current understanding. Those are questions best left to someone more knowledgeable."

"When is Mr. Quinn coming home?" Anita asked.

Her father shrugged his shoulders.

"Well," Halima said, closing her book, "while we wait for Mr. Quinn and Bukya to return, how about if all of you help me with my own investigation?"

"And what investigation would that be?" Lawrence asked.

"Remember that necklace I found the other day? Mr. Quinn took it with him when he left."

"Why would he take that old dog tag?" Anita asked.

"He didn't say," Halima said. "But I copied down the name, and I need some help finding out who the owner was."

"That tag was probably there since before the Great Disruption," Anita said. "It's impossible to find out anything about people from that far back. All the records were destroyed."

Halima was not happy with the lack of encouragement. "Come on, Anita. I need you to help me find Sumsari Baltik!"

"Finding Sumsari Baltik," Hypatia said. Everyone turned and watched as a single ladder on the western wall began to move. It stopped near the northwest corner of the room. A solitary red laser emerged from the dome and pointed to a book on the top shelf. "*The Unexpected Life*, written by Felix and Maria Quinn in 2029."

"Why would his name be in a book in here?" Halima asked.

"And one written by Felix and Maria?" Anita added.

"Those are excellent questions," Lawrence said, before turning to Halima. "*The Unexpected Life*, all twenty volumes of it, contains the writings of Mr. Quinn's parents in which they recount their extraordinary adventures." He smiled. "It would seem, my dear, that your innocent search is about to become a very interesting investigation."

There was a big grin on Halima's face as she walked across the library and started climbing the ladder.

22

Has everything that can be done been done?
If so, why are you here?
We assure you, there is much more to do.

—THE CHRONICLES OF SATRAYA

NEW CHICAGO, 9:20 A.M. LOCAL TIME, MARCH 22, 2070

"They did a brain scan, and there are no signs of tumors or edema or cellular damage due to the fall," Logan said to Valerie on his PCD. "They're going to do a couple more tests. I'll call you when we get the results."

He ended his call and smiled at Jamie, who was reclining in an examination chair and had a neuro cap with numerous electrodes on her head.

"You look like you're heading into outer space," he joked.

When Jamie had complained about another severe headache last night, Logan decided not to take any more chances. After dropping Jordan off at school, he'd brought Jamie back to the neurologist who had examined her yesterday. The doctor had recommended that Jamie undergo further testing with his colleague, Dr. Timothy Zepher. Logan remained concerned about her, the images he had seen in the mirror the night before still fresh in his mind. The last time he had had such a vivid vision was in July, when he'd seen Valerie's funeral. That hadn't happened, but still, Logan wondered who the man in his vision was and what his daughter's face appearing in the Munch picture meant. And worse still to think, what else had he seen that he didn't remember?

"OK, Doctor, we're all set," the physician's assistant said.

Dr. Zepher walked over to Jamie, gave her a set of earphones, and positioned the neuro cap's visor over her eyes. "Jamie, we're going to start a series of visual tests. Different-colored lights are going to flash in those special eyeglasses you're wearing. You don't have to do a thing; just sit back and relax."

The doctor returned to the four monitors and the 3-D projector, and the test began. Logan watched as telemetry lines began to register activity. The assistant manipulated the controls, and portions of the projected image of the brain became colorized.

"As we run through the visual tests, we can see if Jamie's brain is reacting properly to outside stimulus," the doctor told Logan. "We can gauge her reactions by seeing which areas of her brain become colorized."

"Hey," Jamie called. "I just saw a giraffe. Oh, and there was a lion."

"Very good, Jamie," the doctor said. "Let us know if you see anything else." He turned to Logan to reassure him. "Sometimes the light sequences cause the brain to fire patterns of recognition. It's perfectly normal for people to see things that aren't really there. In fact, we'd probably be more concerned if she didn't."

Logan's PCD vibrated and began to make that annoying chirping sound. "Sorry, my PCD's been acting flaky," he said, reading a message from Jasper.

"We're going to start a series of auditory tests now," the doctor said to Jamie, and then he turned to Logan. "Sound affects a different part of the brain. While visual processing takes place at the back of the brain, auditory takes place in the right and left hemispheres. We're cycling through tones that humans don't consciously hear."

"Interesting," the assistant remarked as the telemetry was displayed.

The doctor sat up straighter in his seat. "Wow."

Logan's concern did not exactly dissipate. "What is it? *Interesting* and *wow* are usually not words you want to hear during a doctor's exam."

"It looks like Jamie is more sensitive to sound than most people," Dr. Zepher said.

"That's pretty impressive," his assistant added, nodding his head in agreement. "These low-end frequencies don't register with most people."

"Ouch!" Jamie yelled.

"Hold up," the doctor said to his assistant. "Jamie, does your head hurt?"

"No, not anymore," she answered. "It did for a second, but now it's OK. I saw a really bright orange light."

"Again, interesting," the doctor said in a low voice. He rewound the time-lapse recording of Jamie's brain response and then moved it forward second by second. "We need to find the exact moment her pain centers fired."

Logan leaned in for a closer look.

"There!" The doctor leaned back in his chair as he looked at a particular reading of Jamie's auditory cortex. "What are the odds of that?"

"Odds of what?" Logan asked.

"We saw the same thing last night," the assistant explained. "One of the people who came in last night complaining of headaches reacted the same way as Jamie when we ran the test on him."

"And at this same tone," the doctor said. "Eight Hertz. No one is supposed to react to those frequencies."

"What does that mean?" Logan asked.

"I don't know," the doctor said. "We sent off his results to the Calhoun Medical Center in Washington for analysis. They have more advanced equipment than we do. Looks like we have another set of results to send to Calhoun. For some reason, Jamie's auditory cortex is hypersensitive."

"As a result of her fall?"

"Maybe," the doctor said. "But the man who came in last night hadn't suffered any trauma to the head."

Logan could hear his daughter humming something. It was a short sequence of notes that she repeated over and over. "What are you humming?" he called to her.

"Just some tune that's in my head," Jamie answered. "Grandma taught me to play it on the violin."

"She plays an instrument?" the assistant asked.

"Yep, the violin," Jamie said proudly. "Just like my grandma. Why do you ask?"

The assistant glanced at the doctor, who seemed equally intrigued by Jamie's musical ability. "The man who came in last night complaining about headaches is a famous musician," the doctor said.

"He ended up having to cancel his concert last night," the assistant added.

"Ming Peera?" Logan asked. That was the musician whose performance Jasper had been planning to attend.

"Yes," the doctor said, with a bemused expression on his face.

23

A seed must be planted for the coming rains to nourish it.
Much like philosophy, which needs the nourishment of
experience before truth can grow.

—THE CHRONICLES OF SATRAYA

WASHINGTON, D.C., 11:17 A.M. LOCAL TIME, MARCH 22, 2070

"How were the agents killed?" Valerie asked Zurich-based WCF field
agent Colette Hasburg, whose image was projected on her PCD.

"Each was shot and killed with a flux round to the base of his skull,"
Colette said, her Swiss-German accent cutting the words sharply. "A
very precise strike through the spine."

"What is a flux round?" Chetan asked.

"It's like a melting bullet," Valerie said, shaking her head. "Imagine
if you were shot with a bullet made of ice. It would do the same damage as a lead bullet, but within a few minutes, it would melt away. There
would be nothing but water left behind."

"No bullet to analyze, no evidence," Sylvia said. "Flux rounds came
on the market three years ago. They are made from a composite alloy.
The heat from the gunshot causes a chemical reaction in the casing
of the bullet. Within twenty minutes, the bullet disintegrates; the only
thing left is a big old hole in the victim, which looks like an acid wound."

"We found the two agents stuffed in a barred tunnel under the dock," Agent Hasburg said.

"Under the dock?" Valerie repeated. "Did any of the Château's cameras pick anything up?"

"No. At this point, we have no evidence that indicates that the intruder entered the house. We have agents going room by room to see if anything is missing. So far, nothing."

"What about the tunnel? It's clear that the assailant knew about it."

"We're mapping the tunnels now. There is more than one tunnel down there, and they lead to various parts of the estate. It's going to take some time."

"Thanks, Colette. Keep us posted." Valerie disconnected the call.

"Who would want to break into the Château?" Sylvia asked. "Why take such a risk and kill two agents?"

"We'll have to let the team in Switzerland deal with it for now," Valerie said. "Did we get anything more from the Commonwealth?"

Before either Sylvia or Chetan could answer, a portly agent with a thick mop of unruly red hair walked over. "Hey, Val," he said, with a defeated look on his face.

"What's wrong, Darvis?" Valerie asked. "You look like someone stole your puppy."

"I wish that was my problem," he said. "I need some help, or at least some advice." Seeing Sylvia, he made an attempt to smooth down his hair. She gave him a slight wave and a smile. "You know those earthquakes we've been having?"

"You mean, like the one that almost killed me?" Valerie said.

"Sorry, didn't know that." Darvis pointed over at the large 3-D image of the globe rotating in the northeast corner of the Cube. "See the red, green, blue, and yellow circles overlaid on the map? They represent the global seismic events that we've been recording for the last three days. The red indicators were the first ones we recorded. Then came the greens, the blues, and most recently the yellows."

"Looks like the frequency of seismic events has been rising," Valerie observed. "Many more yellow circles than red."

"And the circles are clustered in certain regions of the world," Chetan said. "China, Egypt, Mexico, southern England, and southern India have experienced the most earthquakes."

"So how can we help you, Darvis?" Valerie asked.

"I was wondering if any of you have ever heard of an earthquake without an epicenter?"

Sylvia and Chetan frowned. "What do you mean, without an epicenter?" Sylvia asked.

"That's impossible," Chetan added. "Which one didn't have an epicenter?"

"That's just it," Darvis said. "None of those earthquakes that you see recorded on the map had epicenters."

"How is that possible?" Sylvia asked.

"No idea," Darvis said, exasperated. "I've been working with the geologists at the E-QON II center in Brussels, but they're as stumped as we are."

An alarm blared, interrupting the conversation. Valerie looked around, trying to determine what was wrong. Lab technicians were moving quickly to the southwest corner of the facility, where a series of bright red and white lights were flashing. "There's something going on over at the Chromatography Bubble," she said.

"Goshi is in there," Sylvia said. "He's testing the foreign residue samples we received from North Africa."

Valerie had an incredulous look on her face. "What do you mean, testing? Those samples are still supposed to be in quarantine. Who authorized the testing?"

"Goshi told me he received a call from Director Sully. She was adamant that he start. She told him that you knew about it."

Valerie rushed to the Bubble, followed by Sylvia and Chetan.

The Chromatography Bubble was an airtight portion of the lab where compounds and other materials could be vaporized for analysis. A single large window made of two-inch-thick tempered glass provided a view into the five-square-meter room.

"What in the world is going on?" Valerie asked, as she arrived at the window.

Two men were rolling on the floor, gagging and struggling to breathe. Goshi was kneeling beside one of them, trying to help him. A fine gray ash was floating in the air.

Sylvia took a seat at one of the control panels, joined by Chetan. "The oxygen level is at fifteen percent and dropping," she reported. "I'm going to turn up the supply in there."

Valerie watched as Goshi moved to the other technician, trying to help him sit up. But it was too late. The man was dead. A moment later, the first technician became motionless.

Sylvia hit a button on the control panel, turning on the microphone. "Goshi! Go over and get into a bio suit, and hook it up to one of the oxygen tanks."

"What happened to the oxygen?" Valerie asked, as Goshi followed Sylvia's instructions. "I thought you increased the supply. It's still only at fifteen percent!"

"I did," Sylvia said. "I don't know what's going on." More gray ash swirled through the air, and now it was accumulating on every surface in the Bubble. It was even sticking to the window, making it difficult for people on the outside to see what was going on inside the Bubble. Sylvia pushed the oxygen supply to max.

Goshi had put on the bio suit and attached a portable oxygen tank to his back. He stepped over the bodies of the technicians and stood by the window.

"Are you all right?" Valerie asked. "What happened?"

"We were running our tests on the substance that we received from the Commonwealth." Goshi's voice sounded muffled. "Then, suddenly, these specks of dust were in the air. April and Jonathan began to have trouble breathing." Goshi used his glove to wipe clean the window and the visor on his bio suit. The gray dust continued to fall, now more rapidly than before.

"I think we have a big problem," Chetan said, working frantically on the computer. "We are picking up a biological life form in there, and it is not Goshi."

"What are you talking about?" Valerie asked.

"Whatever exactly that gray dust is," Chetan said, reading the computer display, "it appears to be a living organism."

"Goshi," Sylvia said, "can you put some of that dust on the electron screen?"

Goshi nodded. He walked over to the electron microscope and removed its plastic cover. He opened the test sample chamber and allowed some of the airborne particles to float in. He turned the device on and walked back to the window, which he had to wipe clean again. He gave the thumbs-up sign.

Sylvia projected a 3-D holographic image. Chetan slid his chair over. They were looking at fifty spherical objects moving in random directions. Each one had six arms protruding from it. At the end of each arm was a cone-like structure. Also, attached to each object was a long, thin appendage that looked like a tail.

"What are they?" Valerie asked, incredulous. Before she could express another thought, the fifty spherical objects somehow multiplied to one hundred.

"They're alive, all right, but they don't look like anything I've ever seen," Chetan said. "And they are reproducing at an alarming rate."

Valerie looked into the Bubble and saw confirmation of what Chetan was saying. Goshi continued to wipe the gray dust from the window and his visor. The dead bodies on the floor were now almost completely covered.

"They just reproduced again," Chetan said. "What are they feeding on?"

"Looks like they have a very short life span," Sylvia said. "About a third of them stop moving every few seconds. They are some kind of biological nanite, man-made living organisms designed for some purpose."

A loud snapping sound grabbed their attention. The glass window of the Chromatography Bubble had cracked. Chetan looked at a biometric display. "The pressure is falling in there," he said. "A vacuum is forming."

"How is that possible?" Valerie asked. "Where is the oxygen going? What is sucking it out?"

"The only other organic things in there with Goshi are the nanites," Chetan said.

"Maybe the nanites are feeding on the oxygen," Sylvia said, frantically working the computer display. "I'm killing the O-two."

More popping sounds could be heard. Valerie watched as the crack in the window began to spider.

"The pressure is still dropping," Chetan said.

"We need to get everyone out of here," Valerie said. "If the vacuum keeps increasing and that window shatters . . ."

"Then the nanites will be released out here." Sylvia finished Valerie's thought. "They'll start consuming all the oxygen in the lab!"

"How much time before that window breaks?" Valerie asked.

"Impossible to say," Chetan replied. "Minutes, maybe."

Valerie turned and addressed the other technicians who were standing nearby. "All of you need to get out of here and take everyone else in the Cube with you." She turned to Sylvia. "Sound the evacuation alarm. Everyone needs to vacate this facility right now! Go!"

Sylvia called in the evacuation order, and the technicians scrambled. Within moments, a voice came over the loudspeaker, ordering everyone to evacuate. Only Valerie, Sylvia, and Chetan remained by the Bubble, with Goshi trapped inside.

"How do we kill these things?" Valerie asked.

"Goshi," Sylvia said, "how were these nanites transported to us?"

Goshi didn't answer; his face showed fear.

"Goshi!" Valerie yelled. "We need to stay focused here. How were the nanites transported to us?"

"Nitrogen," he answered, regaining his thoughts. "The samples were maintained in liquid nitrogen capsules."

"Can we flood the room?" Chetan asked.

"That may stop the nanites," Sylvia answered, "but Goshi's bio suit wasn't made to withstand such a low temperature. It will shatter within seconds."

"We need another idea!" Valerie said.

Another snap sounded as two more large cracks formed along the outer edges of the window.

Sylvia grabbed Chetan's arm. "Help me get a few thermal suits. They will be able to withstand the low temps." The two of them hurried off, leaving Valerie near the Bubble.

"Hold on, Goshi, we'll figure out something." Valerie received a call on her PCD. It was Director Sully.

"Did you just order the evacuation of the building? You had better have a good explanation for this, Agent Perrot."

"I don't have time to justify anything to you right now," Valerie shot back. "You can blame me later if you want. But right now, two analysts are dead, and a member of my team is in grave danger because he's conducting a test you authorized." Valerie hung up her PCD.

Sylvia and Chetan returned, wearing thermal suits and oxygen tanks strapped to their backs. They had brought back two more for Valerie and Goshi.

"What's the plan?" Valerie asked.

"We need to get Goshi into one of these suits and then flood the Bubble with liquid nitro," Sylvia said.

"How are you going to do that without opening the door?" Goshi asked, stepping over the bodies of his fellow agents and moving to a control panel on the wall. He pressed a few buttons. A yellow strobe light began to flash. The inside of the Bubble began to frost up.

"Goshi!" Sylvia yelled. "What are you doing?"

"He's releasing liquid nitrogen into the Bubble," Chetan said, looking at a monitor.

"Turn off the nitrogen supply," Valerie ordered.

"I can't," Chetan said. "He jammed the valve."

Goshi's muffled voice came over the intercom. "This is the only solution, Val. You can't take the risk of letting these nanites out of here, and you know it. If only one of them gets out, then a lot more people are going to die."

Valerie placed her hand on the window. She could barely see Goshi's face through the ash that had accumulated on his visor.

"It's all right, Valerie. I once watched Dominic Burke give his life for me. Now it's time to pass that favor along." Goshi walked calmly over to his two fallen coworkers and squatted beside them. He gently wiped the dust off their faces. When he was done, he sat in a chair close to where they lay. He undid the latches to the helmet of his bio suit.

"No!" Sylvia shouted. She put her hands over her face and turned away.

Chetan looked on silently. Valerie watched Goshi remove his helmet. He glanced over at the window, which was almost completely coated with frost, then smiled at Valerie and closed his eyes, leaning back in his chair. Valerie could see the puffs of Goshi's breath in the cold of the room. Frost now, instead of gray dust, began to accumulate on everything in the Bubble. Goshi's breaths grew smaller, until they ceased entirely. The gray dust that once floated in the Bubble fell innocently to the floor and onto Goshi's lifeless body.

"We have to find out who did this," Valerie whispered. "We have to make sure they pay."

24

Be certain and then become.

—THE CHRONICLES OF SATRAYA

"You've had a lot to deal with over the last few days," Mr. Perrot said to Logan. "The narrow escape in Mexico and Jamie's injury, your mother's recordings, Mr. Quinn's picture, and now the vision of the man in a laboratory."

"I'm definitely at some kind of nexus point," Logan said. "It feels sort of similar to when you knocked on my door the morning after the auction and the Council murders."

After Jamie's doctor visit, Logan had taken his daughter for a late lunch and then brought her back to the studio with him. While Jamie was delighted to miss the rest of the school day, she was disappointed about missing orchestra practice. She decided to make up for that by practicing her violin at the studio. Jasper was giving a short tour to a group of visitors who had come to see the restored replica of the *Creation of Adam* fresco. Logan hadn't told anyone that Sebastian Quinn, its previous owner, had informed him that it was actually the original. He thought it prudent not to broadcast that information.

Logan took a tin box off a shelf in the work room and set it on a stainless-steel table. It contained the broken relic that Mr. Montez had hired Logan to restore. Behind them, Edvard Munch's *The Scream* was on an easel next to a few of Cassandra's mosaics, which they had brought out of the vault.

"Have you told Valerie about the vision you had last night?" Mr. Perrot asked.

"No," Logan said. "Just you. Valerie's dealing with her own issues right now. She called earlier and said there was a big accident at the lab. Three scientists are dead, including a valued member of her team. Plus, she's under tremendous pressure to figure out what caused the natural gas explosion in northern Africa. Not a good time for her or the WCF."

"Is she all right?" Mr. Perrot asked, concerned. "That's the second member of her team she has lost in less than one year."

"She's doing fine," Logan replied, opening the tin box, which contained many smaller containers. "Have you heard from Madu again?"

"No," Mr. Perrot said. "You can add him to our list of curious developments."

"Why, after all these years, would he suddenly contact you?"

"I doubt we will know the answer to that question until I speak to Madu again."

Together Logan and Mr. Perrot removed thirty-eight small containers from the tin box and set them on the table. Logan opened one up. Inside were five small broken pieces of stone packed in protective black molded foam. He set it down and opened another. Mr. Perrot followed suit, and within a few minutes all thirty-eight were open. The stone fragments, which varied in shape and size, had rough edges, and most of them had various hues of pigment on one side—blue, red, yellow, and black. Logan ran his finger across a fragment on which a flower had been painted.

"Reminds me of something I saw in my vision last night," Logan said. "The scientist I told you about was drawing a cross that looked something like this in his notebook. Except he drew a circle around it. It also vaguely looks like an image we saw painted on the walls of the chamber that Jordan and Jamie fell into in the pyramid. At that time, we thought it was a snowflake. Which doesn't make sense, now that I think about it, because it doesn't snow in Mexico."

Logan looked at the hundreds of pieces in front of him and sighed, wondering where to start. "It's not going to be easy to put all of this together."

"When do you have to complete this restoration job?" Mr. Perrot asked.

"Mr. Montez didn't give me a deadline," Logan said. "But I suspect that he is under some pressure from the Tripod Group, the think tank that funds his research."

"Hey, Dad." A voice suddenly interrupted. It was Jordan.

"How did you get here?" Logan asked.

"I asked Ms. Sally to drop me off when she picked me up at school," he answered, waving at Mr. Perrot and tossing his green backpack onto the floor. He took a notebook from his backpack and started rifling through its pages enthusiastically. "Dad, did you know that there are pyramids in China? They're flat-toppers just like the ones we saw in Mexico. There are hundreds of them around the world."

"Jordan is writing a report on pyramids for a school project," Logan explained to Mr. Perrot.

"Well, seeing as you are somewhat of an expert on pyramids," Mr. Perrot said, "perhaps you'd like to assist your father and me in putting these pieces back together."

Jordan's face lit up as he took the fragment that Logan was holding. "This looks like the snowflake we saw in the mural in the secret chamber."

"That's what I thought," Logan said. "Mr. Montez said these fragments were found in a tunnel they discovered in the Pyramid of the Moon several months ago."

Jordan reached into his backpack and pulled out his PCD. "I have an idea. Let's use the Puzzler!"

"The what?" asked Logan.

Jordan projected a cube-shaped grid over the table with his PCD. "It's a puzzle solver," he said. "My friend Zack showed it to me at school." He took one of the pieces from the box and set it near his PCD. He then pressed a button, which caused a red laser to scan the surface of the stone fragment. Within moments, its 3-D image was projected within the grid. He reached into the projected grid and, with various hand gestures, was able to rotate and size the image as he desired. "We need to scan all the pieces, and the Puzzler will help us put them together."

"Can't hurt to try," Logan said. They moved the pieces into the projected grid and then at Logan's suggestion, separated them by color according to the painted sides. After an hour, they were able to make out the figure of a man and what appeared to be flowers. It took some time, but with determination and assistance from Jordan's PCD, the artifact was taking shape.

"It looks like the last piece goes here," Jordan said, using his finger to slide the projected piece into place. The 3-D image was now complete, revealing a thirty-centimeter-tall cylindrical object, which had an almost eight-centimeter-long stem jutting from its side. It was intricately painted and depicted a man standing under a blue sky, with flower-shaped objects floating around him.

"What is it?" Mr. Perrot asked.

"It's a whistling vessel," Logan answered. "There were a bunch of them in the secret chamber." He had a quizzical look on his face. "Not to take anything away from the Puzzler, but it seems to me that Mr. Montez could have pieced this together himself. Why did he need me to do it?"

No one had an explanation to offer.

Jordan examined the vessel. "This one's much bigger than the ones we saw," he said. "And it's shaped differently, too. The others were more rounded; this one is cylindrical, like a fat tube. The man painted on the vessel looks like one of the priests that were painted on the wall. And those are the same snowflakes we saw."

Mr. Perrot squinted and maneuvered to get a closer look at something. "Are those the Satraya symbols?"

"Where?" Logan asked.

Mr. Perrot pointed at the head of the man depicted on the vessel. "Jordan, can you zoom in on the man's head?"

Jordan did so, and Logan nodded at what they saw. "The fundamental four, along with the main Satraya symbol, all of which also appear on the headband of the praying man statue."

"Praying man?" Mr. Perrot asked.

"Mr. Montez showed us a statue that he found near these fragments. Valerie said that it looked like a man on his knees praying. I think Mr. Montez is going to be disappointed. He suspected that these fragments were going to help him figure out some kind of radiation source." Logan turned to Mr. Perrot, who was deep in thought. "What is it?"

"Why would a person who was familiar with these symbols two thousand years ago sculpt a man who was praying?" Mr. Perrot said. "If the sculptor possessed that kind of knowledge, wouldn't he have depicted something else?"

"It looks like something is written on the stem of the whistle," Jordan said. He zoomed to the spot he was referring to, but the words were incomprehensible: *QUITETEUHQUIMILOA CANAHUAC COHUATL TOCONMONEXTILIZ ITOZQUI TLALLI.*

"What does it mean?" Jordan asked.

"I don't know," Mr. Perrot said. "I'm not even sure what language it is."

"Valerie and I saw words from this language carved in the base of the praying man statue. Mr. Montez said it was a form of Nahuatl.

Let's see if we can get a translation." Logan pulled out his PCD and started typing, waiting a moment for the results. "There are a few different interpretations, but they all seem to allude to the same thing: 'Wrap thin serpent to discover earth voice.'"

"Remember that image of a snake we found on the platform?" Jordan said. "The one with the red eye? Maybe this has something to do with that. Not sure what *earth voice* means, though."

Just then, Jamie walked in, carrying her violin and bow. "What are you doing?"

"Solving a puzzle," her brother answered.

"I want to help," she said. But before she could make her way over to the table, her attention was caught by the Munch pastel. She stopped and stared at it. Logan noticed her fascination and walked over to her, while Mr. Perrot and Jordan continued to ponder the meaning of the writing on the whistle.

"Are you all right, Jamie?" Logan asked. "This is one of the most famous works of art in the world."

"I know. I once saw Grandma looking at it in a book," Jamie said. Her voice was nonchalant, but her gaze was fixed on the picture. "That's sort of how I feel when my head hurts."

Logan put his hand on his daughter's shoulder as he stood behind her. "You feel like screaming?" He wondered if that was why he had seen his daughter's face merged into the picture during his vision.

"Yeah," Jamie answered. "Grandma said this is what happens to some people when the earth loses its voice. She said her music teacher told her that."

Logan looked down at Jamie, who walked over to the table to join her brother and Mr. Perrot. "The earth's voice," Logan repeated, murmuring. He looked at the projected image of the whistling vessel and then turned to the picture. In Edvard Munch's own words, this image was about the scream of nature, and the stone whistle seemed to have something to do with the earth's voice. *Could these two works of art, created almost fifteen hundred years apart, be related somehow?*

25

Here, at the edge of your faith, is where you will find what you
are looking for. Remember that truth and wisdom lie outside
of your conjecture and your belief.

—THE CHRONICLES OF SATRAYA

PEEL CASTLE, 9:30 P.M. LOCAL TIME, MARCH 22, 2070

"The art of Reflecting, like the Satraya Flame, can only be achieved with
singularity of mind and purpose," Sebastian said, standing between two
sheets of water falling silently from a source above. With twelve pillars
and twelve statues standing ever watchful along the perimeter, the Arcis
Chamber was held to be the most sublime room on the castle grounds.
It was here that Sebastian Quinn had been taught the metaphysical arts
associated with exploration of the mind and here, after spending many
years mastering those arts, that he passed them on to others.

The smooth falling sheets of water reflected the subtle images of
Anita and Halima, who sat in front of them. The two eager students
had made themselves comfortable, sitting cross-legged on cushions on
the black and white checked floor. White sheets were draped over their
shoulders.

"In olden days, before mirrors and looking glasses, any reflective surface was sought out to reveal the extraordinary to an adventurer who had
the eyes to see," Sebastian explained. "Before you is such a thing. It is

called Jaladarz, the water mirror. In it, you will see your purest reflection. Firmly press your finger to your forehead, just above your nose, and hold it there. As with the Satraya Flame, it is from this place"—Sebastian touched his own forehead, and his listeners did likewise—"that you will perceive the most interesting things about yourself and about the world of the seen and the unseen that surrounds you."

Sebastian walked away from the waterfalls and took his own seat on the floor out of Anita and Halima's view.

"You may lower your hands, but keep gazing upon the reflection of your countenance," he said. As Anita and Halima looked at their reflections, Sebastian began to tell a story. "In a kingdom long ago, there lived a beautiful princess. On the day of her twenty-first birthday, the king declared the Swayamvara of his daughter. She was to choose the man she would marry. Many suitors traveled from far and wide, seeking the hand of the most dazzling woman in all the land. But the king was wise and knew the true hearts of men. Fame, fortune, and power were what most of them desired. And so the king devised a test. Only one who could pass it would be allowed to marry his beloved daughter. He began by having constructed a small circular pool filled with oil, its surface as still and reflective as a mirror."

"The king made his own Jaladarz," Halima said, turning to Sebastian. "An oily mirror."

Sebastian smiled and motioned to Halima to look back at her reflection in the waterfall. "You mustn't lose your gaze, or my tale will lose its meaning." Halima turned back around. "Directly above the pool of oil, suspended from the high ceiling of the arrival hall of the palace, was placed a carved image of a fish, its eye prominently outlined in gold leaf. Halfway between the fish and the pool was a large spinning wheel with twenty-four spokes. The king declared that any man who wished to marry his daughter would have to prove his worth by shooting an arrow through the spokes of the rotating wheel and piercing the eye of the fish. The king further decreed that a contender could only look upon the target's reflection in the pool, not gaze at it directly. And to make the test more challenging, handmaidens stood near, waving large feathered fans, stirring the air and sending ripples across the surface of the oil.

"The wise king knew that if a contender attempted to focus only on the eye of the fish, the shimmer of the oil and the flicker of the wheel would obstruct his view, and the contender would fail. If a man were to concentrate on gaining a clear glimpse of the fish through the gaps of the wheel's spokes, he would lose sight of the eye, and his arrow would miss. Leaning forward over the pool to gain perfect alignment would prove futile, as the bowman's own reflection would overshadow the intended goal. And so it was that an impossible path had been laid for any man seeking his daughter's hand, a secret that only the most sincere of heart would know.

"And so it is today and with you," Sebastian said, addressing Anita and Halima. "The art of Reflecting presents to you the same challenge as the king's. Should you get caught up in the grandeur of your own countenance, you will lose the moment. Should you be distracted by the many faces that you will surely see, you will lose the moment. Should you grow impatient for something to happen, you will, again, lose the moment."

Anita and Halima meditated on Sebastian's words, gazing intently at their own reflections.

After a lengthy pause, Sebastian continued. "The hours of trial turned into days, which turned to weeks, then into months. Each suitor was given ten chances, but no one in the kingdom could pass the king's test. Arrow after arrow went astray. Most plunged into the spokes of the spinning wheel. Those that passed missed the fish and struck the ceiling high above. The fish and its eye remained untouched. The learned priests and holy men of the realm pleaded with their king to lower his expectations. But the wise king was not dissuaded."

Sebastian interrupted his storytelling and addressed Anita and Halima. "There is a milepost that you will pass when gazing upon your reflection. There will come a moment when you lose track of who is looking at whom. You will wonder if you are you or the reflection of you looking back at you. But should you persist in your quest, you will reach the point at which you realize you are both. It is this moment that should be sought. This is when all things can be known and wizardly powers can be yours."

Sebastian took a light breath and then continued. "Early one morning, on the one hundred twentieth day of the Swayamvara, a young man dressed in simple garments arrived. He carried a crudely made bow and had but a single arrow in his quiver. The king stood and addressed him. 'You, who have traveled here for my daughter's hand, how do you believe that you will be able to accomplish this task with such a meager bow and a single arrow?'

"The young man looked up at the king. 'I cannot say, your grace,' he answered. 'I only know that at the time I heard of the trial, I had not a bow or an arrow to my name. What I hold now, I myself freshly fashioned. I do not presuppose my worthiness that I will pass this test and your daughter will choose me.'

"'Choose you?' the king asked. 'Do you believe my daughter has a choice in this matter? Is it not your assumption that should you hit the target, you will possess my daughter's hand?'

"'No, my king,' the young man answered without hesitation. 'All have choice. One's heart can never be possessed but must be tendered freely. Hitting the eye will only allow me the opportunity to greet your daughter with the air of possibilities.'

"A slight smile came to the king's face. He turned to his daughter, who had moved forward in her seat, keenly intrigued by the young man, and could not take her eyes off of him. The king retook his seat. 'Proceed, then,' he said. 'And let us see the virtue of your intent.'

"The young man knelt down and looked at his shimmering reflection in the oil. He saw the spinning wheel above and the dancing eye of the fish. He pulled the single arrow from his quiver and positioned it on his bow, then raised the bow above his head and pulled back on the string. The handmaidens continued to disturb the surface of the pool with each stroke of their feathered fans. The young man grew still, holding his gaze on the surface of the pool. He did not immediately let the string go as the other participants had done. Instead, he held steady. Those watching in the hall grew silent. They wondered what the young man was waiting for—the shimmer of the oil to lessen, the spinning of the wheel to slow, the appearance of the fish? The young man remained steadfast, until suddenly, everyone in the hall heard the snap of his bow and the wisp of the arrow as it flew upward."

Sebastian paused, allowing the silence and stillness of the Arcis Chamber to overtake the moment. Anita and Halima sat motionless, intently staring at their reflections. He knew they had attained singularity of mind and were about to fire their own arrows.

✳   ✳   ✳

Anita had lost awareness of her surroundings. She had let go of the thoughts that tugged at her and was now completely entranced by her reflection in the falling water. Sebastian's voice had faded, and the edges of her vision began to darken. The image before her began to morph, and a scene unfolded.

Anita found herself in a place she had vowed never to return to. She was standing next to the dilapidated old red phone booth at the northeast corner of a park she had known as a young child. The soft ticking of a clock could be heard. The people walking down High Street seemed unaware of her presence. Apartment buildings surrounded the square, and to the south, she could see one of the spires of the cathedral she had attended in her youth. She was only a short distance from the house where she had grown up and spent the worst years of her life.

Anita looked up at the sky. It was pitch-black, yet the town and surroundings were brightened as if on a sunny day. Lightning flashed. She listened for thunder, but it never arrived, nor was there any rain. The faces of the people passing were blurred, their voices muffled and their words not discernible. She was startled by the sudden blaring of an organ. It was a disturbing, off-tune sound. No one on the street seemed to notice, though, or else they did not seem to mind it. She looked around and realized that the noise was coming from the cathedral. She felt a tug on her waist and was abruptly catapulted inside it.

In the blink of an eye, she found herself standing behind the organ console, which was not in its usual place. It now stood on the stone floor in front of the nave, which was full of parishioners, men, women, and children, some dressed in pure white robes. Anita wondered how the organ was still producing sound when it was not connected to its pipes. Despite the awful din, she could still hear the ticking clock. The ceiling of the cathedral was gone, and when she looked up she saw the same black sky and the streaks of lightning.

A young man dressed in a grungy blue jumpsuit sat at the helm of the organ's four-layered keyboard. His dirty left hand frantically pulled and pushed the various knobs of the console, altering the sound that bellowed forth. Anita noticed his right hand repeatedly striking the same seven-note pattern on the second tier of the organ's keyboard.

Anita felt a great pressure building in her head. A burning smell was filling the nave, and smoke was rising off of the people who had gathered. She attempted to stop the young man's playing by grabbing his arm, but her hand passed through him as if he were a ghost. The children had started shrieking. The smell grew more pungent as the smoke thickened, more distinguishable: it was burning flesh. The men and women clutched their heads, some crying out in agony. The young man pulled and pushed the knobs more frantically, repeating the same terrible pattern of notes. The pressure in Anita's head turned excruciating, worse than anything she had ever felt. Flames erupted throughout the nave, and in an instant, every one of the parishioners exploded into dark ash.

The harsh, discordant sounds of the organ stopped, yet the ticking of the clock continued. Anita screamed.

26

*If you had a handful of fleeting moments to speak to the
world, what would you say?*

—THE CHRONICLES OF SATRAYA

WASHINGTON, D.C., 5:35 P.M. LOCAL TIME, MARCH 22, 2070

Valerie and the others were finally allowed back into the Cube after
a decontamination squad confirmed that none of the nanites had escaped the Chromatography Bubble. As an added precaution, a resin-
based compound was sprayed inside the Bubble, setting and hardening
like amber and freezing the corpses of Goshi Tambe and the two other
technicians like insects fossilized from prehistoric times.

"What am I going to tell Goshi's family?" Valerie said, as she watched
thick white drapes being installed over the Bubble's window until a
proper disposal protocol could be performed. "He had a wife and kids."

"How many more people are we going to lose?" Sylvia's voice was
muffled but angry. She sat at her desk, with her head buried in her crossed
arms. "Charlie, Director Burke, and now Goshi. What is happening?"

Similar thoughts were coursing through Valerie's mind. In less than a
year, she'd lost three people she'd been close to, none to natural causes.

Director Sully walked into the lab with several aides. "What's the
update? People are demanding answers."

"No real update," Valerie said, allowing some disdain to show in her voice. "We'll be looking at this from top to bottom."

"Starting with why Goshi began his testing early," Sylvia added, sitting up and wiping the tears from her eyes.

"Are you suggesting something, Agent Brookes?" Director Sully asked.

"She's not," Valerie interjected, "but I am. Protocol is clear. The infectious disease team is supposed to quarantine and then clear all material before any investigation is allowed to be done."

"I know the protocol, Agent Perrot," Director Sully said. "It was my call. Sometimes you have to set aside protocols for expediency. We couldn't afford any delays in finding out if the natural-gas disasters were a result of sabotage. Based on the nanites that were found, I would say we have the answer to that question. I'm sorry for your loss, Agent Perrot, I really am. But you're not the only one who has been affected by this gas crisis. The body count is up to four hundred in the North African Commonwealth and even more at the Derby site."

"What Derby site?" Valerie asked.

"You and your team are supposed to be leading this investigation. I would expect you to be aware of what is going on in the world." Director Sully shook her head. "One of the Deep Horizon gas refineries in Western Australia imploded twenty-three minutes ago. Five hundred people are dead." An aide showed Director Sully something on a PCD. She finished, "Get it together, Agent Perrot. Find out whoever is sabotaging these gas wells."

"You're the one who should have been promoted to director," Sylvia said to Valerie when Sully and her aides were gone.

Valerie gave no sign of acknowledgment. "Have we got any more of that amber foam? I'd love to bury her in some of it." Sylvia tried to smile. "She is right about one thing, though," Valerie continued. "We need to figure out who or what is behind all this."

Sylvia took a deep breath and slid her chair in front of a computer station. She pressed a few controls and brought up a projected image of a round gray object. It was the same image they had looked at earlier, a sphere with six legs with a longer and thinner protrusion that looked like a tail. "Goshi was analyzing the fuel samples we received from the North African Commonwealth. This is a magnified image of one of the nanites that is causing all this chaos. This afternoon, after we were kicked out of the lab, I did some more analysis on these little monsters at home. This is a methanophiles cell. It's classified as a prokaryote, a unicellular organism. The nanites appear to be a molecularly modified version of methanophiles."

"Methano-what?" Valerie asked.

"Methanophiles are able to metabolize methane," Sylvia explained. "We learned a lot about them during the 2010s, when the world was dealing with global warming. Some governments deployed forms of methanotrophs to reduce the release of methane into the atmosphere."

"I remember learning about that in history class," Valerie said. "Rice fields, landfills, and swamps were blamed for emitting huge amounts of methane. Several countries in Europe sponsored an effort to deploy methane eaters into the ecosystems in 2020. Are you saying this is what's messing up the natural-gas supply?"

"I think so," Sylvia answered. "Natural gas is seventy percent methane. As these nanites consume the methane, the natural gas is rendered useless."

"You said these nanites were modified."

Sylvia nodded. "In a couple of ways. First, as they consume the methane, they multiply profusely. In theory, you would only need a single nanite to take out a whole natural-gas field. But they don't live very long, as we witnessed in the Bubble. All that gray soot in there is dead nanites."

"And second?" Valerie asked.

"Second, these little things also consume oxygen," Sylvia said. "But what's even stranger is that when they absorb either gas, they don't release anything back into the atmosphere. Unlike humans, who consume oxygen and release CO-two, these nanites hold on to whatever they consume. That's why a vacuum formed in the bubble. The more O-two we pumped in, the faster the nanites metabolized it and the faster the vacuum grew. The beasts consume, multiply, and die."

"And we're positive these were man-made?" Valerie asked.

"I found mutations that do not occur naturally. There were also what we call watermarks in the DNA of the nanites. Watermarks are genome sequences added to DNA so that the synthetic organisms can be differentiated from the normal ones. They're not easily accomplished. These things are man-made, I'm certain of it."

"What about the mutations?" Valerie asked.

Sylvia rotated the image and zoomed in. "You see this thing that looks like a tail?" she asked. "I think it's some kind of antenna. One of the big questions is how you turn these organisms off once they come alive," Sylvia said. Valerie gave her a quizzical look. "Once these things start consuming oxygen, if left unchecked, they wouldn't just stop at one gas well. They would keep going until the air on the whole planet was consumed."

"You could freeze them like we did," Valerie said.

"It would take a tremendous amount of nitrogen to do that. The only nitrogen in the samples we received from the Commonwealth was put there by the North African WCF lab technician for transportation. There has to be another way to turn them on and off."

"And you think this antenna has something to do with it?" Valerie considered that possibility for a moment. "I wonder if Goshi accidentally activated one during his testing."

Just then, a call came in on the HoloPad next to Sylvia, projecting an image of Alex. "Hey, Val," he said. "Just heard about Western Australia."

"What's the update from the Commonwealth?" Valerie asked.

"Tensions are pretty high over here. The politicians are bent on blaming this whole thing on the Republic of South Africa. They're convinced that the RSA is attempting to destabilize their country. I've had a tough time getting anyone to consider any other possibility."

"Not surprising, considering the escalating tensions between the two countries since the first President Jabral was assassinated," Sylvia said.

"There are very few leads here," Alex said. "No one saw anything out of the ordinary. I've talked to at least thirty people, and none provided anything more than what the technicians said. This is all pointing to someone on the inside. Which is not hard to believe with the political atmosphere around here."

"I'd agree with you if it wasn't for the Australian site," Valerie said. "They're not embroiled in any power struggles. And the fact that two different companies were attacked makes a disgruntled employee less likely." She thought for a moment. "Why destroy the energy supplies around the world? Who benefits from that?"

"Terrorists," Sylvia suggested, "or a competitor."

Valerie nodded. "Alex, I need to you to go to Western Australia as soon as you can. Since that attack just happened, there might be fresh evidence there." Alex nodded, and the call ended. Valerie grabbed a chair and sat down next to Sylvia. "Bring up a list of all the companies in the world that are in the natural-gas business."

Sylvia did so quickly:

NAF Atlantic, Inc.
North African Commonwealth, LLC
South America Holdings
Kimberly Gas
Harlen Oil and Gas
Siberian Drilling and Exploration, Inc.

"Siberian Drilling and Exploration is the one heavily invested in the Western Australia site," Sylvia said. "Not a very long list."

"I'm not surprised," Valerie said. "With all the regulations put into place after the Great Disruption, energy exploration is a capital-intensive business and not easy to get into."

"All of these companies emerged right around the same time. About twenty years ago, after they figured out how to fracture rock by using sound. Little-known fact, but sound is an underappreciated science. If you find the right frequency of sound, you can break apart anything."

"What about alternative energy companies?" Valerie asked. "Wasn't there a company trying to deploy a solar collector in space?"

Sylvia manipulated her display. The list in front of them tripled in size:

NAF Atlantic, Inc.
Oceanic Breeze
The Tripod Group
Solar Navigation
South America Holdings
Arbatro of India
Kimberly Gas
Harlen Oil and Gas
NovaCon International
New Light Wind and Power
Siberian Drilling and Exploration, Inc.

"Not sure that helps us," Sylvia said.

Valerie's eyes widened. "What about those DNA watermarks you talked about? Is there any way to trace them?"

"We may not be able to trace the watermarks, but . . ." Sylvia thought a moment, then began to manipulate her display. "There is only one company in the world that makes the equipment to insert watermarks of this kind: BioGen, Inc. They have a device called a DNA spectrometer. We may not be able to track the watermark itself, but we can see who has purchased one of these devices." Sylvia brought up another list:

SimCon, Inc.
Albiet Research
Kilakore Pharmaceuticals

The Tripod Group
Bentley Pharma, LLC
NovaCon International
Zolton Five
Medi-Tech, Inc.

"In theory, each of these companies has the capability to create those killer nanites," Sylvia said.

Valerie nodded, scanning rapidly. Suddenly, she stopped. "Tripod," she said softly, placing her hand on Sylvia's shoulder. The name was on both lists. "That's twice in the last three days I've heard that name. The Tripod Group is behind the excavation of the pyramid Logan and I visited in Mexico. Mr. Montez, the archaeologist at Teotihuacán, said Tripod is funding his work."

"Did I hear you mention the Tripod Group?" Chetan asked, as he arrived at his desk. "I almost went to work for them. They are one of the world's leading think tanks. Rigel Wright is an impressive man."

"Impressive or not, he might be behind what's been happening at the gas wells," Valerie said.

Sylvia projected her findings for Chetan. "Man-made methanophile nanites," she said. Chetan shook his head in disbelief.

"What do we know about the Tripod Group?" Valerie asked.

Sylvia brought up a picture of a short man with beach-blond hair and a confident smile that showed off his pearly white teeth. "This is Rigel Wright. He is forty-seven years old and a billionaire many times over. He started the Tripod Group eight years ago after he sold off his interests in his stem-cell organ replication company."

"He is a genius," Chetan said. "I heard that the Tripod Group holds thousands of patents."

"Twenty-two thousand five hundred forty-four, to be precise," Sylvia read. "He's not married, he has an older sister, and both of his parents are dead."

"Where is the Tripod Group located?" Valerie asked.

"They have offices all over the world," Sylvia said. "But their primary office is in London."

"Well, then, looks like we're going to London," Valerie said.

"Mr. Wright is not there," Chetan said, shaking his head. "He lives on a boat. A two-hundred-meter yacht called the *Water Shadow*. He travels around the world doing pretty much whatever he wants."

"Where is his yacht now?" Valerie asked.

"It's currently docked in Southampton, United Kingdom," Chetan answered.

"Why in the world would you know that?" Sylvia asked.

"I read that Mr. Wright is retracing the path of the RMS *Titanic*. He had a special submarine constructed that is going to attempt to raise the ship from the bottom of the ocean. He is going to start in a few days. I've been tracking the expedition for the last year."

"Well, then, looks like you and I are going to Southampton," Valerie tried again. Chetan nodded. "I'm also arranging a little side trip for us."

27

Move past the roadblocks of your own expectations. Only there
will you find something new.

—THE CHRONICLES OF SATRAYA

NEW CHICAGO, 7:20 P.M. LOCAL TIME, MARCH 22, 2070

After supper, Ms. Sally took the children to a movie, and Logan used
his time alone to listen to more of his mother's recordings. He hoped
to come across one that revealed what she and her music teacher knew
about the Munch painting and the voice of the earth. Based on Jamie's
reaction to the picture that afternoon and her telling him that it represented what happened to people when the earth lost its voice, Logan
suspected that his mother's music teacher possessed a deep understanding of Munch's work, and he wanted to gain more insight into it before he and Mr. Perrot returned to Mexico the next morning with the
restored whistling vessel. He had much to discuss with Mr. Montez,
especially now that Valerie had told him of her suspicions concerning
the Tripod Group.

Logan didn't hear anything related to his line of inquiry until the
third recording on a chip dated February 15, 2036, at 3:34 P.M. He
heard his mother say:

'Bye, Madu . . . You know I'm going to get Nadine to tell me what you and Sumsari are working on.

There were male voices laughing and talking in the background, followed by the sound of a door closing. Logan's mother continued:

That was Madu. He's working on some top-secret project with Sumsari and won't tell any of us about it. Anyway, Sumsari said that I could record our lesson today. I've been having trouble mastering a few of the techniques he's been teaching me. I'm hoping that if I record the lesson and listen to it again later, I'll stand a better chance of picking up what I've been missing.

Logan heard a gentle male voice and figured it was Sumsari Baltik's:

Sumsari: *I smell a delicious aroma coming from your bag.*
Cassandra: *I baked you raisin scones. I thought they might remind you of England.*

The rustling of a paper bag could be heard.

Sumsari: *These are wonderful, as good as the ones I enjoyed at a castle I frequented during my travels in the British Isles.*
Cassandra: *I brought you something else.*
Sumsari *(laughing): Where in the world did you find that? I haven't had a good London porter since the Great Disruption.*
Cassandra: *Camden brought it back from Switzerland. He just got back a couple of days ago.*
Sumsari: *Thank you for this, and please thank Camden. I hope he had a productive trip.*

The recording had been made two days after an entry Logan had read in the pages that had been ripped out of his father's journal. Camden had

traveled to Switzerland because he suspected that Fendral Hitchlords
had lied about how he discovered his set of the *Chronicles* at the Zurich
train station. During that trip, Camden had spoken to several people
who lived in the station's ruins and uncovered evidence indicating that
Fendral stole the *Chronicles* from the man who had originally found
them, Giovanni Rast, and then killed him.

*Sumsari: So how is our mother-to-be? I can see by the glow on your face that
motherhood agrees with you already.*

Cassandra: I'm fine. I have a few more months to go.

Sumsari: Boy or girl?

Cassandra: We don't know.

Sumsari: Would you like to know? I can show you how to find out.

Cassandra: Do you have an ultrasound machine in here?

Sumsari: No, but I do have a piano.

Cassandra: How can your piano tell?

*Sumsari: Music can tell. More precisely, we can tell from a fetus's reaction to
particular musical sequences called the Coffa and Solokan progressions. Girls
react to one, and boys react to the other.*

Cassandra: Even in the womb?

*Sumsari: Oh, yes. Would you like me to show you? Place your hands on your
belly, and tell me when you feel your baby move. This first one is the Coffa
progression.*

Logan heard seven notes being played on the piano. There was a slight
pause, as the sound faded away.

Sumsari: Nothing? All right, this one is the Solokan progression.

There were more notes, different now and repeating.

*Cassandra: Oh! I felt two strong kicks! When you played the second sequence.
Play the first one again . . . Now the second . . . Yes! The baby is kicking and*

moving. What does that mean, boy or girl?

Sumsari: *It means that you will have a boy.*

More notes sounded again, of the second sequence.

Cassandra: *Where did you learn to do that? I've never heard of anyone predicting the gender of a fetus that way.*

Sumsari: *I just tickle their souls. There is a sound constantly flowing all around us. These sequences enhance that constant melody surrounding us in a very subtle way. Babies are quite aware of it. They know when their soul is moved. One day, I will tell you more about my journey through Europe and what I learned at the castle. But that is not why you are here today. We are here to continue your violin training.*

Cassandra: *Yes, that's right. But I'm having trouble with the son filé. I'm just not able to get the proper bow angles, the pressure, the speed, or even the contact. I even went to the Library of Congress, or what's left of it, and found a few books on it. I followed the explanations to the letter, but it didn't seem to help.*

Sumsari: *You are trying too hard. Stop attempting to become what you think a good musician should be. Instead, you must find your own voice. The great secret of the grand composers and musicians was that they created their own ways of playing. They created their own styles, rhythms, and techniques. Do you think that Mozart ever wrote a book about how to do what he did? What about Beethoven or Bach? Can a great poet ever write a poem about how to be a great poet, when the reason he is great is that he has found distinctiveness? Uniqueness makes one great, not conformity to what others say you should do or should be. There is only one way to play that violin sitting next to you, and that is Cassandra's way! Stop trying to do it like someone else. What would Mozart have been if he tried to emulate Bach? What would the Beatles have been if they had attempted to emulate Beethoven? Each had their own sound, each had their own voice, each had their own groove. As it must be with you. Those books you read can only teach you what the author knows. But what if your destiny is to be greater than the author? Or simply different from the author?*

Cassandra: *I'm not sure about that.*

Sumsari: Then I will be sure for you. I do not teach my students so that I can remain their teacher forever, I teach them so that one day, I can become their student.

Cassandra: That is a wonderful goal. But I'm a long way from being your teacher.

Sumsari: You are closer than you think. You only need to find your musical voice. If you wish to learn how to move a child in his mother's womb, you need to listen for the voice of nature around you. Once you hear the voice of the earth, you can express it in unique ways.

This was what Logan was waiting for—Sumsari's understanding of the voice of nature. He listened as his mother queried further.

Cassandra: Are you saying that the earth makes an actual sound?

Sumsari: Yes. Science calls it the Schumann resonance. The earth is like a massive tuning fork. Understand it this way. The conductor of an orchestra tunes the entire orchestra to middle A before the concert begins. But once the performance starts, each musician must express his own singularity and uniqueness yet still stay in tune with the rest of the orchestra. The earth does the same with every insect, animal, and human ever born. It endeavors to keep us in tune. The voice of nature runs through all of us, even though we may not hear it.

Cassandra: What happens if we stop being in tune? Or worse, if the earth goes out of tune?

Sumsari: I think we would look like the screaming man in a picture I once saw.

There was an extended moment of silence on the recording. The image of Munch's "The Scream" flashed through Logan's mind. Could it be that Jamie's headaches were a result of the earth going out of tune? Were the earthquakes with no epicenters being caused by the same thing? And could all of this be linked to the mysterious phrase that was painted on the shaft of the whistle, *Wrap thin serpent to discover earth voice?*

Cassandra: How long did it take you to hear the voice of nature? How long should I expect it to take me?

Sumsari: *That, my lovely lady, is called the journey. If any of us had the answer to the question of how long anything might take, we could have written the* Chronicles *ourselves. But until then, evolve, create, and teach yourself to play in a way the world has never witnessed before. It is the only way to engage in any task you undertake. If you teach that to your son, you will do him a great service.*

With that, the recorder clicked off. Logan looked at it and saw that there was another recording on this chip. It was from later that afternoon. He pressed the Play button and heard the rustling of papers before his mother spoke.

After my lesson with Sumsari, I went over to Deya's. I told her what Sumsari had told me about the voice of the earth and that I needed to discover my own way of playing the violin. She smiled and told me to follow her and to bring my violin with me. We went downstairs to her meditation area. She told me that when she was a child, she dreamed of becoming a singer. But she wasn't able to accomplish her goal. I didn't understand what she was talking about. I told her that she'd sung beautifully at our wedding a few months ago. She grinned and told me that she couldn't have done that two years before. She agreed with Sumsari: as long as we have expectations of how things should be, we will always be disappointed. She told me that before the Great Disruption, she and Babu traveled to a city in southern England. While they were strolling down a street there, they came upon a poem stamped into the concrete.

I wrote down the poem Deya recited so I wouldn't forget it. It went like this:

> Arise from the earth like water,
> Give birth to your sacred dreams,
> This world is an ocean of mirrors,
> An invitation to create and be seen.

Deya told me that she'd never forgotten the words, but it wasn't until she read the Chronicles *that she fully understood what they meant. She agreed with Sumsari's assertion that we have to create something new; we can't create something that already exists. That is not creating, that is duplicating, just as it says in the* Chronicles. *She told me that she learned to put these words into practice. I asked her how, and she pointed to the mirror. She repeated some of the words from the poem again:* The world is an ocean of mirrors, an invitation to create and be seen.

She told me to look at three words in that sentence: mirror, create, *and* seen.

She turned, looked into the mirror, and closed her eyes. Somehow I knew to step back from her. Her body began to sway slowly back and forth, as if in time to music that only she could hear. She opened her eyes and looked at her reflection just as she had instructed me to do. Several minutes passed as she gazed into the mirror and then began to sing. I have no words to describe the purity of her voice and how utterly transfixed I was by it. I didn't understand a word of what she sang in her mother tongue of Hindi, but I felt her emotion. I felt lifted. She continued to sway in front of the mirror, staring at her reflection. When she was finished, she closed her eyes and stood motionless for a few moments. Then she turned to me and said that simply watching your own reflection perform a task can train your brain to help you become what you desire.

She repeated the three words from the poem: mirror, create, seen. *She told me that the secret to the art of Reflecting is to reach the moment when you don't know if you are the reflection or the one looking at the reflection. She said that sincerity and lack of expectations were the keys to reaching that state. She picked up my violin and handed it to me.*

I knew what she wanted me to do, but I was too uncomfortable to play in front of anyone. Deya didn't take no for an answer. So I tried. It didn't work. Deya told me to stop trying to play the violin perfectly, stop trying to imitate what she had done. She told me that I needed to play as Cassandra the creator and not Cassandra the imitator. It was the same thing that Sumsari had said. I closed my eyes and took a deep breath. The short musical sequence that I had heard Sumsari playing for Madu when I had entered Sumsari's studio earlier that afternoon came into my head.

Logan heard his mother hum the sequence a few times. It was the same melody that Jamie had been humming at the doctor's office that morning.

I opened my eyes and began to play. I played better this time, but I was still too conscious of Deya's presence. She was right, though. There were moments when I felt as if I was the person in the mirror looking back at me. It is very unnerving for your perspective to shift like that. At one moment, I'm looking at my reflection in the mirror, and in the next moment, I'm the person in the mirror looking at myself. I lost track of who and what was real.

Deya told me it would take practice. I see how the fundamentals of Reflecting can be a very powerful training tool. There is a lot to be gained from watching yourself perform a task. It's as if an objective part of you gets to observe the emotional part of you. It's like being two different people at the same time. I'm not sure if that makes sense. Nonetheless, I can't wait to try this again when I am alone tonight.

The anamorphic nature of Reflecting, along with what Deya is teaching me about the mirror, has given me an idea for a new mosaic. I'm not planning to tell anyone what it's going to be. Let's see if they can figure it out!

Logan remembered his mother's abstract mosaic, which was headed to the commemoration. What did it have to do with Reflecting and what Deya taught her?

He also remembered Mr. Perrot's comment about how quickly his mother had learned to play the violin. Now he knew her secret method.

28

Would you search for God if someone had never
told you he was there to search for?
What, then, is it to search for enlightenment?
Are you searching for it because someone else said you should?

—THE CHRONICLES OF SATRAYA

CHÂTEAU DUGAN, SWISS ALPS, 9:00 A.M. LOCAL TIME, MARCH 23, 2070

"We found the bodies of both agents near the entrance to the tunnel below the dock," said WCF field agent Colette Hasburg.

"Was anything found on the dock or in the tunnels?" Valerie asked.

"Nothing yet. Our dive teams are still combing through the lake."

Valerie and Chetan had arrived at Château Dugan, the former home of Simon Hitchlords, via a WCF transport helicopter from Zurich. The sprawling estate, in the foothills of the Swiss Alps directly to the south, had been of great benefit to Simon's father, Fendral, during the tumultuous years leading up to the Great Disruption and after. The dense forest and lake had sheltered the Hitchlords family from much of the unrest in the nearby villages and towns. As the world recovered during the Rising, Château Dugan had served as the chrysalis in which Federal and then Simon plotted to regain their family's power, wealth, and position in the world. Now the palatial grounds were the property of the WCF, seized after Simon's crimes had come to light.

"It took us more than ten hours to map the extensive tunnels below the Château," Agent Hasburg said. She projected the map for Valerie and Chetan, as the three of them stood in the Château's dungeon.

"Looks like you can access just about any portion of the grounds from down there," Valerie said.

"The fact that the bodies were found in the tunnels leads us to believe that the killer entered that way."

"What was this place used for?" Chetan asked, glancing around the shadowy square room, where an open well was located. Loose wiring was attached to lights mounted on the ceiling that dimly illuminated eight iron doors. Another light fixture was perched on the wall alongside the set of stairs they had used to enter the dungeon.

"Whatever dungeons are used for these days," Agent Hasburg said mirthlessly. "We believe that the intruder used the tunnel to access this spiral staircase inside the well." Agent Hasburg turned her PCD into a flashlight and directed the beam over it. "If you look carefully, you can see that the mildew growing on the steps has been disturbed." Valerie joined her at the edge and peered over, spotting footprints. "And if you look at the floor here, you can see traces of that mildew."

"Why would someone put a water well in the middle of their home?" Chetan asked.

"My guess is that this well was one of the first things built on the grounds," Valerie said. "Over time, the house was constructed around it. Doesn't smell very good down there, does it?"

"There is a good reason for that," Agent Hasburg said. "After the plumbing in the Château was modernized, the owners used the well for other purposes. We found four more bodies down there. We have only been able to identify one so far, a Lokesh Sarin from Banaras, India. He was reported missing in July of last year."

"That's Deya Sarin's son," Valerie said. "That's how Simon knew to look for the books in Deya's garden in India. Long story," she added, catching Hasburg's look at the mention of books.

"As I was saying," Hasburg went on, "the other corpses are just skeletal remains. Two men and one woman. We believe they have been there since the pre-Disruption era."

"Assuming that the intruder used the tunnels and climbed up this well to the dungeon, what was he looking for?"

"Good question," Agent Hasburg said. "As far as we can tell, nothing was stolen from the Château. None of the video surveillance systems on the grounds or in the house picked up any unauthorized persons. The dungeon is the only place in the Château that is not monitored by video cameras, but we believe the intruder entered this room." Hasburg led them to the third iron door to the right of the staircase. "The WCF security tape was ripped off the door."

They entered a room where empty metal buckets lay on the floor and a metal chair stood directly over the metal grate of a drain in the stone floor. Chetan was squatting down by the wall opposite the doorway. "Look at this scribbling."

Valerie took out her PCD and videotaped the writing on the wall. The initials *GSR* were etched multiple times. "Well, we know that at least one person was kept here against his will." Under the initials was a series of twelve vertical lines.

"We found trace evidence of blood on the chair and the floor near the drain," Agent Hasburg said. "Turns out the blood is Mr. Sarin's. Whatever happened to him, it probably happened here."

Valerie finished videotaping what she now realized was a torture chamber. "All right, let's recap this," she said. "Some guy approached the Château via the lake, killed two agents, and used a secret passage under the dock to enter the dungeons."

"We can't be certain that this was the *only* place he went," Agent Hasburg said. "The hidden passageways lead in every direction. The dungeons are the only place we have evidence that he went."

Chetan had risen and continued around the room and was now standing in the far corner.

"What are you looking at?" Valerie asked him.

"There seem to be some fresh marks here," Chetan said. "At least, they look recent."

Valerie walked over and ran her fingers along the corner where most of the marks were concentrated. Chetan took out a pen and began to scratch along the grout line between the bricks. Suddenly, it was plucked from his fingers and stuck to the wall. "Well, that's interesting," he said, as Agent Hasburg walked over. Chetan moved the pen up and down along the corner. "Looks like this particular brick is magnetized," he said, then went and grabbed the metal chair in the center of the room.

Valerie moved out of the way. "You plan on smashing the wall down?" she asked sarcastically.

Chetan raised one of the legs of the chair and moved it close to the magnetized brick. It was immediately attracted and made a clinking sound as it stuck. With a strong pull, Chetan dislodged the brick from the wall. To the left, the wall moved a few inches, revealing a door they hadn't realized was there.

"Well done," Valerie said, impressed, giving Chetan a pat on the back. "Let's see what other secrets Château Dugan holds."

Valerie pushed the stone door open and entered the room first. As she did so, bright, overhead lights came on and illuminated what was inside. Chetan followed close behind her.

Valerie turned to Agent Hasburg in the doorway. "You'll need to bring the forensic team down here; there's a lot to bag and tag."

While Agent Hasburg placed the call and spoke on her PCD, Valerie and Chetan began to investigate the Hitchlordses' treasures. Soon enough, Chetan found a box filled with leather pouches containing diamonds and other gems. "If someone broke in here, why would they leave all these valuables?" he asked. "What would have been of more value than these gems?"

"I have my suspicions," Valerie said. "Do you remember when I told you that we never recovered the three missing sets of the *Chronicles*? I bet they were in here."

"But Simon's dead. Who else could have known about this place?"

"I'm more certain than ever that Simon and Andrea weren't working alone," Valerie answered gravely. "Someone else knew about this safe room."

Chetan nodded, sharing her concern. After he opened another box, his concern deepened. "I think you'll want to see this." Valerie turned and saw that he had pulled some photos from an orange envelope. He handed her one and pointed to someone in it. "Isn't that Logan's mother, Cassandra? And I think this one is of Logan's father."

Valerie sighed. She went over to the stainless-steel table and laid the photographs on top of it. She turned one over and read the handwriting on the back: *July 21, 2066, Freedom Day Rally, New Chicago.* "This was taken just a few months before they were murdered," she said softly. "After all those years, Simon managed to track them down."

"I am not so sure he was the one who did the tracking," Chetan said, as he read a note he had taken out of the orange envelope.

"What do you mean?"

Chetan set the note and the envelope down on the table beside the photos. He pointed to the upper left corner. "Look at the return address."

1211 East Cicero, New Chicago, IL 60611, North American Federation. Valerie didn't recognize it. She picked up the note and read it.

May 1, 2065

Mr. Simon Hitchlords,

　　It's been a while since we've seen each other. You were just a boy the last time. I heard your father is at the pearly gates or as I suspect, somewhere much warmer. But I'm sure you're having a good old time spending your family's money.

　　I've found some people you might have forgotten about. But I sure bet your father would want to see them again if he were alive. Have you got any interest in doing so in his place? If someone were to go missing who was already missing, what can be the harm in that?

Let me know. I'm sure a guy like you won't have a problem getting in touch with me.

RJ

Valerie and Chetan looked at each other for a few moments before Valerie said what both of them were thinking. "We need to find out who RJ is."

29

He who asks in belief is praying.
He who commands in knowingness is creating.

—THE CHRONICLES OF SATRAYA

TEOTIHUACÁN, MEXICO, 8:40 A.M. LOCAL TIME, MARCH 23, 2070

Logan carefully set the stone whistle that he and Mr. Perrot had pieced back together on a table in the pyramid-shaped room of the National Institute of Anthropology and History's research center. Mr. Perrot closed the lid of the metal suitcase in which they'd transported the ancient artifact and placed it on the floor. The two of them had caught the first flight from New Chicago to Mexico City that morning. On the way, Logan had filled Mr. Perrot in on Valerie's suspicion that the Tripod Group might be involved in the natural-gas disasters. Personally delivering the whistle to Mr. Montez would afford Logan the opportunity to question him about Tripod directly.

While they waited for Mr. Montez to arrive, Mr. Perrot walked over to the large white statue. "So is this the statue that you spoke about? It's very impressive."

Logan nodded, walking over. "Mr. Montez said that they found it in a chamber very close to the one Jordan and Jamie fell into during the earthquake."

"He does resemble the priests depicted on the stone whistle." Mr. Perrot pressed the backs of his hands against the palms of the statue's hands. "The statue's hands are a good twenty-five centimeters apart."

"Why is that important?"

"If this statue is praying, as you suggested, why are its hands so far apart? I would have expected them to be closer." Mr. Perrot stepped back to take it in more fully. "This is not your standard praying posture."

Logan shook his head. "Mr. Montez believes that the pyramids here and around the world were used to extract power directly out of the atmosphere. At first, I was skeptical, but after my experience with the mirror the other night, I'm becoming more open-minded."

Mr. Perrot walked around the statue and studied its back. "The presence of the Satraya symbols suggests that the sculptor had insight into the *Chronicles*."

"Or at the very least to the philosophy presented in them," Logan said. "It still fascinates me that the Satraya symbols were known two thousand years ago. I incorrectly assumed that the books were a gift given to humanity in our time."

"The knowledge in the books is ancient. We can assume that the symbols are also. Perhaps the gift to us is that the symbols were made more accessible."

Logan nodded and then added, "At least, some of them."

"What about this sixth symbol that is carved into the headband?" Mr. Perrot asked.

"Yeah, that's the one I told you was similar to what was painted on the whistle and what I saw in my vision." Logan walked to Mr. Perrot's side. "I wonder," said Logan.

"Wonder what?" asked Mr. Perrot.

"Could this be one of the veiled symbols? As you said, the sculptor of this statue possessed knowledge of the *Chronicles*. What if he knew it all? You even said you didn't think this man was praying. What if he is more than a priest?"

"You think this man is a Rasatya?"

"Not the statue," Logan said. "But whoever sculpted it."

"But the *Chronicles* only *allude* to the existence of such people," a familiar voice said. Logan turned and saw Mr. Montez and Elvia walking through the doorway.

"Hello, Mr. Montez," Logan said, stepping out from behind the statue with Mr. Perrot. "I was just telling Mr. Perrot about your theories. Mr. Perrot, I'd like to introduce you to—"

Logan stopped abruptly. Mr. Perrot and Mr. Montez were staring at each other.

"Madu Shata and his wife, Nadine," Mr. Perrot finished for Logan.

30

At the heart of every living cell lies the
power of a thousand suns.

—THE CHRONICLES OF SATRAYA

TEOTIHUACÁN, MEXICO, 9:00 A.M. LOCAL TIME, MARCH 24, 2070

"I was hoping that Nadine and I would be able to keep our secret a little longer," Madu said. "We have been Juan and Elvia for more than five years now."

"My husband did everything he could to resist calling you after we learned about your reappearance," Nadine said to Mr. Perrot, and Madu smiled. "Just recently, we learned that Simon and Andrea died. Only then did I allow Madu to come forward."

"Like you, we'd been in hiding, too," Madu added. "After the splintering of the original Council, Nadine and I returned to Egypt and took on new identities."

"It was difficult at first," Nadine said. "Madu and I were very famous and easily recognized in Cairo. We had to spend years in disguise until we faded from people's memories. Since then, we have changed our identities numerous times, as we have traveled from place to place pursuing Madu's energy theories."

There was a lull in the conversation—strange, it seemed, for such good friends.

"You're awfully quiet," Logan said to Mr. Perrot.

"I am still rather stunned by all of this," Mr. Perrot said, then addressed Madu. "I have so many questions. After you called me a few days ago, I wasn't sure if I would actually see you again."

"Speaking of your call the other day," Logan said, "Mr. Perrot said that you were on your way to a business meeting. Did it happen to be with Rigel Wright?"

"Yes, it was," Madu answered. "Why do you ask?"

"I can't say too much," Logan said, "but the Tripod Group has been mentioned a few times in relation to the recent natural-gas well explosions."

"Rigel couldn't be involved in those disasters," Nadine said. "He has been nothing but supportive of Madu's work."

Madu nodded in agreement.

"That's part of what we are afraid of," Logan said, stealing a glance at Mr. Perrot.

"I agree with my wife," Madu said. "I don't believe that Rigel is involved in the explosions." The reconstructed whistle on the table caught Madu's eye, and he walked over to it. He put on his glasses, adjusted the overhead swivel lamp, and started inspecting it. "Excellent work."

"It turned out to be rather easy to put the fragments together," Logan said, as he and Nadine joined Madu at the table. Mr. Perrot remained near the statue. "Perhaps a little too easy."

"Easy, yes, as in an easy way to meet you," Madu admitted with a grin.

"Before you and Nadine arrived," Mr. Perrot said, "I told Logan that I don't think this statue depicts a man who is praying."

Madu removed his glasses and looked at Mr. Perrot. "You don't think this statue represents a holy man? He is quite in line with the images of the priests painted on the walls of the secret chamber we recently discovered and also the priests painted on this whistle."

"Robert, you are always questioning everything," Nadine said fondly.

"He might be a holy man," Mr. Perrot said, "but a holy man with great insight into Satrayian philosophy. Remember, the *Chronicles* had a very different explanation of prayer and communion."

Madu did not look convinced. "But we know that during the construction of Teotihuacán, the priests led large and elaborate prayer sessions and even sacrifices."

Mr. Perrot looked at the statue's face and then its hands. "He who asks in belief is praying . . ."

"He who commands in knowingness is creating," Madu said, completing Mr. Perrot's quote from the *Chronicles*.

Mr. Perrot put his hands up in the same position as the statue's. "I asked Logan this earlier. If this man is indeed praying, why are his hands so far apart? No, I think he is doing something else."

"And what do you think this statue is doing, Robert?" Nadine asked. "When we walked in, did I hear one of you refer to the statue as a Rasatya? Do you really believe that this statue or the person who sculpted it was someone who possessed absolute truth, as the *Chronicles* define a Rasatya?"

"Perhaps," Mr. Perrot said. "I think there are always such people with us in the world, guiding and urging us forward." He gave Logan a knowing look.

"What do you make of the phrase painted along the air stem of the whistling vessel?" Logan asked, turning everyone's attention back to the restored artifact. "I translated it after we restored it. It means *Wrap thin serpent to discover earth voice*. I'm not sure how that relates to the radioactive source you told me you were looking for the last time I was here."

Madu looked disappointed. "This is a curious phrase indeed. I did not expect the broken pieces to form a whistle. While interesting, it does not advance my research in any perceivable way."

"What about the pyramids and their electrical qualities?" Mr. Perrot said, walking over to the table. "Maybe something on that front will spur us forward as we try to figure out what the stone statue depicts."

Nadine's PCD rang. "Excuse me. I need to take this," she said, and walked out.

"I was taught that electricity is created by the motion of strong magnets," Mr. Perrot resumed. "Have you located any rotating gears or mechanisms that could have held something magnetic? Any levers or pendulums?"

"As I told Logan during his last visit, I think the energy came right out of the atmosphere," Madu said. "Are you familiar with the work of Nikola Tesla in the late nineteenth century? He once said, 'The desire that guides me in all I do is the desire to harness the forces of nature to the service of mankind.' He proved that a measurable amount of electricity exists between any two points of different heights off the surface of the earth. It is my contention that the pyramids worked in much the same way as Tesla described. I believe that these pyramids were devices that somehow captured the earth's electricity, which exists between the pyramid's apex and its base and possibly below it. The major question I have been grappling with is how the ancients amplified that relatively weak current of energy into something more useful."

"You said that you thought the people of Teotihuacán did that by using some kind of radioactive core," Logan said. "Rocks and gems of some kind."

"Yes," Madu said. "I still believe that. Once amplification takes place, the capstone of the pyramid would become supercharged. And once that occurred, electricity, as Tesla suggested, could then flow between the capstone and the base of the ionosphere."

"The ionosphere?" Logan asked, surprised.

"Yes, there is an almost unlimited supply of electrical energy between the surface of the earth and the ionosphere seventy kilometers above it. This space is known as the Schumann cavity."

"You're talking about the Wardenclyffe Tower that Tesla built," Mr. Perrot said.

"Yes, Robert. And had Tesla been allowed to complete the construction of that tower, he would have demonstrated the true extent of free energy."

"And you believe that this pyramid is like Tesla's tower?"

"Not just this one," Madu replied, "but many other pyramids around the world."

"And how did the pyramids transmit the energy they captured?" Logan asked.

"Tesla answered that question, too," Madu said. "He claimed that the earth itself could be used in place of a wire. He even demonstrated it with his wireless lightbulb."

Wireless lightbulb, Logan thought, suddenly realizing where he'd seen that very thing. The man in his vision—he was Nikola Tesla. Logan had suspected that the man was the one Mr. Quinn had referred to in his note as the person halfway around the world who had somehow caused "nature to scream" and inspired Munch to create his masterpiece.

Logan interrupted the conversation. "Assume that you're right and devices such as this one could in fact extract energy from the atmosphere. Would there be any side effects?"

"Plenty," Madu said. "Tesla wrote copious notes concerning what could happen if the proper precautions were not taken. One side effect of atmospheric energy induction is the release of stray electrical discharges. They appear as lightning. During one of Tesla's experiments in Colorado, he produced millions of volts of artificial lightning. As he refined his work, he was able to induce various weather phenomena: rain, windstorms, hail. That same work led to the creation of the resonance machine."

"If I remember correctly," Mr. Perrot said, "that work was of keen interest to the military. Resonance machines are capable of shaking buildings and bridges."

"They could do much more than that," Madu said. "Tesla was able to shake the earth and produce earthquakes. He once wrote that isolating the exact resonances and sounds was an important part of his work."

"In what year did Tesla do all this?" Logan asked.

"Tesla immigrated to the United States in 1884," Madu replied. "The Wardenclyffe Tower was built in 1901. I would assume that Tesla did a great deal of experimenting in that seventeen-year span."

Logan looked at Mr. Perrot and lowered his voice. "Munch created *The Scream* in 1895 . . ."

Mr. Perrot nodded. "Please continue, Madu."

"We recently found records that refer to a time, two thousand years ago, when the area around Teotihuacán was much lusher and more fertile than it is today. Sometime around A.D. 536, that suddenly changed, and droughts took over the land. We have also discovered skeletons with signs of malnutrition from the sixth century. Some scholars and archaeologists have attributed this decline to naturally occurring climate change."

"But you don't," Logan observed. "You think it had something to do with this pyramid."

"Yes," Madu said. "I believe, as Tesla wrote, that the pyramids could be used to control the weather in the area surrounding Teotihuacán. And this is not the only place, I believe, where pyramids were used to effect a change in the weather. Did you know that Egypt's deserts were once fields and prairies? I believe that the pyramids of Giza and others around the world once acted in much the same way as those built here."

"So what happened?" Logan asked. "Why did the climate change?"

"That I don't know," Madu said, shaking his head. "There are indications that Teotihuacán was invaded during the sixth century. I suspect that the destabilization of the civilization had something to do with the drought and eventual crop failures."

"The pyramid stopped working," Mr. Perrot said, looking at Madu. "Or it was turned off."

Logan returned to the statue of the kneeling man. "What if *he* knew the secret?" He put his hands up, the same distance apart as the statue's, then turned and eyed the whistle sitting on the table. "What if Mr. Perrot is correct, and this is not a statue of a man praying?" Mr. Perrot grabbed the whistle and walked it over to Logan, who in turn placed it between the open hands of the statue. It fit perfectly. The air stem from the whistling vessel touched the statue's lips. "What if this is a statue of a man playing an instrument?"

Madu said nothing. He just stared at the statue. Logan turned and looked at him. "You said earlier that Tesla believed that sound and resonance played a key role in his theories. I don't mean to insult you, but maybe you missed something over the years. Maybe sound, and not radiation, is the missing ingredient."

The silence after this was long and tense, broken finally by Mr. Perrot. "I suggest that we visit that secret chamber," he said.

Logan nodded. "What if *that* is the place, as the name Teotihuacán suggests, where men went to become gods?"

31

There is no final exam for life. All you need
to do to pass is give it a whirl.

—THE CHRONICLES OF SATRAYA

"Since the site has been put off limits by the government, we haven't been able to do much down here," Madu explained to Logan and Mr. Perrot after they had descended into the secret chamber of the Pyramid of the Moon that Jordan and Jamie had discovered. A metal cage elevator that accommodated a single person had been installed, along with bright lighting. Tables had also been set up to hold archaeology tools, empty boxes, and packaging materials, so that artifacts could be wrapped and transported to the research center. "As you can see," Madu said to Logan, "everything is as we found it during your last visit."

Mr. Perrot walked around the chamber. "Fascinating," he remarked, as he looked up at the many small openings in the ceiling, which angled off in different directions. When he reached the middle, he inspected the mica platform with the carving of the coiled serpent at its center. He moved on to the archway where the skeletons lay. After looking them over, he glanced at the wooden cart, which resembled a wheelbarrow, in the corner nearby. Then he walked over to the murals and began to study them.

Logan carefully set his backpack and the box containing the whistle on a long table that also held an array of broken pottery and other artifacts. He picked up a long piece of tangled string that lay on the table. Parts of it were discolored and worn through. "What was this used for?"

"I don't know. We found it in the wooden cart," Madu said.

Logan finished untangling it and put it back on the table. "One thing this chamber and the praying man statue have in common is a round mica platform." He stepped onto it. Looking down, he saw the red stone that served as one of the eyes of the image of the serpent carved into the platform.

"Since your last visit, I have been able to determine that this chamber sits directly under the apex," Madu said. "And the platform that you are standing on is in perfect alignment with it. The red eye of the serpent aligns exactly with the pyramid's apex."

Logan knelt down and raised his hands in front of his mouth. "Look familiar?" he asked.

"Yes, but you're missing something," Madu said, and he picked up one of the ceramic whistles in the corner of the room and placed it between Logan's hands. "Now your pose is complete."

"The praying Logan," Mr. Perrot said with a chuckle.

Logan looked over at the skeletons. "Those two must have known what this place was all about."

"Let's continue with the train of thought concerning sound," Mr. Perrot said.

"Agreed," Logan said. "What if something down here acts as the pyramid's on-and-off switch? And what if the statue is demonstrating how that switch works?" He blew into the whistle. The three of them looked up at the chamber's ceiling, surprised by the reverberation of the sound.

"Excellent acoustics," Mr. Perrot said. The harmonic continued for a few moments before fading. Mr. Perrot pointed to the ceiling. "It is possible that these shafts extend throughout the pyramid somehow, allowing the sound to spread."

Madu picked up two more whistles from the ground. "Try the one with the painting of a goat on it," he said as he handed it to Mr. Perrot. "I'll try the one with the picture of an ox." The two of them joined Logan near the mica platform. They all blew into the stems of their whistles. A richer sound now echoed throughout the chamber. The three different sounds from the whistles blended together to create a completely new reverberation and harmonic.

Mr. Perrot spotted the four other whistles on the ground. "I don't know much about music, but I can safely say there are potentially thousands of harmonics that could be created by combining the sounds of these whistles."

Logan rose to his feet, set the whistle he was holding on the mica platform, and walked over to a pair of long, thin sticks that were leaning against the wall. "Have you been able to determine what these rods were used for?" he asked Madu.

Mr. Perrot handed his whistle to Madu and walked over to Logan. He took a handkerchief from his pocket and wiped some of the oxidation off the rod, scratching it with his fingernail. "It looks like copper."

"Did this pyramid ever have a capstone?" Logan asked.

"I suspect it did," Madu replied. "But as with the other pyramids around the world, the capstone was probably stolen by raiders long ago. Egyptologists speculate that the capstone of the Great Pyramid in Giza was wrapped in metal—some say gold, others say copper."

"Wouldn't one of Tesla's theories come into play, then?" Logan asked Madu, who nodded. "You said earlier that an electrical charge naturally exists between two metallic points positioned at different heights."

"And we know that this room is in perfect alignment with the apex," Mr. Perrot added.

"May I see the end of that rod?" Logan requested. Mr. Perrot handed it to him. He ran his finger over it from top to bottom. "Look at how the last quarter of the rod is thinner than the rest of it. You can feel the change in diameter at this point here." He put his index finger on the point in question. Madu came over to inspect it.

Mr. Perrot went over to the mica platform where Logan had been kneeling. He squatted and examined the image of the coiled serpent carved there. "In certain metaphysical teachings, coiled serpents represent energy," he said.

"Isn't there something in the *Chronicles* about that?" Logan asked.

"A coiled river of energy waits eagerly to be released in the tiniest of cells to the stoutest of men. With simple decree, the power of a thousand suns can be rallied forth into the reality of life. It is the spiral serpent known as Zakti," Madu recited.

Mr. Perrot rose and stepped off the platform. As he did so, he accidentally kicked the red stone that formed the eye of the serpent, dislodging it. Water could be heard running under the floor. "I hear the trickle of water."

"Yes," Madu said. "We suspect that a strong river used to flow under the pyramid, not just the trickle you hear now."

Logan watched Mr. Perrot bend back down and put his right index finger into the hole. As a thought occurred to him, he carried the rod over to the platform. Mr. Perrot stepped back. "You said the eye was in perfect alignment with the apex. Assuming that this copper rod represented the point of conductivity beneath the capstone"—Logan positioned the thinner end of the rod above the hole—"this would be a perfect place for it to go." He inserted the thinner end of the rod into the hole. When he removed his grip, the rod stood vertically on its own.

"So in theory," Mr. Perrot said, "if there were a capstone at the apex, a small yet measurable amount of electricity would be detectable, correct?"

"That is what Tesla proved," Madu acknowledged.

"So now the only thing we need is a way to amplify the current," Logan said, picking up the whistling vessel from the platform and

blowing into it as he had done before. The harmonic echoed through
the chamber, and the copper rod began to vibrate, making a twanging
sound. Logan blew into the whistle again, with more force. The rod
vibrated more vigorously. Taking Logan's cue, Madu handed Mr. Perrot a whistling vessel and picked up another one. They blew into them
simultaneously, and an intense harmonic was created. The copper rod
oscillated back and forth. Logan stepped off the platform, not wanting
to get hit by the now rapidly swaying rod. Suddenly, the rod sprang out
of the hole and flew across the chamber, crashing into the sealed opening near the two skeletons.

"Well." Logan watched in amazement. "I think we are definitely onto
something."

"Not only do these whistles cause a harmonic that is enhanced by
the acoustics of this chamber," Mr. Perrot said, "but the harmonic affects the copper rod in a very profound way."

"I doubt if an out-of-control copper rod is what the people who
built this chamber intended, though," Logan said.

"No, this must be one of the side effects that Tesla warned about,"
Mr. Perrot said. "Without the proper harmonic, who knows what can
happen?"

"The lack of a proper capstone in place could also account for unpredictable results," Madu added.

Mr. Perrot walked over to the sealed doorway. A piece of its thin
plaster façade had broken off where the rod had struck it, revealing the
head of a painted horse. "There is something beneath this plaster."

Madu turned toward Mr. Perrot and the sealed doorway. His eyes
widened. He went over to a table and picked up a few scraping tools. In
five minutes, he and Mr. Perrot were able to remove the plaster.

"It's a mural," Logan observed from behind them. They stepped back
and saw that it was a painting of a battle. Below it, another scene was
depicted: two men in robes constructing a wall. "What does it mean?"

Madu pointed to the top of the mural. "Teotihuacán was attacked.
This shows a king leading his marauding army down the Avenue of the

Dead toward the Moon Pyramid. They are killing everything in sight. Look at the burning fields and the slaughtered cattle."

"This supports your theory that Teotihuacán was sacked," Logan said.

"And it was surrounded by lush farmland." Mr. Perrot gestured to the scenery in the background.

Madu pointed to the middle of the mural. "Here are two people running into the Moon Pyramid." He moved his finger farther to the right. "Here they are pulling a cart and running through a tunnel toward a room."

Logan looked away from the mural to the small wooden cart in the corner near the two skeletons. "Looks like we know what room these two were fleeing to," he said.

After a solemn pause, Madu continued with his interpretation of the mural. "The last scene shows them constructing this wall."

"They buried themselves in here." Logan looked at the two skeletons.

"They didn't want the invaders to find this room." Mr. Perrot agreed, squatting down next to one of the skeletons. "They're dressed similarly to the two people running in the mural. Look at this." Both Logan and Madu squatted down next to Mr. Perrot. "Look at the copper headband this man is wearing."

"The Satraya symbols along with the snowflake. Just like the statue and the wall paintings," Logan said. "I think there's more to this snowflake than we are giving credit to."

Mr. Perrot attempted to lift the headband up over the skull. As he did so, the skull fell off the corpse and rolled to the ground. The men jumped back, startled. "I apologize," Mr. Perrot said, "but I believe we are about to learn something significant."

"This one also has a headband," Madu said of the other skeleton. He carefully removed it, leaving the bones intact. Suddenly, the ground began to shake. The three men stood still, looking at one another for several seconds, but the shaking didn't stop.

"Another earthquake," Logan said. "We have to get out of here!"

The shaking intensified. Chunks of stone fell from the ceiling. Logan ran to the table for his backpack and the silver case containing the reconstructed stone whistle.

"Take as much as you can!" Madu shouted. He grabbed the copper rod and the three whistles. But before he could get to the other four, a large rock fell and crashed down on them.

Logan grabbed some of the broken pottery off the table and stuffed it into his backpack. He used the worn string to better secure his overflowing pack. A monstrous rumbling filled the chamber as the ground shifted beneath their feet. More stones dropped from the ceiling, one landing on the mica platform. Logan handed the silver case to Mr. Perrot. One by one, they stepped into the small metal cage elevator, hoping it would rise as the Moon Pyramid broke apart around them.

32

How do you expect to find what you're looking for if you never start looking for it?

—THE CHRONICLES OF SATRAYA

NOVACON ISLAND, 4:05 P.M. LOCAL TIME, MARCH 23, 2070

"This is too dangerous, Doctors," the technician warned. "We have already seen what introducing more radioactive isotopes has done. I'm shutting down the core." The technician frantically maneuvered a set of controls in front of him.

"There is . . ." said the male doctor, dressed all in black.

"No proof of that," continued the female doctor, who was dressed all in white.

"The earthquakes . . ." said the male doctor.

"Are simply coincidental," said the female doctor.

"Coincidental?" The technician raised his voice. "Are you kidding me? Each time we do this, the seismic activity on the island spikes, and within moments, we hear reports of earthquakes from all over the globe. Just look at what is happening out there. We're killing people. We have to stop this now!"

The doctors exchanged glances before turning back to the rebellious technician. "People die . . ." said the male doctor.

"Every day," finished the female doctor, and she motioned to two armed security guards standing nearby. "Discharge this man. Martin does not serve us any longer."

The two guards quickly walked over to the technician. One grabbed him by the arm. The other grabbed his briefcase. Martin was forcibly escorted to a set of doors that automatically opened as they approached. The three men stepped into the elevator car, and the doors closed behind them.

Just then, another set of doors to the control center opened. Dario entered, a humming emanating from his black business suit as he walked in. Catherine and Yinsir accompanied him. Rashidi followed them.

"Hello, Doctors," Catherine said. "How goes the testing?"

The two doctors turned simultaneously and walked over to her in unison. Yinsir gazed in amazement at the odd pair.

Catherine smiled. "Yinsir, I would like to introduce you to Dr. Rosa and Dr. Josef. The world's first set of neurologically conjoined twins."

The doctors bowed. Yinsir responded in kind. The twins were exactly the same height, standing a meter and a half tall. They had flawless pale skin and matching green eyes. Their short brown hair, which barely covered their ears, did nothing to soften their identical cold, expressionless faces.

"Do not let their size or appearances fool you," Dario said in his raspy voice. "While the twins may have been born with some physical deficits, their neuro interface allows their brains to act as one."

"From an intellectual point of view," Catherine added, "these two might be the smartest single person on the planet."

"An interesting way to put it," Yinsir said.

"Please, turn around, Doctors. Show our friend here what we are talking about."

The doctors turned in unison. At the base of each of their skulls was a small disk-like device flashing a series of green, blue, and red lights.

"They act as one," Dario said. "Their brains are fused together to the point where they complete each other's thoughts."

"However, when they analyze a problem," Catherine said, "each can process a different part of the problem at the same time. Their thoughts are transmitted back and forth to each other almost instantaneously. Their combined brain power is exponentially greater than that of any single person with the IQ of a genius."

"It must get pretty loud in their heads," Yinsir said with a laugh.

The doctors turned back around. "Thoughts are . . ." said Dr. Josef.

"Not loud," Dr. Rosa stated.

"Feeble minds . . ." continued Dr. Josef.

"Are loud."

"Yes, Doctors, you are right, as always," Catherine said. "Please continue with your work. We don't want to hinder your progress."

The doctors walked to a group of technicians who were seated at numerically identified work stations on a circular platform fifteen meters in diameter. Each technician sat in an ergonomically designed chair in front of a computer whose thin glass display showed a variety of readings. The technicians wore contact lenses optically connected to the displays in front of them, which made their eyes glow neon green.

Catherine, Dario, and Yinsir went to the side of the room and observed.

"Let us . . ." said Dr. Rosa.

"Try again," added Dr. Josef.

The technicians began to perform their tasks. "What is the status of . . ." said Dr. Rosa.

"The radical EM wave?" asked Dr. Josef.

"Zero hertz. No wave is present, Doctors," answered the female technician seated at console fourteen.

"Binary fission rate is normal," a male technician answered from console number three.

The technician at console one looked at a few readings on the display in front of him. "Should we open the core?" he asked.

The doctors walked over to him. Dr. Rosa stood to his left, Dr. Josef to his right. They looked at the display, analyzing it for several seconds.

"Yes," said Dr. Rosa.

"Proceed," added Dr. Josef.

"Moving to low output," said the technician at console one. As they began to manipulate their controls, the image of a slowly rotating white pyramid was projected over the platform where the technicians were seated.

"EM wave normal," a technician said.

"Fission rate normal," another added.

"Opening the core," announced the technician at console one. As he worked the controls, a gentle rumbling sounded for several seconds. "Core exposure at ten percent."

"Ten is not enough," said Dr. Rosa.

"Open to twenty," said Dr. Josef.

The technician gave the doctors a questioning look.

"Do . . ."

"It."

The technician did as the doctors requested. The white pyramid turned yellow. "Electrical induction has commenced," the technician said. "Output is at low yield, one megahertz."

"Open the core . . ." said Dr. Rosa.

"To thirty," said Dr. Josef.

Another momentary rumbling occurred as the core was opened further. The technicians worked feverishly, calling out their readings to one another. "Power collectors at seven thousand megawatts," one announced.

The doctors looked at the projection of the pyramid as the color of the capstone changed from yellow to golden brown.

"When you asked me to join you on the island, I did not know what to expect," Yinsir said. "And though I still can't say that I understand a word of what these people are saying, I'm impressed."

Dario laughed. "This, my friend, is the latest in energy supply."

"This structure that we are standing in is called a zero-point frac-turing node," Catherine said. "It has the ability to extract electricity directly from the atmosphere. Once this device is operational, we will be deploying identical devices at strategic locations all over the world."

"And fret not, my friend. Neither Catherine nor I make any attempt to understand what is being said by these people." Dario motioned around the room. "All I know is that we are standing at the center of the world's newest pyramid."

"There is a large copper capstone fifty meters above us and a nuclear core fifty meters below," Catherine explained. "And somehow, through the miracle of science, electricity is produced."

Yinsir chuckled. "Did Simon know about this?"

"Heavens, no," Catherine replied. "This is my and Dario's baby."

"Simon thought he had all the answers," Dario said. "We gave him some rope to see what he would do with it."

"Turns out all he could do with it was hang himself," Catherine said.

A loud crack of thunder startled everyone in the control center. The technicians glanced at one another. A man seated at console nine pressed a button, and the shutters over the windows along the periphery of the control center opened, providing a panoramic view of the island. A heavy rain pelted the windows as a storm raged outside. The technicians rotated in their chairs to gaze out. Just to the north was Ponta do Pico, a large stratavolcano that rose more than two thousand meters in the air. The crashing waves of the ocean could be seen to the south. Another thunderclap boomed and then another.

Yinsir noticed the twin doctors standing by the large windows, looking out at the storm. "And where did you find them?"

"That is a rather long story," Catherine answered. "Let's just say that we liberated them from their last employer, who was not using them to their full capacity."

"If this device works as you say," Yinsir said, "then those two might have come up with the most radically innovative power-generating tech-nology the world has ever seen."

A bolt of electricity was discharged from high above, appearing to come from the capstone. A moment later, another. "Fission rate is decreasing," a technician said.

The two doctors turned to each other and then to the projection of the pyramid rotating above the platform. The capstone was rapidly alternating color from deep gold to pale yellow.

"Radical EM level at fifty hertz," the technician at console fourteen announced, disappointed.

"Fission rate is dropping further."

"Power collectors holding at seven thousand megawatts," said the technician at console one. "Dropping back to low yield."

Catherine left Dario and Yinsir, quickly walking over to the doctors, who had moved back over to the technicians. "No, we must push forward," she insisted. "Doctors, we must be able to harvest more energy. Seven thousand megawatts isn't even enough to power a small city!"

"If we push any further, we have no idea what will happen," said the technician at console fourteen. "We're going into uncharted territory here. Martin wasn't joking around."

"There are workers outside," said the technician at console one. "An increase in output could cause more electrical discharges."

"Would the two of you like to join Martin outside?" Catherine asked, giving them a glare that made them cower in their chairs. "I don't care about side effects or discharges. We need results. Move the output to high. I want to see what my money has bought me after six years."

"We agree," said Dr. Rosa.

"We must push on," said Dr. Josef.

The technician at console one shook his head. "Opening core to fifty percent," he said.

The capstone of the projected pyramid above them transitioned from gold to red. Electrical discharges now fired at random in rapid succession. The stormy sky grew darker.

"Radical EM level now at one hundred fifty hertz," technician fourteen announced.

"Fission rate is zero," technician three said.

Two electrical discharges were expelled from the capstone and struck the ground near the control center. One of the technicians rose from his seat and ran over to the eastern-facing windows that overlooked the complex's arrival and departure platform. He put his hand on the window. "Martin!" he called. Others joined him there, seeing their colleague's lifeless, charred body lying faceup on the ground with steam rising from it. Martin had been struck by one of the electrical discharges. The briefcase he was carrying lay open beside him, the wind scattering his papers in all directions. Two other, more fortunate workers had taken refuge underneath a nearby awning, waiting for the violent storm to pass.

The doctors turned to Catherine and took two quick steps forward. "We must stop," said Dr. Rosa.

"Agreed, we must stop now," reiterated Dr. Josef.

"We cannot risk . . ." said Dr. Rosa.

"The integrity of the ZPF," said Dr. Josef.

Catherine's face was red with anger as she stared at the doctors. "Shut it down, then," she said reluctantly. The technicians returned to their computers and started working. The capstone of the projected pyramid transitioned from red to deep gold and then to yellow. The lightning and thunder ceased, and the rain and battering wind eased. The capstone transitioned from yellow to white.

Dario walked over to Catherine, and Yinsir made his way to a table where a technician was putting away a few pieces of equipment.

Catherine pointed at the doctors and said, "The two of you had better figure this out."

"A timetable has been established according to your promises," Dario added. "Events have been set in motion and cannot be stopped now."

"The plans you provided . . ." said Dr. Rosa.

"Are incomplete," Dr. Josef finished.

"A critical piece . . ."

"Is missing."

"Can't the two of you figure out what it is?" Yinsir said loudly from across the room, as he picked up an odd-looking piece of equipment. "I am told you're the smartest people on the planet."

Neither Catherine nor Dario appeared pleased with Yinsir's off-the-cuff comment.

The doctors turned and looked at him. They put up their hands and spoke in unison. "Please do not play with that device."

Yinsir heeded the warning and put the device back down. "The others will be arriving soon. You will have to tell them that your project has been delayed."

"Doctors, you both knew when you started working here that the plans had not been tested," Catherine said sternly. "The two of you assured us that was not a problem."

"Wait," Yinsir interrupted. "The doctors did not draw up the plans for this device?"

Catherine and Dario exchanged looks. "No," Catherine said. "The plans for this device come from another source."

"An old Satrayian," Dario said.

Yinsir raised an eyebrow. "Then it might be time to get back in touch with him."

33

The only reason the wise sage told his student to climb the highest of mountains was that the student refused to believe that what he was looking for was within himself.

—THE CHRONICLES OF SATRAYA

TEOTIHUACÁN, MEXICO, 11:20 A.M. LOCAL TIME, MARCH 23, 2070

Logan, Mr. Perrot, and Madu didn't stop running until they were more than a hundred meters clear of the Moon Pyramid. Seven minutes had passed since the earthquake had started. Electrical arcs, similar to the ones Logan had witnessed on his first trip to Teotihuacán, were shooting out of the apex of the Moon Pyramid. Another, more intense series of arcs shot into the sky. A loud crackling sound rent the air as bolts of electricity scattered. Light crept along the outer surface of the pyramid. The pyramid began to glow.

"It looks like one of Tesla's static electricity experiments," Mr. Perrot said, not believing what he was witnessing.

The three men moved farther back, holding their arms out to their sides to maintain their balance as the ground shifted and rippled beneath their feet. Cracks appeared at the apex of the pyramid. Within seconds, the cracks grew wider and longer, running down the sides of the ancient structure. Stones continued to topple down off the pyramid's façades.

"It's falling apart," Madu said in disbelief, taking a step forward.

Mr. Perrot grabbed him by the shoulder and pulled him back. "There's nothing we can do," he said, recalling what it was like watching old skyscrapers being demolished after the Great Disruption. A haunting and eerie moment of stillness occurred, as if they were standing at the eye of a hurricane, before a series of blue lights exploded overhead. Logan, Mr. Perrot, and Madu ducked as the light passed over them. A mere five seconds later, the Moon Pyramid, which had once jutted into the sky, imploded. A massive dust cloud rose into the air and spread into the twilight sky.

"It's gone," Madu said in shock. He closed his eyes, falling to his knees and whispering. "And all of its secrets along with it. . . ."

* * *

Logan and Mr. Perrot helped Madu, still distraught, back to the museum's research center. "It doesn't look like there was much damage here," Logan said, as they entered the pyramid-shaped room.

He set his backpack on a table, and Madu set down the three whistles he was carrying and the headband he'd taken from the skeleton, then lowered himself into a chair and buried his face in his hands. Logan untied the string he'd wrapped around his backpack and took out the pieces of broken pottery he'd salvaged. Mr. Perrot leaned the copper rod against the table and placed the metal case containing the restored whistle on the floor.

"Do you have the other headband?" Logan asked.

Mr. Perrot held it up to show him and placed it on the table next to the one Madu had taken.

"There you are!" Nadine ran into the room and rushed over to Madu and hugged him. "Are you all right?"

"I'm fine," he replied. "I'm fine."

While Nadine and Madu spoke in hushed tones, Logan and Mr. Perrot turned their attention to the items they had salvaged from the hidden chamber. Logan inspected one of the headbands. He ran his fingers over the Satraya symbols, which had been pressed into the copper along with the mysterious symbol that could be a snowflake or a flower. He looked at the inside of the headband and saw a familiar phrase. He pointed it out to Mr. Perrot: *QUITETEUHQUIMILOA CANAHUAC COHUATL TOCONMONEXTILIZ ITOZQUI TLALLI.*

Mr. Perrot picked up the second headband. "The phrase is also written on this one: *Wrap thin serpent to discover earth voice.*"

Logan sighed, still unsure what it meant. His PCD sounded, and he started to worry when he saw who it was from. "Ms. Sally," he said, typing a reply. "Jamie had another one of those splitting headaches."

Madu and Nadine joined Logan and Mr. Perrot at the table.

"It cannot be a coincidence that this phrase is found on both headbands and also on the stem of the stone whistle," Mr. Perrot said.

"The term *earth voice* is curious," Madu said. "I suppose it could be referring to many things. Sound, music, even poetry . . ."

"I recently learned that my mother took violin lessons from a man named Sumsari Baltik when all of you were on the Council," Logan said.

"Yes," Madu said. "Sumsari was a musical genius."

"He told my mother that the earth had a voice. The message on this stone whistle and also on these headbands alludes to the same thing. What if the earth's voice is the activation harmonic for the pyramid?"

Nadine gave Madu a skeptical look. "I thought a source of radiation was the key. Isn't that the assumption behind all your work over these last many years?"

Madu sighed. "It is possible that my initial theories were incorrect. Based on what we discovered before the pyramid collapsed, sound and resonance might have played a more pivotal role. Sumsari knew a great deal about these things. Perhaps I should have listened to him more closely back then. I wonder if he's still alive. He might be able to shed more light on what we have discovered here."

"I'll send Valerie a message," Logan said, pulling out his PCD. "She'll be able to tell us if Sumsari is still alive and, if so, where he lives."

"Until then, we need to push forward," Mr. Perrot said. "I wonder if the serpent that was carved into the mica platform is what this phrase is referring to."

"A serpent could mean a lot of things," Nadine said, straightening up the mess of artifacts on the table. "In those days, people spoke allegorically when they wanted to veil certain truths. The term *serpent* could mean anything from a real snake to the symbol for energy to a piece of jewelry."

"We may never know," Madu said. "What if what we're looking for is now buried under the Moon Pyramid?"

"Then we will dig it up," Nadine said emphatically.

Logan watched as Nadine wound the discolored string around her fingers. His eyes lit up in realization. "A Spartan scytale," he said out loud.

"A Spartan what?" Mr. Perrot asked.

"A Spartan scytale was a ciphering technique used more than twenty-five hundred years ago," Logan said. "It involved wrapping a string or ribbon around an object, usually a cylinder on which a secret text had been imprinted. The text was transferred to the thread. Then, when the thread was unwrapped, the message was encrypted; the message would look like a bunch of random marks on the string." Logan pointed at the string wrapped around Nadine's fingers. "You see these dark marks we thought were dirt? What if it's a cipher? *Wrap thin serpent to discover earth voice,*" Logan said, repeating the phrase as Nadine began to unwind the thread.

"What if the earth voice is—" Mr. Perrot started.

"The activation harmonic," Madu said, completing his thought.

"The key to deciphering a message like this one is to wrap the string around something that is the same shape and size as the object on which the message was originally imprinted," Logan said. "The string was originally found in the wooden cart in the secret chamber."

"What about the copper rod?" Mr. Perrot suggested.

"Worth a try," Logan said.

Nadine quickly finished unwrapping the thread and handed it to

Logan, who then carefully twisted it around the copper rod, making sure the marks faced outward.

Mr. Perrot examined it when Logan was done. "Doesn't look like we have the right object. There is nothing decipherable."

Logan tried again at the thinner end of the rod, but the results were the same. "This rod is not the key."

"Other than the copper staff," Madu said, "we were only able to salvage the three whistling vessels and some broken pieces of pottery."

Logan set the string on the table. He surveyed the items beside it for anything that might serve as the key to the Spartan scytale. "The broken pottery clearly won't work. The whistling vessels are a possibility, but their odd shapes would make it difficult to wrap the thread around properly."

Nadine and Madu tried several whistle stems and even set two next to each other and wrapped the string around them both, but neither way worked.

While they did that, Logan looked at the praying man statue and the mica platform on which it stood, wondering if they should try it. But he discarded the idea, because the platform was too large and the thread would only go around it a couple of times. Then, recalling something, he walked over to the statue and knelt down near the base. "What did you say this phrase said?" he asked Madu.

"The wise man of stone holds the nest of the snake," Madu replied.

Logan smiled. "And what does the stone man hold?"

"The whistle," Madu said.

Mr. Perrot took the reconstructed stone whistle from its case and set it on the table. "The nest of the snake," he said, sharing Logan's smile.

Nadine quickly took the string and started wrapping it around the cylindrical body of the praying man's whistle. Logan walked back over to the table to join Mr. Perrot and Madu. They watched anxiously as, loop by loop, Nadine meticulously wound the thread.

"The marks are lining up," Logan said. "It looks like a series of animals."

"We've seen these before," Madu said. "These are the animals that were painted on the seven whistling vessels we found in the chamber."

"This might be the sequence in which the whistles need to be played in order to activate the pyramid," Mr. Perrot suggested.

Logan looked at the three whistles they had taken from the chamber. "Without the other four, this sequence is meaningless." He turned to Madu, regret on his face as he spoke. "I'm sorry, Madu."

Everyone was silent. All of Madu and Nadine's efforts at Teotihuacán over the last seven years seemed to have been for naught. Madu stood with his head bowed, and Nadine gazed at him with concern in her eyes.

"The two of you should come to the commemoration in Washington," Mr. Perrot gently told them. "Put all of this aside for now, and rejoin us as Madu and Nadine Shata, the finders of the *Chronicles* and the only people to have survived the Pyramid Run."

"You remember that story?" Nadine said.

"Of course I do," Mr. Perrot replied. "It is the inspiring true story of two people who didn't give up in the face of hopelessness."

Madu looked up. "Robert is correct," he said to Nadine. "There is nothing more for us here. Even if we are able to persuade Rigel to fund the excavation of the Moon Pyramid, it will be months before we can start. There are other pyramids where I can continue my research."

Nadine nodded and took his hand.

Just then, Logan received a reply from Valerie on his PCD. "Here's another reason for you to go to Washington with us: Valerie says that Sumsari Baltik is alive." He sighed, turning to Mr. Perrot. "He was a victim of the satellite malfunction last July, though. He is now at the Calhoun Medical Center undergoing therapy."

"Still, that should be our first stop when we arrive in Washington," Mr. Perrot said.

Madu looked at his old friend and nodded in agreement.

34

Can anything you have ever done in your life be forgiven?
Yes.

—THE CHRONICLES OF SATRAYA

SOUTHAMPTON, UNITED KINGDOM, 6:00 P.M. LOCAL TIME, MARCH 23, 2070

"So this is where that famous ship began its maiden voyage?" Valerie asked, looking out the helicopter window. "The one that collided with an iceberg?"

"Yes, it sank, killing more than a thousand people," Chetan answered. "It was called the *Titanic*. It's been at the bottom of the Atlantic for almost one hundred sixty years."

"And Rigel Wright thinks he can raise it after all this time?"

"Of course. He even has plans to build a gigantic museum for it."

A WCF transport plane had flown them from Zurich to London, where they'd boarded a helicopter to take them over the city of South-ampton on the southern coast of England. While social unrest had spread through most of Great Britain during the Great Disruption, the southern coast had been relatively unscathed. The city of London, one hundred forty-four kilometers to the northeast, did not fare so well. A series of earthquakes had shaken the city and caused the Thames River to surge, flooding many of the landmarks along its banks. The fabled timekeeper, Big Ben, had stopped at half past four on the day of the first major earthquake. It remained that way to this day to remind everyone of the moment when the Great Disruption struck. London Bridge had collapsed into the river, along with portions of the nearby Tower of London. During the worst of the city's riots, the Beefeaters who guarded the Tower had been overrun, and the Crown Jewels had disappeared, never to be seen again.

"There are hundreds of boats down there," Valerie said.

"You cannot miss Rigel Wright's," Chetan said. "Do you see that boat with the multitiered deck and the long bow? There is a helicopter landing pad on it."

"That's not a boat," Valerie said. "That's a whole island."

"That is the *Water Shadow*," Chetan said. "It has a crew of eighty and can house thirty guests. It's the fastest ship ever constructed. It can reach speeds of more than two hundred knots. It is where Mr. Wright spends most of his time."

"What about his family?" Valerie asked.

Chetan chuckled. "He is a bit of a playboy billionaire." Valerie gave him a look. "That's what I read, at least."

The helicopter banked to the left as it descended toward the *Water Shadow*. Valerie and Chetan could hear the pilot announce their arrival to the ship's captain. The copter dropped its landing gear and softly touched down on the ship's bow. Valerie and Chetan hopped out and were greeted by a middle-aged woman wearing a full-length white dress and a black scarf tied around her neck.

"Welcome to the *Water Shadow*. My name is Karen," she said loudly over the sound of the whipping helicopter blades. "I am Mr. Wright's assistant. He is not here just yet, but I have notified him of your arrival. Please follow me."

Valerie and Chetan followed Karen down a stairway to a lower deck. As they walked toward the stern, they caught glimpses of lavishly appointed staterooms and passenger cabins through tinted windows. After two more sets of stairs, they stood on a deck almost level with the sea.

"Do we know how long Mr. Wright is going to be?" Valerie asked.

"Shouldn't be much longer," Karen replied.

Valerie gazed out on the English Channel, expecting to see an approaching boat. Then she looked up and saw a plane in the sky. "Is he planning to parachute in?"

"No, not today." Karen laughed. There was a disturbance in the water behind the ship. Hundreds of air bubbles broke to the surface. Valerie and Chetan stepped back to avoid being splashed by the incoming waves. "In fact, here comes Rigel now."

Valerie and Chetan watched as the glass dome of a submarine rose out of the sea. "Like I said, a lot of resources," Chetan whispered. Valerie remained silent.

The twenty-meter-long submarine bounced out of the water, causing a very large wave to splash onto the platform. Four boat hands rushed to attach mooring lines to the submarine, while two others set up a walkway. The side door opened, and out walked a short, muscular man. His tanned skin contrasted with his platinum-blond hair. He wore white knee-length shorts and a black golf shirt with *Titanic Rising* printed above the breast pocket. As he stepped off the walkway, he handed Karen a leather bag and said something to her that Valerie and Chetan couldn't hear, then walked over to them.

"I'm Rigel. Is the WCF here to assist me in the raising of the *Titanic*?" He smirked.

Valerie ignored his question. "I'm Agent Perrot, and this is Agent Jah."

"I didn't realize that WCF agents come in such classy, attractive packages." Rigel put his hand out to shake Valerie's. "You didn't tell me your first name."

"Valerie," she answered reluctantly.

"Please, Valerie, let's dispense with formalities on this beautiful spring day. You have lovely hair. I hope you let it down occasionally." He gave her a suggestive smile, then turned to a wide-eyed Chetan, who was eager to shake the hand of the man he admired and had read so much about. "Let's go to the Observation Room, where we can talk more comfortably."

Valerie and Chetan followed Rigel and Karen to an elevator that took them to a conference room on the top deck, with panoramic views glinting through the windows.

"Would you like a drink?" Rigel asked, as he poured himself one. Both Valerie and Chetan declined. Rigel took a sip of his drink. "So what brings the WCF to the *Water Shadow*?"

"We understand that one of your companies owns a DNA spectrometer," Valerie said.

"Which company? I own many and imagine a number of them might have purchased such a device."

"You only own one DNA spectrometer," Valerie said. "It was purchased by the Tripod Group."

"This is a very specialized machine, used for only one purpose," Chetan added.

"I know what it's used for," Rigel said arrogantly. "What I don't know is why it matters to the WCF that TTG owns one. Did you find some kind of DNA watermark somewhere you shouldn't have?"

Valerie could see that despite his flamboyant playboy demeanor, Rigel Wright was quite intelligent and well informed. "Are you familiar with the natural-gas well problems in northern Africa and Australia?"

"Of course. Two of the largest fields in the world have halted production." He took another sip from his glass. "I can't say I've been adversely affected by it, though. My energy stock portfolio is up thirty percent in the last week. What does this have to do with TTG and a DNA spectrometer?"

"We believe that someone intentionally sabotaged the gas fields," Valerie said. "We have evidence that the gas supply was contaminated."

"How do you contaminate a natural-gas source?" Rigel asked.

Chetan pulled out his PCD. "With this," he said, projecting an image of the nanite. "This is a—"

"An altered methanophiles cell," Rigel interrupted. He took a step closer to get a better look, then turned to Karen. "Fascinating. Are you seeing this?"

"I am," Karen said, rising from her chair at the exquisitely polished conference table. "This didn't come from one of our labs."

Valerie looked at her. "I'm surprised that your assistant is so familiar with the work that is going on in your biotech companies," she said.

"Sorry about the confusion," Rigel said. "Karen is actually one of my attorneys. She oversees our patent portfolio."

Karen smiled at Valerie.

"And you've never seen this thing before?" Valerie asked.

"No. But it is creatively manufactured. What has it been modified to do?" Rigel asked Chetan.

"It ingests methane and also oxygen. As it consumes the gas, it multiplies at an incredible rate. A three-to-one ratio over five seconds. It also dies shortly afterward."

Rigel seemed confused. "What does it do with the gas it consumes?"

"Retains it," Chetan said. "No by-product is released."

Rigel raised his eyebrows. "So a perfect vacuum is created. What an intriguing modification. I can envision some very interesting applications."

"You mean deadly applications," Valerie said. "Maybe even an application that would send the value of your portfolio skyrocketing."

"I don't need the money," Rigel said.

"What about the power?" Valerie asked. "I recently learned that the desire for control keeps people like you up at night."

"I think this meeting is over," Karen broke in. Her smile was gone.

Rigel motioned for her to sit back down. "I find Valerie's forthright manner very appealing . . . and invigorating."

"If I were you, Ms. Perrot," Karen said, "I would be investigating whoever would benefit most from the disruption of the natural-gas supply."

"Most likely a direct competitor," Rigel added. "Maybe an old oil company looking to reestablish its dominance in the world. Maybe a new one with some emerging technology. . . ."

"You mean a company that might be trying to leverage its alternative energy technology with some help from Mr. Montez?" There was a tense pause. Valerie could see that her knowledge of the Tripod Group's association with the Mexican archaeologist had surprised them. "I think a company with the ability to extract electricity out of thin air would have a strong motive to see the gas fields destroyed."

"Our work with Mr. Montez is far from completion and even farther from commercial application," Rigel stated. "Years, maybe even a decade."

"Why would we destroy an important energy source that we're not in a position to replace?" Karen asked. "That would go against every lesson of Business 101."

"The WCF is free to investigate me, the Tripod Group, or any of my companies and foundations," Rigel said. "I assure you that you will turn up nothing criminal. In fact, I was invited this morning to attend an emergency meeting that President Salize is holding tomorrow to discuss solutions to the energy crisis."

Valerie heard her PCD ping. A message had arrived from Sylvia. She took a moment to read it, then turned to Chetan. "Can you bring up the BBC-SKY news feed?"

The projection of the nanite was replaced by the image of a newscaster beside a large screen showing people running down a street where buildings were shaking and collapsing.

"Fifteen earthquakes—perhaps more—struck around the world nineteen minutes ago," the newscaster stated. "Scientists cannot yet explain how so many temblors could occur simultaneously. Areas west of Cairo and east of Mexico City, which were both hit hard last week, have suffered again. Here in the U.K., a modest seismic event was reported near the city of Salisbury, where—" The newscaster touched his earpiece. "We can now confirm that China, India, and an archipelago in the South Pacific have also been shaken by earthquakes." The images behind the reporter changed to depict people lined up at hospitals and medical pods. "Outside the earthquake zones, hospital administrators and medical professionals are reporting an influx of patients complaining of excruciating headaches. Due to the volume of complaints, the Centers for Disease Control is launching an investigation into whether the headaches could be related to the earthquakes. The CDC has written off as speculation questions as to why the majority of the people seeking treatment for the headaches are pregnant women. President Salize of the NAF, who will be addressing the nation about the energy crisis two days from now, has not yet commented on the recent catastrophes or concerns that another Great Disruption is upon us. Government offices and news organizations, including this one, have been receiving a high volume of calls from citizens worried that another is imminent because of—"

"Turn it off," Valerie said. Chetan did as she ordered.

Rigel looked at Karen. "I think I'll be going to that meeting," he said.

Valerie remained silent, wondering about Logan and her father, who were in Mexico.

Rigel looked at Karen. "Maybe we should have gotten into the earthquake insurance business," he said sarcastically.

Karen turned to Valerie. "It looks like your president has a great many problems to deal with. And I suspect that means that you do, too."

35

How can anyone have power over you if they don't
understand your motivations?

—THE CHRONICLES OF SATRAYA

NOVACON ISLAND, 6:06 P.M. LOCAL TIME, MARCH 23, 2070

"Aye," said one man.

"Aye," said another. Four more people expressed agreement.

Dario stood in the spacious conference room of the NovaCon facility. He was flanked by two men on his left and two women on his right.
"Catherine, you have the final vote."

Catherine and six others sat in high-back crimson leather chairs with
polished mahogany arms and arranged in a circle. Yinsir sat to her left,
and Klaus was next to him. Ilia sat across the circle from Catherine, and
Rashidi stood stoically behind one of the five empty chairs. To the left
of each was a small table holding a carafe of water and a glass turned
upside down on a white linen cloth. A small wooden mallet also lay on
each table.

"Aye," Catherine responded.

"Then it is unanimous and confirmed," Dario announced. "I present to all of you the newest members of Reges Hominum." Simultaneously, the seated individuals picked up their mallets and struck the

ends of their armrests in a show of approval. Dario motioned to those standing next to him to take their seats, then made his way to the chair behind which Rashidi was standing, his metal prosthetics humming as he walked. The twelve chairs were positioned around the circumference of a ten-meter circle. The ceiling was slightly vaulted. Five illuminated orbs floated above the group, providing light. The opaque floor beneath them looked like a sheet of black ice. The shutters on the windows were closed, and two tall doors were opposite each other on two of the four walls. "Long live Reges Hominum," Dario said, before lowering himself into his chair.

"Long live Reges Hominum!" the eleven others repeated.

"As all of you know, the plan to replace the world's electrical supply is under way."

"I still do not understand what you are proposing to replace it with," said one of the newly appointed members, an elegantly dressed woman with shoulder-length curly brown hair. While there was not a line on her face, her eyes lacked the sparkle of youth. "Catherine graciously articulated what we were doing but did not detail *how* we were doing it."

"Yes, Madame Sinclair," Dario said, "it is time to unveil the Nova-Con device to all of you before we unveil it to the world." He pressed a button on the control panel attached to his chair. The shutters retracted from the windows, revealing a view of the island. The shiny dark floor beneath their feet turned translucent, causing everyone a moment of trepidation as they observed what appeared to be volcanic lava flowing well beneath them. "I had the same reaction when I first saw it. But fear not," Dario reassured them. "We are safe. This floor is made of a one-meter-thick specialized heat-reflective polymer." He stomped his foot on the floor, his metal prosthetics humming loudly as he did so. "It will protect us from the thousand-degree lava that is flowing below us."

"This is the project that Dario and I have been funding for the last six years," Catherine said. "This is the next step in energy exploration."

"The pyramid you saw as you entered NovaCon headquarters is more than an architectural marvel of someone's fancy," Dario explained.

"It is an energy device. If you look down, you can see the nuclear core and, below that, the flowing lava of Ponta do Pico."

"This device will allow us to harness all the electricity that the world could ever consume," Catherine said. "When fully functional, this will be the world's first zero-point fracturing node."

"Zero-point what?" asked a man with a deep Southern drawl. He moved forward in his chair, adjusting his large golden belt buckle and running his fingers along his bushy horseshoe mustache.

"They are talking about free energy, Mr. Harlen," Madame Sinclair said. "Scientists have been chasing that myth since before the Great Disruption. I know about it firsthand. My family spent a king's ransom when a man once told us he could somehow extract energy directly out of the air. My father was a fool to have listened to him."

"It is not a myth," Catherine said. "What you see around you is working. The power to run this island is coming from the device itself. There are no power lines running from either Spain or Portugal, I can assure you."

"The president of the NAF has called an emergency meeting to discuss the energy crisis," Dario said. "Catherine will be leaving here shortly for Washington to attend Enrique's meeting. She will unveil our energy device and announce that NovaCon is prepared to fill the energy shortfall."

Yinsir chimed in. "Are you sure that is wise? Based on what I witnessed earlier, this energy device is not entirely ready."

Everyone looked to Dario for a response. "We have made contact with the individual who can sort out a few issues," he said. "Rashidi here will be accompanying Catherine to ensure cooperation."

"For our plan to work," Catherine said, "we will need certain types of assistance from our members."

"What kind of assistance?" Mr. Harlen asked.

"From you, Mr. Harlen," Dario said, "we require your vast land holdings. You see, we plan to build a great many more of these pyramids around the world."

"Will we then need to call you Pharaoh Dario the Second?" Klaus asked. The others in the group laughed, including Dario.

"I might have to build a much grander pyramid to bury myself in," Dario joked.

Just then, the door to the conference room opened, and two men entered, walking quickly to the center of the room. One of them had a hideously scarred face.

"Yes, Dario, I would love to see you buried in a pyramid," the man with the scarred face said, as he stood in front of Dario.

The other intruder eyed the group for anyone who posed a threat. He held a large silver gun in his right hand.

Dario tried to rise to his feet, but Rashidi, who was standing behind him, pushed him back into the chair. The man with the scarred face leaned down and looked coldly into Dario's eyes.

"Simon! You're supposed to be dead," Dario whispered. "How did you find this place? How did you get in?"

Simon pulled back his shirt sleeve to reveal a thin gold bracelet, then shook his head. "You really should be more careful about whom you hire," he said, glancing up at Rashidi.

Dario looked over at Yinsir, who sat with a blank, cold look on his face, unlike the others, who appeared surprised by what was taking place. Yinsir was the one who had recommended Rashidi to him.

"I was told you were dead," Dario repeated, realizing the extent of Yinsir's betrayal. "I only meant to keep moving the group along."

"Without me, you mean," Simon said, "If you were going to move on, you should have done so with another group of people."

"Another group?" Dario looked around the room. The others were all still and silent.

Simon straightened. "You're in my seat."

Rashidi took a large knife from his pocket and, in one swift motion, ran it across Dario's throat. The blood flowed, and Rashidi pushed Dario forward off the chair. His body struck the floor with a thud. The glow of the lava coming through the translucent floor eerily illuminated Dario's pooling blood. Simon stepped over his corpse and sat in his chair. He looked around at the faces of the members of Reges Hominum.

"I feel as if another vote is in order," Simon said. "I nominate myself as head of the order. What do you think, Catherine? I am told you were Dario's biggest supporter."

Kashta moved to stand behind Catherine's chair.

She took a deep breath before speaking. "It's too risky to bet against someone who somehow defies death," Catherine said, and then added, "I'd like to be the first to welcome you back, Simon."

Simon nodded and smiled and then looked at the others. "Don't worry, almost everything that Dario has told you is true," he said coldly. "Everything, that is, except the part about me being dead."

36

Love is not a process.

—THE CHRONICLES OF SATRAYA

PEEL CASTLE, 10:10 A.M. LOCAL TIME, MARCH 24, 2070

Bukya led the way through the unusually quiet corridors of Peel Castle. With his paw, he pushed open the door to a bedroom in the west wing.

"Bukya's back!" Halima exclaimed.

The dog quickly trotted over to the four-poster bed positioned between a set of floor-to-ceiling windows. He placed his front paws on the edge of the mattress and gave Anita a loving but slobbery kiss. Halima, who was also lying on the bed, near Anita's feet, moved closer to Bukya and rubbed his ears. Anita's friend Britney, who was helping Anita deal with the lingering effects of a terrible headache, sat in a chair next to the bed. Lawrence, who was also seated nearby, set down the book he was reading and looked at the doorway. He knew that Bukya did not travel alone.

The door to the bedroom opened wider. "We were wondering where the denizens of Peel Castle had gone to," Sebastian said in his typically calm, comforting voice. Halima leaped from the bed and rushed over to greet him. "It would seem that Bukya has unraveled that mystery."

Sebastian squatted down and gave Halima a hug. Anita was sitting up, holding a cup of steaming rose-colored liquid in her hand. She was wearing a red sweatshirt adorned with the emblem of the Isle of Man University. Her hair was pulled back in a ponytail, and a blanket covered her legs. "I see that Sara has brewed you one of her famous elixirs."

"It seems to be working," Anita said. "I'm feeling much better."

"She got a terrible headache yesterday when she was playing Devavani," Halima said, pointing at Anita's violin case, which lay on a table in the sitting area of the bedroom. "She went out of tune again."

Anita took a sip from her cup. "It was more intense than the last time."

"I was concerned," Lawrence said. "So I called Dr. Henry. By the time he got here, Anita's headache had abated, and he couldn't find anything wrong. Nonetheless, based on the severity of the pain, he prescribed a couple of days of bed rest."

"Halima told me that before you left, you mentioned that the voice of the earth had been disrupted," Anita said. "Did that happen again?"

"Has Sarvagita changed somehow?" Halima added.

"Does it have something to do with the Munch picture?" Britney said shyly.

Sebastian grinned; he looked at the three of them. "I see all of you have been busy." He took a seat by the edge of the bed. Bukya comfortably positioned himself at his side. "Yes, the voice of the earth is being disrupted. And yes, the picture is very much tied to it. Sarvagita is more than just a metaphysical convenience; it is an empirical and scientific phenomenon in this physical world. Without it, life on earth would be very different, and most species would not thrive here. Sarvagita is a vibration and a resonance that is key to everything."

"That's what Uncle Lawrence told us, too," Halima said.

"I've never heard the earth speak to me," Britney said.

"The first question to consider," Sebastian offered, "is if you would even understand the language of the earth if you heard it. Think of it this way. When we speak, the words that usher forth are simply vibrations put in a particular sequence. When we are young, we are taught by our parents and teachers how to create and recognize these patterns. We call it language, and we use it to communicate our thoughts and desires to those around us. When you and Anita are at university and sitting in a crowded place, I would imagine there are people from all around the world speaking in a variety of languages. Even though your ear hears every conversation around you, your brain only focuses on what you understand—the language you can process. Perhaps even a voice of a particular frequency; I'm certain you would be able to pick out Anita's voice from across a crowded room. And so it is with Sarvagita, the earth's voice. Your ear has the capability of picking up all sound; it is your brain that has not been trained to process all of it."

"And you can train yourself to do this?" Britney asked. "Hear the earth?"

"Not only hear the earth but speak to it, too," Sebastian replied. "Have you not heard the story of the American Indian witch doctor who brought the rains upon the lands?" Britney nodded. "He had to do more than just say words. He was trained in the art of shadow talking, trained to communicate with nature, among other things."

"What's shadow talking?" Anita asked.

Sebastian smiled. "That is a subject for another day," he said.

"So what does the earth say when it talks to you?" Halima asked.

"Have you ever wondered how animals know that an earthquake is imminent? Or how they know that a storm is approaching when the sky is sunny and clear? How do birds know which direction is south?"

"The earth is telling them," Anita suggested.

"Yes. And the earth is also speaking to you. But its language is not English or French or German. The language of the earth is a very low-sounding vibration."

Halima looked up at Lawrence. "The Schumann resonance," she said.

Sebastian smiled. "I see that Lawrence has advanced your knowledge of Sarvagita very well. Science claims that the Schumann resonance is constant, but that is not correct. The voice of the earth is changing at every moment. Each time a new creature is born, the resonance is modified. And anytime a creature passes away, the resonance is modified again. The tools and instruments of science are not yet capable of measuring such infinitesimal shifts. Only the most sensitive of beings are attuned to these alterations. Those masters, whom history speaks of and who have reached the zenith of their understanding, know when any creature is born and when a single leaf falls from the tree. They hear the change in the voice of the earth."

"Like you," Halima said.

"No," Sebastian said humbly. "Those whose statues stand in the Arcis Chamber: Yeshua, Buddha, Germaine . . ."

"Don't forget the Lady of Light," Halima added.

"Yes, her, too. All of them are able to hear and understand the language of Sarvagita. But it is important to remember that each of us hears the voice of the earth to some degree; it is just that some of us are more sensitive than others."

"Is that why not everyone is affected by shifts in the resonance?" Britney asked.

"Yes."

"But musicians are?" Anita asked.

"Musicians in particular. You, and those like you, are more reliant on Sarvagita and the Schumann resonance than you know. When you play your violin and reach that moment of singularity of mind described in the *Chronicles*, you have opened yourself up to the voice of nature. Some have mistakenly correlated singularity of mind with silence, but I assure you, it is filled with treasures that could tempt even the richest of kings."

"'The music is not in the notes but in the silence between them,'" Anita quoted in a contemplative voice. "Mozart had it right, didn't he?"

"Yes, he understood," Sebastian said. "Every creature in the world reacts to the voice of the earth to varying degrees. Whatever has been disrupting the resonance is growing stronger. Yesterday many more people felt the change. If the disruption to the Schumann resonance continues, eventually everyone will be affected."

Lawrence said, "The news reports from around the Isle stated that a large portion of those who sought medical treatment were pregnant women."

Sebastian nodded slowly. "That is of great concern. The amniotic fluid within the womb of a woman is very sensitive to the Schumann resonance. It acts as an amplification chamber for the growing fetus. The amniotic fluid is a conductor of sound and vibration. Food is not the only nourishment required by a child growing inside his mother's womb."

"That is why expectant parents often play music for a child who is still in the womb," Lawrence said. "And why mothers sing lullabies and why people are so moved to place their hands gently on a pregnant woman's belly and whisper welcoming words."

"That is correct," Sebastian said. "Expectant mothers fell ill yesterday because their unborn children were trying to communicate to them that something was wrong in their environments."

"What will happen to the fetuses if the resonance continues to be disrupted?" Anita asked.

Sebastian's silence answered her question.

"What about animals?" Halima asked. "What about bees, and ants, and squirrels, and—"

"And horses," Britney interrupted. "What about Biscuit?"

"All living things are touched by Sarvagita," Sebastian answered. Anita put her hand over Britney's to comfort her friend. "None is free from its wonder. You cannot tinker with the fabric of life. It is a lesson that has been taught over and over again throughout time."

"You make it sound as if this is no accident," Anita said. "Has this happened before? Has the voice of the earth been tampered with before?"

"Yes," Lawrence answered her. "A very long time ago, in a forgotten past, in a place that no longer exists."

"There was an island in the ocean beyond the Pillars of Hercules," Sebastian explained. "An ocean we now refer to as the Atlantic."

"You're talking about Atlantis, aren't you?" Anita asked. "The city that Plato wrote about."

"The city existed long before Plato was born," Lawrence said.

"What happened to it?" Halima asked eagerly.

"Atlantis was home to people of great culture and scientific understanding," Sebastian related. "The city was laid out in concentric circles of alternating land and water canals. A main water causeway connecting the circles led from the sea to the sensational citadel at the center of the city. Ships of all kinds arrived with treasures and spices from around the globe. At the height of this civilization, Atlantis was a beacon of prosperity to the rest of the world."

"That doesn't sound bad at all," Britney said.

"It wasn't bad then," Sebastian continued. "But in the citadel, which was shaped like a mighty pyramid, were stored the treasure troves of Atlantis. And in the civilization's later days, the citadel was converted into something far different."

"Something that led to the downfall and destruction of the entire Atlantean civilization," Lawrence said. "They endowed the pyramid with special powers."

"They gave it the ability to extract energy from the resonance of the earth," Sebastian said. "With that energy, they were able to control the weather and induce crops to grow at an alarming rate, and there were rumors of healing chambers that used electricity."

"Electrotherapy," Britney said. "One of our professors was talking about that the other day."

"That's right. While construction of the pyramid should have been a great resource for all of mankind, it was sanctioned during the reign of a king who became corrupted by the information that was imparted to him. It was information he should have never received."

"What information?" Anita asked.

"A symbol," Sebastian said. "One that should have remained hidden."

"Who gave it to him?" Halima asked.

"This is beginning to sound like the story you told about Alexander the Great and the king of Magadha," Anita said. "Is this another story where one of the hidden symbols from the *Chronicles* was revealed?"

"What hidden symbols?" Britney asked, completely engrossed and not wanting to be left behind in the story.

Anita looked at her. "You can't tell anyone about any of this."

"Who would believe me?"

"True," Anita said. "But don't tell anyone."

Sebastian smiled at their banter. "The symbol is called the Rokmar. It was given, along with instructions on how to activate it, to the king by the very same brotherhood that would eventually have to destroy him."

"You see," Lawrence said, picking up the explanation, "because the king did not take the time to fully understand the Rokmar, he created a device that could indeed extract electrical power from the atmosphere, but it also had terrible side effects."

"It interrupted the song of the earth." Anita understood.

"Yes," Sebastian said. "It produced radical waves that interfered with the Schumann resonance and thus interfered with nature."

"The result of which is exactly what we are experiencing today," Sebastian said. "The earth is convulsing, and everything that lives upon it is feeling that discomfort."

"Why did that brotherhood give the king such information?" Anita asked. "Didn't they understand that the most powerful of the Satraya symbols are veiled for a reason? What leads those who purport to be wise to commit such careless, irresponsible acts?"

Sebastian grinned. "That irresponsible brotherhood is the brotherhood of my ancestry."

The expression on Anita's face did not soften but actually hardened. "Are you telling me that *Enuntiato de Tutela*, the very words we follow, was written by those who were derelict in their duties of stewardship to the world?"

"No, not exactly. *The Manifesto of the Guardians* was indeed written by our ancestors but only after they were cast out of the brotherhood. The lineage from which I was born understood that mankind is to be nurtured toward realization and is not simply entitled to it. But there were other members who believed that quantum jumps in knowledge would serve the people better."

"Members of what?" Britney asked.

"Ever since man has walked on this earth," Sebastian said, "there have been those entrusted with its guardianship. Throughout the annals of time, they have been known by many names: the Schintati Order, the Council of Light, the White Brotherhood, to name a few."

"In recent history, you might have heard other names," Lawrence added. "Such as the Rosicrucians, the Illuminati, the Freemasons . . ."

"The members of these groups reached certain levels of understanding concerning the divine nature of man," Sebastian explained. "From time to time, when needed, they step forward to change the course of humanity."

"Doesn't seem like they do a very good job," Britney said. Anita gave her a disapproving look. "I'm just saying."

"There is some truth to your observation," Sebastian said. "It is a difficult task guiding humanity and yet allowing people's free will to flourish."

"Which of the groups do you belong to?" Halima asked.

"We," Anita corrected, turning her gaze to Sebastian. "We're a part of whatever group you belong to."

Sebastian smiled. "None of them," he said. "Our group is without a name, and our history is without a marketer."

"So what happened to the king of Atlantis?" Halima asked.

"When the king refused to shut down the device," Lawrence said, "those who provided him with the secret knowledge had no choice but to sink the island into the sea and into oblivion."

"How did they do such a thing?" Anita asked. "How do you sink an island?"

"It was another one of the Satraya symbols," Halima said, "wasn't it?"

Sebastian smiled cryptically. "A particular device was used to send a particular signal along a particular sonorous line."

"Causing the island, along with the pyramid, to implode," Lawrence added.

"And what is a sonorous line?" Britney asked.

"Think of it as the nervous system of the earth," Lawrence replied.

"What device did they use?" Anita asked. "And what signal did they send? Has someone recently built a pyramid similar to the one in Atlantis? Is that why I am losing my ability to hear and play music?"

"I cannot say," Sebastian said. "But it is clear that something or someone is wreaking havoc with the Schumann resonance."

"Then we have to do something," Anita said emphatically.

"Like the brotherhood did something for Atlantis?" Lawrence asked.

"If we must," Anita quickly responded. "We cannot allow the earth to suffer like this."

"I agree that it must be stopped," Sebastian said. "But not with the kind of action you are alluding to. It is dangerous to tap the power of the Rokmar. Even with knowledge and proper instruction, there are risks. Unlike the old brotherhood, we will carry forward in trust. We will trust that the good people of this world can and will rise to the moment."

"We, *too*, are part of the good people of the earth," Anita retorted, dissatisfied with Sebastian's answer.

"Anita, my dear," Lawrence said, knowing his daughter, "heed Sebastian's words."

Britney nodded.

Anita gave both her father and Britney an exasperated look before turning back to Sebastian. "Is the old clan who gave the king information still in existence? Are they somehow behind this?"

"I do not know," Sebastian answered.

"So what do we do?" Anita asked impatiently.

"You, my dear, are to continue your studies. And that goes for you, too," he said to Halima. "When the moment is right, you will be called into service."

"How will we know?" Halima asked.

Sebastian smiled. "Focus on the Satraya Flame, and use the Jaladarz as I've instructed. More information will arrive when it is ready to arrive."

37

*You should start every day with a smile and end every day with
thoughts of why you did so.*

—THE CHRONICLES OF SATRAYA

WASHINGTON, D.C., 9:00 A.M. LOCAL TIME, MARCH 24, 2070

Valerie hit a few buttons on her PCD and showed Logan the video that
she took in Château Dugan's dungeon and the surrounding rooms.

"What's all that writing on the wall?" Logan asked.

"Not exactly sure," Valerie said. "But it looks like people were kept
down there against their will."

The video played on. Logan and Valerie sat across from each other
at a table in a small meeting room at the north side of the Cube. They
had met up at the WCF lab after Logan, Mr. Perrot, Madu, and Nadine had flown in from Mexico City. Valerie and Chetan had returned
only a few hours earlier from their visits to Château Dugan and Rigel
Wright. After Logan and Valerie were finished sharing information at
the Cube, they planned to take Mr. Perrot and Madu to the Calhoun
Medical Center so they could see Sumsari Baltik before the Council of
Satraya commemoration that evening. Mr. Perrot, Madu, and Nadine
were waiting anxiously at a nearby hotel.

"Here is the hidden vault we discovered," Valerie said. "I was certain that we were going to find the missing three sets of the *Chronicles*, but they weren't there. I'm more convinced than ever that Simon and Andrea had others helping them with the Freedom Day plot. Do you remember that e-mail message Fendral Hitchlords wrote to a man named Dario that we found last year?"

"Yes, the one in the old FBI archive retrieved from the Akasha Vault that dated from before the Great Disruption," Logan replied.

"Well, it's gone. The message is no longer in the archive."

"It has to be there. Did it get moved to another system?"

"No." Valerie looked up at him. "It's been expunged."

"By whom? Someone in the government?"

"I don't know." She shook her head. "But we did find something else in Simon's vault that you need to see." She shut off the video and slid an orange envelope across the table.

Logan opened the envelope and pulled out two photographs. One was of his mother, and the other was of his father. The disturbed look on Logan's face reflected his inner anguish. Simon, it seemed, was still taunting Logan from the grave.

"Believe me, this was not what I was expecting to find at the Château," Valerie said. "If anything, I thought we would discover information about who might have been helping Simon and Andrea with the Freedom Day plot. If Simon had any pictures of your parents, I would have expected them to have come from the time of the first Council forty years ago. But they didn't. Look at the date on the photos." Valerie turned over the one of Logan's mother. "I grabbed these before the WCF team in Switzerland could enter them into evidence."

Logan nodded in thanks as he read the date: *July 21, 2066, Freedom Day Rally, New Chicago.* "That's only a couple of months before my parents were murdered," he said. He looked more closely at the photo of his father. "This was definitely taken in New Chicago. You can see the Cloud Gate in the background. I took the kids there for dinner the other day."

"We found something else," Valerie said, pulling out a handwritten letter from the orange envelope and handing it to him. "The return address on the envelope says it also came from New Chicago."

"That's a few blocks from the house," Logan said, alarmed as he continued to read the letter.

"We ran the address," Valerie said. "It's a rental property. Sold in 2067. We're attempting to track down the previous owner." Logan's eyes widened. "What is it?"

"RJ," Logan said in a low voice. "My mother mentions an RJ in a few of her recordings." Logan looked up at Valerie with dread in his eyes. "And your father told me that there was a young man named RJ who was a Forgotten One and arrived in Washington with my mother." Logan's mind raced, trying to reconcile the photos, the note, and his mother's recordings. "Do you remember when we confronted Simon in India? He denied killing my parents. Remember his saying to us that someone else—"

"'Performed that necessary deed,'" Valerie finished. "I remember. I also remember Simon's saying that it was *love* that might have gotten your parents killed."

Logan looked at the note. "Whoever wrote this might be the person Simon was alluding to. We need to figure out who RJ is."

Valerie nodded. "I'll have Chetan and Sylvia analyze the photos. They were taken with a plenoptic camera; we might be able to analyze something more out of them." She gathered up the pictures and the letter and put them back in the envelope. "The problem is, I'm not supposed to be working on this case. My team is supposed to be completely focused on the natural-gas investigation. Don't worry, though," she said, moving around the table and kissing the top of Logan's head, then looking into his eyes. "I'm not going to let this go until we figure it out."

Before he could answer, there was a knock on the door. Valerie reached over and opened it, and Chetan poked his head into the room. "We have something you need to see," he said.

Logan stood and slung his backpack over his shoulder. He and

Valerie followed Chetan to where Sylvia was sitting. The motionless image of a single nanite was projected in front of her.

"Do you remember Mr. Wright mentioned activating and deactivating the nanites?" Chetan asked. "Well, I think we've made some progress."

"We're still working to isolate the exact signal," Sylvia said, "but we're getting close."

"We've isolated one of the nanites from samples we received from the North African Commonwealth," Chetan said, and he continued before Valerie could protest. "Don't worry, we've taken all the precautions this time."

Sylvia pressed a few keys on the control board in front of her. "Check this out. If we create an ELF of seventy-nine point six-five-four hertz . . ."

Everyone watched as the nanite seemed to come alive and move around in random directions.

"It appears that these nanites are programmed to activate when a certain ELF signal hits them," Chetan explained.

"How do you turn them off?" Valerie asked.

"You just kill the signal," Sylvia said. She hit a control, and the nanite went motionless. "These things are really simple; they're either on or off."

"We found something else," Chetan said, taking a seat next to Sylvia. "Maybe the clue we have been looking for. As you know, the Akasha Vault satellites are constantly recording telemetry off the surface of the earth."

"Included in the telemetry are ELF signals," Sylvia said. She activated another display, which projected jagged lines moving from left to right.

"It looks like a heartbeat monitor," Logan commented.

"It sort of is," Chetan said. "Extremely low frequencies, or ELFs, are a common occurrence on the earth. This yellow line represents the normal ELF range of the planet, between three hertz and sixty hertz."

"What is that straight dark blue line?" Logan asked.

"It is a constant signal known as the Schumann resonance," Sylvia said. "It always stays at seven point eight-six hertz. It is the frequency that exists between the surface of the earth—"

"And the ionosphere," Logan finished. Everyone turned to him, wondering how he knew that. He shrugged. "I learned it when I was down in Mexico yesterday."

Chetan resumed. "As you can see, unlike the steady blue line, the yellow lines fluctuate and have peaks and valleys. But they remain within the normal range. Now, watch as I move the time lapse forward." Chetan slowly slid his hand across a set of controls. The images of the gas field and the graph advanced in unison. "There's the spike," he said, pointing to the display.

"And ELF at seventy-nine point six-five-four hertz is detected," Sylvia said.

"That's the same frequency that activated the nanites," Logan said.

Chetan nodded. "If we advance further, we will see that as the radical ELF continues, the gas wells begin to shake, until tower two implodes." He continued to slide his hand. "Twenty seconds after the collapse, the wave disappears, and once again, we are within the normal ELF range."

"So someone planted the nanites at the site," Valerie clarified, "and then activated them by turning on some kind of signal?"

"That's correct," Sylvia said, and Chetan nodded in agreement.

"Can we tell where the signal originated?" Valerie asked. "How close would whoever activated the signal have to be to the natural-gas well?"

"Based on the satellite readings, the signal was localized within the vicinity of the imploded well tower in a radius of about one hundred meters," Chetan replied. "The device was at the center of that area. It could have been on a timer or activated remotely. Which means whoever did it might not have been on the premises. We have no way of telling. Either way, the device is probably buried under tons of rubble now."

"What about the well in western Australia?" Valerie asked. "Have you been able to determine if the same thing happened there?"

"We have, and the answer is yes." Chetan brought up the image of another graph. "The exact same ELF was detected there just before the implosion of that well."

Valerie thought for a moment. "We have some answers, but I'm not sure if we are any closer to knowing who did this or why."

"How would you test something like this?" Logan asked suddenly. Everyone looked at him, not understanding his question. "If I were building a killer machine, I'd want to test it out first, right?" Logan set his backpack down and sat in a chair next to Chetan. "Just like what Simon and Andrea did with their frequency generator in that Indian village."

"That is an interesting thought," Chetan said. "In theory, we should be able to search for seventy-nine-point-six-five-four-hertz ELF anomalies."

"I would imagine the initial engineering of these nanites took place in a laboratory," Sylvia countered. "Which means that those ELFs would have been isolated and not detectable. But if any real-world tests were run, we could theoretically detect them. Follow me—we need to use Bertha."

"Who is Bertha?" Logan asked.

"That's the nickname they've given the big projected image of the earth over there," Chetan told him.

Sylvia led everyone to a control pod near the large display of the earth. "Hi, Darvis," Sylvia said. "Any chance we can get hold of Bertha?"

Logan looked at the revolving image of the earth. Numbers, letters, and indicators of all sorts were sprinkled over the surface. "Wow, that is some map," he said. The continents of North and South America slowly rotated into view. "I'm not sure how anyone can make heads or tails of it."

Darvis rose from his chair, and Sylvia took his place. "Yeah, it can get very confusing when all the telemetry is displayed," Darvis said.

"We track everything from satellite positioning to aircraft patterns. We also bring up weather and atmospheric conditions."

"Which of these controls brings up the ELF map?" Sylvia asked. Darvis leaned over and showed her.

"See all those red markers?" Valerie said. "Those are where the earthquakes have been taking place." She pointed to the two red markers near Mexico City. "The larger one is the quake you and my father experienced."

Logan looked at other markers on the globe as it continued to rotate. "The earthquake markers seem to be clustered in certain areas. Most spots have three or more indicators."

"Yes, we've noticed that pattern," Darvis said. "Each time a rash of earthquakes strikes, they occur in the same locations. During the last round, a few additional locations popped up."

As the globe rotated, the Atlantic Ocean came into view, along with the western coast of Africa. Logan pointed to a spot in the ocean due west of Portugal. "Looks like a large number took place there."

"Not too surprising," Chetan said. "That is the Azores archipelago. There is a tremendous amount of volcanic activity there. During the Great Disruption, all the islands were flooded, and the inhabitants had to flee. After the disruption, the volcanic activity increased, and it remains strong to this day. Those islands are uninhabited. Volcanic and seismic activity go hand-in-hand." Darvis nodded in agreement. "Any progress on explaining the epicenter-less earthquakes?" Chetan asked him.

Darvis shook his head. "No, it is still a mystery."

The ELF signal map was now projected on the rotating globe. "There we go," Sylvia said.

"What are you guys looking for?" Darvis asked.

"ELFs at seventy-nine point six-five-four hertz," Chetan replied.

Different-colored indicators showed up on the globe as the African and European continents rotated away and the continent of Asia appeared. Sylvia leaned back in her chair and gazed at the results. "We're looking at two months' worth of data. Any ELFs of seventy-nine point six-five-four hertz are identified by those orange markers."

"There must be more than two hundred orange markers," Valerie observed. "It's going to take forever to investigate all of them."

"Do we have a choice?" Sylvia asked, sounding resigned.

"I thought you said the Schumann line was always supposed to be straight," Logan said, referring to the fact that the dark blue line and the yellow lines contained a series of closely grouped spikes.

"That is strange," Sylvia said. She pressed a few buttons, stopping the rotation of the globe and the time lapse of the ELF graphic. "The spikes don't line up with any seventy-nine-point-six-five-four-hertz anomalies."

"Nor do they line up with the times the gas wells collapsed," Chetan added.

"Must be some kind of glitch in the readings," Sylvia said, about to resume the search for the 79.654-hertz signal.

"Wait," Darvis said. "The Schumann spike may not line up with your gas well problems, but they do line up with the last round of earthquakes."

"What does that mean?" Valerie asked.

"Could you expand the view for the Schumann reading?" Darvis requested. "Make it for four days ago, when we first started to see an unusual amount of seismic activity . . . There, look at that. Every spike in the resonance correlates to when we detected seismic activity."

"Since when does the Schumann resonance have anything to do with earthquakes?" Sylvia asked, looking at Darvis.

"I have no idea," he said. "I've never seen anything like this before."

Logan pointed at the globe, which had stopped with the Atlantic Ocean in view. "Look at the Azores. Why are there so many orange markers there? Does it have something to do with the volcanic activities you mentioned?"

"No," Chetan said. "While the Azores do have a great deal of earthquakes due to the volcano in the area, those ELF markers shouldn't be there."

"I think you guys might have found a good place to start your analysis," Valerie suggested. "You may want to stay with them, Darvis. Looks like the earthquakes might be related to all this."

"Where are you two going?" Sylvia asked.

"We are heading to the Council of Satraya commemoration," Valerie said, a smile coming to her face. "My father has a big night ahead of him."

38

The limits of perception are just that, limits.
Push through them, and discover that they are illusions.

—THE CHRONICLES OF SATRAYA

WASHINGTON D.C., 12:20 P.M. LOCAL TIME, MARCH 24, 2070

"We would like to see a patient by the name of Sumsari Baltik," Valerie said to the elderly woman sitting at the reception desk at the Calhoun Medical Center. "I think the spelling of his last name is—"

"B-a-l-t-i-k," the receptionist cut in. "He's suddenly a popular man. Are all four of you here to see him? Because we only allow two visitors at a time."

Valerie pulled out her WCF badge. "Official business," she said.

"Did you say he was a popular man?" Mr. Perrot asked.

"Until two days ago, he hadn't had a single visitor in the nine months he's been here," the receptionist replied. "Then someone came to see him a day or two ago, and now the four of you." She turned to her communications pad and spoke into her headset, then handed them four visitor badges. "Dr. Bradley is coming to speak with you," she said.

"May I ask who else has visited Mr. Baltik?" Valerie said as she clipped the badge to the pocket on her suit jacket.

"I'm sorry, we aren't allowed to give out that information. Privacy laws. But seeing as this is official WCF business, you might try Dr. Bradley."

The doors behind the receptionist opened, and a man in scrubs approached them. "Good afternoon, I'm Walter Bradley, one of the center's senior physicians. I understand you wish to see Mr. Baltik?"

"That's correct," Valerie said, shaking his hand. "I'm Valerie Perrot, a senior agent of the World Crime Federation."

The doctor eyed Valerie's badge. "Follow me," he said, without hesitation.

They followed the doctor through a set of heavily fortified doors and down a long hallway to the main ward, where orderlies and nurses were manning the monitoring stations and three corridors branched to the sides. Logan could see patients in green gowns and slippers pacing up and down, others simply standing in the doorways of their rooms. All of them had pale, expressionless faces. A red light started flashing above a set of open metal doors at the end of one of the hallways. Two orderlies and a nurse quickly rose from their seats and darted down the hallway.

"Please wait here," the doctor said. "I will log you in."

"Do you think all these people were affected by the frequency pulse?" Logan asked, when the doctor walked off.

"Probably," Valerie whispered in answer. "I know the victims were rounded up and brought here first for further examination."

"They don't appear to be doing very well," Mr. Perrot said.

Madu looked at them both quizzically. "A frequency pulse?"

Logan didn't have a chance to explain; he was bumped from behind by someone tugging at his backpack. "Are you Benjamin?" Logan turned and saw that it was a young woman. "Are you Benjamin?" she asked again, more loudly.

"No, I'm Logan," he said gently, tightening his hold on his backpack. "What is your name?"

"Are you Benjamin!" the woman yelled, pulling harder and drawing the attention of the staff.

The doctor motioned to two orderlies, who rushed over and grabbed the woman by her arms. She struggled to free herself, blurting out nonsensical words and phrases, but they were finally able to take her away.

"Sorry about that," the doctor said.

"It's OK," Logan said. "I understand these are the people who were exposed to the frequency pulse last Freedom Day and experienced alterations in their DNA?"

The doctor looked at him hesitantly, without answering.

"It's all right, Doctor," Valerie said. "We're well aware of what took place at Compass Park on Freedom Day, even though the administration chose not to release the whole story to the public. It was my team, along with Logan and my father, who worked that case."

"So you're the ones," the doctor said softly. "They left all the names out of the reports that we received."

Valerie nodded. "Are you going to be able to help them? I had hopes an antidote would be created using the green pills we discovered at the hidden laboratory in North Carolina."

"It has been very tough," the doctor said. "As far as we can tell, the DNA alteration these people experienced is a one-way science."

"What about the rest of the population?" Logan asked. "Almost everyone in the world is still carrying those DNA collars."

"We're still working on that," the doctor said. "We've enlisted the help of other medical facilities around the world."

Logan and Valerie exchanged dissatisfied glances. The doctor could only avert his eyes, as he continued leading them down one of the three hallways.

"Were you here when Mr. Baltik had a visitor a day or two ago?" Valerie asked.

They stopped in front of a door marked 169. The doctor nodded. "His nephew came to see him two days ago. He brought his service dog, which Mr. Baltik seemed to enjoy as much as the piano we gave him when he first arrived. Music is the only thing that seems to calm him. I have to warn you, on that note, Mr. Baltik does not communicate very coherently."

The doctor turned and placed his right hand on a security pad. The door to room 169 opened, and he entered, followed by Valerie.

"Mr. Baltik?" the doctor said as he looked around the empty room. He checked the bathroom and then opened the closet door.

"Is there a problem?" Valerie asked, already knowing the answer.

"He's supposed to be here," the doctor said, his worry clear. "Please remain here while I find out where Mr. Baltik is."

The doctor left the room, giving the others room to enter. Logan's attention was instantly drawn to something on the wall above a vintage piano. It was a hand-drawn copy of *The Scream* by Edvard Munch.

Scattered on the floor were writing markers and their caps. The walls were covered with hand-drawn musical notes and some kind of mathematical formula, which was repeated over and over again. "Robert," Madu said, examining the scribbling. "This is the same note sequence that Sumsari spoke to me about more than forty years ago." He walked over to the piano, lightly touching the keys. "It went something like this . . ."

Logan recognized the melody instantly. "That's the Solokan progression," he said.

Madu looked at him. "How did you know that?"

"That's what Sumsari called it in one of my mother's recordings. There was another sequence, too."

"The Coffa progression," Madu said, and Logan nodded.

Dr. Bradley looked perturbed. He was followed by an orderly carrying an electronic clipboard. "It looks like Mr. Baltik has been transferred to our sister facility in Tennessee," he said.

"Transferred?" asked Valerie. "What do you mean, transferred? When?"

"This morning," the orderly replied, inspecting the display on his clipboard. "We received the transfer order at nine this morning, and a gentleman arrived at nine thirty to escort him. We didn't think much about it; transfers happen quite often."

The doctor still looked worried.

"What is it?" Logan asked.

"When we contacted the facility a few moments ago, we learned that Mr. Baltik still hadn't arrived there," the doctor said.

"Who authorized the transfer?" Valerie asked.

Dr. Bradley looked at the electronic clipboard. "A Dr. Kline," he said, staring at the name. "I've never heard of him."

"What about the person who took him? Have you tried to contact him?"

"I'd never seen him before," the orderly answered. "But he could have been a new guy."

"Why would someone take Mr. Baltik out of the Calhoun Center?" Logan asked.

"Probably for the same reason we wanted to speak to him," Madu suggested. "Might I ask if Mr. Baltik ever discussed what he was writing on the walls?"

"He started doing that a few days ago," the orderly said, "when he started complaining about severe headaches. He also did that drawing and hung it up there at about the same time."

"All right, Doctor, all privacy issues are out the door now," Valerie said seriously. "We need the name of the man who came to see Mr. Baltik a few days ago."

"Mr. Quinn. I think his first name was Sebastian," the doctor answered, and the others exchanged glances. "Yes, I remember him because of his service dog. Mr. Baltik really seemed to connect with the dog." The doctor pointed to the top of the piano. "And those," he said, "those are the military service tags he returned to Mr. Baltik."

39

One thing impossible in the Kingdom of Heaven is to be
abandoned. Someone will always be with you.

—THE CHRONICLES OF SATRAYA

GORNERGRAT, SWITZERLAND, 7:11 P.M. LOCAL TIME, MARCH 24, 2070

There was only one way to get to Gornergrat, and that was by railway. The once-popular Kulm Hotel, built in 1897, still stood on the
ridge in the Pennine Alps at an altitude of 3,120 meters, overlooking
the Gorner Glacier. A high-altitude research station and astronomical
observatories had been located in the north and south cupolas of the
building. During the Great Disruption of 2027, the open-air railway
leading to the majestic hotel had been destroyed. Gornergrat had become inaccessible, and the hotel had been abandoned. During the Rising, in 2056, a prominent Japanese family had purchased the defunct
hotel and converted it into a private retreat. The magnificent views of
the mountain peaks of Dom, Weisshorn, Mont Rosa, Lyskamm, and
the Matterhorn were no longer viewed by hordes of visitors. Only one
person had that privilege now.

"This is your new PCD and ID glass," Kashta said. "As you requested,
the world will now know you as Adrian Finch. Simon Hitchlords will
remain dead to the world."

"For now," Simon said, taking the thin Plexiglas card from Kashta and looking at it. He grimaced at his ID photo, which depicted him as he currently appeared, his face disfigured by burn scars. Simon was sitting behind a large Victorian twin pedestal desk. In front of him was the silver case that Kashta had retrieved from the Château. He looked up at Kashta. "Are you satisfied that your men searched the art studio adequately?"

"Yes, the books were not there," Kashta replied. "I suspect that Logan Ford is keeping them at his home. He was not at the studio, either."

"Catherine has informed me he and his children will be at the Council of Satraya offices this evening, attending a commemoration in honor of the original members of the Council."

"Shouldn't you be attending, then?" Kashta asked. "You, too, were an original member."

Simon laughed. "I'm not sure how welcome I would be."

Kashta shrugged. "I will have our men search the house tonight. If the books are there, we will find them."

Simon nodded, gazing at Kashta intently. "You will find them indeed. At any cost."

There was silence as Simon gestured for Kashta to leave. "Remember, the new staff will arrive tomorrow. As you instructed, none of them worked at the Château." Kashta walked out of the room.

Simon leaned forward and pulled the silver box closer to him. He typed an access code into the keypad on the box, and the lid opened. It had been a long while since he had seen his prized possessions. He carefully removed the three original copies of *The Chronicles of Satraya* and set them on the desk. Then he removed a blue journal. The bloody handprints on its cover reminded him of how the journal had come into his possession. Simon paged through Camden Ford's notes and paused when his attention was drawn to a short paragraph that Camden had written on June 23, 2036.

I still wonder about the blue orb I encountered in the woods and the enigmatic light it gave off. I wonder what it was, maybe even who it was. Deya has been very open about her healing experience; Madu is more reserved about sharing his. I think about the man named Giovanni Rast and the gold coins the orb gave him before Fendral killed him and stole his copy of the Chronicles. *I remember Marilyn and others saying that a strange blue light had come from the abandoned train car Giovanni called home. When they queried Giovanni about it, he could only say it had magically appeared from the books. I wonder if any of us will ever see the orb again.*

Maybe I can find the secret to the orb in the Satraya Flame or one of these hidden symbols. I am certain now that the partial symbol on the last page is meant to be fragmented. After three and a half years of effort, I still don't see anything when I look at the blank pages of Deya's and Madu's sets. I doubt that I will ever be granted access to Fendral's books. Maybe no one person is supposed to possess all of them. I can see how that could be a terrible thing.

Without the personal account of Logan's father, Simon would never have learned about the finer utility of the Satraya Flame and the veiled mysteries of the *Chronicles*: the hidden symbols on the blank pages that promised extraordinary abilities to anyone able to see them. He was particularly interested in Camden's mention of the blue orb, because he believed that the mysterious blue light he had seen when he'd fallen into the cremation pyre along the Ganges River had something to do with his surviving that ordeal. Could the mysterious blue light have been the light of the blue orb?

The journal entry was also a reminder of something that Simon would rather have forgotten: the day he overheard his father explain to Andrea why they had to abdicate their seats on the Council of Satraya. With Camden, Madu, and Deya already having resigned from the Council, Simon's father and his close friend Andrea Montavon could have seized control of the most influential group in the world at that time. But Fendral had been forced to admit to Andrea that he had stolen the books from a handyman named Giovanni Rast, who used to work for him. Logan's father, Camden, had somehow uncovered Fendral's crime and threatened to expose it if Fendral did not step down with the others. Simon had never told his father that he knew of his shame. Until recently, Simon had believed that his family's secret was safe. But the ruse perpetrated on him by Logan Ford and his comrades revealed that at least three others now knew the secret. All three of them would be at the commemoration, which was supposed to start in a few hours.

Simon gazed at the three original sets of the *Chronicles* on the table in front of him. Logan Ford possessed the fourth, which had once belonged to Deya. Simon disagreed with the conclusion Camden had drawn about one person possessing all four sets of the *Chronicles*. It would be excellent for one person to possess all four sets, as long as that one person was him.

Simon stood and walked over to the large picture window and looked out at the night sky. He reached into his pants pocket and removed a small plastic bag of painkillers. He took out one of the pills and popped it into his mouth, swallowing it whole without any water.

40

The finest moment of your life will be when you are alone and
still realize that you are loved.

—THE CHRONICLES OF SATRAYA

Logan and Valerie walked through the main entrance of the Council
of Satraya building, which was at the corner of 18th Street and New
York Avenue. Ms. Sally and the children were right behind them. The
iconic redbrick building, which had once been the Octagon Museum,
was given to the Council a few years after the Great Disruption to use as
a base of operations. It was here that Camden Ford and the other eleven
original Council members organized their mission to deliver copies of
the *Chronicles* to every corner of the world.

Wearing a black suit and a white collared shirt, Logan had spruced
himself up for the event. He had resisted Valerie's efforts to get him
to wear a tie, but after seeing how elegant she looked, he had relented
and was now sporting a red and black paisley silk tie. Valerie wore a
full-length black dress, with lace sleeves and a slit along its left side that
came up to just above her knee. Her hair was in an up-do, revealing a set
of amber and gold earrings that matched the necklace she was wearing.

Mr. Perrot, who had arrived earlier, was standing in the foyer with Madu and Nadine. "You look beautiful, my dear," he said to his daughter, giving her a kiss on the cheek. "All of you are well turned out this evening." He patted Logan on the shoulder, hugged the children, and shook hands with Ms. Sally, thanking them all for coming.

Adisa Kayin, the current head of the Council of Satraya, who was wearing his usual colorful African attire, quickly approached them. "Salutations, friends. All of you must come with me quickly. I am told they will not be staying very long."

"Who?" Logan asked, as they followed Adisa into an elegant drawing room. A large Oriental rug covered most of the dark wood floor, a crystal chandelier hung from the ceiling, and an ornate fireplace dominated the wall to the left of the doorway. Logan smiled as he entered, seeing three of his mother's mosaics prominently displayed on easels. Adisa took them to a group of people milling around the mosaics, admiring them.

"Mr. President," Adisa said.

Enrique Salize, the president of the North American Federation, turned around. Accompanying him were Director Sully and about ten other people. Four WCF agents dressed in black suits stood nearby.

Valerie grabbed Logan by the arm. "These are the business leaders the president invited to Washington to help him work out a solution to the energy crisis," she explained in a whisper.

"Did you know they were coming to the commemoration?" he asked.

"No. The founder of the Tripod Group, Rigel Wright, should be with them, but I don't see him."

"Mr. President," Adisa said. "I would like to introduce you to Logan—"

"Logan Ford," President Salize said, loudly enough for everyone in his group to hear. He shook Logan's hand and then Valerie's. "Good to see you again, Agent Perrot."

Valerie could see Director Sully's surprise that the president knew her name. Logan noticed a blond woman standing at the back of the group and craning her neck to get a better look at them.

President Salize turned to Mr. Perrot. "And you must be the man of the hour."

"Nice to meet you, Mr. President," Mr. Perrot said.

"I wanted to stop by and pay tribute to the original Council of Satraya," Salize said. "As you know, I don't always see eye-to-eye with the current Council, but no one can deny the contributions the organization made to the world during the Rising, the years when the *Chronicles* were most meaningful."

"Some would say those meaningful years are still going on," Mr. Perrot said.

"How did your energy crisis meeting go?" Valerie asked, changing the subject. She could tell that her father was about to start lecturing the president about the value of the *Chronicles*.

"Very well," Salize answered. "We have a solution in the works that will be announced in the next few days."

"That doesn't mean your investigation stops," Director Sully said to Valerie. "You and your team are still expected to bring the perpetrators of the gas well explosions to justice."

"Of course," Valerie said. "We are not slowing down."

"I'm glad to hear that," the president said. He turned back to Mr. Perrot. "Congratulations to you, sir. I hope your term on the Council of Satraya is all you wish it to be." He nodded farewell to Logan and Valerie, and with that, his group turned and dispersed in the growing crowd.

"The president's stopping by was a nice surprise," Logan said to Adisa.

"Yes, it was quite unexpected. I'm glad to see he realizes the Council is a force to be reckoned with. Of course, it would not be in the strong shape it is in today if it hadn't been for your support," he added warmly, glancing from Logan to Mr. Perrot to Valerie. "The three of you breathed new life into the Council during those dark days following the murders of Cynthia and the others. And now, with the emergence of original Council members Madu and Nadine Shata, I am confident we will grow even stronger."

"Where are they, by the way?" Logan asked.

"Over there," Valerie said, pointing to the corner of the room. "They're talking to Rigel Wright. I bet they have a few things to explain to him about Mr. Montez and Elvia."

Logan laughed.

"Dad," Jordan said, tugging on Logan's arm. "Can Jamie and I go upstairs? Someone told us there's food up there."

"Yes," Logan said, "but Ms. Sally has to go with you."

Jordan made a face but walked off with his sister and Ms. Sally.

Mr. Perrot pointed to a large framed photograph that hung on the wall above the mantelpiece. "I see you were able to find a group shot of all the original Council members."

"Yes," Adisa said, leading them over to it. "We found it among some old photos we had in our files. We plan to leave it up permanently. They all look very happy in that picture."

"It was indeed a happy time for the Council and those who worked closely with us," Mr. Perrot said. "I'm so glad that we are honoring Camden, Cassandra, and the other original members tonight. It makes my second induction into the Council, this time as Alain Perrot, even more gratifying and poignant."

Logan was looking not at the smiling faces of his parents but at the expressionless face of the teenage boy standing at the center of the enlarged photo. It was fourteen-year-old Simon Hitchlords, standing with his arms straight by his sides, between his father, Fendral, and his father's friend Andrea Montavon.

Valerie leaned in close to Logan and whispered, "I can't believe she was my mother. I don't look anything like her."

Logan examined the face more closely. "I don't know," he said. "I can sort of see a resemblance."

Valerie shook her head disapprovingly.

Adisa turned eagerly toward the fortified glass display case at the center of the room. Logan and Valerie took one last look at the photograph of the first Council members before joining him and Mr. Perrot. The case contained Logan's set of the *Chronicles*, which had originally belonged to Deya Sarin, and a distressed wooden box. "The books are the jewel of the commemoration exhibit. The Council cannot thank you enough for allowing us to display them, even for only a few hours."

Logan looked over at a man who was standing near the case, admiring the books. His shoulder-length gray hair was neatly combed behind his ears and he held a silver-handled cane in his right hand. He looked familiar to Logan, although Logan couldn't place him. "Even though the books are in my care," Logan said, "I still consider them to be Deya's. I am certain she would have wanted them to be part of the commemoration."

"I wish her husband, Babu, were here tonight," Mr. Perrot said. "He, too, deserves to be honored."

"He politely declined our invitation," Adisa said. "But he did send us the box in which Deya found the books."

"It's great to be able to see the books along with the box. I've wondered if the pouches and boxes the original books were found in represented something."

"That is an interesting thought," Mr. Perrot said.

"Speaking of the other copies," Adisa said, "is there any word about the whereabouts of the copies of the *Chronicles* that Simon Hitchlords possessed? The Council would like to purchase them from his estate, if possible."

"No," Valerie answered. "They haven't been located."

"That's a shame. However, it will not cloud this evening." He reached into his coat pocket and took out a handful of programs, which he passed out to his companions. "Here is the program for tonight's commemoration. Now I must circulate among our guests. I will catch up with you later."

Valerie's PCD rang. She took it out of her purse and walked a few steps away to take the call.

"Looks like you're up first," Logan said to Mr. Perrot, who was also looking at the program. "You're getting sworn in to your Council seat in a half hour." Mr. Perrot nodded and turned to the photo of the original Council members over the fireplace. Logan could sense it was spurring a flood of memories. "Shall we take another look at it?"

They started over and Madu and Nadine joined them. "To think that was just one year after we all arrived in Washington," Nadine said, giving Logan and Mr. Perrot each a kiss on the cheek.

"We saw you talking to Rigel Wright," Logan said. "How did that conversation go?"

"Not very well," Madu said, sounding disheartened. "I think something must have happened at the conference with the president this afternoon. He indicated that there was going to be some big announcement that would render my research into the pyramids obsolete. He didn't say anything more."

"Logan Ford," a female voice interrupted. Logan turned and saw the blond woman from the president's contingent approaching, the one who had been trying to get a better look at him and Valerie. "My name is Catherine Bribergeld," she said, extending her hand.

While Logan returned her handshake, he could not help but notice the thin gold bracelet she was wearing. The large letter N caught his eye. Logan was surprised that she didn't acknowledge Mr. Perrot, Madu, or Nadine. Out of the corner of his eye, he saw Rigel Wright talking to Valerie. Actually, the two of them were laughing together. He turned back to Catherine Bribergeld. "I understand from the president that you all had a successful meeting this afternoon. It's not easy saving the world."

"I've heard through the grapevine that you have some firsthand experience with that kind of challenge," Catherine replied, smirking. Logan forced himself not to react. "I suppose the Council of Satraya has its own theories on how to save the world, voodoo and all."

Logan didn't reply. Catherine glanced at Mr. Perrot, Madu, and Nadine.

"Voodoo is an interesting choice of words," Mr. Perrot chimed in. "I take it that you don't subscribe to the philosophies put forth in the *Chronicles*? Or perhaps you are not familiar with them? One of the original sets of the books is on display right over there." He gestured to the glass case. "You should have a look. And the Council keeps many copies on hand. We can give you one to take home and read if you like."

Catherine glanced at the display. "Yes, maybe I will take a look at the original. I have read the books, but I was brought up by my father to be more of a pragmatist. Philosophers and prophets never put food on my table or money in my hands."

"What does put food on your table?" Logan asked.

"The financial industry," Catherine answered. "Everyone can always use a little more money."

Logan turned to Madu. "There you go," he said, half in jest. "Maybe Catherine would be willing to fund some of your work."

"I'm sorry," she said, "but my company doesn't fund the digging up of old things. We are focused on new construction." She smiled at them knowingly. "Anyway, I must be off. I just wanted to say hello to the son of Camden and Cassandra Ford." She turned, the smile still on her face, and disappeared into the crowd.

"Interesting lady," Mr. Perrot said.

"Interesting indeed," Madu agreed. "I've never met her, and yet she acts as if she knows my business."

"She does seem to know a lot," Logan said, thinking of Catherine's comment about his having experience in saving the world. He wondered just how close she was to the president, if she knew about that.

Madu shrugged it off. "Come, Nadine, let us take a closer look at Cassandra's mosaics." He took Nadine by the arm and pulled her away.

Valerie came over with Rigel Wright. "Logan, Dad," she said, "I'd like to introduce you to Rigel Wright, the founder of the Tripod Group."

"It's nice to meet you," Logan said. "But I think you drove Madu and Nadine away."

"I'm sorry if they're angry at me for refusing to fund his research any longer, but you can't invest in something forever," Rigel said. "Sometimes you have to recognize when you've been beaten to the punch. But more to the point, tell me, Logan, how does an art restorer score the hottest-looking agent in the WCF?"

Logan smiled, unfazed. "Well, first, your parents have to be best friends with her father. Then, as the two of you grow up together, you have to let her make fun of you every day and let her think she's the boss. Then she has to go off and disappear for fifteen years. In the meantime, you need to struggle with life and have your whole world essentially fall apart. Then a series of events has to bring you back together." Logan caught his breath, and Rigel smiled in turn. "After that, it's easy—you just ask her out. There's always more to a story than how the story appears to end."

There was some commotion as the WCF guards started to clear the area by the doorway. "Looks like the president is leaving," Valerie said. "You'd better go, Rigel. You don't want to miss the big dinner."

"It was great seeing you again, Valerie," Rigel said, before rejoining the president's contingent and departing.

Logan saw Catherine Bribergeld glance over her shoulder at him again before she left the room.

"You let me *think* I was the boss?" Valerie said to Logan, before giving him a kiss on the check.

A chime sounded. "We are about to start," Adisa announced, as he walked to a podium that had been placed in front of the fireplace.

Valerie adjusted Logan's tie.

41

Agreement among people is not advantageous when it is the
unknown that is being sought.

—THE CHRONICLES OF SATRAYA

WASHINGTON D.C., 7:55 P.M. LOCAL TIME, MARCH 24, 2070

The people in the drawing room applauded when Logan finished telling stories about Alain Perrot, his father's best friend, and the wonderful times he and his family had shared with him when they all lived in
New Chicago. As Logan left the podium, he gave Mr. Perrot a warm
hug. Then he made his way through the crowd, stopping occasionally to
shake a few hands, moving back to where Valerie, the children, and Ms.
Sally were standing with Madu and Nadine. Valerie had been reading
something on her PCD when he approached.

"Good job," she said, adding with a grin, "You must have inherited
your speech-writing skills from your mother."

Logan gave her a quizzical look, but before he could ask her what
she meant, Jordan and Jamie stepped between them.

"Dad!" Jordan said excitedly.

Logan put his finger to his lips, indicating that he should speak
more softly.

"Can we go see the Egalitarian Round Table?"

Jamie eagerly nodded her head.

"Didn't you see it when you went upstairs earlier?"

"There were too many people in the way for us to get a good look at it," Jordan replied.

Logan turned to Ms. Sally. "Would you mind taking them?"

She nodded and led Jordan and Jamie out of the drawing room.

Logan turned to Valerie. "What were you reading on your PCD?"

"We received some video footage from the Calhoun Center," Valerie answered.

"Is there any word about Sumsari?" Madu asked.

"No. But we might have a lead on the man who took him."

"Good," Logan said, and he pointed to Valerie's PCD. "But now it's time to put that away. Your father's about to begin his acceptance speech."

Valerie did so and repositioned herself to gain a clearer view of the podium. Logan slipped his arm around her waist.

"My friends," Mr. Perrot began, "I am deeply honored to be invited to join the Council of Satraya and to sit in a chair at the Egalitarian Round Table. Over the last few days, I have struggled to come up with the words that would convey my appreciation for this opportunity. My struggle might have continued until this very moment, had I not remembered a speech that Camden Ford gave to a gathering of world leaders during the Rising." Mr. Perrot removed a folded piece of paper from the breast pocket of his jacket. "It is a little-known fact that this speech was actually written by Camden's wife, Cassandra."

Valerie turned to Logan and smiled.

Mr. Perrot flattened the paper on the podium. "So, with your permission, I would like to read the beginning of what I now think of as Camden *and* Cassandra's speech. The words are as relevant and poignant today as they were back then."

"I remember that speech," Logan heard Madu whisper to Nadine behind him. "'The sun rose this morning and illuminated the sky with opportunity . . .'"

"The sun rose this morning and illuminated the sky with opportunity," Mr. Perrot said.

Logan turned and gave Madu and Nadine a fond look. After all these years, they still remembered what his father had said, what his mother had written.

As Logan listened to Mr. Perrot read his parents' speech, he couldn't help thinking about all the unanswered questions related to his parents that had recently arisen. Who had sent the photos of his parents to Simon? Who was RJ, and what had happened to his mother's music teacher, Sumsari Baltik? Logan took a deep calming breath. Now wasn't the time to think about all of that. He turned his attention back to Mr. Perrot.

A woman in front of Logan and Valerie started coughing. The man standing next to her handed her the glass of water he was holding.

The high-pitched beep of Valerie's PCD indicated that an urgent message had come in. Valerie took her PCD out of her purse and looked at the screen. "It's from Sylvia," she whispered. "I have to call her. I'll be right back."

As Valerie walked out of the drawing room, Mr. Perrot finished his recital of Camden and Cassandra's speech. "Thank you," he said. "With those words, which I have borrowed from two outstanding former Council members, I would like to accept my seat on the Council of Satraya."

Before the audience could applaud, a loud voice broke in. "Not so fast, sir. I think we should hear from this man standing next to me, who says he has a stronger claim to a seat at that Satraya table than you do."

Logan moved to his left to get a better view of whoever was talking. Madu and Nadine did the same. The man stood more than two meters in height, was wearing blue jeans and a black leather vest, and had long, stringy brown hair. Logan immediately recognized him as Randolph Fenquist, the head of the Sentinel Coterie.

Randolph had his hand on the shoulder of a much shorter man, who had long gray hair and was holding a silver-handled cane. Logan had seen him earlier in the evening, admiring Deya's set of the *Chronicles*. "I would like to introduce my friend Giovanni Rast," Randolph shouted.

There was a tense silence as the members of the crowd turned to look at the two men. No one seemed to know the second man's name. But Logan did. Giovanni Rast, one of the original finders of the *Chronicles*, who'd presumably been killed by Simon's father. How could Giovanni Rast still be alive? And why did Giovanni Rast look familiar to him?

He was about to speak but was momentarily distracted by the swarm of flies in his face, which he tried and failed to swat away. The woman in front of him started coughing again, this time more severely, and the man who had handed her a glass of water started coughing, too. Logan's heart was racing as he struggled to hear what Randolph was saying.

Adisa Kayin rushed to the podium and spoke into the microphone beside Mr. Perrot. "The Council does not appreciate your interrupting our ceremony with these spurious claims . . ."

His voice was quickly drowned out by the sounds of more people coughing. The woman in front of Logan collapsed on the floor. The people next to her bent to assist her, but soon they were coughing, too. Logan's attention was ripped away from Randolph and Giovanni, and he watched in horror as more people fell to the floor.

"Everyone has to get out of here!"

Logan turned at the sound of Valerie's voice. Holding a tissue over her mouth, she was pushing her way through the crowd, holding out her badge.

"I'm WCF! Everyone has to exit the building right now!"

Most people rushed the door, but a handful of guests were helping the afflicted to their feet or carrying them to the exits. Logan was about to pick up an elderly man who had fallen, when Valerie ran over to him.

"Logan! Grab as many people as you can, and get out of here!" She turned to the podium. "Dad! Adisa! You do the same thing!"

"What's going on?" Logan asked.

Valerie grabbed the handkerchief from the pocket of Logan's suit jacket and put it over his mouth and nose. Madu covered his mouth and nose with a handkerchief, and Nadine used her shawl. "Sylvia called. They detected a seventy-nine-point-six-five-four-hertz ELF pulse coming from 18th and New York."

"That's right here!" Logan said.

Valerie nodded. "Those aren't flies you're swatting. They're killer nanites. We have to get everyone at least fifty meters away from this building and out of range of the ELF pulse."

Four police officers had arrived and were carrying people who were gasping for breath out of the room.

"Dad! What's going on?" Logan turned and saw Jordan, Jamie, and Ms. Sally.

"Go!" Valerie said. "Get them out!"

Mr. Perrot rushed over.

"What about you?" Logan asked Valerie.

"I need to find the activation device, Sylvia and Chetan are en route. They'll be here in two minutes. Now, get out of here!"

"I'm not going anywhere without you," Logan said. "That device could be anywhere in the building and we have no idea what it looks like." He turned to Mr. Perrot. "Take the children and Ms. Sally. Madu, Nadine, can you help a few of these people to the exit? Follow Mr. Perrot."

"And get as far away from this building as you can," added Valerie. "You have to get out of the range of the signal that is activating these nanites."

Madu and Nadine nodded, helping an elderly man to his feet and moving quickly, as Mr. Perrot took Jamie's and Jordan's hands and led them and Ms. Sally out of the drawing room.

Two more uniformed officers appeared in the doorway.

"You two," Valerie said, "start checking the other floors. Make sure that everyone vacates the building."

Logan looked around the drawing room and saw that there were still about ten people on the floor, gasping for air, struggling to breathe. Their faces were turning blue.

"They must have breathed in the nanites," Valerie said. "And now the nanites are multiplying and consuming all the oxygen in their lungs."

Logan heard a loud cracking sound to his right. He looked over and saw a woman with an unnaturally flat chest, as if it had caved in. An empty water glass lay next to her. He gazed around again; he saw no sign of Randolph Fenquist or the man he claimed was Giovanni Rast.

"We have to find the activation device. Sylvia said the signal was coming from the Council building and extending approximately fifty meters in all directions." As Valerie looked around, she saw an ashy substance floating in the air. "This is what happened in the Chromatography Bubble when Goshi died."

Sylvia and Chetan sprinted through the doorway, wearing gas masks. "Put these on!" Sylvia shouted, handing a pair to Valerie and Logan.

Chetan bent down next to a woman on the floor who had gone still. "The nanites are creating a vacuum in their lungs," he said. More cracking sounds could be heard, as chest and rib bones continued to break.

"Should we seal the doors and windows to this room?" asked Valerie. "We need to try and keep the nanites isolated."

"Too late for that," replied Sylvia. "I saw nanites everywhere when we entered the building. Even if we could isolate them, it wouldn't take long for a vacuum to form—these wooden doors and glass windows wouldn't stand a chance. We need to find the activation device."

A WCF agent wearing a gas mask entered the room and handed Sylvia a device, which she placed on the floor at the center of the drawing room. The shiny, black, half-meter-tall cylinder had a timer attached to it.

"What's that?" Logan asked.

"An explosive," Sylvia said grimly. "If we can't find the activation device in the next eight and a half minutes, we're not going to have any other choice. It's the only way to deactivate any nanites that might be on your clothing or you might have inhaled."

"You're going to blow up the Council of Satraya building?" Logan said incredulously.

"It might be our only option," Valerie said. "These nanites are not going to stop multiplying.

"In ten minutes, all the oxygen in this building will be devoured and a vacuum is going to collapse this room along with the entire building," Sylvia said with no uncertainty. "The nanites are not going to stop there, they will keep sucking the oxygen from the surrounding area. If we can't turn the nanites off, we need to neutralize the activation device."

Another officer came to the doorway. "We've put out the order to evacuate everyone within a two-hundred-meter radius of this building. We're going door to door. It should take about an hour."

"We don't have that much time!" Sylvia said, as she began to enter a code into the keypad. Logan saw that the ash-like substance was getting thicker.

"What's the blast radius of the device?" Valerie asked.

"Forty meters," Chetan said.

"Set the timer," Valerie ordered. She turned to the officer. "You have seven minutes to get everyone at least a hundred meters away from here."

The officer ran out of the room.

"I can't believe we're about to do this," Logan said.

"Let's go," Valerie said. "We need to get a safe distance away from here."

"What about searching for the device?" asked Logan, still in disbelief. "We can't just blow up this historic building!"

"We have no choice! We need to be long gone before the timer goes off." Valerie grabbed Logan by the arm, and they headed to the main entrance. Sylvia and Chetan finished setting the timer and followed them.

As Logan left the building, he could see police vehicles with flashing lights blocking the streets in all directions. Valerie led everyone south on 18th Street just past E Street, where two black WCF vehicles were parked in the intersection. Logan and Valerie took off their gas masks and turned to look at the building.

"Four minutes," Sylvia said, as she looked at her PCD.

"The seventy-nine-point-six-five-four-hertz signal is still going strong," Chetan said, looking at the display of a small device he was carrying.

Logan spotted his children and Ms. Sally standing next to Mr. Perrot. Madu and Nadine were standing with him behind a police barricade. Adisa Kayin was not far away. Logan looked at the redbrick building two hundred meters from where he was standing. He could not imagine that the Council of Satraya building, which had stood for more than two hundred years, was about to be destroyed, and all its history with it. He suddenly remembered something.

"The books!" he yelled. In all the chaos, he had forgotten to take the original set of the *Chronicles* out of the glass case in the drawing room. "I have to get the books!" He started running.

Valerie ran after him and grabbed him by the arm. "No way! There's no time!"

"I have to!" Logan insisted, looking down 18th Street at the Council of Satraya building. Valerie continued to bar his way. Logan shook his head in disbelief, as a numbness came over him. Not only had he failed to protect his father's copy of the *Chronicles*, but he had failed to protect Deya's. His vision began to blur. It was similar to what had happened to him in the ocean in Mexico, when he'd somehow seen Jordan's feet underwater. His vision took on another perspective, and it suddenly seemed as if he was looking out of the glass case in the drawing room where Deya's set of the *Chronicles* was displayed. The gray ash was no longer floating in the air. It had settled on the furniture and the floor. Some of it had landed on the glass case. Logan's vision zoomed in on the gray ash, and he could make out the individual nanites. None of them was moving; they were all dead. Suddenly, his perspective shifted back to normal, and he was looking down 18th Street. "The nanites are dead!" he said to Valerie. "They're dead. Turn off the explosive!"

"How do you know that?" she asked.

A uniformed officer walked over to Valerie. "We got everyone out of the building," he said.

Sylvia announced the countdown. "Ten. Nine. Eight. Seven . . ."

"They're dead, I'm telling you!" Logan shouted.

"Just got a call from Darvis," Chetan said. "The seventy-nine-point-six-five-four-hertz signal is gone."

"What? The signal is gone?" Valerie asked.

Chetan held up his PCD. "Darvis says the signal is no longer there."

Valerie turned to Sylvia. "Kill the timer!"

42

It only takes one person to see a situation differently for the
universe to unleash a rainfall of possibilities.

—THE CHRONICLES OF SATRAYA

WASHINGTON, D.C., 9:04 P.M. LOCAL TIME, MARCH 24, 2070

"One more second," Sylvia said, as she inspected the explosive device,
"and all of this would be gone."

Valerie had led her team back inside the Council of Satraya building
after the 79.654-hertz signal had suddenly stopped. Everything on the
first floor was covered with fine gray soot.

"You and Chetan gather as much evidence as you can," Valerie said
to Sylvia. "Then go home and get some rest. We'll pick things up in
the morning."

As Valerie walked back outside and down the front steps of the
building, she saw many of the people who were at the commemoration
talking to a WCF agent who was trying to calm them down, as they
asked about what had happened inside and the conditions of others
who hadn't made it out. In the distance, by the barricades, she saw police
officers holding back news reporters and camera crews. She made her
way over to Logan, who was standing with his children and Ms. Sally.
Mr. Perrot stood a few meters away, talking with Madu and Nadine.

"Dad," she said, "take everyone back to my apartment. It will be crowded, but everyone can spend the night there. I'll assign a protection detail to take you."

"Do not worry about us," Nadine said. "Madu and I have to return to our hotel to prepare for our flight back to Cairo tomorrow morning. Our plane leaves very early."

"In that case, I'll have someone take you back to your hotel tonight and then to your flight in the morning." Valerie gestured to a group of uniformed officers standing nearby, then turned to Logan. "I'll see you back at the apartment."

He shook his head. "I'm going with you. The books are still in there."

Logan gave his children a hug and said good-bye to Madu and Nadine, before the police officers escorted them away. Then he and Valerie slipped through the crowd and entered the Council building.

When they reached the drawing room, Logan went to the display case, carefully lifted it, and set it on the floor. He grabbed the first of the three books of the *Chronicles* and put it in his backpack.

"How did you know the nanites were dead?" Valerie asked him. "How did you know that the signal had stopped?"

Logan looked at her a moment before answering. "It's that problem I've been having with my vision. That perspective shift. When it happened tonight, I found myself looking out at the room from inside the display case. I could see the nanites. They weren't moving."

"Maybe I was wrong," Valerie said. "Maybe you shouldn't see a doctor. Whatever it is, you might just have saved not only this building but many lives."

Logan smiled, but he remained silent, placing the remaining two books into WCF evidence bags.

"We found it!" a voice called out from the hallway. A female agent dressed in a blue jumpsuit entered the drawing room. In one hand, she was carrying a wand-like device, and in the other she held up a dark green object the size of a lunch box. "We found it under the sink in the first-floor bathroom."

Sylvia and Chetan, who were about to leave, turned around and went over to her and examined the device.

"Bag it. Chetan and I will take it back to the lab," Sylvia said. "I'll start looking at it tonight."

"No," Valerie said. "Both of you go home and get some rest. We have a lot to deal with tomorrow, and I need both of you alert and well rested."

Sylvia and Chetan acknowledged her instructions and exited.

"Same for you," Valerie said to Logan. "Go back to the apartment and get some sleep. You have the books now."

"Easier said than done, knowing that someone tried to kill everyone at the commemoration ceremony," Logan answered. "I'm not going anywhere."

"I'm running out of brain cells trying to keep track of everything that's happening," Valerie said. "The natural gas crisis, worldwide earthquakes, Goshi's death, the break-in at the Château, the abduction of your mother's music teacher, and then all of that followed by a mass-murder attempt. What is going on?"

"What about the appearance of Randolph Fenquist and the man he claimed was Giovanni Rast?" Logan added.

Valerie shook her head, uncertain.

"The most important question is why the same people who destroyed the natural-gas wells would also want to kill everyone at the commemoration."

"Yes, the same weapon was used in both attacks—the nanites," Valerie said. "We need to find out who planted the activation device here tonight."

"It's not going to be easy," said Adisa Kayin, who had joined them. "More than two hundred people were arriving and departing all evening, and that doesn't include the service staff we hired. And there are no cameras near the bathroom where the device was found." Adisa shook his head as he watched WCF personnel lift the deformed bodies of the victims off the floor and put them into black body bags.

"Are you all right, Adisa?" Logan asked.

"As well as can be expected," he answered. "I apologize for listening in, but I don't understand who could commit such a despicable deed."

"Neither do we," Valerie said.

"Logan, I know that this may not be the proper moment to mention it, but while we were outside, I was approached by Giovanni Rast. He has an outlandish claim and wants to meet with the entire Council as soon as possible."

"I would advise you to proceed cautiously," Logan said. "Giovanni's association with Randolph Fenquist makes me skeptical of anything he has to say."

"So you know him?" Adisa asked.

"I know of him," Logan replied. "His claim may have some merit, but I would suggest that you not include Randolph Fenquist in the meeting. The Sentinel Coterie has no right to be involved in the Council's business."

Adisa nodded. "I will be in touch," he said, before he walked away.

43

*If you close your eyes and meditate all the days of your
life like the ascetic, you might miss the very thing you
are living your life to learn.*

—THE CHRONICLES OF SATRAYA

WASHINGTON, D.C., 11:10 P.M. LOCAL TIME, MARCH 24, 2070

Logan unlocked the door to Valerie's apartment and entered quietly.
He walked to the den, where a lamp was on, and set an evidence bag
that contained the three volumes of the *Chronicles* on the coffee table.
Then he made his way to the master bedroom and peered through the
partially open doorway. Jamie was sleeping on the bed next to Ms. Sally,
and Jordan was sprawled on the floor in a sleeping bag. Logan was relieved that they were safe and sleeping peacefully after witnessing the
attack on the Council of Satraya offices.

Back in the den, he poured himself a glass of wine and sat on
the couch. Valerie had remained at the Council of Satraya building
to continue the investigation. It was going to be a long night for her,
and Logan didn't expect her to return home anytime soon. Mr. Perrot hadn't made it back, either, and was probably still with Madu and
Nadine.

Logan took a big gulp of wine and leaned back. The evening's horrific events were fresh in his mind. *Who in the world would want to kill ev-*

eryone at the commemoration? The people he loved most could have all died tonight—his children, Valerie, Mr. Perrot. He felt angry, outraged, and, he had to admit, a little frightened. *Or was the real target President Salize or one of the members of his energy advisory council?* Logan was also troubled that in the heat of the moment, he had forgotten the books. They were within seconds of being destroyed and would have been the second set of the *Chronicles* he'd failed to protect. Logan picked up one of the books on the table in front of him and fanned through the pages with his thumb. He stopped when something on one of the pages caught his eye. He ran his finger over a small spot of blue wax. He grinned; he knew exactly where the wax came from: Deya's Manas Mantr candle. A thought struck him like a bolt of lightning. He could have kicked himself for not thinking of it before.

Logan went over to the corner of the den where he'd left his backpack and took from it the plastic box containing his mother's recordings, Deya's small mirror, and her blue Manas Mantr candle, which he had carefully wrapped in tissue paper. He found a candle holder in one of Valerie's cabinets and put the blue candle in it. The candle was just like his father's. Logan had learned from an entry in his father's journal that the Manas Mantr candle was mysteriously linked to a man named Bate Sisan, who he'd later figured out was Sebastian Quinn. In one of Logan's candle visions last July, when he was trying to unravel the Freedom Day conspiracy, Bate Sisan had given him some cryptic advice that had later been instrumental in foiling the plot. Logan pinched the burned wick, straightening it out. He cleared the table and lit the candle, then sat down on the floor and stared into the flame. Almost immediately, a ringing sound came to his ears, and his peripheral vision began to darken. He looked forward to going back to the old study his father's candle had taken him to.

* * *

Instead, Logan found himself standing in a lush, well-tended walled garden. The sun shone brightly in the cloudless sky. There was a stone pergola to his right and urns containing young banyan trees at the corners of the garden. Logan walked over to one of the six free-standing concrete pillars at the center of the garden and read the words inscribed on it: *Perfection is an illusion theorized by your personality.* It was from the *Chronicles.* Logan looked around. Where was he? Beyond the pillars, he spotted a small pond with a bench next to it. He stepped between two of the pillars and walked over to the pond. The water in it was crystal-clear, allowing him to read a message that had been stamped there:

> In the once Great House,
> Where fire is and ashes rise,
> Where the ear stone fell,
> Will hold your prize

Logan's eyes widened. He was in Deya's garden. Mr. Perrot had told him that he had found this riddle in Deya's garden, and it had led him to other riddles and eventually to the place where she had hidden her set of the *Chronicles.*

The wind kicked up, rustling the leaves on the trees. The sunlight faded. Logan looked up at the sky and saw ominous dark clouds. Then he noticed mist forming on the other side of the pond. He tensed, and his heart began to race as the mist coalesced into a shadowy human figure. It was the same haunting figure he had seen in the old study. He recalled what it had told him during their last encounter, that this was a place of sincerity, of humbleness, and that one should not presuppose one's entitlement to be there. Logan closed his eyes and calmed his mind. As suddenly as the wind started, it died down. He opened his eyes, squinting because of the sunlight that had reemerged through the scattered clouds. The shadowy figure was now more defined.

"Mr. Quinn?" Logan took a step forward, almost tripping into the pond. "You look much clearer to me this time, although still a little blurry."

"You look clearer, too," Sebastian said.

"I was expecting the candle to bring me to the old study," Logan said.

"That is where Camden's candle led," Sebastian replied. "Deya's candle is linked to her garden." Sebastian stretched out his arms, gesturing to the surroundings. "The fact that you are here and that you no longer see me as a shadow indicates that it is working for you. Your perspective is expanding."

"I'm not sure I understand."

"The A-Tee-Na and the Sin-Ka-Ta. Have you not been able to see the marks?"

Logan's eyes widened. "You mean the hidden symbols. Yes, I can see them now."

"And do you remember my telling you that it is a progression?" Sebastian said. "First, you will see them, and then you must experience them?"

"My blurry vision—my perspective shifts," Logan said, realizing what Sebastian was referring to. "Are those the experiences you're talking about?"

"The Sin-Ka-Ta is an invaluable companion should you learn to harness its power. You will have the ability to see the world through many eyes."

"And what about the other symbol, the A-Tee-Na? And the fragmented symbol on the last page?"

"Patience. That will come in time. The power of the symbols must emerge gradually in one's life. Otherwise, the wisdom to administer them will run aground on a ship called power."

"I understand," Logan said with a sigh. "I could certainly use some wisdom now. The world is in trouble again. Someone is destroying the world's energy supply, and the same person or people attempted to kill everyone at the Council of Satraya commemoration tonight. On top of that, people are getting sick, and no one knows why. I can't help but wonder if it is related to the DNA collars that were injected into people as part of the Freedom Day plot." He waited for Sebastian to say something, but Sebastian remained silent. "I don't know what to do. Is there anything you can tell me?"

"Have you unlocked the mystery of the Munch picture I sent you?" Sebastian asked. "Did you discover why the screaming man was screaming?"

"The scientist, Nikola Tesla," Logan said. "The experiments he was conducting had something to do with it."

"Something to do with it?" Sebastian repeated. "You cannot make nature scream and expect it to have no effect upon the world. Your daughter, along with many others, can attest to this truth." With the tip of his index finger, Sebastian began to draw something in the air in front of him. As his finger moved, a gold tracing appeared, and Logan saw an image that was familiar to him.

"That's what I saw at Teotihuacán and also in Tesla's journal." The gold tracing pulsed with light. "What does it represent?"

"It is the Rokmar, one of the nine veiled symbols of Satraya. Whoever possesses the secret of this symbol can draw energy seemingly out of thin air." The golden symbol pulsed brighter and brighter, to the point where Logan raised his hands to protect his eyes from the dazzling light. "Be vigilant of the man who taught your father the King's Gambit. It is his sincere pursuit that could mark the onset of dark times."

The intensity of the light diminished, allowing Logan to lower his hands. The mist had returned, obscuring his view of Sebastian.

Logan quickly asked, "Who are you talking about? I don't know who taught my father that!"

*   *   *

The opening of the apartment's front door coincided with Logan's return from his candle vision. Mr. Perrot walked into the den, and Logan leaned forward and blew out the flame of the candle. Without stopping to inhale, he said, "Who taught my father the King's Gambit?"

Mr. Perrot was taken aback by Logan's abruptness, but, noticing the blue candle on the table, he understood his urgency. "Madu. He was our chess master."

"When are Madu and Nadine leaving for Egypt?" Logan asked.

"Tomorrow morning," Mr. Perrot said.

Logan nodded. "You'll need to pack your bags."

44

Life is not a test. That idea comes from the notion that life can
be passed or failed.

—THE CHRONICLES OF SATRAYA

After spending a restless night at Valerie's apartment, Logan and Valerie returned to the lab. Mr. Perrot, who had slept on Valerie's couch, left the apartment with them but went instead to the Council offices to help Adisa deal with the aftermath of last night's attack. Later, in the afternoon, he would fly to Cairo.

In the WCF Cube, Valerie stood in front of a large glass writing board. Chetan and Sylvia sat at their desks while Logan stood nearby eating a muffin. Sliding the tip of her right index finger across the glass, Valerie scribbled a list, which appeared in radiant blue writing:

1. *Attack on Council offices*
2. *Man kidnapped from Calhoun Medical Center, Sumsari Baltik*
3. *Earthquakes*
4. *People getting sick*
5. *Australian gas field explosion*
6. *Nanite infestation, Goshi dead*

"Anyone have anything else to add?" she asked, stepping back from the glass.

Although Logan had a few suggestions—the photos of his mother and father that had been found at Château Dugan, the surfacing of Madu Shata and the mystery of the pyramids, the Munch picture Sebastian Quinn had sent him, his mother's recordings, and his own mirror visions—he remained silent.

"I would add the seventy-nine-point-six-five-four-hertz signal's suddenly stopping, not that I'm complaining about it," Sylvia said.

"I've analyzed the device that was found under the sink in the bathroom," Chetan said. "It is remotely activated. Whoever turned it on and off had to have been relatively close to the device."

"Obviously, the nanites link items one, five, six, and eight on the list," Sylvia said, as she took a sip of her coffee. "Chetan and I confirmed that the nanites unleashed in the Council building have the same watermarks as the ones that were found at the gas refineries. I'm not sure about the other items on the list; they might be coincidences."

With the tip of her finger, Valerie circled items one, five, six, and eight.

"We can infer that whoever is bent on destroying the world's energy supply is also bent on destroying the Council of Satraya," Chetan said.

"I only know of one person who had that aspiration," Valerie said, "and he's dead."

Logan tossed his muffin wrapper into a nearby trash can, sighing before he spoke. "We still haven't identified everyone involved in the Freedom Day plot. We know that Victor Ramplet was helping Simon and Andrea. We heard Simon mention a man named Dario. And we found an old e-mail message from Simon's father to Dario in which a woman named Catherine was mentioned."

"A message that mysteriously vanished," Valerie added. "We originally found it in an old FBI archive stored at the Akasha Vault. But now it's gone."

"How does something like that vanish?" Sylvia asked.

Valerie shook her head.

"We also need to add Randolph Fenquist to the list," Logan said. "Until eight hours ago, we thought he might have been killed in the pulse that hit Compass Park last year."

"That's quite a suspect list," Chetan said.

"And there's one more," Logan said. "In my mother's old recordings, I heard her mention a man in a wheelchair who used to visit Simon's father and Andrea from time to time. That same unnamed man was in a newspaper photograph we found. He was pictured alongside Andrea and Simon at Andrea's husband's funeral six years ago."

"Your mother's recordings?" Sylvia asked.

"Long story," Valerie said, as her PCD sounded. "Looks like the team just retrieved the video surveillance from the Calhoun Medical Center. They say to start looking at time marker fourteen." Valerie handed her PCD to Sylvia, who brought the video up on the large glass display next to the list Valerie had written. Everyone watched as a dark-skinned man with shoulder-length dreadlocks and a white orderly uniform pushed a wheelchair down one of the darkened hallways of the Calhoun Center. His back was to the cameras as he moved, preventing them from getting a good look at him.

The man stopped in front of a door with a small window, where a dim light shone through. The room number, 169, was stenciled on the door frame. Sumsari Baltik's, they knew. They continued to watch as the man set the brake on the wheelchair, looked up and down the hallway, and then peered through the door's small window, before opening it and entering. Rapidly moving shadows on the floor indicated that a struggle was taking place inside. After a few moments, the man emerged, dragging the body of an older man dressed in a pale green robe.

"That must be Sumsari," Logan said, leaning closer to get a better look.

The man swung the limp body into the wheelchair. The old man's head flopped backward.

"Pause there," Valerie said. "What is that on the side of his head? Near his left temple."

Sylvia zoomed closer. "Looks like some kind of neuro implant. Impossible to say what for."

The video continued rolling. The dark-skinned man in white shut the door and bent down to put Sumsari's feet into the wheelchair's footrests. Now he was facing the surveillance camera.

"Hey," Logan called out, placing his finger on the glass where the face of the man with the dreadlocks appeared. "I've seen that guy before."

Sylvia paused the recording. "Where?"

Logan shook his head, unable to place it. It was recent, he knew, but he couldn't take it any farther.

"At the beach in Mexico," Valerie suddenly said. "He looks very similar to the photographer we met on the beach, the one who insisted on taking our picture. But he didn't have dreadlocks then."

"Are you sure it's the same person?" asked Sylvia.

Logan took a closer look. "They look awful similar," he said, before something else caught his attention. He squinted and pointed at the man's right wrist. "Can you zoom in here?" Sylvia obliged. The man was wearing a thin gold bracelet with the letter *N* attached to it. Logan turned to Valerie with alarm. "I saw this same bracelet being worn by a woman at the commemoration last night."

"Who?" Valerie asked.

"She introduced herself as Catherine Bribergeld," Logan said quickly. "She was in President Salize's group."

"Are you sure it's the same bracelet?" Valerie asked.

"I'm positive. The letter *N* was very distinctive. It's the reason I noticed it in the first place."

Chetan began manipulating the controls on his display to project a list. "These are the people who attended the president's conference yesterday."

"Catherine Bribergeld," Sylvia said. "Fourth name from the bottom."

Valerie looked at Logan. "You're telling me that this guy in the video is linked with Catherine Bribergeld, who was at the commemoration last night?"

"That's what it looks like," Logan said. "Your father, Madu, and Nadine were all there when she spoke to us."

"So a guy who kidnaps people and hangs out with the rich and powerful is also a beach photographer in his spare time?" Chetan said incredulously.

Sylvia looked at Valerie. "And didn't you just say a Catherine was mentioned in a note that magically disappeared?" she asked.

Valerie nodded. She and Logan continued to look at the image of the dark-skinned man with dreadlocks; he had been spying on them in Mexico, they now realized.

"Let's see what we can find on this Catherine Bribergeld," Sylvia said. Within moments, a series of images appeared on the glass display. "She is definitely rich. CEO of the Bribergeld Bank of Spain. One of the largest financial institutions in the world."

"The bank's recent investments include these," Chetan said, as another list appeared:

The John Mason Institute
Miracle Fitness Centers
AB Control Systems
ComData
NovaCon International."

"NovaCon was on that list we pulled up the other day," Valerie said, turning to Sylvia. "When we were looking into which companies had recently purchased a DNA spectrometer. We zeroed in on the Tripod Group, but I'm sure NovaCon was on the same list."

"And you all remember AB Control Systems, don't you?" Logan asked. "That was Andrea's husband Alfred Benson's technology company. If Catherine Bribergeld knew Alfred and Andrea, she also would have known Fendral and Simon Hitchlords."

They stared at the picture of Catherine Bribergeld being displayed next to the frozen image of the man who had abducted Sumsari Baltik.

"Agent Perrot," a stern female voice called out. It was Director Sully. She approached with two WCF agents and saw the image on the glass board. "Why do you have a picture of Ms. Bribergeld up there?"

"We believe that she's working with this man," Valerie said, pointing to the frozen video footage. "Who happened to have been involved in an abduction yesterday at the Calhoun Medical Center."

"The Calhoun Center?" Director Sully said in a raised voice. "Do you understand priorities, Agent Perrot? We're in the middle of a global energy crisis. You're supposed to be investigating the gas wells."

Logan was about to jump in, but Valerie did so first. "We also believe that Ms. Bribergeld is involved in a company called NovaCon. They're involved in alternative energy research and—"

"I know who they are," the director responded. "You must know that Ms. Bribergeld is a valued member of the president's crisis panel. In fact, at the meeting yesterday afternoon, Ms. Bribergeld presented NovaCon and its newly constructed energy device. NovaCon has offered to let the NAF use this device at a reduced charge until we can get the natural-gas crisis under control."

"What kind alternative energy device?" Sylvia asked.

"I don't know the particulars," the director answered, annoyed by the question. "She called it zero-point fracturing. You will hear all about it this afternoon at the president's news conference, where he will be announcing the plan and introducing NovaCon to the world."

"What if the crisis never ends?" Logan suggested. "What if the destruction of the natural-gas wells continues?"

"I couldn't have made the point better myself," Director Sully said, turning her gaze to Valerie. "You need to focus exclusively on the destruction of the gas wells. Let the agent assigned to the Calhoun Medical Center handle the kidnapping. And leave Catherine Bribergeld out of this. NovaCon is the only hope the Federation and the rest of the world have at the moment." The director turned and began to walk away. "Get focused, Agent Perrot. Or I'll find someone else who can."

No one said anything as Director Sully left the Cube. Logan couldn't help but notice the look of defeat on Sylvia's and Chetan's faces. Chetan manipulated some controls, causing the images of Catherine Bribergeld and the video feed from the Calhoun Medical Center to disappear from the glass board.

"What are you doing?" Valerie asked.

Chetan shrugged. "The director just said—"

"We're not done! Get those images back up here."

Logan and Sylvia both smiled. They knew Valerie too well. She was not going to be deterred from pushing forward with her line of investigation.

"Bring up everything you can find on NovaCon. Let's find out exactly who this Catherine is and what NovaCon does."

"Yes, boss," Chetan said, also letting loose a smile as he displayed some documents on the glass wall beside the restored image of Catherine. "Looks like NovaCon International is registered in Spain. Over the last six years, the Bribergeld Bank has invested more than five hundred million Universal Credits in the company. Also looks like NovaCon has filed more than two hundred patents in that same period. Most of the filings concern atmospheric electrical induction, something to do with pulling electricity right out of the atmosphere."

Logan turned to Valerie, his expression grave. "That's the same thing that your father and I were investigating with Madu in Mexico."

"You need to bring them up to speed," Valerie said.

Logan turned to Sylvia and Chetan. "For the last forty years, Madu Shata has been developing a theory about the large pyramids around the world. He believes they were used in ancient times to harness an endless supply of electrical current directly out of the atmosphere."

"Free energy," Sylvia said.

"That's right," Logan said. "It's similar to the research into energy production that Nikola Tesla was doing in the late 1800s."

"Tesla did a lot of work in the areas of free energy and wireless energy transmission," Chetan said. "Some say he even figured it all out."

"Why didn't his work come into the mainstream?" Valerie asked.

"According to historians, his funding got pulled," Chetan said. "But I think it was more than that. As Tesla performed his experiments, he began to see negative side effects of his work. If he didn't do his calculations precisely, things would go haywire. He claimed that one of his experiments caused an earthquake in New York City in 1898. Scientists dismissed the claim, because it didn't have any epicenter, and—" Chetan broke off suddenly.

Sylvia had the same stunned look on her face. "That's what's happening now," she blurted out. "None of the recent earthquakes has had a seismic epicenter."

Valerie looked at the list and circled point number three, *earthquakes*. "Where is this NovaCon company based?" she asked.

Sylvia read from her display. "The Azores. NovaCon spent a massive amount of money buying property on one of the islands from the Spanish government."

Logan looked over at the large globe rotating at the northwest corner of the Cube. "Isn't that where we noticed all those earthquakes and the frequency spikes?"

"Yes," Chetan said.

"Here is the latest aerial view of Pico Island, where they bought all the property," Sylvia said, as she projected it on the glass board. "It is one of the few islands left in the archipelago after the Great Disruption. There's a big volcano at the center of it."

"What's that shiny thing to the west of the volcano?" Valerie asked. "It looks like a square building."

Sylvia zoomed in.

Logan understood what it was at once. "They built themselves a pyramid," he said.

"We need to get to that island," Valerie said, staring at it.

"I'm not sure they're going to just let us show up in a row boat and then escort us around," Sylvia said. "There is no way Director Sully is going to authorize a raid on NovaCon and Catherine Bribergeld."

"There might be another way," Chetan said. Everyone turned and looked at him. "But I'm not sure anyone is going to like it."

45

If you truly forgave someone, you would never have
to let anyone know that you did.
Forgiveness is a state of mind and does not have
to be broadcasted.

—THE CHRONICLES OF SATRAYA

PEEL CASTLE, 2:18 P.M. LOCAL TIME, MARCH 25, 2070

"I don't see anything here about the story Mr. Quinn told us about
Atlantis," Halima said, flipping through a large book. Its pages were
made of thick parchment on which text had been handwritten and il-
lustrations hand-drawn.

"Not surprising," Anita said, scanning a chapter in a science book
that explained the finer points of electromagnetic waves. "Recorded
history is more about what those in power were doing at the time than
what actually happened. People want to be remembered, so the vain and
powerful tended to control the quills of antiquity. I'm not sure that will
ever change."

Anita and Halima were sitting at the illuminated table under the
dome of the Alexandria Room. The surface was covered with books
and manuscripts they had been pulling from the library's shelves for
the better part of the day. Britney had been helping with the research
but she'd had to return to the university to attend a class. Sebastian's

explanation of the voice of the earth being disrupted and the story he had related about the downfall of Atlantis concerned Anita. She was determined to understand what was disturbing the world and, more important, what she could do to help stop it. While assisting Anita in the Alexandria Room, Halima had taken the opportunity to retrieve several volumes of *The Unexpected Life*, the writings of Sebastian's mother and father. She was particularly interested in volume eight, which contained the references to Sumsari Baltik.

"It says here that the Schumann resonance is a series of electromagnetic waves that bounce between the surface of the earth and the bottom of the ionosphere," Anita said, her eyes widening. "The waves are caused by lightning emitted from the thousands of storms constantly taking place around the world at any given moment. It goes on to say that as the waves bounce and flow around the earth, the crests and troughs eventually align to create a collective resonance that amplifies the original signal. The resonance can be as low as eight hertz."

Halima blinked. "And that's important because . . . ?"

"Because it's the same frequency range as the alpha and theta waves in our brains," Anita said, looking up and sitting back in her chair. "If the Schumann resonance is somehow being altered, as Mr. Quinn suggested, that would explain why people are reporting hallucinations and headaches and are having trouble falling asleep."

"Just like you," Halima said. "What are alpha waves?"

"They are the waves that our brains produce when we close our eyes and relax. Theta waves occur when we fall into a deep sleep."

Halima stopped reading from her book and looked up. "What about Bukya? Does his brain produce waves? What about other animals?"

"Yes. Alpha and theta waves are found in every biological system, from bacteria to humans."

"That's why Mr. Quinn was so concerned." Halima understood the gravity of what Anita had just told her. "Our brain waves are clashing with the brain waves of the earth."

Anita nodded. "Well put. Whoever is disrupting the field is causing all the trouble. Mr. Quinn said that a brotherhood stopped this once before. The question is, how did they do it?"

"This might help," Halima said. "Do you remember when Mr. Quinn told us that the brotherhood used a device to send a signal?" Anita's attention was piqued; she watched Halima look through volume eight of Sebastian's parents' autobiography. "And remember when I was looking for information about that man named Sumsari Baltik? Well, it turns out that he spent a lot of time with Mr. Quinn's mother and father. Listen to what they wrote." Halima began to read.

Three years ago, Sumsari came to us a war-torn man. The ravages of combat had taken an immeasurable toll on him. Life here on the Isle of Man seems to provide him with some relief from his memories of the loss of life he witnessed while he was in the city of Kiev. We wish Sebastian were here to meet him, but his studies with Makesh prevent him from returning home.

"Who is Makesh?" Halima asked. When Anita shook her head, she continued to read.

Sumsari has devoured all the books and documents we have given him about the spiritual nature of the world around us. It is a rare evening that passes in which we do not converse for hours about these subjects and more. While Sumsari is not certain what he is searching for, he is venturing into sacred territory at a blistering pace. He is certain that sound, music, and resonance hold some kind of key and that his pursuits are going to lead him to some startling discovery, though he doesn't know what that is. His past as a piano and guitar player has provided him with a starting base of understanding. Sumsari spends countless hours on the piano in our study, and, based on our observations of him, we believe that he is one of those few people whose brains perceive music as colors and geometric shapes. We made a big decision today to give Sumsari access to certain pages of the Enuntiatio de Tutela *in hopes that it will help guide and advance his learning.*

A few weeks ago, Sumsari showed us a simple-looking item that he crafted out of two old brass urns he purchased in town. It looked like a Christmas tree ornament. He said his inspiration for it is a Helmholtz resonator, which he read about in one of the books from the library.

"Stop," Anita interrupted. "What's a Helmholtz resonator?"

"Not sure," Halima replied. "But Hypatia will know." Halima turned and activated the librarian of the Alexandria Room. "Finding Helmholtz resonator," said a female voice. A moment later, an image of a brass ball with openings on opposite sides was projected above the table.

Hypatia's voice continued: "In 1850, Herman von Helmholtz created this device to isolate singular frequencies and pitches in complex musical systems. The device demonstrated the phenomenon of air resonance in a cavity or closed space."

"Keep reading," Anita requested.

As the image continued to hover over the table, Halima picked up where she left off.

Sumsari indicated that he had altered the design a bit. He struck the end of a tuning fork and placed it near the larger of the two openings. The resonator did not simply increase the sound coming from the tuning fork by a fractional amount, it amplified the sound exponentially. Whatever alterations he had made, they were strikingly evident. As Sumsari moved the fork back and forth across the opening, the harmonic wavered. But when the fork was held at the perfect position and distance from the opening, the resonator performed flawlessly and fully. We didn't immediately tell him, but the harmonic being emitted was that of the Rokmar.

"That's the symbol that Mr. Quinn spoke about," Anita said. "He called it the Rokmar."

"Yes, the one they gave to the ruler of Atlantis." Halima read on.

> *Somehow he gained an understanding of one of the secret Satrayian symbols and had duplicated the harmonic associated with the legendary Brahmastra device.*
>
> *This is the main reason we are going to make the* Enuntiatio de Tutela *available to Sumsari. Anyone with such knowledge and a device like the one Sumsari crafted would be able to activate any of the sonorous lines around the world. We closely observed Sumsari for several weeks after he showed us his resonator. We needed to know his heart—we needed to know if and how he intended to use his wizardly amplifier, which we are now calling the Sumsari resonator.*

"See," Halima said excitedly, "doesn't this remind you of what Mr. Quinn said about how the old brotherhood destroyed the pyramid on Atlantis?"

"My father used the word *implode*," Anita said. "Is there any more?"

"Yeah, but I need to find it." Halima quickly flipped forward through the pages. "Okay, here it is."

> *Two months ago, we took Sumsari to Salisbury Cathedral so that he could hear what kind of sound his device could produce inside this acoustic treasure.*

Anita recalled the vision she had had in the Arcis Chamber a few days ago, when Mr. Quinn had taught her and Halima the technique of Reflecting. The cathedral in her vision was the one in the city of Salisbury. Anita turned her attention back to what Halima was reading.

> *We were granted access to the cathedral when it was empty. We took Sumsari to the center of the church, where he struck his fork and activated his resonator. He was not disappointed by what he heard. It was then that we explained more about what he had discovered and introduced Sumsari to the workings of the sonorous lines. We explained to him how those major and minor lines connect*

the entire surface of the earth in a complex grid. We explained that the sonorous lines are very much like the nervous systems in our bodies. There are major nerves within the spine that are connected to secondary nerves that extend to all the other parts of the body. Signals are constantly being sent back and forth. And so it is with the earth. There is no place on earth that is not connected to another place on earth. We explained to him that just like an acupuncturist uses meridian points on the skin to provoke a reaction in the body, certain points along the major sonorous lines do the same to the earth.

We then took a chance and took Sumsari to the Altar of the Bluestones. We waited until the witching hour, when, again, we had him strike his tuning fork to vitalize his resonator. Instantly, he experienced all that we had explained to him. He witnessed firsthand the power of the Rokmar and the effect it had on one of the major sonorous lines of the world. The standing wave that was created rocked the entire site. Sumsari understood the true nature of what he had created.

We never saw the device after that day; he told us that a device such as that should be concealed and only used at the most urgent of times. We were relieved that Sumsari had arrived at that conclusion on his own. He stayed with us for a few more months and then left, telling us he was headed to Washington, D.C.

Halima stopped reading. She turned the page. "That's it," she said, looking up at Anita. "That's all they wrote about Sumsari, at least in this volume."

"I wonder if his resonator could stop what's going on in the world now," Anita mused. "Just like what the brotherhood did with the device in Atlantis. As Sumsari said, this is certainly the most urgent of times."

"We would have to figure out where the Altar of the Bluestones is," Halima said.

"First things first," Anita said. "Where did you say you found Sumsari's chain and tag?"

Halima's eyes widened. She hopped out of her chair. "Buried in the tunnel under the old armory!"

They quickly made their way to the northern part of the castle grounds. They stopped at the gardener's shed, where they grabbed a lantern, a small shovel, and a pick, then continued past Saint Germaine's cathedral over the ruins of the old armory. Halima pulled on the iron door leading to a tunnel that had been dug into the ground during the construction of the original castle. The door opened easily. Anita turned on the lantern and followed Halima in. The ground was muddy. They stopped about ten meters in, when Halima bent down near a little hole that had been scratched into the ground. "This is where Bukya found the chain," she said.

Anita knelt down and set the lantern next to the shallow hole. "Let's dig deeper. Maybe there is something more down here."

"Like the resonator," Halima said with excitement.

They dug together with the pick and the shovel. It did not take long before they struck something hard. They set their tools aside and used their hands to clear more dirt from the hole. They pulled out a large, flat stone the size of a dinner plate. "There's something written on it," Anita said.

Halima brushed more dirt off the stone and read the message:

THE CATHEDRAL KNOWS
THAT THOSE WHO HAVE IT
CANNOT SELL IT,
THAT THOSE WHO WANT IT
CANNOT BUY IT,
AND THAT WHICH SHOWS IT
CANNOT HIDE it

"What does that mean?" Halima asked, as she read it again.

"It's a riddle," Anita said. "And I'm sure it has something to do with the resonator device."

"We need to talk to Mr. Quinn," Halima said. "He'll know the answer."

"Mr. Quinn's gone again, and I don't know when he'll be back. My father might know, but we can't wait. People are suffering now. I have to go and find the resonator and figure out where the Altar of the Bluestones is."

"I'm going, too," Halima announced.

"No, you're not," Anita said. "One of us leaving is going to cause enough trouble."

"Well, you can't go alone."

Anita thought for a moment and replied, "I won't be alone."

46

There are words that you will not like to hear. We are going to
say them anyway because we love you.

—THE CHRONICLES OF SATRAYA

CAIRO, 9:23 A.M. LOCAL TIME, MARCH 26, 2070

"Nadine and I were surprised that you decided to come visit us so
soon," Madu said. "Have your daughter and Logan recovered from the
attack at the commemoration?"

"Not entirely," Mr. Perrot said. "They are still preoccupied by many
unanswered questions."

"Well, I'm happy you are here and hope you stay for a while. Nadine
is at home preparing dinner for us."

The details of Logan's candle vision and Mr. Quinn's suggestion
to keep an eye on the man who had taught Logan's father the Queen's
Gambit were enough to persuade Mr. Perrot to visit Madu and Nadine as soon as possible. Madu had picked him up at the Cairo airport, and they were heading to their home in the residential district
known as Garden City. Mr. Perrot looked out the window of Madu's
little electric-powered red car at the numerous buildings that had been
constructed after the Great Disruption. The streets were crowded with

vehicles, bikes, and pedestrians. And on just about every street corner, vendors were selling food or souvenirs to tourists and locals alike.

"You said you went back to Cairo after the splintering of the council?" Mr. Perrot asked.

"We did at first," Madu replied. "As you know, after my experience with the blue orb, I was consumed with trying to solve the mystery of the pyramids. It was why I agreed to become a member of the original Council of Satraya. I hoped that the other finders might provide additional insights to assist me in my quest. But I soon realized that the others had their own questions about the orb and the *Chronicles*. Camden, Deya, and Fendral knew as much as I did, which at the time was not much."

"Yes," Mr. Perrot said. "We were all flying blind to some degree back then. Did you speak much to Fendral?"

"A little at first. But it didn't take long for me to realize I didn't have much in common with him. I'm not sure any of us did. Based on what you told me about his son, I wonder if those men who interrupted the commemoration are somehow linked to the Hitchlordses?"

"Yes," Mr. Perrot said. "Linked by the man who claims to be Giovanni Rast. Logan found a note written by his father indicating that Fendral actually stole Giovanni's set of the *Chronicles* from him and presented it as his own discovery. Camden's learning of Fendral's crime contributed to the Council's splintering. But based on the information in the note, we all assumed that Giovanni Rast was dead. It seems now that assumption was wrong."

"So it does," Madu said, nodding. "After the splintering, Nadine and I returned to Cairo. We followed Camden's suggestion and changed our identities. I subsequently donated the *Chronicles* to the museum, where I thought they would best serve the people of Egypt during the Rising. I continued to study the pyramids, working tirelessly to unearth the secret of free energy that I knew was possible from my experience with the blue orb. At first, my work progressed very quickly. The plans for my device were coalescing. But there were certain questions that I just couldn't answer. Time passed, and I wasn't making any headway. After twenty years, my plans were still incomplete. I could see that my obsession had put a tremendous strain on Nadine, who was working at a local bank to make ends meet. One day, she came home and suggested that perhaps I could find the answers I needed elsewhere in the world. She had met a man who she thought might fund my work."

"Rigel Wright."

Madu nodded. "I showed Rigel a portion of my plans and explained what my work could eventually do for humanity. It didn't take long for him to agree to back my work financially. He even supported my intention to provide the results to the world for free."

"And you believed him?" Mr. Perrot asked. "It is unusual for a man with such power and wealth to do anything without the prospect of gaining something."

"I had to. I couldn't bear to see Nadine under such stress any longer, and I wasn't yet ready to give up my pursuit."

"Is it possible that Rigel might have stolen your plans?"

Madu thought for a moment. "I don't think so. I never actually gave my plans to Rigel. I only showed him a portion of them and explained a few of the basic concepts. Why do you ask?"

"Logan and Valerie are on their way to the Azores to investigate what they believe is a newly constructed energy extraction device," Mr. Perrot said. "They believe that whoever constructed it is behind the gas well explosions and that the device is also causing the earthquakes around the world."

"So that's why Rigel was so dismissive when Nadine and I talked to him at the commemoration and asked him to continue funding my work in spite of the losses I suffered at Teotihuacán," Madu said. "He intimated that my work is obsolete." Madu laughed mirthlessly. "And you think that that device is based on my plans? Why would Rigel fund my work in Mexico if he secretly was constructing his own device?"

"We don't know," Mr. Perrot said. "But one reason might have been to keep you distracted."

Madu sighed. "People may be suffering because of my work," he murmured.

Mr. Perrot shook his head. "Not because of you, my friend. Because of those who would use your work for ill." He paused. "Tell me more about what happened after Rigel initially backed your exploration."

"As a result of my partnership with Rigel, Nadine and I spent the next fifteen years traveling around the world to other pyramids. We spent time in China, Europe, India. But Teotihuacán is where my research progressed most. Until the destruction of the Moon Pyramid, that is. I sensed we were close to solving a very profound mystery."

"So did I," Mr. Perrot said warmly. "So did I."

"Still, I feel reinvigorated," Madu said. "The information that you and Logan helped me uncover has given me valuable insight into the original vision I had when I first found the books and the blue orb took me to that secret chamber. I realize now that the waves of energy that I saw emanating from the center of the room were not radioactivity but sound." Madu slowed the car and pointed toward a redbrick building. "The Cairo Museum is open again. This is where the *Chronicles* were kept before they were stolen."

"Yes," Mr. Perrot said, looking at a long line of people waiting to enter.

"Had I known of Simon's desire to possess them, I would never have donated them in the first place," Madu said regretfully.

"You could not have known what Simon would become."

"No, I suppose not. But I always had reservations about his father, and the apple does not fall far from the tree. Do you know why he wants the books so badly?"

Mr. Perrot did know the answer to Madu's question, but he thought it best not to open that door. "No one can fully understand the pursuits of madmen," he said.

"Deya knew, didn't she?" Madu reflected. "She always seemed to know things. She never let those books out of her sight."

A black vehicle sped by, narrowly missing a group of bikers, who yelled out expletives. Madu pointed toward a plaza with food stands and vendors and a nearly fifty-meter-tall obelisk. "That is Tahrir Square," he said. "That is where the Egyptian Spring started fifty years ago. It was tragically cut short by the Great Disruption, which opened the door to the rise of the twelve ruthless Khufus. The obelisk was erected to remind the citizens of Egypt not to take for granted the sacrifices of those who helped create a free Egypt."

"Then your name should be at the very top," Mr. Perrot said. "A new-generation pharaoh." They both laughed.

"You should extend your stay here and help me, Robert. The government has undertaken a massive effort to restore the Giza pyramids. Two weeks ago, they even placed copper capstones at the apexes of all three. Please stay. I am certain that together we can bring forward the greatest discovery since the finding of the *Chronicles*."

"That is an enticing thought," Mr. Perrot said. "You said that the information we uncovered in Mexico could help you here?"

"Yes," Madu said. "My two years in Egypt before leaving to join the Council were spent searching for the secret chamber where the blue orb had taken me. Despite Nadine's urging, I wanted nothing to do with politics or the government that was emerging after the fall of the Khufus. I only wanted to locate that chamber. My fame provided me with access to all of the sealed areas of the pyramids and also to the many tombs and chambers at the Valley of the Kings and the Temple of Hathor. At each of those places, I uncovered more clues that confirmed what the blue orb had demonstrated to me: that the pyramids of Giza were more than large gravestones." With traffic building up, Madu slowed the car and rolled down his window to let in some fresh air. "All the clues pointed to the likelihood that the pyramids had been used as energy devices. When I finally discovered the room under the

Menkaure Pyramid, I was even more inspired to find the key to its activation."

"You actually found the room?" Mr. Perrot asked.

"I did, Robert. But unfortunately, at that time, I didn't possess the knowledge or the insight to decipher the mystery further. That was also when Camden contacted me and proposed establishing the Council of Satraya."

"Do others know about the room?" Mr. Perrot asked.

"Only Nadine and Rigel. No one else. The entrance remains a secret even to this day."

Mr. Perrot took all this in, gazing out at the square. "And how does Cassandra's music teacher fit into all this?"

"Yes, Sumsari seemed to understand a great deal about the energy lines that cover the surface of the earth. At the time, I believed his knowledge would assist me with my design. I theorized that a radioactive core would be even more energized if it was located at certain places on the globe. Sumsari talked about something called Sonorous Lines, which I had never heard of. Many years later I came across a reference to something called ley lines, which I think are the same thing. His explanation did help me to understand why pyramids and temples around the world had been erected in certain locations."

"In her recordings, Cassandra indicated that Sumsari had gained his knowledge during his travels in Europe just after the Great Disruption."

"Sumsari told me the same thing. Had I known back then that sound, music, and resonance were the actual key, I would have paid much more attention to what Sumsari was explaining to me." Madu smiled. "If we could find him, I now know what questions I would ask him. Has Valerie made any progress in locating him?"

"Not that I know of. As I said, her main focus is finding the people responsible for the gas well explosions. Another group of agents is looking into Sumsari's abduction."

The traffic cleared, but before Madu could accelerate, a black vehicle screeched to a stop in front of them, and Mr. Perrot saw two men jump out. Madu's car jolted forward, and Mr. Perrot and Madu were whiplashed backward as a second black vehicle crashed into their rear. Before they could make sense of what was happening, the driver- and passenger-side windows were smashed, and the doors opened. Their assailants stuck small silver objects onto Mr. Perrot's and Madu's temples. The last thing either one remembered before falling unconscious was a beeping sound.

47

If no one understands you, why do you lament? Does the
rain lament when you tell it to go away?

—THE CHRONICLES OF SATRAYA

"We're approaching from the south," Rigel Wright said, looking at a
3-D map of Pico Island displayed in front of him. Logan, Valerie, and
Chetan stood around a small table at the center of Rigel's submarine,
which he affectionately called *Nemo*. Surrounding them, at several control stations, were eight crew members performing various tasks.

Chetan had been right. While neither Valerie nor Logan had liked
his idea about how to get to NovaCon Island, it had turned out to be
the best option available. Rigel Wright had remained in Washington,
D.C., after his meeting with President Salize, and his yacht, the *Water
Shadow*, was docked in Chesapeake Bay. Logan had put aside his dislike
of Rigel, and it hadn't taken much effort on Valerie's part to persuade
the billionaire to transport her, Logan, and Chetan to the island in the
Azores that Sylvia had identified. The *Water Shadow* lived up to its billing
as the fastest ship ever constructed and was able to complete the forty-
five-hundred-kilometer trip in less than twenty-four hours. Director
Sully and the rest of the president's cabinet were busy crafting the of-

ficial statement they would deliver to the public about the energy crisis. An announcement that NovaCon was working on an energy solution was going to take place in less than twelve hours.

"What's the plan for entering the facility?" Logan asked. "From what we saw at the lab, their pyramid seems to be pretty isolated and I would assume pretty well guarded."

"The outer perimeter of the island is covered by heavy vegetation, which will provide you with sufficient cover to get onto the island," Rigel said, as he zoomed in on the image and panned the map. "But once you make your way toward the volcano and the pyramid device to the west of it, you'll be on the open lava fields. They'll be able to spot you for sure."

"What about a nighttime landing?" Chetan asked.

"You could try, but the terrain is rough. The lava rocks are jagged, and maneuvering over them is treacherous, even by day."

"We'll have to risk a daytime approach," Valerie said.

"What are those green dotted lines on the map?" Logan asked. "They seem to go in all different directions."

Rigel paused for a moment before answering. He zoomed in on the western portion of the island and one of the dotted green lines that Logan was referring to. "Now, there's an interesting thought. You might be able to use Gruta das Torres to conceal your approach."

"Gruta what?" Valerie said.

"A lava tube," explained Rigel. "All over the western part of the island is a series of interconnected lava tubes, which were formed more than a thousand years ago. Before the Great Disruption, locals and tourists walked through them. Gruta das Torres was the longest recorded lava tube in the Azores, more than thirty-three hundred meters long. And that is just what they were able to explore. Some estimates have it at double that length."

"How do we know if any of these tubes will lead to the NovaCon device?" Logan asked.

"That we can easily figure out," Rigel said. He projected another image next to the one of the island. "This is a more detailed map of the Gruta and its tributaries. If we overlay the two maps, we can see how close you'll be able to get to the pyramid."

Valerie examined the merging of the two maps. "The end of the tunnel looks like it brings us pretty close to the pyramid."

"The opening to the vent tube is near the old tourist center, located here." Rigel pointed to it. "Based on this map, there is a vent tube at the end of the tunnel that you can use to get back to the surface. It looks like you'll only be about fifty meters away from the device."

"Pretty lucky, if you ask me," Chetan said.

"They must know about the lava tube," Logan pointed out. "Especially since they built the device so close to it."

Valerie thought for a moment. "The Gruta is still the best option. Walking across the open lava rock field, by either day or night, seems too dangerous."

"We'll surface about four hundred meters from shore," Rigel said. "The underwater volcanic activity in these parts makes it too risky for us to take *Nemo* any closer." Logan looked out the huge portals of the submarine and could see large bubbles of steam rising from the sea floor. "Maurice will take you the rest of the way on the skid."

"ETA ten minutes, Mr. Wright," one of the crew said.

"We'll provide you with some equipment—ropes, lights, and such," Rigel said. "The three of you should get ready. We'll remain submerged, but we'll stay in the area until we hear back from you." Rigel sat back in his chair and crossed his arms over his chest. "You're really convinced that Catherine is behind the destruction of the natural-gas wells? That she's bent on destroying that industry in order to corner the market with her own alternative energy?"

"We are," Valerie said firmly, as she checked her weapon and put it back into her holster.

"We also think this pyramid device NovaCon built is responsible for the recent earthquakes and the health problems people have been having," Logan added. "It's time to see if we're right."

Rigel nodded. "Good luck to all three of you. And try not to let Valerie boss you around too much," he added, looking at Logan.

✳   ✳   ✳

"This must be the old visitors center," Valerie said, as she, Logan, and Chetan walked up to a large, vine-covered building with toppled welcome signs out front.

"I feel like a modern-day explorer," Chetan said.

They tore down the brush growing over the door of the abandoned building, and the words *Gruta das Torres* appeared, etched into the wall next to the door. Logan entered the building, followed by Valerie and then Chetan. Their steps crunched quietly on the scattered debris.

Chetan knelt down to examine something. "These are fish bones and the remnants of shellfish. They must have become trapped in here when the Azores were flooded by the tsunami."

Valerie held up a glass bottle. A mangled bicycle and rusted cans lay at her feet. "The floodwaters must have carried this stuff from the nearby town." Valerie walked over to a sheet of tin roofing and lifted it up. She quickly stepped backward. "Along with a few dead bodies."

Logan looked over and saw a human skull and what appeared to be the rib bones of a human chest cavity. The rest of the body was nowhere in sight. "Let's keep moving," he said. "The entrance to the lava tunnel should be really close."

The rest of the visitors center looked much the same, except that farther into the building, large portions of the roof had collapsed. Logan could see the sky through large holes in the walls. Birds were flying around, and the dirt that had been carried there now gave life to lush vegetation.

"There's a set of stairs over here," Chetan said. He used his hatchet to chop away at an overgrown thorny bush. Logan and Valerie cleared away the branches until they could see the crumbling concrete steps that zigzagged downward.

"The tunnel must be down there," Valerie said, peering into the pitch-black darkness.

Logan opened his backpack and pulled out three small head lamps that Rigel had provided. They strapped them around their heads and turned them on.

Valerie pulled out her PCD and projected the image of the tunnel map they had studied on the submarine. "If the map is accurate, we have about a two-thousand-meter trek from here."

They started down the stairs, the air thick and humid. Soon they reached the bottom and were walking on a smooth, shiny floor. "I would have expected the ground to be rougher," Logan said.

"We're walking on a pahoehoe flow," Chetan said. "This kind of lava flow has a very slow velocity, which allows the outer skin to cool and form a smooth surface."

Logan glanced over his shoulder at the natural light that illuminated the bottom of the staircase they'd descended. He was certain that this was the last bit of daylight they were going to see for some time.

"It's pretty warm down here, isn't it?" Valerie said. She took off her jacket and tied its sleeves around her waist.

"It shouldn't be," Chetan said. "Underground lava tunnels are usually more temperate. I'm not sure where the heat is coming from."

Valerie led everyone forward. Some portions of the lava tube were quite tall, nearly fifteen meters, while others didn't break two. From time to time, they heard whistling from above as wind passed through an upper lava tube. Small openings created by gas bubbles allowed air to flow between the layers of tunnels. Logan paused to look at a portion of the wall where tourists had scribbled their names and the dates of their visits into the white bacteria that grew there. Stalactites hung from the ceiling, and the once-smooth ground was now dotted with basalt rocks of various sizes that had fallen from the ceiling.

"I don't see any indications that this tunnel is being used by Nova-Con," Chetan said. "It doesn't look as if anyone has been here recently."

"Let's hope it stays that way," Valerie said.

They ventured deeper into the lava tube. Bats scurried off as the trio's head lamps shone into their dens, disrupting their sleep. Valerie pulled out her PCD from time to time to make sure that they were headed in the right direction and that every step took them closer to the NovaCon device.

"It's getting hotter," Logan said, stopping to take a sip of water from his canteen before handing it to Chetan.

Valerie glanced at her PCD. "I wonder how my father is doing. He told me he would send me a message once he arrived at Madu's house."

"He's fine," Logan said, reassuring her and partly himself as he re-called Sebastian's cryptic words concerning the teacher of the King's Gambit. "They just have a ton of catching up to do." Logan put his canteen back into his backpack. "How much farther do we have to go?"

"About eighty more meters," Chetan said. "In theory, the exit vent is just up there. With any luck, we'll be right next to—" Chetan stopped and turned off his head lamp. He took a few steps forward, peering down the tunnel.

Logan and Valerie followed. "What is it?" Valerie asked.

"I see a faint light down there."

"Very faint," Valerie said, removing her M&P40 from her shoulder holster. "Let's go."

She quietly led the way, and the light in the distance grew brighter. Some fifty meters down, the tunnel opened into a spacious cavern il-luminated by a floodlight above a stainless-steel door. When they were close enough, Valerie stopped, squatting behind a large boulder. Chetan and Logan joined her there. They turned off their head lamps.

Chetan leaned around the boulder to get a better look. "I don't see any security cameras by the door."

They stayed silent for a few moments; all they heard was the whis-tling of air that passed over the numerous holes in the cavern's ceilings and upper walls.

Valerie peered over the boulder. "I don't see anything, either. Let's take a closer look." She raised her gun, and they moved forward, Chetan now brandishing his gun, too.

"How does this thing open?" Logan asked, eyeing the stainless-steel door, which had no handles or hinges. "I don't even see a security panel."

"Probably proximity," Chetan suggested. "You need to have a proximity device to open it."

Valerie holstered her gun and turned her head lamp back on. "Wasn't there supposed to be an exit vent here leading to the surface?" She pulled out her PCD and looked at the tunnel map. "Yeah, right here."

"It's probably behind the door," Logan said, placing his hand on it.

"So now what?" Chetan asked, discouraged.

"Now we find another way out." Logan turned his head lamp back on and surveyed the ceilings and walls. He sniffed the air. "I smell sulfur. Do you?"

Valerie nodded. "The whistling is much louder in here."

"That's because there are many more holes in the walls and ceiling here than there were in the narrower part of the tunnel. There must be other lava tubes above us," Logan said. "Tributaries of the Gruta."

"Where there is flowing air, there might be a way out," Chetan suggested. "We just need to find a hole up there that we can fit through."

"And then get up there," Valerie added.

Logan looked back at the boulder. "Boost me up. I have an idea." Chetan interlocked his hands, providing Logan with a step to climb up. Standing on top of the boulder, Logan looked up at the ceiling. His head lamp illuminated an opening there.

"Could we fit through it?" Valerie asked.

"I think so," Logan said. "It's still about three to four meters up there. Are you in the mood for a little rock climbing? We'll need that rope and grappling hook that Rigel gave us."

Valerie unhooked the rope from her belt, and Chetan tied one of the ends to a small grappling hook.

Logan reached down and took the hook and the rope from Valerie. He steadied himself atop the boulder and began to spin the rope with the hook attached. After building speed, he launched it toward the hole and missed terribly. The hook bounced off the ceiling with a clank and fell to the ground. After a few more failed attempts, Valerie grew impatient. "Let a trained professional give it a try."

Logan gave her a look, but he jumped off the boulder and helped Valerie climb on top of it. She took a few moments to study the hole in the ceiling and the hook on the end of the rope. Then she whirled the rope. On her first try, it sailed into the hole and wedged itself.

Chetan whistled appreciatively. "That why she's one of WCF's finest."

Valerie pulled on the rope to make sure that it was secure and began climbing up. A humbled Logan followed and found a wide smile on Valerie's face as he made it through and joined her in the upper lava tube.

"It's hotter up here. The sulfur smell is more pronounced, too."

"Yeah, and you can really feel the breeze," Valerie said, then called through the opening, "Come on, Chetan. Your turn."

Chetan grabbed the rope and started climbing. When he was barely a meter and a half off the ground, he jumped down and turned off his head lamp.

Valerie leaned over the opening. "Chetan, what are you doing? Get up here right now!"

"Pull up the rope!" he said, his voice low. "The door just opened. I count six men. They have guns and spot lamps."

Logan and Valerie turned off their head lamps. They could hear muffled voices. "Hurry up and start climbing. That's an order!" Valerie whispered.

"No time. They're coming this way. I'm going to make a run for it. You and Logan need to keep going." Chetan shot off into the darkness.

"Someone's down here!" one of the men yelled. "He's running down the tunnel."

"Stop!" another yelled.

Logan pulled Valerie back from the opening. More shouts followed, and then a round of gunshots echoed in the cavern. They heard people running below on the cavern floor. Logan squeezed Valerie's hand. A moment later, there were more raised voices and more rounds of gunfire.

"I'm going after him." Valerie pulled away from Logan and prepared herself to climb down. "I can't leave him."

"Wait," Logan said. "Listen."

They heard people approaching below. "Who else is down here with you?" a deep voice asked.

"No one," Chetan said. "I'm a geologist. I'm just exploring the island."

"This island and everything on it is private property," another male voice said.

"Here's his badge. He's WCF."

"A geologist, eh? Keep searching the tunnel. I'll send more men down here. Where there's one WCF agent, there's bound to be more. I'll take him up and let the boss know."

Logan and Valerie remained still and silent until they couldn't hear any more voices. "He's still alive," Logan whispered. "We'll get him back. We have to keep going." When he turned on his head lamp, he saw the anguish on Valerie's face.

"I'm not losing another member of my team," she said, determined.

Logan turned on her head lamp and grabbed her hand.

The upper lava tube was lower and narrower than the one they had come from, and it was much hotter. The smell of sulfur was also more pronounced. Barely able to stand without knocking their heads against the ceiling, Logan and Valerie walked in the direction of the breeze. The tunnel curved right and then left as they proceeded. They heard a rumbling sound before a faint orange light appeared about thirty meters ahead of them. The tunnel then grew even smaller, and they had to hunch down in order to move forward until they couldn't go any farther. They gazed awestruck at the gigantic pit that was the source of the heat, the sulfuric smell, and the orange light. Lava poured out of an opening like a waterfall in slow motion, falling in a river of molten rock. The heat was almost unbearable.

Logan looked up. Metal beams and girders were supporting a retractable flooring system, perfectly square in shape. Catwalks and ladders led up to small hatches on its perimeter. Hanging from the center of the flooring system was a fifty-meter tube that was attached to a large cylindrical object. "Where in the world are we?"

Valerie pulled out her PCD. "According to the map, we are directly below the pyramid." She frantically pushed the buttons of her PCD, trying again and again and sighing in defeat when she put it away.

"What is it?" Logan asked.

"They deactivated Chetan's PCD," she said. "I'm not getting any signal from it."

48

If you saw a man steal some food from another man and then saw that man robbed by someone else, would you deem that justice? Or would you offer him some bread?

—THE CHRONICLES OF SATRAYA

CAIRO, 1:15 P.M. LOCAL TIME, MARCH 26, 2070

Mr. Perrot awoke with a terrible headache. He opened his eyes and saw that he was lying on a stone floor facing a wall covered with hieroglyphics. He reached to the right side of his head near his temple and could feel that a small piece of metal, about the size of a bottle cap, had been placed there. He tried to remove it, but it hurt too much to touch the skin surrounding it. He heard a sound from behind him, and he tensed. Not knowing what to expect, he turned cautiously. To his relief, he saw it was Madu lying beside him, trying to sit up. "Are you all right, my friend?" Mr. Perrot asked groggily, still trying to get his own bearings.

Madu blinked slowly. "What happened? The last thing I remember is someone breaking the windows of the car." Madu felt the right side of his head. He, too, had a small piece of metal on his temple. "What is this?"

"I'm not sure." Mr. Perrot mustered the strength to rise to his feet. "Whoever brought us here must have affixed these devices to us. Not that I'm even sure where *here* is." Large copper urns spouting flames sat in front of massive pillars at the four corners of the room. No doorway was visible, and the ceiling was so high the light of the flames could not illuminate it.

Madu brought himself to one knee and gazed around the chamber. "It can't be," he said in awe.

"Do you know this place?"

Madu quickly turned to the hieroglyphics on the wall closest to him. "I have studied this pattern a million times," he said, running his hand over it affectionately.

He extended his hand, and Mr. Perrot helped him to his feet.

"This is the secret chamber I told you about, the one I was brought to when I first discovered the *Chronicles* . . ."

"How is that possible?" Mr. Perrot asked. "You said only Nadine and Rigel knew about this place."

Madu did not answer. Mr. Perrot felt a tingling on the back of his neck. He reached back to see if an insect was crawling up his neck.

"There is nothing there, Robert," Madu said. "I believe that what you're feeling are charged particles in the air. Do you remember I told you that capstones had been placed on top of all the Giza pyramids as part of the restoration work?"

Mr. Perrot looked at him, astonished. "Are you saying that the pyramid is generating electricity?"

"Yes," Madu said. "This chamber is directly under the apex. Now that the capstone has been put into place, a tiny amount of electricity is flowing."

The sound of mumbling caught their attention. Mr. Perrot could see someone's shadow on the wall near one of the large pillars at the opposite end of the room. He pressed his index finger to his lips, and then he and Madu quietly made their way across the chamber. Madu grabbed Mr. Perrot by the shoulder and moved him slightly to the side to avoid a raised platform on the ground that he was about to trip over. Mr. Perrot looked down and saw an image of two men playing flutes on it. It reminded him of the platform he'd seen in the Moon Pyramid at Teotihuacán. As he and Madu continued past it, they saw a large unzipped canvas bag filled with excavation supplies and hand tools. They assumed that the man, who was now mumbling more loudly, had brought it with him. When Mr. Perrot peeked around the pillar, he saw a man kneeling on the ground, facing the wall. The man's thinning gray hair floated in the air due to the static electricity in the chamber. He was drawing something on the wall with a piece of white chalk. Madu looked over Mr. Perrot's shoulder. The mumbling man seemed unaware of their presence and continued to draw over the ancient hieroglyphics.

"What is he writing?" Madu asked in a whisper, unable to see clearly in the dim light.

Mr. Perrot shook his head, unsure. "Hello," he called to the man, but he got no reply. "Hello," he called again, moving closer and placing his hand on the man's right shoulder.

The man screamed and jumped to his feet, dropping the piece of chalk. He stepped backward and pressed himself tightly against the wall, holding his arms rigidly by his side. Startled by his actions, Mr. Perrot and Madu also stepped back. The man was wide-eyed, his gaze rapidly shifting between Mr. Perrot and Madu. He seemed to be afraid of them. Mr. Perrot noticed that he, too, had a small metallic device attached to his right temple.

"It is OK, my friend," Mr. Perrot said in a calming tone. "We are not going to hurt you."

Madu took a few steps forward and bent down to better see the scribbling on the wall. "This is the same writing we saw at the Calhoun Center," Madu said, looking up at Mr. Perrot and then at the other man's face. "And this is Cassandra's music teacher, Sumsari Baltik."

49

Mind is Mind.

—THE CHRONICLES OF SATRAYA

CAIRO, 1:31 P.M. LOCAL TIME, MARCH 26, 2070

"What are you doing here?" Madu asked Sumsari. "How did you get here?"

Sumsari didn't answer. He continued to shift his gaze between Madu and Mr. Perrot.

"Sir," Madu persisted, "you must tell us how you came to be here."

"He's lost his faculties," Mr. Perrot said, turning to look around the chamber. "What is certain is that all of us have been brought here against our will. We need to get out of here." He checked his coat pockets for his PCD. He was unable to find it. Madu searched for his, but it was gone, too. "Where is the door to this room?"

"There is a small passageway close to where we awoke," Madu replied. "That is how I entered the second time, when I located the chamber on my own after much searching."

Mr. Perrot tried to take Sumsari by the arm to lead him to the passageway, but Sumsari knelt back down and once again started to scribble and mumble, this time more loudly. "Must find . . . suffering . . . death."

"Sir, you must come with us," Mr. Perrot implored. "It is not safe for you to stay here."

"Madness has overtaken him," Madu said. "I wonder what he is trying to say."

"He's saying the same thing that he has been saying since the moment we took him," a loud voice answered, echoing in the chamber.

Mr. Perrot and Madu turned around. A man stepped from behind one of the pillars, his face shadowed. Another, taller man emerged and stood by his side.

"Who are you?" Mr. Perrot asked. "Why have you brought us here?"

"Come now, Robert," the man said. "I thought you enjoyed the challenge of a good riddle. Or has something changed since our last encounter? You remember. By the river . . ."

Mr. Perrot squinted, trying to get a better look. "I'm afraid you have me at a disadvantage."

The man stepped over to one of the large fire urns and picked up a torch that lay on the ground next to it. He placed one end into the urn, allowing it to catch fire. Then he walked over to the platform at the center of the chamber and stepped onto it. The taller man joined him there. The light from the torch cast an eerie orange glow on the man's scarred face. But despite his disfigurement, Mr. Perrot recognized who it was.

"Simon," he said, not believing his eyes. The man smiled crookedly. "It can't be—I saw you fall—into the pyre."

"How does that quotation go?" Simon thought for a moment. "'The rumors of my death have been greatly exaggerated' . . . or something like that. I was never a big fan of Mark Twain."

"Why have you brought us here, Simon?" Mr. Perrot asked defiantly. "Have you not done enough damage?"

"Relax, Robert," Simon said in a casual tone. "I'm not really that interested in you at the moment." He turned his piercing dark eyes to Madu. "I'm more concerned with the man standing next to you. The one and only Madu Shata."

"What do you want from him?" Mr. Perrot persisted. "Speak plainly."

"Our friend here," Simon said, gesturing at Madu, "sold the plans for an energy device to a couple of my colleagues. And as it turns out, the schematics are unfinished. At first, we thought that decrepit man was all we needed to complete the plans. But as you can see, his communication skills are somewhat lacking." Simon gave Sumsari a good long stare before turning back to Madu. "That's why we had to secure your support, too."

Mr. Perrot looked aghast at Madu.

"I did no such thing," Madu insisted, a confused look on his face. "I would never have sold away my life's work to anyone. Especially not the likes of you!"

"Rashidi"—Simon motioned to the tall, dark-skinned man who accompanied him—"show our good friends what we are talking about." Rashidi pulled out his PCD and used it to project the image of a pyramid surrounded by a series of elaborate mathematical equations. "Are these not your plans?" Simon asked. "Is this not the device that you have been secretly designing for the last many years?"

Madu recognized his work. "Where did you get these?" he shouted in anger.

Simon stepped off the platform and walked through the projected image, stopping just a few meters from Madu. "The wheres and hows are unimportant. What is important is that you fix your broken device."

"It cannot be fixed," Madu said. "My original plans were wrong."

"Anything can be fixed," Simon said, smiling and running a finger down the side of his scarred face. He pointed to a particular spot on the 3-D image that was marked *Activation Chamber*. "Now, I am told that this cylindrical thing hanging underneath the device is not working properly. You need to show us how to fully energize the pyramid."

"I don't know how," Madu said. "It is what I have spent years trying to figure out."

"But he knows, doesn't he?" Simon glanced over at Sumsari, who continued to scribble on the walls. "I was told that somewhere in the head of that miserable creature over there is the key to perfecting your design."

"Who told you that?" Mr. Perrot asked.

"Once again, Robert," Simon said, as he gave him a baleful look, "a truly unimportant question."

Mr. Perrot shook his head. "And why should we help you?"

"Now, that is a much more interesting query." Simon motioned to Rashidi. The projected image of Madu's plans disappeared, and suddenly, Mr. Perrot and Madu both heard a beeping sound. The next thing they knew, intense pain shot through their entire bodies. They both grabbed their heads. "One reason to help me is that you will feel better if you do," Simon said. The excruciating pain continued, and then it ceased when the beeping did. "Those devices on your heads are calibrated with the sensory centers of your brains. I was told they are quite effective, and judging by your reactions, I can see that I was not misled."

Mr. Perrot and Madu recovered their composure.

"The energy pyramid is not a toy," Madu said. "You must know that there is a point of no return. I would not attempt to build one without first solving all the equations."

"I actually agree with you, but I fear it is too late," Simon said. "A couple of my rather rash colleagues have already constructed one. It seems they've been trying to turn it on for some time now, without much success."

"So it's true," Madu said, hearing his worst suspicions confirmed. "The unexplained earthquakes, the sickness, and the turmoil—it is all being caused by an energy device."

"I'm afraid so," Simon said. "But I am here to put an end to the world's suffering. My colleagues have turned to me for help. If you were to assist me, we could end the world's troubles and at the same time solve the current energy crisis. Everybody wins."

"You are the only person who will win, Simon," Mr. Perrot said.

"I will not help you," Madu said.

Simon smiled. "I think you will." Rashidi activated his PCD, and Mr. Perrot and Madu saw a holographic projection of Nadine. She was bound to a chair by silver straps, her mouth covered with tape and a neuro device attached to her right temple. "Your wife would be most appreciative if you completed your work." Rashidi pulled out a PCD from his pocket. He manipulated it to project the current time. "If you don't help, Rashidi here is going to send a signal to the neuro device attached to your wife's head. Keep an eye on this clock, and know that at the top of each hour, your wife will be squirming in pain. You'll find some tools in that bag we brought down here for him," Simon said, with a gesture at Sumsari, "but it looks like he's only interested in a piece of chalk. When you figure something out, call us on this PCD—it's a one-way connection to a single HoloPad device." Simon turned and walked away.

"What if I can't?" Madu asked.

Simon stopped and turned. "It would be a shame to see such a beautiful woman suffer pain. Maybe I'll be merciful and end it quickly for her."

Mr. Perrot and Madu watched silently as Simon and his man left through a small doorway.

Simon poked his head back through the opening. "Robert," he said. "I feel like you and I have done this before."

Mr. Perrot and Madu could hear laughter until the stone door swung closed.

50

Uniqueness is not in the challenges that people face but in the
way they deal with them.

—THE CHRONICLES OF SATRAYA

SALISBURY, U.K., 11:49 A.M. LOCAL TIME, MARCH 26, 2070

"Are you sure we should be doing this?" Britney asked.

"Come on," Anita said, adjusting the blue book bag slung over her
shoulder. "I think they went this way."

After Anita and Halima had made their discovery in the tunnel
under the armory, Anita had called Britney and persuaded her to ac-
company her on an outing the next day. Anita had hated lying to her
father, but he would have been upset if she'd told him she was going to
search for the Altar of the Bluestones. She couldn't get out of her mind
the look of love and concern on his face when she'd told him she'd been
asked by the head of the university's chemistry department to fill in for
a professor who was ill.

"But what about you, my dear?" her father had asked. "Are you sure
you feel up to it? I don't want you risking your health by overdoing it."

"I feel fine," she'd assured him. "Plus, this is a great opportunity for
me, and I don't want to pass it up."

Her father had given her a kind look. "If it means that much to you, by all means go."

Anita had hugged him with all her might before running out the door to meet Britney.

She had reasoned that if she were to find the Altar of the Bluestones, the best place to start would be to follow the path that the Quinns had set forth for Sumsari. She and Britney boarded a plane, which flew them a short distance from the Isle of Man to London, where they continued by high-speed rail to the historic city of Salisbury in southern England. The whole trip took just a few hours.

Upon arrival, the two girls spotted someone they did not expect to see. They followed stealthily and watched from across the street as an iron gate leading into the renowned Salisbury Cathedral was opened.

"What is Mr. Quinn doing in Salisbury?" Britney asked as she watched Sebastian enter with Bukya walking at his side. "And why did he go into the very place we're going? Did you tell him anything?"

"No," Anita replied. "I didn't say a word to him. I didn't even know he'd returned from his trip."

The girls waited a few moments before making their way across the street and walking over to the iron gate. Anita tugged and set it rattling. "It's locked." She peered through the gate's intricate latticework and down a walkway that led to the cathedral's tall wooden side doors. "The doors look locked, too."

"How did he get in?" Britney asked, gazing down the walkway.

"Someone must have already been inside and opened it for him," Anita said. "Let's try the main entrance. It's just around the corner."

"The cathedral is closed for ten more days," a voice called out to them. "The restoration of the choir, presbytery, and chapter house are all under way." A teenage boy dressed in blue work clothes approached them. A gardening rake was resting over his right shoulder, and a bulky set of keys was attached to his belt loop. His hands were dirty, and there was a smudge on his face. "They've moved the Magna Carta off site for safekeeping, if that's what you were aiming to see. The organ is also being restored, so there will be no concert this evening. You'll have to come back in a few weeks."

Anita froze, staring at the young man. She recognized him as the person who had been playing the organ in the vision she'd had while looking into the waterfall in the Arcis Chamber. He wore the same blue jumpsuit, and his hands were dirty, just as the organ player's had been.

"Maybe you can let us in for a quick peek." Britney jumped in, unsure why Anita had gone silent. She smiled and put her hand on the young man's arm. "We've come an awful long way to see the cathedral."

"Yes," Anita said, following her friend's lead. "We've journeyed all the way from the Isle of Man. We are writing a paper about the cathedral, and it's due in less than a week. Plus, this might be your only chance to press the keys and pull the knobs of the organ." The young man gave Anita an odd look. "I know you've always wanted to do that," she added, smiling.

"How could you know . . . ?" The young man stopped himself and shook his head. "I still don't think I can allow you in. The dean would be furious if he found out. Plus, I have a ton of work to finish around the grounds."

"Just for a few minutes," Britney persisted, squeezing the young man's arm. "We only want to take a little peek inside."

The young man took a quick look around. "I'm going to get into so much trouble." He sighed, relenting. He tossed the rake to the ground and approached the iron gate. He searched through his ring of keys and used one to open it. Anita and Britney followed him inside. "I will meet you both back here in a half hour," he said. "You have to leave then."

Britney gave him a quick kiss on the cheek. "You're a doll," she said. "And if you're ever on the Isle, I know this great castle we can show you." Britney gave Anita a wink. The two girls walked through the doors.

"Remember, thirty minutes!" the young man said, closing the doors behind them.

Anita and Britney entered the southern side of Salisbury Cathedral. Many of the interior lights had been turned off because of the restoration work, but the magnificent stained-glass windows allowed in sufficient light for them to be able to appreciate the exquisite architecture.

"Amazing," Britney said, pointing up at the vaulted and ribbed ceiling. Her voice echoed as she spoke.

"Hush." Anita pressed her finger to her lips. "We're not supposed to be in here, remember. We need to find where he went."

Anita slowly walked across the stone floor. Britney followed her, awestruck by the multitude of statues lining the walls. Hanging above the lifelike sculptures of saints, dukes, and duchesses were paintings and icons from the early days of the church.

"It's sort of spooky in here," Britney whispered, reading the names of people that had been carved into the floor. "Are people really buried under these markers?"

"Yes," Anita said. "But the more famous people are entombed in those chests along the walls." Britney looked at the large stone sarcophagi with sculpted effigies on their lids. Some were simple, others far more elaborate. Anita pointed to one that seemed newer than the others. "The man and woman who are entombed in that one don't deserve to be in here."

"Why would you say such a thing?" Britney walked over to a large white marble sarcophagus with the faces of a man and a woman carved into its top. She read the names on the plaque affixed to its front, before turning back to Anita. "Charles Pottman, Steward of Gravely House, 2045, and Lady Guinevere Pottman, 2045. Who were they?" Anita didn't answer, as she stared coldly at the stone crypt. "Were they involved in whatever happened to you before you came to the Isle?" Again, Britney waited for an answer, but none was forthcoming.

Anita turned toward the central aisle of the cathedral. "There's the organ," she said. "Just like in my vision."

"Well, our gardener boyfriend did say they were restoring it."

Anita and Britney made their way toward it. They passed more crypts, more paintings, and what was believed to be the oldest working clock in the world, constructed in 1386. Anita heard the sound of voices. She grabbed Britney by the arm and quickly led her to the canon stalls at the center of the cathedral, stopping when they reached one of the massive central pillars. Anita peeked around it in the direction of the voices. She pulled back and whispered to Britney, "I see him. He's standing at the other end of the nave talking with a few people."

"What people?"

Anita shook her head, unsure. "We have to get closer."

"Are you bonkers?" Britney whispered. "What we need to do is get out of here."

"Come on." Anita was not deterred by her friend's trepidation. She left the cover of the pillars and moved down a side corridor running parallel to the nave. Britney reluctantly followed. The girls ducked down and tiptoed their way from pillar to pillar. They finally came to a stop behind a massive, intricately carved sarcophagus and squatted down. A placard on the stone monument indicated that it belonged to Bishop Beauchamp, who had died in 1481.

Anita and Britney peered around the sarcophagus and saw Sebastian standing in front of a uniquely designed water font. It was a cruciform vessel roughly three meters wide and a meter and a half tall, crafted from bronze, with faded green oxidation on its surface. Streams of water flowed from its four corners, and its shiny surface reflected the cathedral's architecture and the colorful stained-glass windows. Next to Sebastian sat Bukya, ever watchful. Standing across from them were two men and two women. Anita and Britney were close enough to eavesdrop.

"You are failing, Sebastian," one of the men said. "We warned your parents, and now we give you the same warning. The house of Quinn should have allowed the world to falter after the Great Disruption. Nature is speaking again as it did then, but your house chooses not to listen."

Sebastian remained silent. A woman with short red hair said, "Makesh is correct. Had your parents allowed what was necessary to occur, they would still be alive today, and we would not be dealing with such an ominous threat to the earth itself."

Makesh? thought Anita. That was the name she and Halima had come across in Sebastian's parents' autobiography. He had been Sebastian's teacher.

"The ill-fated Rising is over," Makesh added. "Mankind could not stand but a single generation before reverting back to its selfish and arrogant patterns of life. This should be evident to you now."

"A great storm is coming," the second man said. "And I see that this latest threat will finish what was left undone by the Great Disruption. I advise you not to interfere. A new age for mankind will be ushered forth. Much that requires cleansing shall be cleansed."

Anita watched Bukya leave Sebastian's side and approach the woman who had remained silent. She had long blond hair that fell to the small of her back and knelt down gracefully at the dog's approach, greeting him with a gentle stroke across the fur and a rub of the ears. It was clear that these two were not strangers. The woman whispered something to Bukya, causing him to press his nose to her cheek.

"There is nothing new under the sun or on the lands of earth for these people, Sebastian," said the other woman with the short red hair. "They have abused this planet for far too long. It is time for it to end. It is time for this lot to pass into the annals of time and for a new group to come forward. Why do you resist the cycles that have been taking place since time immemorial?"

Sebastian spoke for the first time. "We are not separate from them, Satia. There are more things between heaven and earth than are dreamt of in even *our own* philosophy." He gestured to the font with both hands. "The flowing water of this altar knows this truth. Even if you watch the water fall for a thousand years, the streams will never be the same. Each cascade, each tumble, is made from different droplets of different rains of different rivers and of different tears. No, Satia," Sebastian said, lowering his arms, "everything is always different and ever-changing under the sun. And should one ever become bored by what one sees under the light of Ra, one should then be implored to appreciate the world by the light of the moon."

Who are these people? Anita wondered. *They are so cold to let the world suffer.* She watched as Bukya walked back over to Sebastian.

The woman with the long blond hair rose to her feet and spoke, her voice gentle. "You speak as you always have, Sebastian. But you cannot deny, as Qumron said, that the world is not clean. You cannot deny that a change must take place."

"A change is taking place," Sebastian said. "There are those fighting for their land as we speak."

"But not enough of them," said the second man, the one named Qumron. "Most are unaware of what is currently taking place around them, just as they were unaware of what was coming forty years ago."

"The populace doesn't even question why thousands died a few short months ago," Makesh said. "They have no idea that they all walk around with altered DNA."

"Altered DNA?" Britney whispered. "What is he talking about?"

Anita didn't answer her, even though she was well aware of what Makesh was talking about.

"They have been lied to," Sebastian said.

"Being lied to does not excuse people from responsibility," Qumron said. "People know deep down when they are being deceived; they choose to ignore it because it's the expedient thing to do."

"We love the world as much as you do," Satia said. "But sometimes the end must be allowed to come so that a new beginning can unfold. That is why nature spoke so loudly during the Great Disruption."

"Your efforts and those of your parents have only staved off the inevitable," Qumron said. "The blue orb is fickle, Sebastian. The Quinns have benefited from its presence. But you know as well as the rest of us that this prosperity will not last indefinitely."

"So the brotherhood would see humanity perish?" Sebastian asked. "How—"

"If need be, yes," Satia interrupted with her voice raised. "It will not have been the first time."

"That cannot always be the answer, Satia," Sebastian said. "There must come a time when the solution of extinction is wiped off the table of options."

"I know what you are thinking, Sebastian," Makesh said. "You cannot have the Brahmastra. That device has not been used in a very long time and will not be allowed now."

"What are they talking about?" Britney whispered into Anita's ear. "What device?"

"Shhhh," Anita said, noticing that Bukya's ears had perked up, his eyes alert.

"The Brahmastra? No, you can't have that," Qumron said. "Even your parents would have given you the same counsel. The Altar of the Bluestones has aged. And the utility of the Brahmastra would be unpredictable at best."

"The Brahmastra will stay sealed," Satia said.

"I am not asking for the device, nor do I need it," Sebastian said.

"Then why did you call us here?" Makesh asked.

"To ensure your noninterference," Sebastian said.

"Noninterference?" Satia repeated. "You will not get any interference from us. With what is about to happen to the earth's voice, the final chapters of the Great Disruption will finally be written. Why would we interfere with that?"

"Let the world go, Sebastian," the woman with the long blond hair said. "You have already given up far too much for them. And if you continue, I fear that you will lose even more. Was it not you who once counseled that people should be left to find their own way? That the intermixing of lives is a tricky and messy business?"

"Heed her warning, Sebastian," Makesh said. "If you will not listen to us, then at the very least, listen to her. We have no more to discuss here."

"Peace be with you," Qumron said.

Anita watched as the two men and the woman named Satia turned and walked way. The woman with the long blond hair remained. She and Sebastian stood and looked at each other.

"You have not changed, my Sebastian," she said, taking a few steps forward and gazing at her reflection on the surface of the still water in the font. She bent forward and blew on the water, causing a ripple to radiate outward and disrupt the reflection of the cathedral ceiling. She gazed upward. "This pool reminds me of that archer's story you so like to tell. We only need a spinning wheel and a target." She smiled, looking back at him. "Do you really trust the Ford boy? Do you believe he will be able to fire his arrow and accomplish his task?"

"I do," Sebastian replied. "I am certain that more than just Logan will step forward."

"And if they fail?" the woman asked.

"Then they fail, and the brotherhood will have been correct. But what if they succeed? Will you see things differently then? Or will the people of the world still not have proven their worth? When was the last time the brotherhood shot their arrow?" Sebastian waited for a response, but none came. "At least, my archers are fighting to learn how."

The woman nodded. "Peace be with you, Sebastian," she said, and she walked away in the same direction as her companions. "Good-bye, Bukya."

Sebastian remained alone. He placed his hand on Bukya's head and began to whistle a tune that reverberated under the vaulted ceiling. As he continued to whistle the same sequence of notes over and over, the echo grew louder, causing a soft harmonic to spread throughout the cathedral. Anita and Britney stared in amazement as the harmonic lingered for an extended and inexplicable amount of time. Anita recognized the sequence of notes Sebastian whistled; it was the same progression she had heard during her vision in the Arcis Chamber. Except this time, the notes were harmonious, not gut-wrenching. Sebastian closed his eyes, seeming to immerse himself in the vibration.

After a few more seconds, he turned and walked to the exit with Bukya by his side.

Anita and Britney emerged from behind the sarcophagus and walked over to the font.

"What was that all about?" Britney asked. "Who were those people?"

"People who aren't going to do anything to stop what's happening to the world," Anita answered.

"Doesn't sound like Mr. Quinn is, either," Britney said.

Anita nodded solemnly. "We're going to have to do something ourselves."

"Do what?" Britney asked, afraid of the answer.

Anita pulled a small piece of paper from her book bag. "First, we need to find Sumsari's resonator," she said. "Then we need to figure out where the Altar of the Bluestones is."

51

Divine intervention does come, but only to those
who invite it with divine sincerity.

—THE CHRONICLES OF SATRAYA

"Didn't you hear what those people were saying?" Britney asked, exasperated. "Messing around with all of this is dangerous."

Anita shook her head. "I'm not going to sit around and watch as people all over the world die and suffer. I'm doing this. With or without you."

Britney looked at her friend. "You're so stubborn. Fine." She swiped the note out of Anita's hand, unfolded it, and read it out loud.

> THE CATHEDRAL KNOWS
> THAT THOSE WHO HAVE IT
> CANNOT SELL IT,
> THAT THOSE WHO WANT IT
> CANNOT BUY IT,
> AND THAT WHICH SHOWS IT
> CANNOT HIDE it.

Britney studied it incredulously. "This is all we have to go on?"

"It's a riddle," Anita said. "It was written on a stone that Halima and I found buried under the old armory tunnel at the castle. We're pretty sure it was written by Sumsari Baltik, the man I told you about."

"You forgot to capitalize the last word," Britney observed.

"That's how it was written on the stone," Anita said. "I think Sumsari intended it to be that way. As if the lowercase *it* is referring to something different from the uppercase *IT*."

"And you think his resonator, or whatever that thing is that you showed me a picture of, is here in the cathedral somewhere?"

"Yep," Anita said. "The riddle points to it: *The cathedral knows.*"

"So what can a person have that they cannot sell?" Britney asked, reading a line of the riddle. "Clearly nothing material."

"Agreed." Anita squinted as she sought the answer. "What about a person's voice? A person can't sell his voice."

"Wrong," Britney quickly responded. "You can record a song and sell it. I also suppose you could cut your voice box out and sell it."

Anita shook her head. "That's just gruesome. What else do people have that they can't sell? A house, a car, an animal, a pet, money?"

"No, no, no, and no," Britney replied in frustration. "All I know is that we need to get out of here. Our boyfriend is probably wondering where we are. What time is it, anyway? The clock is ticking."

Anita spun and looked at her friend with a gleam in her eye. "Ticking," she said, remembering the clicking of the clock during her vision in the mirror. "Time!"

"Yeah, what time is it? We have to get out of here."

"No, *time* is the answer to the riddle. Those who have *it* cannot sell *it*—time. Those who want *it* cannot buy *it*—time. That which shows *it* cannot hide *it*—time. And what shows time?" Anita asked, already knowing the answer.

"Brilliant! A clock," Britney said. "Isn't there a clock in here somewhere?"

"Yes, the oldest one in Europe," Anita said. "We passed it on the way in."

They quickly turned back to the center of the cathedral and made their way down the aisle where they'd entered, stopping in front of the old iron-framed clock. Anita looked at the two large stone weights hanging from the taut ropes that snaked through the pulleys attached to the cathedral's ceiling high above. The two massive windows on either side of the old timekeeper were being restored, and scaffolding surrounded it.

Britney inspected the main gears and trains looking for anything that resembled Sumsari's resonator. "Do you see anything?"

"Nothing down here," Anita replied. She tracked the ropes that supported the weights and counterweights of the clock. They stretched above the windows, reaching almost to the cathedral ceiling, where they were attached to a small wooden platform. "I wonder if he hid it up there." Before Britney could say anything, Anita adjusted her book bag and began climbing the scaffolding. She maneuvered up the rungs quickly until she reached the top, but the scaffolding was not high enough for her to reach the wooden platform. "I need to find something to stand on," Anita called to Britney. She grabbed an empty bucket that was on the top platform of the scaffolding and turned it upside down.

"Be careful," Britney called from below, as she watched Anita step onto the bucket and reach up to the wooden platform. "Do you see anything?"

"It's still too high, but I think I can feel something. Maybe even two things." Anita stood on her toes and stretched her arm further, almost losing her balance as she did so. Britney let out a short gasp. Anita regained her footing, then grabbed the items and placed them in her bag. She carefully stepped off the bucket and made her way down, a smile on her face. She reached into her book bag and pulled out a brass ball and a tuning fork.

"You found it!" Britney said excitedly. "OK, I have to admit, this treasure-hunting business is pretty fun. Now what?"

"Let's see how it works," Anita said, walking to the center of the cathedral. They stood next to the organ. "Here goes."

Anita struck the tuning fork against a stone pillar, holding it near the larger of the two openings on the brass resonator. She passed the tuning fork over the aperture until she found the correct position. As she and Halima had read, an exquisite harmonic filled the entire cathedral. Anita struck the tuning fork again, this time with more force. The resonator's harmonic seemed to be amplified by the cathedral's unique design, causing the hundreds of stained-glass windows to shake almost as if at a small tremor in the earth. The two girls listened in awe as the resonance continued. After about forty seconds, it began to dissipate.

"What are you two doing in here?"

Anita quickly stuffed the resonator and the tuning fork into her book bag. She turned and saw the young groundskeeper.

"All the windows were shaking."

"Must have been a minor earthquake," Britney said. "There have been so many of them lately, you know."

"We're finished with our research," Anita said. "We really appreciate your letting us in."

"You have to leave right now," the young man said. "The dean's about to show the stonemason where he wants the bluestone sculptures to go."

"Did you say bluestone?" Britney asked, her eyes widening.

"Yes, the city commissioned a few sculptures made from dolerite stone. Some of them will be placed outside on the lawn, and others will go in here."

Anita turned to her friend. "I think I know where the Altar of the Bluestones is."

52

It is all right to sit under the shade of a tree and be called lazy.

—THE CHRONICLES OF SATRAYA

NOVACON ISLAND, 1:16 P.M. LOCAL TIME, MARCH 26, 2070

Logan and Valerie used the ladders and catwalks to maneuver their way to a hatchway in the floor. After climbing through it, they found themselves in a small computer room. The ceiling was covered with large bundles of colored wires spread in multiple directions, and there was a single door with a security access panel attached to it. At the room's center was a cluttered desk with a single chair behind it. An open bag of crackers and a cup of coffee sat among the jumble of electronic parts, computer chips, and a soldering iron. Valerie walked over to the table with her gun drawn. She felt the side of the cup. "It's still warm. Whoever this belongs to didn't leave that long ago."

"We need to get out of here and find Chetan," Logan whispered. He tried the handle of the door, but it didn't open.

"We can't without an access card," Valerie said.

They heard voices and a few beeps coming from the other side of the door. Valerie grabbed Logan and took a position to its side. The door opened, and a heavyset man entered, carrying a plate of pastries.

Valerie pressed her gun to the man's head. "Don't say a word. And don't drop the pastries," she said.

Logan shut the door behind him. Valerie led the man to the table and pushed him down into the chair. Logan grabbed the plate from the man's hand and set it next to the cup of coffee.

Valerie took out her badge and showed it to the man. "Valerie Perrot, WCF," she said, walking to the other side of the desk to face him. "Where have you taken my agent?"

"M-madame," the man stammered in broken, accented English, clearly afraid. "I do not know who you are referring to. I only look after the electrical systems on the island. I am no more than a janitor to my employers."

"Who are your employers?" Logan asked.

"Catherine Bribergeld and Dario Magnor pay the bills around here."

"Did you say Dario?" Valerie said, glancing quickly at Logan.

"Yes," the man replied. "Dario Magnor. He's a nice man, always says hello to me. It's quite inspiring to see him walking around after spending most of his life in a wheelchair."

"Wheelchair?" Logan repeated.

"Yes. I don't know the whole story, but I heard he was injured during the Great Disruption while trying to save his family."

Now Logan and Valerie finally knew who the man in the wheelchair was. The man they had seen with Andrea and Simon in the newspaper clipping, the man Logan's mother had mentioned in her recordings as a frequent visitor to Fendral during the days of the first Council of Satraya, was Dario Magnor.

"Where is he now?" Valerie asked.

"Can't really say. He and Catherine are probably with the twins."

"What twins?" asked Logan.

"The doctors. They are the ones who designed the ZPF device."

Logan and Valerie exchanged looks. Valerie looked at the name plate on the table. "OK, Mr. Pastor," she said, "where is Catherine now?"

"She could be anywhere," Mr. Pastor replied. "Her office, the control center, the Hades Room."

"The Hades Room?" Logan repeated ominously.

"Let's start with her office," Valerie said, putting her badge away. "Where is it?"

"The other side of the pyramid. You will have to use the angle-vator cars to get there."

"The what?" Valerie asked.

"When you work inside a mostly hollow pyramid, you cannot get around by traditional means," Mr. Pastor explained. "The angle-vators are electrostatic cubes that travel in angular directions along the inner shell of the pyramid. You type in the destination point, and it takes you where you want to go. There is an entry bay just outside the door. But you'll also need one of these to move around here." He held up his wrist, displaying a gold bracelet. "It's a security device."

"Well, that answers a question," Logan said, recalling that he had seen a similar bracelet on Catherine Bribergeld at the commemoration and on the man who had kidnapped Sumsari.

"Stand up," Valerie said, nudging Mr. Pastor with her gun. "You're going to be our guide."

He reluctantly rose from his chair and led Logan and Valerie out of the electrical room and down a long, narrow hallway that, Logan realized, had no ceiling. Both the inner and outer walls angled up and inward toward the apex. Twenty meters above them, they could see the cars Mr. Pastor was referring to: small square cubes zipping on various tracks, their only sound the slight whipping of air as they moved.

Valerie stood behind Mr. Pastor with her gun drawn, pressing the barrel into his back. "Now what?"

Mr. Pastor moved to a set of closed doors in the inner wall and pressed a button on the security panel. A cube paused directly above them and began to descend. When it stopped the doors slid open, and a walkway emerged from the angle-vator, extending to the doorway across from it. The three of them entered. A numerical display was projected, and a computerized female voice came on, requesting a destination code. Mr. Pastor entered the numbers 3-0-1 into the keypad. "Office level three, room zero one," the female computer voice announced. The cube smoothly began to ascend and picked up speed. Within twenty seconds, after a series of momentum changes, the cube slowed again and started its descent. Valerie readied her gun and waited for the door to open. "You have arrived at your destination," the female voice announced.

"Behind us," Mr. Pastor said. "We've traversed the apex and are on the other side of the ZPF."

"What are you talking about?" Valerie asked. Before he could answer, the set of doors behind Valerie opened. Surprised, she quickly spun around. To her relief, the doorway was clear. She grabbed Mr. Pastor by the shirt and took him across the newly extended walkway to a door on the other side. "Is that the room?" she asked.

"Yes," Mr. Pastor said. As they approached, the doors opened to a spacious office. Valerie entered cautiously, holding Mr. Pastor in front of her. Logan followed. As they walked in, they saw a woman standing near the corner, looking out of an open window at the ocean in the distance.

Valerie quickly pushed Mr. Pastor into a chair and pointed her gun at the woman. "Don't move," she said.

The woman turned around.

"Nadine!" Logan called. "What are you doing here?"

"Thank the stars!" Nadine said. "They kidnapped me. Barged right into our flat in Cairo and abducted me."

Valerie's gun was still on Mr. Pastor, keeping him quiet. Logan noticed that a silver object with a blinking red light had been placed on Nadine's right temple. "What's that?"

"I don't know," she replied, touching it with her hand. "They placed it there when they took me."

"What about my father and Madu?" Valerie asked.

Nadine shook her head. "Madu had already left to pick up your father at the airport when all this happened. I have not spoken to him since he left the flat."

Valerie pulled out her PCD and attempted to call her father, but there was no answer. "It doesn't even ring," she said.

"Do you have any idea who brought you here?" Logan asked.

"Yes," Nadine said. "After I arrived, they took me to see that blond woman we met briefly at the commemoration. I don't remember her name."

"Catherine Bribergeld? Is she here on the island?"

"Yes, yes, that's the woman. I asked her what she wanted, but she wouldn't say. They locked me in here. Why are they doing this?"

"We don't have time to go into it now," Valerie said. "The agent we arrived with was captured. We have to find him."

"Do you remember where you saw Catherine?" Logan asked.

"It looked like a large conference room," Nadine said. "The room had a very shiny floor, and the chairs were positioned in a large circle. Strange balls of light were floating in the air, and there was a strange reddish glow under the floor."

"That," Mr. Pastor said, "is the Hades Room."

53

A boy using his gadget was judged by his father who used
a typewriter, who was judged by his father who used a pen,
who was judged by his father who used a quill, who was
judged by his father who painted on walls.
Change. Your children will be happy you did.

—THE CHRONICLES OF SATRAYA

CAIRO, 4:30 P.M. LOCAL TIME, MARCH 26, 2070

Madu and Mr. Perrot were alone again with Sumsari, who continued to mumble and write the same thing on the walls. "Must find . . . suffering . . . death."

"How could Simon have known about this chamber?" Madu asked. "And how could he have known about Sumsari?"

"We will have to answer those questions at another time," Mr. Perrot said. "At the moment, we have to figure out the information that will save Nadine from harm."

Madu knelt on the ground. "This is the current design of the device that Simon has built." He drew in the sand with his finger. "Like at Teotihuacán and here at Giza, my plans called for the main pyramidal structure to be aboveground, with a conductive gold capstone placed at its apex. Fifty meters underneath the pyramid is the activation chamber. The chamber is made of lead to isolate the radiation, but it is plated with two centimeters of pure gold."

"So the gold in the capstone and in the activation chamber creates the initial current of static electricity that we are experiencing right now."

"Yes. The activation chamber is connected to the pyramid by these three hollow ion tubes that extend deep into the pyramid."

"Very much like the openings in the ceiling here and in the Moon Pyramid in Mexico," Mr. Perrot said.

"I knew that in order for the pyramid to generate copious amounts of electricity, the air within the pyramid had to be intensely ionized. The ions produced from the radiation would intermix with the naturally occurring static electricity and amplify it. I further postulated that placing the device over an intense, massive heat source, using a process called thermal radiation, would boost the amplification even further."

"How did you come up with all this?"

Madu rose to his feet. "Are you familiar with the Ark of the Covenant?"

"Yes."

"There is an obscure old tale that suggests that it was actually a radioactive device housed in a chamber such as this one that powered the pyramid above it. As the story goes, when Moses and his followers left Egypt, they stole the Ark and took it with them. It was for that reason that the pharaoh pursued them at all costs."

"Egypt lost its energy source," Mr. Perrot said.

"That's right," Madu said. "That tale, along with what I saw during my experience with the blue orb, influenced my original plans." He sighed deeply. "We now know that sound, not radioactivity, was the missing ingredient."

"So what exactly have Simon's associates constructed?" Mr. Perrot asked gravely.

"Whatever it is," Madu replied, "to judge from the way it is affecting the world, it is clearly unstable. If NovaCon's pyramid was built according to my plans, it has the same physical characteristics as the pyramids here and in Mexico. So in theory, it could use sound rather than radiation. If the proper harmonic was introduced within the activation chamber, the pyramid would fully energize."

Mr. Perrot bent down and emptied the bag Simon had left. It contained a couple of flashlights, a small pick, a penknife, a rope, a hand shovel, and three small water bottles. He handed one to Madu. "We are back to the same square where we were at Teotihuacán: What is the proper activation harmonic?" As Mr. Perrot drank some water, he walked over to Sumsari and looked more closely at the mathematical equation Sumsari was repeatedly scribbling on the wall. "Have you ever seen this formula before?" Madu came over, and Sumsari rose to his feet, dropping the piece of chalk and walking over to the open bag and the tools lying on the ground next to it. Madu took a sip of water and looked at the equation that Mr. Perrot was referring to.

$$\omega_H = \sqrt{\gamma \frac{A^2 P_0}{m V_0}}$$

"Yes," Madu said. "This is a famous formula used for the Helmholtz resonance."

"What is that?"

"It describes the phenomenon of air in a cavity. We've all seen it in action." Madu blew over the opening of his water bottle, creating a whistling sound. "The size of the cavity, the volume of air inside it, and other factors dictate the quality and the pitch of the resulting resonance. This formula speaks to that."

Mr. Perrot heard a cracking sound. He and Madu saw that Sumsari was standing on top of the platform at the center of the room and had broken one of the Egyptian flutes in half. He was digging the tip of the small penknife into the portion of the flute he was still holding. Madu turned in alarm. "What is he doing? He's ruining the only clues we have!"

"No!" Sumsari yelled, as Madu rushed over to try to take the flute from him. He pointed the tip of the knife at Madu threateningly before walking off.

"He has lost his faculties," Mr. Perrot said, as he walked over and backed Madu away from Sumsari. "He will not be of much help to us. We must focus on deciphering the Egyptians' amplification secret. The lives of Nadine and many others depend on it."

Mr. Perrot and Madu looked over at the clock that Simon had left. There were forty-two minutes before the top of the hour, at which time Simon was going to activate Nadine's neuro device. "We don't have much time," Mr. Perrot said, picking up the remaining long flute.

"It is called a ney," Madu said. "This particular instrument must be at least three thousand years old."

"The platform in this chamber depicts two men playing similar instruments," Mr. Perrot said, walking over to it.

He took a small scraping tool from the bag and began to scratch the surface, revealing a brownish color that contrasted with the rest of the limestone. Madu took out a chisel and assisted Mr. Perrot in clearing off more of the oxidation. Small sparks flew as they scraped, and the hair on their heads began to stand up straight with the greater charge. "It's copper," Madu said. "It is reacting with the new capstone."

Just then, the lighting dimmed, and a loud clanking could be heard. Mr. Perrot and Madu looked up and saw that Sumsari had toppled over one of the fire urns and was striking at the center of it with the pick. Smoke rose from the smoldering coals on the ground near the pillar as the clanking continued.

Mr. Perrot and Madu turned their attention back to the task at hand. "So instead of inserting a copper rod into the platform to achieve conductivity as the Teotihuacános did," Mr. Perrot said, "the Egyptians poured melted copper directly into the stone."

"It would seem so." Madu sighed. "But it still doesn't answer the question of how they amplified the power."

Mr. Perrot stood and grabbed the burning torch that Simon had stuck in the ground. He held it above his head and looked at the openings in the ceiling. "Would you mind blowing into one of those flutes?" he said to Madu.

Madu picked up one of the neys and did as Mr. Perrot requested. A sound echoed in the chamber and, as at the Pyramid of the Moon, reverberated through the openings in the ceiling, causing a harmonic to form.

"No!" Sumsari yelled. He had stopped striking the urn and was looking at them with a blank expression. "No! No!" He continued to pound the bottom of the urn.

"I would have expected the electricity to have increased," Mr. Perrot said, disappointed. "Please, another note." Madu blew into the flute again, and a different harmonic started. Again, Sumsari shouted, becoming more agitated.

"Remember what we learned in Mexico," Madu said. "The flutes there needed to be played in a particular order to create the proper harmonic." He looked at the ney Sumsari had broken. "And as at the Pyramid of the Moon, our instruments have been broken."

"Move!" Sumsari yelled at them. Mr. Perrot and Madu both rose to their feet and saw that Sumsari had tied the rope to the toppled urn and was dragging it over to the platform. "Move!" he yelled again. Mr. Perrot and Madu stepped away. Sumsari grabbed one end of the urn and lifted it onto the platform.

"What's he doing?" Madu asked.

Mr. Perrot did not answer but looked on in fascination as Sumsari lifted the other end of the urn and adjusted it on the platform. The moment he did so, Mr. Perrot and Madu felt more static electricity fill the chamber.

"The urn is made of copper. It is causing a greater reaction with the capstone . . ."

Sumsari then took the portion of the ney that he had broken off and knelt down next to the urn. He placed the end near a small hole that he'd picked into the base. He blew into the ney. The sound echoed, and a soft harmonic was created. Sumsari placed his ear on the side of the urn and listened. When the harmonic disappeared, he gathered some sand off of the ground and poured it carefully into the hole, then blew into the ney and placed his ear on the side of the urn again.

"I think he is tuning it," Madu said.

"Tuning what?"

"I think he's trying to construct a modified Helmholtz resonator."

Mr. Perrot and Madu watched as Sumsari repeated the process over and over again. He blew on the ney after adding more sand to the urn, and suddenly, an explosion of blue light came through the openings in the ceiling, along with the crackle of electricity. Mr. Perrot and Madu stepped farther away from the platform. Sumsari continued to play until the harmonic seemed to peak. More intense electrical snaps came from the openings above and began to crawl along the walls and large pillars at the corners of the chamber.

"I can't believe it," Madu whispered, astonished. "I think he's figured it out."

Sumsari jumped up and down in jubilation. Although he had stopped blowing into the ney, the current continued building.

His jubilation did not last long. Suddenly, all the energy he'd created began to dissipate. He dropped his hands and placed the ney next to the brass urn. Then he picked up his piece of chalk and resumed his mumbling and drawing on the wall.

"I thought he had it," Mr. Perrot said, disappointed.

"He did," Madu said. "He found the harmonic."

"But shouldn't it last perpetually, then?"

"This is not the same pyramid it was three thousand years ago," Madu said. "The outer surface and much of the limestone have crumbled away."

"How can we be certain this will work at the NovaCon site?" Mr. Perrot asked.

"We can't be certain," Madu said, looking at the clock on the PCD, which now read two minutes to the top of the hour. "But there is one thing I am certain of," he continued softly. "I have to protect Nadine."

Madu picked up the PCD Simon had left and placed a call.

54

Your soul wears a mask so that you can participate in the
playground of life without people holding you to a past.

—THE CHRONICLES OF SATRAYA

NOVACON ISLAND, 2:00 P.M. LOCAL TIME, MARCH 26, 2070

Valerie walked into location 6-9-6 with her gun drawn and holding Mr.
Pastor in front of her. Logan and Nadine entered right behind her. Just
as Nadine had described it, the room had a shiny translucent floor providing a view of the lava flowing beneath it, twelve chairs arranged in a
large circle, and floating illuminated orbs. Two men and a woman were
standing with their backs to the door in front of a HoloPad. Valerie
was shocked by what she saw on the HoloPad. She stepped over a large
bloodstain on the floor near one of the chairs.

"Why is my father on that HoloPad?" she yelled. "Where have you
taken him and Madu?"

The projection disappeared. One of the men turned, his gun already drawn. The light from an orb above him bounced off his highly
polished gold weapon. He was the tall man with dreadlocks who had
abducted Sumsari. His gun was pointed at the bloodied face of the
person sitting in one of the chairs. It was Chetan.

"Your father is safe," the second man said. He was standing near the HoloPad, his back still turned to Valerie and Logan. "For now."

The woman wearing the black business suit turned. "Hello, Mr. Ford, Agent Perrot," Catherine Bribergeld said. "I'm rather surprised to see you here. You could have just called. We would have been glad to give the WCF a tour of our facility."

"Who is the man standing next to you?" Logan asked. "Turn around!"

"I'm not altogether sure you want to see me, Logan. Or, rather, what you've turned me into . . ." The man turned slowly, revealing his scarred face.

"Simon!" Logan called out in shock, as he stepped past Valerie. She stuck her arm out to stop him from going any farther.

Simon laughed. "I still can't get over how much I enjoy the expressions on people's faces when they see me these days. It invigorates me."

"How can you still be alive?" Valerie asked. "We saw you fall into the pyre."

"Your father asked me the same question," Simon said. "Maybe Logan can answer you. How about it, Logan? You must have a theory about how I managed to survive. You, of all people, should be able to solve this mystery. I'm certain that you've realized a thing or two about those blank pages in the *Chronicles*. Perhaps you saw something inexplicable when I fell."

Logan recalled the moment when he'd seen Simon fall into the pyre at the Manikarnika Ghat along the Ganges. He recalled how calm Simon had looked, that he hadn't screamed when he fell. "The hidden symbols," Logan said quietly. "You said you knew about the symbols."

Simon clapped his hands. "Bravo! They're more powerful than even I could have imagined. But I suspect you already know that. I also suspect that some interesting things might be happening to you, no? But I can't take all the credit."

Logan was silent a moment, before he murmured, "The blue light . . ."

"Yes, the light cast me away from certain death," Simon said. "But, as you can see, I was not entirely spared from the flames. My face certainly was not."

"What are you talking about, Simon?" Catherine asked. "Symbols and blue light?"

"Nothing that concerns you," Simon told her.

"You're not going to get away with this, Simon," Logan said. "This device will not work without the proper—"

"Proper activation harmonic," Simon interrupted. "Yes, I know that. With the help of that batty old music man, Robert and Madu were actually able to figure out how to get this device to work. I was just speaking to them." Simon motioned to the HoloPad platform behind him. A quiet rumbling began. "You see, the doctors are already using the information they received."

"With the help of President Salize," Catherine interjected, "Nova-Con will soon be the only credible supplier of electricity in the world."

"People are dying out there because of this device," Valerie said, glaring at Catherine. "And what about the destruction of the gas wells? How many lives did those nanites of yours claim?"

"Those deaths were unfortunate but necessary," Catherine said. "The world can now sleep better knowing that the energy crisis and all the earthly chaos is about to end."

"Necessary!" Valerie shouted. "You people are sociopaths!"

"We people?" Simon said. "We are here because people like you need us. Just like doctors exist because of the ill. Just like teachers exist because of the stupid. Just like missionaries exist because of people who need sustenance for their souls." Simon gave Valerie a smile. "Just like WCF agents exist because of clever villains. Have you ever wondered what God would do if there was no one to save? Did you know that more people died from the Great Disruption than at the hands of any man or woman in all of human history? I don't see you chasing after Mother Nature, though, Agent Perrot. I don't see you trying to sentence her to prison. No, it's people like us who get people like you riled up so you can wake up in the morning and have something to do with your otherwise boring and insignificant lives. We are the reason you people have purpose. Good and bad, Logan. The yin and the yang, the positive and the negative—it is the great waltz of life. Do you know what this world would be like without people like us? Have you considered what the world would be like without struggle and strife? I'll tell you. It would be boring."

Simon shrugged. "You know, I was prepared to let you all die at the commemoration. I was prepared to see the whole Council of Satraya building blown to shreds!"

"You planted the nanites," Valerie said.

"Actually, it was Catherine who planted them, but it was my idea. Don't you want to know why the activation signal stopped, though? It was because of the books. You see, at first, I thought that Deya's books had fallen into the pyre and were gone forever. But while I was recovering, it occurred to me that if I survived the flames in the pyre then perhaps the books survived, too. When Catherine told me at the last moment that they were actually being displayed at the commemoration next to some of your mother's mosaics, I rejoiced and immediately instructed Kashta to kill the signal. You could even say I saved your lives, if only briefly.

Simon turned now to look only at Logan. "You actually saved me a great deal of effort by coming here. I don't really care about all this energy hullaballoo, even though Catherine sees merit in it. My former friend Dario wasn't much of a progressive thinker. My father seemed to like him, but I think it was because of Dario's wine rather than Dario's vision. That is his blood on the floor over there. And to think I once called him Uncle Dario." Simon smiled, as Valerie and Logan could not help but glance at the dried blood on the floor. "No, I really don't care about this energy device. What I really want are Deya's books."

"And why would I ever give them to you?" Logan asked. "I'd more likely burn them myself than do that."

Simon eyed Logan, then turned a smile on Nadine and crossed his hands behind his back. "You've been awfully quiet back there. Perhaps you could give some meaningful advice to Logan and his girlfriend."

Suddenly, a gun was in Nadine's hand and she was pressing it to the back of Valerie's head. Nadine's voice whispered in her ear. "I would advise Logan to tell Simon where the books are. Because he won't be needing them much longer. . . ."

Logan tried to process what was taking place. He felt paralyzed seeing Nadine, Madu's wife, holding a gun to Valerie's head. He wanted to cry out at such an absolute betrayal, but his voice was stuck in his throat.

"I would put your gun down, Ms. Perrot." Catherine was gloating. "As you can see, things are not what they seem. Please hand it over to Rashidi." She gestured to the tall man with the dreadlocks.

Simon laughed. "I know. I couldn't believe it myself when Catherine told me that Madu's loving wife had sold her Madu's plans and insights about the energy device. I was as shocked as the two of you appear to be right now." He laughed again.

Too stunned to offer resistance, Valerie handed her weapon to Rashidi, who held his hand out. He motioned for her and Logan to sit next to Chetan. Two more armed men came through the door.

"That's how they knew about Sumsari," Logan said to Nadine. "You told them."

"How could you do such a thing to Madu?" Valerie asked.

"Do you know what it's like to spend forty years with a man who continually chases a dream and never finds it?" Nadine said, as she walked over to Simon and Catherine and stood beside them. She removed the device on her right temple, clearly a fake. The rumbling grew stronger. "It's tiring, I can assure you. I once thought like my husband and his grandfather, Shai. I truly believed that we could make a difference in the world and that at some point, we would be blessed by the selfless work we performed. But that never happened. Our work on the original Council went unappreciated."

"Amen," said Simon.

"We returned to Egypt with nothing to show for our efforts,"

Nadine continued. "Madu even gave away the most valuable thing we owned: the *Chronicles*. Even then, I still believed what he said, that one day we would find the secret to unlimited energy. But after years of watching him falter and fail, I could not take it anymore. I brought investors to Madu, yet he refused each one."

"What about Rigel and the Tripod Group?" Valerie asked.

Nadine shook her head. "The money Rigel provided to dig holes and move dirt was a pittance compared with what I received from Dario and Catherine for a copy of Madu's plans."

"Rigel Wright is a fool," Simon interjected. "He is just a rich boy with a lot of toys who doesn't know how to leverage what he has. Who cares about raising a ship from the bottom of the ocean?" He walked over to Logan and leaned down, putting his face close to Logan's. "I'm going to ask you again, and this time, please take Ms. Shata's advice. Where are the books, Ford?"

"Like I said," Logan replied, "I'm never going to give them to you. You can shoot me right now. As far as you're concerned, they might as well have fallen into the fire pit."

Simon sighed deeply as he rose. "You are leaving me with few options."

Rashidi pulled his PCD from his pocket. The HoloPad at the center of the room was activated, and an image of Logan's children was displayed. They were sitting on a mattress on the floor of a room Logan did not recognize. Ms. Sally sat nearby.

"What have you done with my children?" Logan yelled. The guard standing behind him pressed his gun to the back of Logan's head. Both of the children and Ms. Sally had small metal devices on the sides of their foreheads, similar to the one Nadine had just removed.

A man who resembled Rashidi entered the frame. "I would like to introduce you to Kashta," Simon said. "He is Rashidi's brother. They look alike, don't they?"

"How did he find them?" Valerie asked Logan. "How did he know—?"

"You have Nadine to thank for that, too," Simon interrupted. "Don't you just love the power of money?" Nadine's face remained expressionless. Logan watched as Kashta grabbed Jordan and brought him closer to the camera. "Has everyone been behaving?" Simon asked sarcastically.

"Unfortunately, yes," Kashta said. "But I don't like this one."

"Leave my brother alone!" Jamie shouted, as Kashta gripped Jordan tighter.

"We're OK, Dad," Jordan said. "They want the books. Don't give—"

Kashta abruptly swung Jordan around and tossed him onto the mattress next to Jamie. Then he pulled out his PCD and pressed a button. The device on Jordan's temple was activated, and the boy screamed, grabbing his head. Jamie started screaming, too. Ms. Sally ran over, crying, and tried to comfort him.

"Stop it!" Logan yelled. "I'll give you the books. Just don't hurt my kids!"

"Now we're getting somewhere," Simon said.

Kashta released the button, and Jordan and Jamie stopped screaming. Jamie leaned over to hug her brother, and the projection abruptly ended. Simon turned and spoke softly to Catherine and Nadine so that neither Logan nor Valerie could hear.

"We'll get them back," Valerie whispered to Logan. "He won't hurt the children while you still have the books."

Just then, they heard a grunt. Logan and Valerie turned to Chetan, who motioned downward with his eyes. The necklace he was wearing was somehow floating in the air.

Logan felt the hair on his head rise.

Valerie could feel her ponytail moving.

The rumbling grew louder, and the floor began to shake. Logan glanced out the window. The sky was overcast, filling with dark gray clouds. The HoloPad was suddenly activated, and the image of two short people appeared. One was dressed in white, the other in black.

"Doctors, is everything all right?" Simon asked.

"We have implemented . . ." said the doctor in white.

"The harmonic," said the doctor in black.

"The energy device . . ."

"Has become overloaded."

"The island . . ."

"Is not safe."

"Then shut the device down!" Catherine said.

"We . . ."

"Can't."

"The harmonic has caused . . ."

"An unstable standing wave."

Suddenly, a lightning bolt shot by the window. A moment later another flashed by and then a third. "I don't think this is what they expected," Valerie whispered. "It might be our only chance." She turned and eyed the two guards who were standing nearby with their guns drawn.

"Take these two to the transport dock!" Simon ordered Rashidi. "We will meet you there in ten minutes."

Simon, Catherine, and Nadine left the room. Rashidi walked over to Logan and pulled him roughly to his feet. The other guards grabbed Valerie and Chetan, and the six of them walked to another door. Two more bolts of electricity flashed by the windows, the sudden light and sonic boom causing the guards to lose their balance for a second. That gave Chetan enough of an opportunity to shove his shoulder into the chest of the guard closest to him, causing him to fall backward. Valerie struck another guard in the throat; he dropped to the floor, unable to breathe, and she immediately snagged his weapon. Shots rang out, and Valerie turned and saw Chetan reel. Valerie fired a round at the guard he'd been struggling with, catching the guard in the head. Rashidi then threw Logan to the side and began firing at Valerie, who dropped to the ground and rolled to safety behind a chair. She fired two rounds, which missed. Rashidi ran to the door, which opened at his approach, an angle-vator waiting outside. Valerie took better aim and fired off three more rounds, but it was too late; her shots struck the closing doors. After seeing Rashidi flee, the guard Valerie had struck in the throat gave up. He stood with his hands raised above his head.

Logan went over and helped Chetan up.

"Are we going after the tall guy with the dreadlocks?" Logan asked, as he walked over with a limping Chetan.

"I'd like to," Valerie said. "He still has my gun. But we need to leave."

"What's the fastest way out of here?" she asked Mr. Pastor, as more bolts of electricity flew by the window.

Before he could answer, a call came in on her PCD, and the image of Sylvia was projected. "What is going on out there? We're detecting electrical readings from your location that are off the charts."

"They managed to activate the device," Chetan said. "And also managed to lose control of it."

"We're leaving now," Valerie said.

"You can't," Sylvia said. "We are detecting deadly electromagnetic readings all across the globe. Each time a spike takes place on that island, spikes follow instantaneously in other places. Two massive earthquakes just struck. One northeast of Xi'an, China, and the other near East St. Louis, right here in the Federation. Reports of more are coming in." Sylvia turned her head as Darvis entered the frame and whispered something to her. Her face grew even more concerned.

"What it is?" Valerie asked.

"People are heading to hospitals in droves," Sylvia said.

"Complaining about headaches again?" Logan asked.

"Not just that," Sylvia said. "People are dying from them now."

Logan bowed his head, thinking about his children, Jamie in particular.

"You have to shut that device down right now," Sylvia said. "You're at ground zero."

The HoloPad at the center of the room was activated. Logan motioned to Valerie to look at it. The image of the two doctors reappeared. "Mr. Simon," one of them said.

"Are you there?" the other one said.

"We'll get back to you," Valerie said to Sylvia, shutting down her PCD. She and Logan rushed over to the projection.

"Where is . . ."

"Mr. Simon?"

"He's abandoned you," Valerie said. "You need to deal with us now if you want to survive."

55

Much learning does not require much teaching.

—THE CHRONICLES OF SATRAYA

AMESBURY, U.K., 3:35 P.M. LOCAL TIME, MARCH 26, 2070

"Are you sure this is the Altar of the Bluestones?" Britney asked. "I don't see anything blue or anything that looks like an altar."

"I'm certain of it," Anita said. They stood outside a chain-link fence that enclosed a ring of standing stones. "The term *bluestones* refers to the smaller dolerite rocks in the inner circle that were brought here from South Wales."

"Wales?" Britney said. "That's a long way to drag them."

"Well, no one is exactly sure how the stones were transported here."

Britney looked up at a large stone that was about five meters tall and seemed to be leaning forward. It stood a good distance away from the main circle. "Looks like they got tired and figured they'd just leave this one out here."

Anita smiled and shook her head. "This one is called the Friar's Heel or Sun-Stone. There's a lot of folklore about it."

After leaving Salisbury Cathedral, Anita and Britney had taken a taxi ten kilometers north to a field in a rural area near Amesbury. It was one of the most famous places in the world: Stonehenge. Clouds scuttled by overhead, as a cool wind blew across the grassy plain that surrounded the circle of twenty-nine stones that had stood there for more than four thousand years. While the site remained open despite the recent earthquake nearby, there were only a few tourists there today, along with a group of about thirty people wearing white robes. Ten of them stood within the ring of stones, holding silver swords and chanting, while the others sat on the grass outside tents they had pitched.

"Who are those people in the robes? And what are they doing?" Britney asked.

"They look like New Age Druids who are carrying out a ceremony. Maybe it's related to the spring equinox," Anita said. While Anita and Britney could not make out what the group was chanting, the combination of the sounds and the setting conveyed an aura of mysticism.

"I wonder if there are other places like this around the world," Britney said. "Prehistoric monuments that were built on those lines Mr. Quinn and the others were talking about."

"The sonorous lines," Anita said. "I suspect that most pyramids, temples, and ancient structures were constructed on those energy lines."

"It's amazing that people way back then knew about all this stuff that somehow we have forgotten."

Anita glanced at her friend with a raised eyebrow.

"What?" Britney said.

"Three days ago, you were telling me all of this stuff was hocus-pocus."

"That was before Mr. Quinn started to explain things. So what do we do now?"

Before Anita could say anything, the ground began to shake, and an arc of blue light passed between two of the stones in the circle. The white-robed people standing inside the stone circle cried out joyfully, as if their chants and prayers were being answered. Other members of the group who were sitting by tents or walking in the fields ran over to join them.

"What was that?" Britney asked, concerned. She turned and looked at Anita, whose eyes were closed and hands were pressed against the sides of her head. "Are you all right?"

"It's happening again," Anita said. "My head is starting to hurt."

Three more electrical arcs rent the sky above Stonehenge. Four more followed. One of the arcs hit a couple of the Druids within the ring of stones, catapulting their bodies into the open field. Anita opened her eyes in time to see the charred bodies crashing to the ground. Other Druids rushed over to stamp out the flames running up the stricken people's robes, while others screamed and ran away. The electrical discharges intensified and now reached all the way to the parking lot, where vehicles were toppled by their intensity.

Anita looked on in horror. "They're being electrocuted! They're burning up, just like in my vision!" She put her hand into her blue book bag and pulled out Sumsari's resonator and tuning fork. "I have to do something!"

"Do what?" Britney asked in panic. "You can't go in there! Remember how dangerous Mr. Quinn said it was to try to stop these forces?"

Anita watched as more lightning struck. "I'm not going to wait to be called into service!" She darted off toward the circle of Stonehenge.

"Anita!" Britney yelled, rushing after her. "Anita!" The ground shook more violently. Britney lost her balance and fell.

Anita struggled to stay on her feet, as the earth convulsed beneath her. The ground continued to shake, and the lightning kept sweeping through the sky. She summoned all of her strength and will to reach the center of Stonehenge. Kneeling by one of the taller standing stones, she held Sumsari's resonator in one hand and the tuning fork in the other. She struck the tuning fork and held it over the aperture of the resonator until she found the right spot, just as she had done at the cathedral. A harmonic began to form. She struck the tuning fork again, and then again. The harmonic grew.

56

There is no absolute truth or wisdom. If there were, the earth
would still be flat and the wheel would still be made of wood.
Truth and wisdom evolve along with all of you.

—THE CHRONICLES OF SATRAYA

NOVACON ISLAND, 3:01 P.M. LOCAL TIME, MARCH 26, 2070

An angle-vator car transported Logan, Valerie, and Chetan to the highest point inside the pyramid, just under the apex. They walked into
the control center and saw the doctors sitting at two of the numerous workstations that surrounded the floating image of the pyramid.
"Where is everyone?" Valerie asked.

"They all fled," said the doctor dressed in black.

"Like Mr. Simon," added the other doctor.

"I am Dr. Josef," said the doctor dressed in black.

"I am Dr. Rosa," said the doctor in white.

Chetan took a seat at one of the consoles. "I'm going to try to get
the Cube online."

An image of Sylvia was projected. "Who are those two?" she asked.

"The only two people in the world who know how this NovaCon
device works," Chetan answered.

"Well, they'd better turn it off fast. The chaos is spreading. Earthquakes are now being reported in the south of England and throughout Africa."

"We need your help, Doctors," Logan told them. "You need to shut this thing down right now."

"We do not . . ."

"Know how."

"Then who does?" Valerie asked, incredulous.

The doctors looked at each other. Dr. Josef said, "Perhaps the one . . ."

"Who provided the harmonic," Dr. Rosa said.

"Madu," Logan said, turning to Valerie. "We need to find your father and Madu. They might be able to help us."

Valerie walked over to the doctors. "We saw Simon speaking with my father, Alain Perrot, and his friend, a scientist named Madu Shata, when we entered the Hades Room. Are they being held somewhere on the island?"

"No, we spoke to them . . ."

"Via HoloPad."

"Bring them up," Valerie ordered. The doctors looked at each other. "Do it *now*."

Dr. Rosa manipulated the controls on the HoloPad. The image of the rotating pyramid disappeared and was replaced by that of Mr. Perrot and Madu huddled together at the center of a violently shaking chamber, ducking flying bolts of electricity.

"Dad!" Valerie called out. "Where are you?"

Mr. Perrot and Madu quickly crawled closer to the imaging device. "Logan, Valerie," Mr. Perrot said breathlessly. "Something terrible is happening. I fear we have somehow triggered the Menkaure Pyramid here at Giza."

"It's not you," Logan said. "Using the information that you and Madu provided, Simon was able to activate the pyramid here on Nova-Con Island in the Azores. But it's wreaking havoc around the world."

"My wife," Madu said. "How is Nadine?"

Neither Logan nor Valerie had the heart to tell him of her betrayal. "She's safe," was all Logan could say. "Right now, we need your help to shut this device down."

Madu nodded. "Did they follow my original design? Does the pyramid possess a radioactive core, and has it been built over a massive heat source?"

"Yes, we have a core . . ." Dr. Josef said.

"And an intense heat source," Dr. Rosa added.

Madu shook his head. "It is as I feared. Adding the harmonic without first expunging the radioactivity and the heat source created more energy than the device can handle."

More electrical discharges sped by outside the window. At the same moment, a bolt flew past Mr. Perrot and struck the ground nearby. The shaking at both locations increased.

"The ELF readings from around the world are way off kilter," Sylvia said. "I can't even get a reading on the Schumann resonance any longer."

"Logan," Madu said, "you must find a way to isolate the radioactive core and then insulate the pyramid from the heat source. It is the only way to reduce the additional ions and bring the device into equilibrium."

"We have already isolated . . ." Dr. Josef said.

"The radioactive core," Dr. Rosa added.

"The lead shielding . . ."

"Is already down."

"Did you hear that?" Logan asked.

"Yes," Madu replied. "You have to remove the heat source!"

Another series of discharges could be seen, this time almost reaching the ocean. Additional static electricity spiraled through the chamber where Mr. Perrot and Madu were trapped. The image started to break up, and then it vanished, suddenly replaced with the image of the NovaCon pyramid.

"Get them back!" Valerie cried.

Chetan tried. "Looks like the imaging device in the chamber was damaged. It's not connecting now."

Valerie turned to the doctors. "What do we do about the lava?"

The doctors looked at each other and then at Valerie. "We do not have . . ."

"A solution for that."

Logan walked over to the window and watched as the storm raged outside. More lightning erupted from the pyramid.

"Oh, no!" Sylvia yelled. Everyone turned to her anguished image in the projection. "They've ordered a Black Star strike. They're going to take out the island. You have twenty-two minutes to get out of there! "

"Who ordered that?" Valerie asked.

Director Sully walked into the frame. "I did, Agent Perrot. We have no choice."

"What's Black Star?" Logan asked.

"It's a laser system," Chetan said. "Part of some Akasha Vault upgrades that were deemed classified. This entire island could be vaporized along with everything on it."

"You cannot . . ."

"Destroy the device."

"We don't have a choice," Valerie said.

"I think what they mean," Chetan said, "is that by blowing up the device, we would blow up the radioactive core and release a huge amount of radiation into the atmosphere."

"Yes!" said Drs. Josef and Rosa at the same time.

"Chetan's right," Sylvia said. "We could take out half of Portugal and Spain if that core explodes. Not to mention the radioactive fallout that could blanket Europe and eventually all of us."

"You still think that Catherine Bribergeld has your back?" Valerie said to Director Sully.

The director ignored her, saying, "You have twenty minutes to stabilize that device, Agent Perrot." Sully walked out of the frame, leaving Sylvia by herself.

"Our only hope is to isolate the lava under the device," Chetan said. "That is the only way to stabilize the device."

"It can't . . ."

"Be done."

"Can we flood the lava pit with seawater? Would that cool it down sufficiently?" Valerie asked.

"I don't see a way to get enough water down there," Chetan said. "Even if we could, the steam that would result from the air trapped in the pit would blow the top off the pyramid like the lid off a pressure cooker."

"Along with the core," Sylvia added.

"A pressure cooker," Logan repeated, thinking quickly. The others turned to him. "Instead of letting the air build up, what if we got rid of it? If we could get the air out of the lava pit, wouldn't that cool the lava? That would suffocate it, right?"

"In theory, yes," Sylvia said. "At the very least, the surface of the pit would cool, and the hotter lava would be trapped underneath."

"But how do we do that?" Valerie asked.

"The nanites," Logan said. "We drop them into the pit and activate them. Let the nanites eat up the oxygen. That's what they do, right?"

There was a long pause. "It might work," Chetan said, breaking the silence. "If they consumed all the oxygen, the lava would cool."

"The dilemma is how to get the nanites into the pit."

"You can use the access . . ."

"Hatch to the core."

The doctors manipulated their controls and zoomed in on the lower portion of the pyramid.

"That's the huge circular tube we saw when we came through the lava tunnel," Valerie said. "Look at how it's swinging back and forth."

"It's going to keep doing that until the rocking and rolling slows down," Sylvia said.

"Inside the access tube . . ."

"Is another smaller tube made of lead."

"It contains . . ."

"The nuclear core."

"How are the charged ions exposed to heat?" asked Sylvia.

"There are thirty translucent conduits that . . . allowing ions to flow back and forth."

"Among the conduits," Dr. Josef said.

"Is an access door . . ."

"Leading . . ."

"To the lava source below," Dr. Rosa concluded.

"We have closed . . ."

"The conduits."

"No ions are . . ."

"Currently flowing."

"Which is the strange part of all this," said Chetan. "With the flow of ions stopped, there is no reason all this chaos should be happening."

"There's no way we're going to get down there with the tube swaying like that," Valerie said. "It's like the pendulum on a grandfather clock!"

Suddenly, Sylvia's look of alarm changed. "I'm picking up another strange reading from the south of England."

"What kind of reading?" Valerie asked.

"Not really sure. It's up in the four-hundred-thirty-two-hertz range, but I'm having a tough time isolating it. Whatever it is, it's creating a massive standing wave that is spreading very quickly. It will hit you guys in three point four seconds."

"Any idea if this is going to be good or bad?" Valerie asked.

"No idea," Sylvia replied.

Everyone waited silently, anticipating whatever was about to hit them. To their surprise, the electrical discharges seemed to dissipate, and the shaking lessened.

"Look at the tube," Chetan said. "It's not swinging as much."

"This might be our only shot to get down there," Valerie said.

Logan looked at the doctors. "Do you have any more of those nanites lying around?"

57

Have you ever looked at yourself through someone else's eyes?
How confident are you that you will like what you see?

—THE CHRONICLES OF SATRAYA

Logan wiped the sweat from his forehead.

"We have fourteen minutes before Black Star is activated." Chetan's voice came through Valerie's PCD.

Valerie led the way down the fifty-meter access tube to the inner chamber of the radioactive core. Logan followed, his backpack slung over his shoulder. They descended a spiral stairway winding around the inner wall. As they descended, they could see the lead shielding of the nuclear core. The swaying of the tube, caused by the instability of the NovaCon pyramid device, slowed their descent.

"Is the standing wave still hitting us?" Valerie asked.

"Yes," Chetan answered. "Sylvia says it's still present."

"Let's hope it stays that way until we can get these nanites deployed." Valerie stepped off the stairs onto a metal lattice platform. Logan stood next to her. Cabinets and locked supply boxes lined the wall.

"The doctors say that you have to crawl under the lead shielding to gain access to the hatch," Chetan said. "Once you have the hatch open, activate the seventy-nine point six-five-seven signal by pressing the button on the device the doctors gave you. The moment the signal is on, you need to drop the nanites into the lava and then close the hatch."

"Did they say to crawl under this thing?" Logan asked, staring at the massive nuclear core only about a half meter above the platform.

Valerie dropped to her knees and looked underneath it. Logan did the same. The core was held in place by thirty of the translucent glass tubes, which the doctors had described, each a quarter meter in diameter. At the center, Logan and Valerie saw a small blinking red light. "That must be the door," Valerie said.

"The doctors say that those support tubes are what allows the radiation from the core to interact with the heat from the lava," Chetan said. "They are closed right now, but they are still very hot. You will have to make your way around them to get to the center where the hatch is located."

"It's like a rat's maze," Logan said, trying to make out a clear path.

"Hand me the nanites and the switch," Valerie said. "I'll crawl under."

"I'll do it," Logan said. He put his backpack on the metal platform, unzipped it, and removed the glass vial containing the nanites and a small activation switch that the doctors had given him. He put both items in his shirt pocket. "You keep an eye on this," he said, handing Valerie his backpack.

She grunted as she swung it over her shoulders. "What the heck do you have in here? Rocks?"

"Just all my important stuff," Logan said, lowering himself to the floor and crawling under the core.

"The doctors say there is a silver handle that will open the hatch," Logan heard Chetan say through Valerie's PCD.

He maneuvered his way toward the center. His right knee hit one of the heat tubes. "Son of a—" he yelled. "The doctors weren't kidding. These tubes are hot."

"The doctors say that you will have to watch out for the initial blast of heat when you open the hatch," Chetan said.

Logan methodically made his way around the heat tubes, taking great care not to touch them.

"How's it going?" Valerie called out. "Not to add any pressure, but we have about nine minutes before Black Star is activated."

"I'm almost at the hatch now," Logan said. He was about to grab the hatch's silver handle when Valerie called out again.

"Logan!" She was whispering. Logan paused and looked back, maneuvering so that he could see her through the jumble of heat tubes. "Someone is coming down here. Hold still, and don't make a sound."

Logan watched as Valerie stood. The only thing he could see now was her legs as she made her way to the other side of the platform. Logan heard a clanking as someone descended the spiral staircase, every step echoing. The core continued to sway slightly back and forth.

"Hello, Agent Perrot, Mr. Ford," said a voice Logan did not recognize. "I know the two of you are down here. Mr. Hitchlords doesn't want to see either of you die on this island. He insisted that I fetch the two of you to safety."

Logan watched as a pair of feet stepped onto the platform from the stairs.

"Don't you want to see your children again, Mr. Ford? I have come to take you to them."

Valerie popped her head down. Her index finger was pressed to her lips, indicating that Logan should remain still. He watched as Valerie walked away from the core and took a position near a large metal cabinet.

"There you are, Mr. Ford," the voice said.

Logan now saw Rashidi squatting down and peering under the core. He was holding Valerie's gun. "Now, how about you come out of there by your own free will? No? Well, we can do it without the free will, too, if you'd like."

Logan remained silent, waiting, watching the gun take aim. Suddenly, there was a shot, and he flinched but felt no injury. Another followed and echoed in the core. Logan heard the bullets ricochet.

"I am not in the mood to play around," Rashidi said. "I was hoping we could do this the easy way."

Logan watched as Rashidi walked a few steps away. He heard the squeak of a door being opened, followed by a loud humming, as the translucent heating columns surrounding him began to glow. The NovaCon device started rumbling again, and the swaying of the core increased. Rashidi squatted back down. "I've bypassed the controls and opened the conduits. I would suggest that you and Ms. Perrot come out right now, or those tubes will burn you alive." Rashidi angled for a better look. "Where is she, by the way?"

"Right here!" Logan heard Valerie say, as she pressed her new gun to Rashidi's head. "I'd like my gun back, please," she said, as she took it from Rashidi's hand. But there was a sudden swaying of the core, and Valerie was knocked off balance, giving Rashidi the advantage. Logan watched as the two of them wrestled, rolling back and forth on the platform. "Logan!" Valerie gasped. "Drop the nanites! Hurry!"

Logan took hold of the silver handle on the hatch and pulled. He turned away as an intense wave of heat burst out of the hatch. He pulled the vial and the small activation device from his pocket. He pressed the button on the device, as the doctors had instructed. Logan could see the nanites beginning to move in the vial; they'd been activated. He wasted no time, dropped the nanites into the hatch, and closed the door. Two shots rang out. Logan looked back frantically and saw Valerie on the ground, with Rashidi on top of her.

"Valerie!" Logan yelled. A series of sonic booms shook the core violently.

58

On the floor of an acclaimed artist's studio lie the tattered
canvases of failed attempts.

—THE CHRONICLES OF SATRAYA

AMESBURY, U.K., 4:20 P.M. LOCAL TIME, MARCH 26, 2070

Britney watched from afar as Anita continued to strike the tuning fork
and place it next to Sumsari's resonator. The sound it generated seemed
to quell the violent lightning strikes and the quaking of the ground. All
of the Druids had escaped the circle of stones now, but a few remained
just outside it, chanting and kneeling on the ground next to the burned,
dead bodies of their friends. Sirens could be heard in the distance.

Suddenly, more electrical arcs filled the sky, and the rumbling grew
louder.

"Oh, no!" Britney cried, as she started to run toward the center of
Stonehenge and Anita. One of the megalithic stones close to where
Anita was kneeling cracked down the center. Half of the massive stone
teetered. Anita scurried out of the way as it toppled, but the resonator slipped from her hand. The Rokmar harmonic instantly stopped.
Another series of lightning bolts rent the sky. People started screaming
again. Britney quickened her pace, determined to help her friend. She
was relieved when she saw Anita stand up. "Anita, get out of there!" she

shouted. But Anita remained by the toppled stone, walking around it, looking at the ground. "Leave the resonator!" Britney screamed. "Just get out of there!"

A series of sonic booms erupted, throwing Britney down. She looked up in time to see a massive electrical arc striking the center of Stonehenge and her best friend illuminated in a brilliant flash of light.

59

Bending an accepted truth is the only way to evolve.

—THE CHRONICLES OF SATRAYA

NOVACON ISLAND, 3:28 P.M. LOCAL TIME, MARCH 26, 2070

"Two minutes until the Black Star strike!" Chetan yelled. The rumbling continued as Logan and Valerie reentered the control center. "What happened down there?" he asked them frantically.

"Why did you . . ." Dr. Josef said.

"Reopen the conduit?" Dr. Rosa asked.

"We didn't," replied Valerie, whose right elbow was bleeding.

"Rashidi showed up," Logan said, setting his backpack down and marching over to the doctors. "*He* opened the core."

"We are trying . . ." Dr. Josef said.

"To close the core," Dr. Rosa finished.

"You guys have to get that device under control!" Sylvia yelled from the HoloPad. "That standing wave from the south of England is gone. The energy readings are off the charts again."

"That rogue signal stopped almost at the same moment the conduits were opened and the charged ions were exposed to the lava," Chetan said.

"Can you close and isolate the nuclear core from here?"

The doctors began to manipulate the controls on a nearby controls panel. "The core . . ." Dr. Josef said.

"Is now closed," Dr. Rosa said.

"Are the nanites working?" Valerie asked.

"Yes," the doctors said in unison. A projection of the lava flowing below the core was displayed. Logan and Valerie saw the familiar ash-like substance begin to appear.

"The nanites are . . ."

"Functioning."

The sparkling increased as the nanites multiplied. Dark spots appeared on the lava's surface. An indicator displayed that the temperature of the core was falling.

"I think it's working," Valerie said. "Do you detect any changes?"

"Yes," Sylvia replied. "It looks like the energy spikes are coming down. I am starting to get a steady reading on the Schumann resonance once again."

"The core . . ." Dr. Josef said.

"Is cooling," Dr. Rosa said.

On the projection, Logan and Valerie could see a dark crust forming on the surface of the lava. There were thin red veins in it, but soon they disappeared.

"The device . . ." Dr. Josef said.

"Is stable," Dr. Rosa added.

Valerie looked at the projection of Sylvia. "Tell Director Sully to call off Black Star right now!"

"Message already sent," Sylvia said. "The satellites have backed down."

"The energy collector is at two hundred thousand megawatts!" Chetan exclaimed.

"Madu did it," Logan said.

"The harmonic . . ." Dr. Josef said.

"Is correct," Dr. Rosa added.

They both turned to Logan, saying in unison, "You must turn off the nanites. Otherwise, a vacuum will form."

"The pyramid, along with everyone in it . . ."

"Will be sucked into the earth."

"There's already a high vacuum starting to form," Chetan said, looking at a display. "Same kind as we saw back at the lab."

Logan pulled the device from his pocket and pressed the button, deactivating the signal.

60

A king will never provide a solution.
In order to keep his power, he will only tell the people
what is wrong and who is to blame.
Listen instead to the one who says that you are the
only solution you will ever need.

—THE CHRONICLES OF SATRAYA

THE AZORES, 5:08 P.M. LOCAL TIME, MARCH 26, 2070

Logan, Valerie, and Chetan emerged from the lava tunnel with the two
doctors. They made their way through the dilapidated visitors center and
walked out the main door. Rigel and some of his men were waiting there.

"We thought we'd lost you along with the whole island," Rigel said.
"Even underwater, *Nemo* almost didn't make it. Massive destruction has
been reported all around the world. Scores of people were struck down
in the global lightning storms. I would imagine that many government
officials are looking for answers. Including your own," he added, glancing at Valerie.

"We'll deal with that when we get back to Washington," she said.

Logan was still anxious, though. He looked at the employees of
NovaCon who had made it out of the pyramid, Mr. Pastor among them.

"Don't worry," Valerie reassured him. "Simon won't hurt the kids as
long as he doesn't have the books. We'll get them back."

Rigel looked at the doctors, who were holding their hands in front of their faces, trying to shield themselves from the bright sunlight. "Who are they?" he asked.

"They built the device," Valerie said. "She's Dr. Rosa, and he's Dr. Josef."

Rigel looked at the implants at the backs of the doctors' necks. "The two of you have a great deal to answer for. Many people have died because of what you constructed."

"We only did . . ." Dr. Josef said.

"What we were told," Dr. Rosa said.

"One day, you might learn that your souls are in your own keeping," Logan said, perturbed by their response.

The doctors looked at each other and then back at Logan.

"We don't believe . . ." Dr. Josef said.

"In souls," Dr. Rosa finished.

Valerie shook her head. Clearly, the doctors' sense of morality was not on par with their intelligence. She turned back to Rigel. "Did you see anyone leave the island? Simon, Catherine, and Nadine fled just as everything started to shake."

"No," Rigel said. "But we were submerged until a half hour ago. We couldn't risk resurfacing during the earthquakes." He looked over at Mount Pico and the NovaCon pyramid at its base. "What's the plan for the energy device? I'd be more than happy to take it off your hands," he added with a smile.

"Yes, yes!" the doctors said in unison.

"We are certain . . ." Dr. Josef said.

"We could make it work," Dr. Rosa said.

"Your friend, Madu . . ."

"Was of great help."

"When we left the device, it was generating more than two hundred thousand megawatts," Chetan said. "Tesla's theory of free energy is now a reality."

"If we could actually fine-tune the device," Rigel said, "we could supply energy to the world for a thousand years."

"Even . . ." Dr. Josef said.

"Longer," Dr. Rosa added.

"But who would ensure that it is accessible to all of humanity?" Logan asked. "Will any of you be alive in a thousand years? No. Now I understand why the pyramids fell into ruin and why their secrets were guarded so closely. Are you two worthy of such a device?" Logan said to the doctors. "What about you, Rigel? Would you have the courage to keep it free, despite your investors' desire to control it exclusively? Could you be the one man whom absolute power does not absolutely corrupt? No, this pyramid needs to go the way of all the other pyramids in history." Logan swung his backpack off his shoulder and pulled out the small activation device.

"All our work . . ." Dr. Josef said.

"Will be lost," Dr. Rosa added.

"Then let it be lost," Logan said, flipping the switch and turning the nanites back on.

Within moments, a rumbling sound filled the air, and boulders began to roll down the quaking volcano. The doctors looked on helplessly as the nanites acted on the NovaCon energy device. Smoke rose around the pyramid, its shiny façades bending and contorting. The rumbling grew louder, until suddenly, a column of lava shot high into the air, and molten rock and rock fragments crashed down in all directions. Everyone but Logan wondered if he had done the right thing.

Valerie received a message on her PCD. She turned to Logan. "A WCF plane with my father and Madu is en route to Lisbon," she said. "It will be ready to take us anywhere we want to go."

Logan's PCD rang, too. But his face darkened when he saw that he'd received a message from Simon.

So, do your children still have a father?

Logan quickly typed the answer: *Yes.*

A few moments later, another message arrived.

Excellent. I will relay that to your children. Here in Washington, D.C.

61

Truth is dependent on the one possessing it.

—THE CHRONICLES OF SATRAYA

OVER THE ATLANTIC OCEAN, 6:43 P.M. LOCAL TIME, MARCH 26, 2070

"It was Nadine," Logan said. "She sold your plans to Catherine Bribergeld and her deceased partner, Dario Magnor."

Madu didn't say anything. He just looked shocked. Mr. Perrot, who was beside him, put his hand on his friend's shoulder.

"Looks like she also told Simon where Logan's children were staying in Washington," Valerie added. "She's put everyone in the frying pan."

They were seated around a table on a WCF transport plane heading back to Washington, where, according to Simon's last message to Logan, the exchange of Logan's children for his set of the *Chronicles* would take place. Simon hadn't provided any further instructions and had refused to discuss specific arrangements. It didn't matter; Logan would do anything Simon said, whenever Simon said in order to protect his children.

The WCF transport plane, which had originated at an air base in Qatar, had picked up Mr. Perrot, Madu, and Sumsari in Cairo and landed five hours later in Lisbon, where Logan, Valerie, and Chetan had boarded it after Rigel had transported them there. Sumsari had been sedated for his journey back to the Calhoun Medical Center and was resting in a row of seats near the rear of the plane. Chetan was in the adjacent row, comparing technical notes with Sylvia and Darvis back at the Cube. An announcement over the intercom informed them that the plane would be landing in Washington in two hours.

"You're saying that she was there on the island?" Madu asked, disbelief on his face. "I cannot believe that my Nadine started this cascade of events. Why would . . . how could she do such a thing?"

"We're sorry," Valerie said. "We were as shocked as you when she turned on us."

"I take it Nadine never gave you any cause for concern that she would sell your designs," Logan said carefully. "We hoped that you would be able to provide some insight into her actions."

"Our relationship was strong," Madu said, struggling to gather his composure. "We had our disagreements, of course. Over the years, she did become more strident in telling me to figure out a way to make some money from my energy work. But I had no idea she would go to such lengths. Where is she now?"

"We're not exactly sure," Valerie replied. "We're assuming that she and Catherine have accompanied Simon back to the Federation. Where she will go from there is anyone's guess."

"Did Nadine ever mention Dario to you?" Logan asked. "It appears that she was dealing with him and Catherine before Simon got involved."

"The name does sound familiar," Madu said, his brow furrowing.

Just then, a call came in on the HoloPad that was sitting at the center of the table. Valerie pressed a button to answer it. The images of President Salize and Director Sully were projected. "Mr. Ford," the president said, "I am told that we have you and Agent Perrot to thank for preventing yet another catastrophe. I'm not sure this is a good habit you are developing." The president smiled.

"You'll have to thank more than us," Logan said. "A lot of other people helped."

"Good answer," the president said. "You have a future in politics."

He smiled again. Logan did not respond. "We're sending a team of scientists to the island. As you know, we are still dealing with an energy crisis, and I'm hoping they can get the NovaCon device working."

"You can certainly try," Logan said, giving Valerie a look. "The device broke apart during the earthquakes and all the electrical activity. The lava from the nearby volcano consumed everything. You can send a team to the island, but I'm not sure there is much there to salvage."

"During the recent summit meeting, Catherine Bribergeld credited two exceptional scientists with the design of the device," Director Sully said. "Do we have them in custody?"

"No," Logan said. "They were lost along with the device."

"Disappointing," President Salize said. One of his handlers came into the projection and whispered something in his ear. Salize rose abruptly and walked away, leaving Director Sully by herself.

"Has my request for the apprehension of Catherine Bribergeld been approved?" Valerie asked. "I need to get word to our field offices as soon as possible."

"We're still reviewing that request," Director Sully said. "As you can imagine, placing the blame for the current energy crisis on an individual within the president's inner circle presents some challenges. Report to me the moment you get back. I want to hear the complete story of what happened." The HoloPad call ended.

"You didn't tell them everything," Mr. Perrot said, gesturing to Madu. "We still have the real designer of the NovaCon device."

"Only bad things can come from owning a device like that," Madu said. "I see that now."

Mr. Perrot nodded in understanding. "And what about the two doctors you spoke about, Josef and Rosa?"

"They're right where they belong," Valerie said cryptically. "Though it might take them some time to get their sea legs."

"And will you be . . ." Madu hesitated. ". . . pursuing Nadine?"

"We have no choice," Valerie said. "She was an accessory to a serious crime. She has to be held accountable."

Madu did not respond.

Just then, Logan heard the odd noise his PCD had recently been making whenever he received a message. He looked at it and saw a number he didn't recognize. He took a deep breath. "This could be it," he said, his heart skipping a beat, his hand shaking as he pressed the buttons to play a prerecorded video.

The image of Simon was projected. "Hello, Logan," Simon's image said. "I hope that all is well. Give my regards to Robert, who I am certain is sitting next to you. I hope he wasn't too shaken and stirred by all that has occurred. Also, please tell Madu that I know how he feels. After everything, your own wife plunges the dagger into your heart. Actually, I've never been married, so I really don't understand what he's feeling. But I've been told."

"Get to the point," Logan whispered. He was interested in only one thing: his children.

"Good news," Simon said. "I checked on the kids, and they are doing splendidly. Kashta hasn't hurt them . . . yet. And that crotchety old woman, she's terrific. She reminds me of the old attendant at the ashram who took care of me. The world could use a few more domestics like her. But I digress . . . You're probably wondering where and when you're going to be reunited with your children. I don't blame you." The image of Simon looked away from the camera. "Kashta, how much more time? Excellent. Kashta has informed me that your plane is going to be landing in Washington at six forty-nine P.M."

Valerie looked at the time on her PCD. "How does he know that?"

"You know," Simon continued, "after I landed in Washington, I realized that I haven't been here since I was a boy. A lot has changed. So how about we celebrate old times by meeting at the Council's favorite ice cream parlor? I've persuaded the owner to rent the place out to me for the night." The video panned, showing an older man, dressed all in white and wearing an old-fashioned straw boater hat. The video continued to pan before returning to Simon. "Let's meet here at nine thirty. I'm not sure where WCF planes land these days, but that should give you enough time to gather the books and allow Ms. Perrot to freshen up. Yes, Agent Perrot, please come along. I look forward to seeing you again. But come alone. If Kashta spots anyone else . . . well . . ." Simon paused, the expression on his face menacing. "Now, Logan, don't be late. That never ends well."

The video message ended.

"Do you know the place he's talking about?" Valerie asked.

"M Street Creamery," Mr. Perrot answered, glancing at Logan. "That was the store's owner, Mr. Newman. Your parents loved that place. The store was abandoned after the Great Disruption. Mr. Newman and his wife took ownership, restored it to working condition, and provided us with a wonderful rendezvous point."

"Looks like the Creamery is between Wisconsin and Thirty-first," Valerie said, as she projected an image of it from her PCD.

"I wonder if Nadine will be there," Madu said forlornly. "I must talk to her."

"We will deal with her after we get the children and Ms. Sally back," Valerie said. "You and my dad can go to my apartment and wait there. I need to get a WCF team ready to apprehend Simon."

"He said to come alone," Logan reminded her. "The books are not worth the lives of the children and Ms. Sally—no way we take that risk."

"I'll have a ghost team ready," Valerie said. "Simon won't even see Luke's squad coming. Once we make the exchange and Simon leaves the building, we'll apprehend him. I'm not letting him get away again."

"Speaking of which," Mr. Perrot said, "where are the books? What did you do with them after the commemoration?"

Logan didn't answer immediately. He grabbed his backpack, put it on his lap, and unzipped it.

"You have to be joking," Valerie said, as Logan pulled out the *Chronicles* and set them down on the table. "You had them the whole time."

Logan nodded, while Mr. Perrot smiled and shook his head.

62

*If you do not have a clear focus, all the great intention in the
world will not help you.*

—THE CHRONICLES OF SATRAYA

WASHINGTON, D.C., 7:15 P.M. LOCAL TIME, MARCH 26, 2070

After the WCF transport plane landed, Logan received a call from Adisa
Kayin, who told him that he and Mr. Perrot were urgently needed at the
Council of Satraya offices. He had two hours until the exchange with
Simon, just enough time to go with Mr. Perrot and Madu.

Logan entered the main conference room of the Council building,
which was still under heavy guard and surveillance after the attack two
days earlier. He was taken aback when he saw who was sitting at the
Egalitarian Round Table with Adisa Kayin. It was Randolph Fenquist
and the man who claimed to be Giovanni Rast, his silver-handled cane
leaning against the table. Adisa and Giovanni rose to greet them, while
Randolph remained seated, with his legs crossed and a smug smile on
his face.

"Gentlemen," Adisa said, "thank you for coming on such short notice. I would like to introduce to you Giovanni Rast, and I'm certain
that you are already familiar with Randolph Fenquist."

"I'm sorry, Adisa," Logan said impatiently, "but I don't have time to discuss Mr. Rast's claims right now. I apologize, Mr. Rast, but I have some pressing issues to deal with."

"You may call me Giovanni," came the answer in a calm voice.

"Too late, anyway," Randolph said, pulling out a cigarette.

"There's no smoking in here, Randolph," Logan said. "And what do you mean, it's too late?"

"During your absence," Adisa said, "Giovanni shared with us the remarkable story of his discovery of the Train Set of the *Chronicles* and recounted the treachery and shocking acts of Fendral Hitchlords. The Council has decided that further investigation is warranted. And if we are able to confirm the legitimacy of Giovanni's story—"

"He gets a seat on the Council," Randolph interrupted Adisa.

Logan looked at Giovanni. He wondered just how much of his account aligned with the information Camden had uncovered.

"I know you must have a great many questions for me," Giovanni said. "I look forward to answering them all in good and proper time. I have no illusions that my claims will be accepted on my words alone."

"Why now?" Mr. Perrot asked. "Why come forward after so long?"

"I suppose he could ask the two of you the same question," Randolph said, looking pointedly at Mr. Perrot and then at Madu. "I don't know what it is about all you old Satrayians, everyone deciding to crawl out at the same time."

Adisa turned to Madu. "The Council would also like to consider your candidacy. If all is confirmed, I am sure that Logan and Mr. Perrot will agree that having two additional finders of the *Chronicles* on the Council would bode well for the organization's future."

Madu took a seat at the Egalitarian Round Table without answering, still presumably consumed by thoughts of Nadine's deceit.

"What's wrong with him?" Randolph asked, gesturing at Madu. "What popped his balloon?"

"What are you doing here, Randolph?" Logan asked with disdain. "Shouldn't you and your Coterie hooligans be causing havoc somewhere?"

Randolph stood, his tall, angular frame towering over Logan. "I've changed my ways, boy," he said. "Mr. Kayin and I have come to an understanding. We brokered a peace accord between the Coterie and the Council."

"And we're supposed to believe that after thirty years of hounding the Council, you've suddenly seen some kind of spiritual light?" Mr. Perrot asked.

"Listen, Robert, or whatever name you go by these days, I got me a new lease on life. After that satellite disaster killed my friend Jimmy, I knew my own sins were going to keep me from the pearly gates. So I figured something had to change. And that's when I met my Swiss friend over there. He told me that we had to let go of the past. He told me his story and convinced me that life is too short to waste on meaningless things. We have to focus on the bigger picture. Ain't that right, G?"

Giovanni nodded with a smile.

"Your Coterie members were outside my studio just last week, demonstrating and causing a ruckus," Logan said. "It didn't sound as if anything had changed."

"Change takes time, boy," Randolph said. "You can't unscrew the past when the only thing you've ever had was a hammer."

"Randolph has assured me that we won't be experiencing any more distress from the Coterie," Adisa said.

"We must move forward together," Giovanni said. "If the Council of Satraya is perpetually fighting with the Coterie, what example does that set for the world at large? If we cannot ourselves live by the precepts of the *Chronicles*, then how can we expect others to do so? *It is hard to change when the people around you keep reminding you of who you are and what you are supposed to be doing.*"

"*You must change in spite of all of it,*" Mr. Perrot said, finishing the quote from the *Chronicles*.

Giovanni nodded. "That is correct."

While Logan could tick off a long list of reasons the Council should not believe Randolph Fenquist, now was not the time.

Mr. Perrot leaned close to Logan and whispered, "I think we need to explain the gravity of the current situation to them. If this man is truly the Giovanni Rast your father wrote about, he might be able to provide us with some valuable insight."

Logan agreed, but not with Fenquist there. "Mr. Perrot and I need to meet with Adisa and Giovanni, alone. Council business, you understand."

"I need a drink and a puff, " Randolph said, sauntering toward the door. "Hey, how come you didn't you bring that dolphin mosaic of your mother's? That's the best one she did." Logan and Mr. Perrot glanced at each other, realizing that it was Randolph who had called the studio offering to buy the mosaic. "You should have brought that one; those others don't make sense to me." No one answered, and Randolph turned and continued out the door.

Madu also rose to his feet. "Please stay, Madu," Logan requested. "You know what we are going to share."

"No," Madu replied. "I am going to my hotel. I am very tired."

"Please consider our offer of a seat on the Council of Satraya." Adisa stopped him.

Madu paused for a moment. "I will," he said, and then he continued out of the meeting room.

"He seems despondent," Adisa said.

"He's been through a lot these last few days," Logan answered.

"Please, everyone have a seat," Mr. Perrot said. "Logan and I have some information to relay and not very much time to do it."

*   *   *

"So Simon is here in Washington," Giovanni said, as he looked out the window at the street below. Logan had just finished taking Adisa and Giovanni through the events of the last few days, from his and Valerie's suspicions concerning the nanites to Logan's arrival at NovaCon Island to the reemergence of Simon Hitchlords to the betrayal of Nadine and the abduction of Logan's children. Mr. Perrot added the events that had taken place in Egypt.

"From what you told us," Adisa said, "Simon already possesses three original copies of the *Chronicles*. Why does he need another?"

Giovanni turned. "I, too, am interested to know why."

Logan and Mr. Perrot did not want to bring up the secret of the hidden symbols. "I don't understand how Simon thinks," Logan replied.

"So you intend to follow through with exchanging the books for your children?" Adisa asked.

"Yes," Logan said.

"Good man," Giovanni said. "I had two children of my own. I lost them and my wife during the Great Disruption. I would give anything to get them back. You are doing the right and honorable thing."

"When is the exchange going to happen?" Adisa asked.

"Nine thirty tonight," Logan said. "I will be leaving shortly."

"Do you have the books with you?" Giovanni asked. "I would love to hold an original set again after all these years."

Logan unzipped his backpack and took out the books, setting them on the table in front of him. Giovanni walked over and picked up one of the volumes. He slowly opened the cover. "I guess the blue orb only shows up once in a lifetime," he said with a smile. Keeping the book, he walked back over to the window, where he flipped through the pages.

"I understand now why Madu seemed to be elsewhere," Adisa said. "He is not dealing well with the situation. I can't imagine how it feels to be betrayed like that."

"And to have Simon benefit from that betrayal," Logan added.

"It is not pleasant, I can assure you," Giovanni said, looking over at the table. "My imprisonment at Dugan almost broke me."

"You were imprisoned at Château Dugan?" Logan asked. He remembered the video that Valerie had taken during her trip there. "What are your initials?"

"My full name is Giovanni Santino Rast," he said.

"GSR," Logan whispered. "Those were your initials carved into the walls of the dungeon."

"So you've seen them? You've visited Dugan?"

"No. Valerie has. She showed me a video she took of the dungeons. I remember seeing twelve marks on the wall, indicating the number of months you spent in the dungeon."

"A year is a long time," Mr. Perrot said.

Giovanni sneered. "No, the marks do not represent months. They represent years. I was held captive in the dungeons of Dugan for twelve long, painful years."

"Twelve *years?*" Mr. Perrot repeated in disbelief. "How could that be?"

"I asked myself that question many times," Giovanni said.

"Other than Fendral, who knew you were there?" Logan asked.

"Not many. Simon knew," Giovanni said. "And a man named Dario, who you say is dead. There was one other, but no more knew of Fendral's deed."

Mr. Perrot shook his head in awe. "A real-life Count of Monte Cristo."

"But without the bitterness," Logan said. "Hard to imagine. In the story, even the noble Edmund Dantes exacted revenge. People don't let go of the past easily."

Giovanni walked over to the table and handed the book back to Logan. "Simon is as crafty as his father. Do not underestimate him."

Logan nodded. Moments later, he received a message on his PCD from Valerie saying that she was waiting for him outside. It was time to confront Simon again.

63

You have been given the vessel of opportunity. What you choose to fill it with is up to you.

—THE CHRONICLES OF SATRAYA

WASHINGTON, D.C., 9:29 P.M. LOCAL TIME, MARCH 26, 2070

Logan received a message on his PCD as he and Valerie turned east onto M Street from Wisconsin Avenue. "It says the door is unlocked."

"How do they know where we are?" Valerie took a quick glance around to see if they were being followed. "They knew exactly where our plane was, too."

They came to the middle of the block and watched as a man and a woman across the street walked to the M Street Creamery and appeared disappointed to find that it was closed. A handwritten sign in the window stated that it would reopen the next day. M Street, usually filled with pedestrians during the day, was quiet at night. Only a motorcycle and a small red sedan were parked on the block. Valerie looked at the windows of the upper floors of the Creamery, but she couldn't see in, because some kind of paper or thick plastic was covering the windows. Logan tightened his backpack, as he and Valerie crossed the street.

Valerie readied her revolver and opened the door. A small bell attached to the top of the door jingled as she entered. Logan followed her inside. An old-fashioned ice cream and soda bar with ten red stools was to the left, bolted into its red and white checkered floor. The bell jingled again as Logan closed the door. The work area behind the bar contained blenders, mixers, cups, spoons, forks, and jars of candy toppings that would delight the pickiest of patrons. The red vinyl booths along the right side of the store had small jukebox music selectors on the tables. Sitting in one of the booths with his back to the door was a man with a black hood over his head and on top of that a straw boater. Suspecting that it was Mr. Newman, the store's owner, Logan quickly walked to the booth, and Valerie followed with her gun drawn. Logan removed the hat and then the hood. It was indeed Mr. Newman. His hands were bound behind him, and a piece of silver tape had been placed over his mouth. Logan removed the tape first and then released the binding on his hands.

"You need to get out of here," Logan said in a whisper, helping Mr. Newman from the booth and handing him his hat.

"Just go outside," Valerie added quietly, showing him her WCF badge. "Do not call the police. I will handle this."

Mr. Newman did as he was instructed, the bell on the door jingling as he left the Creamery.

"Up here," a deep voice called from the top of the stairs at the back of the shop.

Valerie and Logan slowly climbed the creaky staircase to the second floor. The space was in the process of being gutted. The walls were half demolished, and loose electrical wires hung from the ceiling. Broken pieces of drywall and molding lay on the floor.

"There you are," a familiar voice said from the northwest corner.

Logan looked through the gaps in the drywall and saw Simon standing between two windows covered by paint-stained plastic sheets. Logan and Valerie headed toward him, maneuvering around the mess on the floor and ducking through a partially collapsed doorway.

"Where are my children?"

"What?" Simon said. "No pleasantries?"

"No," Logan answered with a glare.

"I wouldn't play games with him right now," Valerie said. She pointed her gun at Simon, the red laser from her weapon striking his forehead. "He's not about to let you do any more harm to his family. And that goes for me, too."

"*More* harm?" Simon repeated. "There you go again, accusing me of killing the beloved Fords." He leaned against the wall, shaking his head as if exasperated by the suggestion. "Ms. Perrot, are you telling me you still haven't solved the murder of Logan's parents?"

"Don't deny it, Simon. We have proof that you were involved," Valerie said. "We found the letter addressed to you, sent from someone in New Chicago in 2065. We also found the pictures of Logan's parents that accompanied the letter. That's all the proof I need."

"Ah, so you did find my little hiding place at the Château," Simon said with a coy smile. "Now, you didn't keep any of the jewelry for yourself, did you?"

"Who wrote the letter?" Logan demanded.

"I suppose I'm going to have to just come out with it, seeing as the two of you are not very good at crime solving. The person who killed your parents was the man who secretly loved your mother since their days in the forest together. He despised your father from the moment he first met Camden and put a gun to his head." Simon waited for a response. "Does any of that help?"

"Are you telling me that a Forgotten One killed my parents?" Logan asked.

Simon *tsk*ed. Then he smiled. "Well, if I must spell everything out for you . . . He's tall and lanky, has stringy hair and beady little eyes. Oh, and he thinks everyone's sins are going to keep them from heaven's gates."

Logan's eyes widened. "You mean Randolph Fenquist? I don't believe you."

"You should," Simon said. "RJ was never to be trusted."

"Did you say RJ?" Logan asked.

"Yes. Randolph Jedidiah Fenquist. But don't tell him I told you. He doesn't like his middle name."

Logan and Valerie realized that Simon was telling the truth, as outlandish as it seemed. The letter from the person who had tracked down Camden and Cassandra was signed with the initials RJ, Randolph Jedidiah Fenquist, the leader of the Sentinel Coterie.

"Excellent!" Simon clapped his hands. "I can see by the looks on your faces that you finally believe me. See, I knew you could figure it out. In his defense, no one was supposed to get hurt that night. All Randolph was tasked to do was to get his hands on your father's copy of the *Chronicles*. You'll have to speak with him about what went wrong. All I know is that instead of receiving the books, which I was promised in exchange for a very handsome payment to the Coterie, I only received a bloodstained blue diary."

"My father's missing journal," Logan said.

"Yes, Camden's journal. I must admit that there are some very interesting entries in it. And, reluctantly, I have to give your father some credit for figuring out the mystery of the blank pages. Everything else he wrote is garbage, just drab writing. I don't care very much for his prose." Simon stepped away from the wall and straightened his shoulders. "Much better. I feel like a great weight has been lifted from me. Now that we've cleared the air and I've been able to help you put to rest the murder of your parents—"

"Put to rest!" Logan said, outraged. "How has anything been put to rest?"

"Have you not been listening to anything I've said? I did not kill your parents. Don't you consider that noteworthy information?"

Valerie shook her head. "You don't understand anything about human beings, do you?"

Simon shrugged. "I see that the two of you are determined to live in the past. Unfortunately, I can't help you with that. At least Nadine was willing to move on."

"Speaking of Nadine, where is she?" Valerie asked.

"Relaxing in the lap of luxury, where any beautiful woman belongs."

"And Catherine?"

Simon's eyes narrowed. "Well, she's not taking things as well. She had her heart set on cornering the energy market. And the two of you messed that up for her. You may want to steer clear of her for a little while."

"You can tell her that her island is gone, along with the energy device," Valerie said. "And the doctors are dead, too."

"As I told the two of you back on the island, I didn't care about the energy device. That was Catherine and Dario's misguided plan. But what I do care about are the books. So how about we get down to business?" Simon's tone turned serious. "Let's have a look at them. I'm sure your children are anxious to be with their father again."

Logan swung his backpack off his shoulder and unzipped it. He took out one of the three volumes of the *Chronicles* and held it up for Simon to see, then put it back in his backpack. "Now, where are Jordan and Jamie?"

"Kashta," Simon called out. From behind a wall emerged a tall, dark-skinned man. He was the one Logan and Valerie had seen in the projection at NovaCon Island and who had posed as a photographer on the beach. Logan's PCD made that strange chirp again, and he quickly shut it down. Kashta had Jordan, Jamie, and Ms. Sally in tow by a rope tied around their waists. All three of them had black hoods over their heads, just like Mr. Newman. Their hands were bound in front of them with plastic ties.

"You see, your children are fine and unharmed," Simon said. "As much as I would like to stay and kibitz with the two of you, I fear that I have some urgent business to attend to. Kashta, please give Mr. Ford his children and his domestic. And you, Logan, please give Kashta the books."

Kashta walked over to Logan and held out the end of the rope. Logan went to grab it, but Kashta pulled it back and raised his eyebrows. "Together," Kashta said, his voice deep and threatening. "The rope for the books."

Logan took out all three volumes and handed them to Kashta, who simultaneously gave Logan the rope. Almost immediately, there was an ear-splitting noise as the two windows on either side of Simon shattered, sending glass flying into the room. Two WCF agents stormed through feetfirst, rappelling from the roof. Logan grabbed his kids and Ms. Sally and pulled them close to him to protect them from the flying glass. Dressed in black jumpsuits and wearing black helmets, the WCF ghost team pointed their automatic rifles at Simon and Kashta. Three more members of the team stormed up the stairs.

"It's over, Simon," Valerie said, lowering her gun. "Nowhere to go now."

Kashta handed Simon the books and stood next to him as if nothing had happened.

Simon nonchalantly opened one of the volumes and flipped through the pages. "You know that I was never really a big fan of the philosophy in the *Chronicles*. But there are a few good quotes." He read one out loud. "*Nothing is ever what it seems to be. That is only because your expectations are anchored to your past. That is why the future is so hard to see.*" Yes, I like that one a great deal—"*nothing is ever what it seems to be.*" Without looking up and continuing to turn the pages, he said, "Don't you want to see how your children are doing?"

Valerie picked up on the implication and quickly removed the black hoods from their heads. "It's not them," she said. Logan and Valerie were looking at the faces of a boy and girl they had never seen before.

"Where are all the cameras?" the girl asked, pointing at Kashta. "He promised that we could sit in the director's chair."

Simon laughed as he closed the book and handed it to Kashta.

"Where are they, Simon?" Logan shouted.

"Did you really think that I would be so stupid?" He directed his question at Valerie. "Did you think for one second that I trusted your word about coming alone? Women. Your gender always thinks you have everything under control."

"The children, Simon!" Logan said again.

Valerie gently guided the kids to her right, handing them over to one of the WCF agents, who escorted them down the stairs.

"Your children are safe for now," Simon told Logan, as Kashta took out his PCD. "We are going to do this my way. Ms. Perrot, you are first going to dismiss all of your henchmen, starting with these four. You will then clear the street outside of any other agents you brought with you. Then Kashta and I are going to leave. If I see any agents following us, the children are going to die. If Kashta sees any agents, the children are going to die. If I believe that we are being followed for any reason whatsoever, the children are going to die. Do you remember the neuro devices that were attached to their heads?" Kashta activated his PCD and displayed an image of Jordan, Jamie, and Ms. Sally. They were all sitting on a mattress on the floor of a nondescript room, the same one they'd been in when Logan had last seen a projection of them on NovaCon Island. The neuro devices were still attached to their temples. "The next move is yours, Ms. Perrot."

Valerie motioned for the remaining agents to exit. She placed a call on her PCD. "Luke, get everyone to stand down and back away. This operation is over."

"Very good. Your mother would have been very proud of you." Simon gloated. "You know, Andrea bedded a lot of men in her day. Robert was not the only one. In fact, I think my father had a few tumbles in the hay with her during their time on the Council. Makes you wonder, doesn't it?"

"Enough, Simon," Logan said. "You have what you came for; now, tell me where my children are."

"Do you still have that mosaic your mother made?" Simon asked him. "You know, the abstract one that is really wide and only about yay tall?" Simon used his hands to describe the dimensions.

"What does that have to do with any of this?" Logan asked.

"It has everything to do with this," Simon said. "Now that your mother and father are gone, I might be the only person alive who knows what that mosaic means."

"How could you know?" Logan asked. "There is no way my mother would have told you. She didn't even complete the mosaic until years after the Council splintered and you and Fendral were long gone."

"But your father figured it out," Simon said. "And as we both know, Camden wrote everything down."

"His journal," Logan said in a low voice.

The sound of screeching car wheels came from outside. Simon smiled. "Ah, my ride has arrived." He took a folded piece of paper out of his pocket and started past Logan and Valerie toward the stairs. "I know you're fond of riddles, so here's one I know your children will want you to solve." He tossed the paper onto the floor by Logan's feet. "By the time you do, we will be long gone."

*   *   *

Simon hopped into the backseat of the black vehicle that had pulled up in front of the M Street Creamery. Kashta took a seat in the front, and the car sped away. A small red sedan, which had been parked across the street, pulled out of its spot and followed the black SUV as it turned left onto Wisconsin Avenue.

64

Success and failure walk down the same garden path
inextricably entwined. One cannot exist without the other.

—THE CHRONICLES OF SATRAYA

"I think you would enjoy coming with us," Simon said. Kashta stood
next to him, carrying a briefcase.

"Simon's right," Catherine added. "We could use a person of your
prowess."

"You mean someone who knows how to deceive?" Nadine asked.

"No," Simon said. "Someone who knows how to deceive convinc-
ingly."

Nadine smiled.

After getting the books from Logan, Simon and Kashta had arrived
at a private jet terminal at Dulles International Airport. Inside hangar
10A, they had joined Catherine and Nadine. Two jets, fueled and ready
for takeoff, were parked outside the brightly lit hangar.

Simon took the briefcase from Kashta and handed it to Nadine.
"Payment for helping me get the books," he said. "I could not have
done it without Logan's kids."

"Have the children been returned to Logan?" Nadine asked.

"I needed to ensure our safe departure," Simon answered indirectly. "The fact that the WCF is not here tells me that he is still looking for them."

"You've made a king's ransom off of us," Catherine said to Nadine. "What are you going to do with all those EBBs?"

"Live," Nadine said. "Something that Madu didn't know how to do."

"If you change your mind about joining us," Simon said, "you know how to contact us."

Just then, a small red sedan sped into the hangar and came to a screeching halt. Kashta stepped in front of Simon and drew a polished silver weapon. The door to the car opened. It was Madu.

"Nadine!" he called. "What have you done?"

"The only thing I could," Nadine replied.

Kashta pointed his gun at him. Madu did not stop. He continued until he stood just before Nadine.

"Kashta," Simon said, "put your weapon down. Can't you see that these two are about to have a tender moment?"

Madu ignored him, his eyes on his wife. "Why didn't you come to me first? It didn't have to be this way. Many people have died because of us."

"I did go to you," Nadine said, showing no remorse. "Many times over the years. You kept telling me to be patient, that money would come, a better life would come, but it never did."

"I took action," Madu said. "I accepted the proposition from Rigel to—"

"Rigel," Simon interrupted, shaking his head. "Right there is your problem, Madu. Rigel Wright is a cheap bastard. How much did he pay you for all your years of work?"

"It wasn't about the money," Madu said softly.

"It's always about money," Simon countered. "And don't fool yourself for one moment. Rigel knows that, too. He lets everyone do the work, while he takes the credit. Have you ever stopped and looked around to see who sets the moral compass that humanity lives by? The very people who live contrary to the morals they spout. I guarantee that it was a king who first said there was more to life than money. I guarantee that the greatest liar in the world was the first to advise people to always tell the truth. You see, Madu, in order for a person to retain his power, he needs to make sure that no one else goes after it. And the best way to do that is to tell people it's better to do something different and not to follow. Your lovely wife finally figured that out."

Madu looked at Simon, then at Nadine. "I hope they compensated you well for all that you did for them, Nadine."

"They did," she answered softly. "They were very generous."

"They've corrupted you," Madu said, shaking his head, still in denial. He grabbed Nadine by the arm, but she pulled away.

"It's over, Madu," Nadine said. "I am not going back to our old life. I'm not going back to promises that only eternity can fulfill."

Kashta leaned over and whispered something into Simon's ear. "Yes, I'm sorry to break up our little party, but I have to leave," Simon said. "Catherine, come along. Nadine, I hope to see you again. Madu, maybe Rigel can find you a morally acceptable project that will help consume the rest of your existence." Simon pointed to one of the jets, addressing Nadine next. "As promised, that jet over there will take you wherever you wish to go."

Madu and Nadine watched as Simon, Catherine, and Kashta boarded the plane. Within moments, the aircraft door closed, and the plane taxied away.

"How much did they pay you?" Madu asked finally, breaking the silence.

"Ten million Universal Credits," Nadine answered.

Madu nodded. "That's a lot of money. Where do you think you will go now?" The engines of Simon's jet revved as the plane tore down the runway.

"Not sure," Nadine said. "Maybe Indonesia—I hear there's a pyramid there." Nadine grabbed Madu's hand. "You could still come with me."

Madu watched the plane take off. "What about what we have done? What about the people we placed in harm's way?"

"After selling Dario and Catherine the original plans," Nadine explained, "I thought that was the end of it. When they contacted me again because the design didn't work, I had no choice. They would have wanted more than just their money back. I did what we had to do to save both of us. Maybe one day, we will be able to compensate the world for our actions. Wasn't it you, my love, who taught everyone that the King's Gambit is a risky move?" Nadine pressed her husband's hand tighter. "Wasn't it you who taught that it is necessary to sacrifice pawns in order to advance? Did we not sacrifice much to see a free Egypt all those years ago?"

Madu stared into his wife's eyes for a long moment. "You're right," he said finally. "You've always been right."

Nadine smiled. The two of them walked to the remaining jet.

"They offered me a spot on the Council of Satraya, you know."

"Really? Well, that would have been interesting."

Madu escorted Nadine up the stairway to the jet.

65

Do not take on another person's need for redemption.
That is a battle he alone must fight.

—THE CHRONICLES OF SATRAYA

WASHINGTON, D.C., 10:32 P.M. LOCAL TIME, MARCH 26, 2070

"Read that journal entry again," Valerie said.

Logan unfolded the page that Simon had torn from Camden's journal and read it out loud. He and Valerie had returned to the Council of Satraya offices and now stood in the drawing room in front of his mother's abstract mosaic. Mr. Perrot, who had remained at the offices, was with them.

May 16, 2040

Today was a fun day. I finally figured out Cassandra's abstract mosaic. The one that looks like an orange sliced down the center. Robert and I have been trying to decipher it for years. During my morning walk, I passed Cloud Gate at the old Millennium Park. I've walked past that odd stainless-steel sculpture a thousand times. But this time, something clicked, and the secret to Cassandra's mosaic dawned on me. I rushed home and tested my theory, giving Cassandra my interpretation at breakfast. She asked why it had taken me so long to figure it out and made me promise not to tell Robert. She wants him to have the pleasure of figuring it out himself. I'm not going to even hint that I solved it. If he knows that I know, he won't let it go until I tell him.

"So Camden *did* know the answer," Mr. Perrot said, shaking his head. "He never even gave me a clue."

Logan continued to read.

After Cassandra told me how she did it, I had to try it myself. It's a lot harder than you think. After a bunch of failed attempts, I finally got it right and drew my first multifaceted triad.

Logan flipped the page around so everyone could see what his father had drawn.

"That doesn't look much like a triad or even a triangle, for that matter," Mr. Perrot said. "But then again, Camden wasn't much of an artist—origami was his strong suit."

Logan continued reading.

I have to give Cassandra a lot of credit. It couldn't have been easy creating a mosaic of the . . . in Washington, D.C. Trying to draw a cascade of triangles was hard enough. To do what she did in a mosaic must have been an incredible challenge.

Cassandra told me that her inspiration came after she had learned a thing or two about Reflecting from Deya. Much to my chagrin, Deya figured out Cassandra's mosaic in less than an hour. I am not surprised. Deya has clearly mastered working with reflective surfaces.

"I think you might have skipped a key word in there," Mr. Perrot said.

"No," Logan said, handing him the piece of paper. "The word has been blotted out. Simon had no intention of making this easy."

"Well, we know one thing," Valerie said. "This mosaic is pointing to a place here in Washington. Simon is holding the kids somewhere in the city." She stared at Cassandra's artwork sitting on the easel.

"That mosaic has always looked like a broken wooden wheel to me," Logan said.

"I think it looks like a half-eaten doughnut," Valerie said, "or a pizza with a hole at the center."

"My mother mentioned it in one of her recordings," Logan said, trying to recall exactly what he had heard. "She said her inspiration came from what Deya had taught her about Reflecting and used the term *anamorphic nature of Reflecting*."

"That conforms with what your father wrote in this journal entry," Valerie said.

"There is a lesson in the *Chronicles* that is very similar to that statement," a familiar voice said. Logan turned and saw Giovanni Rast standing in the doorway. "Pardon my interruption. Did you retrieve your children?"

"No," Logan said. "We were tricked."

"I do know how that goes," Giovanni said. "And the books?"

"Simon has them," Logan said.

Valerie was not as cordial with Giovanni, remembering only his appearance at the commemoration. "Is Randolph Fenquist still with you?"

Logan was also interested in Fenquist's whereabouts after what Simon had told them.

"No," Giovanni replied. "He never returned after he left earlier today. He has a peculiar way of coming and going."

Logan turned his attention back to the mosaic. "Simon said that my mother's mosaic points to where he is holding my children captive."

"And this passage from Camden's journal holds the key to solving the mystery," Mr. Perrot added, handing the journal page to Giovanni, who took a moment to read it.

"You said there was something in the *Chronicles* similar to what my mother said in one of her recordings?" Logan asked.

"While I don't recall the exact use of the word *anamorphic*, there is a lesson that speaks to the pliable nature of our reality. The lesson states that if you learn to see things from a variety of perspectives, the world around you will suddenly bend to meet that point of view. Perhaps your mother was suggesting that people look at this painting from another vantage point. If I remember correctly from my days as a schoolteacher, the word *anamorphic* means 'intentional distortion.' I believe that it is derived from the Latin word *anamorphosis*."

"Which is an art form," Logan said, a gleam of hope entering his eyes.

"That is correct," Giovanni said, walking over to Cassandra's mosaic.

"What is anamorphosis?" Valerie asked.

"Anamorphic art involves a drawing or painting that requires the observer to look at it from a distinct perspective." Logan took out his PCD and began searching. Within a few moments, he projected the image of a painting. "This is a famous painting titled *The Ambassadors* that was done by the German artist Hans Holbein." The projection showed a depiction of two aristocratic-looking men standing next to a double shelf. Among the items on the shelves were a globe of the world, an open music book, and a quadrant. Logan pointed to the lower middle part of the painting. "Do you see this strange distorted shape at the bottom here?"

"Yes," Mr. Perrot said, taking a closer look. "It looks like a large ragged cloth lying on the floor."

"Now, don't move," Logan said, as he rotated the image so that Mr. Perrot was now looking at the painting from the side. "Can you make out what it is now?"

"Unbelievable," Mr. Perrot said, astonished.

Valerie took a look for herself. "From this vantage point, it is a perfect image of a human skull."

"That is anamorphic art," Logan said.

"Camden said that Cassandra's inspiration came after she learned a thing or two about Reflecting, and Camden also wrote that Deya was a master of reflective surfaces," Mr. Perrot said. "That would lead me to believe that the answer to this lies somewhere—"

"In a mirror," Logan said, finishing Mr. Perrot's statement. "Of course." Logan quickly brought up another projection.

"That looks similar to the half-circle in your mother's mosaic," Valerie said. "And just as abstract."

"This is another form of art called cylindrical mirror anamorphosis. Notice how this image seems nonsensical. Now, watch what happens when a reflective cylinder is placed at the center of this image." Logan brought up another image of a tube that had a mirrored surface. "Look at what is reflected on the surface of the cylinder."

"It's the face of a man," Giovanni said. "What a wonderful way to hide a message."

Logan nodded. "Could I see my father's journal entry again, please?"

Giovanni handed it to Logan, who used his PCD to take a picture of the drawing his father had doodled on it. Logan then used his PCD to search for an image of the mirrored cylinder. After a few moments of manipulation, he projected an image.

"Look at the reflection," Mr. Perrot said.

"There's the triad your father said he drew," Valerie said.

"What if my mother's mosaic is also anamorphic in nature?" Logan suggested.

"There's only one way to find out," Mr. Perrot said.

Logan repeated the same process with his mother's mosaic. Within minutes, he projected a new image.

"It looks like the tower of a castle," Valerie said.

"I've see this place recently," Giovanni said. "I believe I walked by it only yesterday. It's the tower of the Smithsonian Museum."

Valerie placed a call on her PCD.

66

A master never forgives. Such an idea would presuppose that a
judgment existed in the first place.

—THE CHRONICLES OF SATRAYA

NEW CHICAGO, 1:30 P.M. LOCAL TIME, MARCH 28, 2070

"How long are we going to have to stay with Mom?" Jordan asked.

"Yeah, how long?" Jamie asked.

"I'm not going to lie to you," Logan said. "It could be a while. I
don't know how long, but I have to make sure it's safe for the two of
you to come back home."

He was speaking to his children via HoloPad from the art studio.
Valerie and Mr. Perrot stood in the doorway.

Jordan, Jamie, and Ms. Sally had indeed been held captive in the
tower of the Smithsonian Castle. After solving the puzzle of Cassandra's abstract mosaic, Logan, Valerie, and Mr. Perrot had rushed over
to the museum. A team of WCF agents had already arrived and started
searching the turret. It didn't take long for the agents to find them
locked in a room on the west side of the tower, dehydrated and hungry.
They were immediately taken to a WCF medical facility, where their
neuro implants were removed. The children and Ms. Sally were not able

to provide significant new information about their kidnapping. They all gave the same account of the events leading to their being locked away in the Smithsonian tower. A day after Logan and Valerie had left them at Valerie's apartment, guarded by WCF agents, they had heard a struggle in the hallway outside the apartment. The door had burst open, and two men had entered. The agents assigned to stand guard had been overtaken and lay unconscious in the hallway. One of the intruders had placed the neuro devices on their heads, while the other had bound their hands. The three of them had been forcibly led from the apartment, shoved into a black SUV, and taken to the Smithsonian tower, where they had been locked in a room. The two men had checked on them every hour for the next two days; after that, they hadn't come back.

After hearing their account, Logan decided that it was not safe to bring Jordan and Jamie back home with him to New Chicago, and he'd sent the two of them to Nevada to stay with their mother. Logan knew what he needed to do, and he was not going to risk the safety of his children while he did it. Logan had tried to persuade Ms. Sally to visit her sister in Cleveland, but she had refused and returned to New Chicago, where she had insisted on continuing to carry out her daily housekeeping duties for Logan.

"Are you going to catch the men who took us?" Jamie asked.

"If he doesn't, Valerie will," Jordan told his sister. Valerie smiled at Jordan's expression of confidence in her.

"Yes, I promise," Logan said. "We will get them." Logan heard his ex-wife's voice calling the children in the background. "You two have to go now. I love you, and I'll talk to you soon."

When the call ended, Valerie walked over to Logan and sat down in a chair beside him. "I'm not sure you should have made that promise to Jamie. We have no idea where Simon is or if he'll ever resurface."

"He'll come crawling out soon enough," Mr. Perrot said. "I'm certain of it."

"I don't think so," Valerie said. "He would be an idiot to show his face again. After what he pulled with NovaCon Island and the destruction he caused, Simon is on every wanted list around the world. He won't show. He has all four books now. Why would he take the risk?"

"It's *because* he has all the books that he will emerge," Logan said. "There is nothing standing between him and the veiled symbols now. You and I both heard what he alluded to on the island, that the power of the hidden symbols had somehow protected him from the flames of the pyre."

"And you believe that story?" Valerie asked. "There were thousands of other people there that day; we don't know exactly what happened as Simon fell into the pit. He might have grabbed onto somebody or caught the ledge and crawled away somehow. We don't know."

"I'm telling you," Logan said, "there's a power that surrounds those books and those symbols. I don't even want to think about what Simon will do if he begins to attain the powers promised by them."

"No, my dear, I have to agree with Logan," Mr. Perrot said. "Very few who attain great power keep it to themselves. They want to bare it to the world so that they can witness firsthand the effects of their power. Simon will be no different. If he is truly beginning to unlock the hidden symbols, he is going to want to see what he can do with them. This is far from over."

"Any news of Fenquist?" Logan asked Valerie.

"Not yet," she replied. "The good news is that with some of the evidence we found at Château Dugan, the WCF is considering reopening your mother and father's murder case."

Logan unzipped his backpack and took out the plastic box containing Deya's mirror, the Manas Mantr candle, and his mother's recordings. "There still may be more to learn about Fenquist and the others."

Mr. Perrot nodded.

"Has Sylvia figured out anything more about the standing wave she detected?" Logan asked.

"No," Valerie said. "She knows nothing more than that it started somewhere in southern England. Whoever or whatever it was, we need to be thankful. It gave us the opportunity we needed to shut down NovaCon."

Logan nodded, wondering if Mr. Quinn had anything to do with it. There was a long silence.

"Have you heard from Madu?" Valerie asked her father.

"Not a word," Mr. Perrot said. "It's been two days now."

"I wonder what happened to Nadine, too," Logan said. "What a tragic story."

Jasper suddenly entered Logan's office. "Hey, I think I figured out why your PCD's been making that strange noise." He walked over and showed Logan something displayed on his PCD's screen. "You got hijacked."

"What does that mean?" Logan asked. Valerie's interest was piqued, too.

"You see this?" Jasper pointed to a red indicator that was flashing on the PCD. "That red dot says that you got the Cheater Virus."

"What's the Cheater Virus?" Valerie asked.

"You know, when you have a boyfriend, girlfriend, husband, wife you think is cheating on you. You infect their PCD with this virus, and you can track every move they make. Sometimes the virus can cause your phone to act up and do crazy things."

Logan turned to give Valerie a look. "Don't look at me," she said. "I know you wouldn't dare cheat on me." She jokingly pulled back her jacket, revealing her holstered gun.

Logan laughed. "How'd it get on there?"

"You had to have allowed someone to transfer it to your PCD," Jasper explained. "I read that most of the infections happen when a person temporarily unlocks his phone to receive a video or—"

"A photograph," Logan said, putting it together. He looked at Valerie. "Simon's bodyguard Kashta, that photographer. I unlocked my phone when he transferred the photos he took of us in Mexico."

"That'll do it," Jasper said. "Mystery solved. Just hit that little button right there, and you will no longer be a cheating spouse."

"That's how they knew what time the WCF plane was going to land," Valerie said. "And when we were approaching the Creamery. He's been tracking you the whole time."

"I need to get rid of this thing," Logan said. He was about to press the button when Valerie grabbed his hand.

"I don't know much about this virus," she said. "But if they've been tracking your signal, I wonder if we could track theirs."

67

*The sun does not pause for the passing of any soul, nor does
the moon halt its forever journey through the night sky.
They continue their eternal tasks, awaiting your assured return
so that they might once again awaken you from slumber and
cradle you to sleep when dreaminess calls.*

—THE CHRONICLES OF SATRAYA

PEEL CASTLE, ISLE OF MAN, 7:12 P.M. LOCAL TIME, MARCH 29, 2070

The wind whipped around the high spire of Peel Castle, where Sebastian stood with his constant companion. Bukya had taken up his usual position on the ledge that faced the unruly ocean. The sun was starting to kiss the horizon, and the sky anticipated the upcoming explosion of hues. The twenty-five-meter yacht named *Everlasting* was anchored two hundred meters offshore. From time to time, moody clouds would float by, shedding mist and rain. Bukya whined as he looked down upon the solitary man standing on a large rock on the beach. Wave after wave rolled in, crashing all around him. A large blue balloon floated next to him, its string anchored to a stone near his feet. The balloon swayed back and forth as the wind tempted it into flight.

"Lawrence is mourning, my friend," Sebastian said, placing his hand on Bukya's back. "The loss of Anita has devastated him. I fear it will take a while for him to return." Sebastian turned and looked at the ruins of the cathedral. "You can still hear Anita's music if you listen carefully." He hummed a few notes of the last melody he had heard her play. Bukya let out a whimper.

Anita Kinelot had not survived the storm that hit Stonehenge. The large electrical arc that struck its center had claimed her life and the lives of many others who had been nearby.

The thick wooden door leading to the spire opened, and Halima walked out onto the rooftop with Britney. The two of them were holdings hands. Both were dressed in black and had just returned from a memorial service for Anita at the Isle of Man University. Sebastian walked over to Britney and gave her a long and heart-felt embrace. "How was the memorial?"

"Wonderful," Britney said, wiping tears from her eyes. "All our friends were there and many of our professors. I miss her terribly." As hard as Britney tried, she couldn't stop the flow of tears.

"She'll be back. Just like my mother and father," Halima said, giving Britney a good, long squeeze around her waist. "Everyone comes back. Don't they, Mr. Quinn?"

"Yes, they do," Sebastian said warmly.

"I don't know how to feel about any of this," Britney said. "I don't know if I'm angry because all of this could have been avoided or inspired because my best friend committed such an unselfish act and helped save a few lives."

"She did more than save just a few lives," Sebastian said. "Because of her, others were given the time to act and prevent a worldwide catastrophe. Anita made a great sacrifice, one that the world may never know about."

Britney nodded, choking back more tears. "I know that Anita would have wanted you to have this." She handed Sebastian Anita's blue book bag. He looked inside and took out Sumsari's resonator and tuning fork.

"Thank you," Sebastian said. "We will keep this safe."

"You seem so at peace after everything that's happened," Britney said. "It's as if you understand why any of this, why all of this, happened. But tell me, how do you deal with the fact that you will never see someone you love again?"

Sebastian could see the pain that Britney was dealing with. "What if you received a message on your PCD from the universe," he postulated, "and in the message, the universe told you that Anita was moments away from returning as a baby girl named Marina Abner of Yorkshire Park. That she would have the opportunity to play her violin again, this time under the tutelage of a great instructor. What if you were assured that she would have doting parents? That she would have a big brother and an older sister who would protect her and look out for her? What if you were told that she would have three dogs and a wandering white cat that would lead her into all kinds of mischief?"

"What happens when she grows up?" Halima asked, eager to know the end of the story. "Does she get married? Does she have kids? What does she do?"

"Only Marina would know how her story will end," Sebastian replied. "But what if the universe sent you such a message?" he asked Britney again. "How would you feel?"

"Still sad that she wasn't with me," Britney replied. After a moment, a cautious smile came to her face. "It is a pleasant thought, though, to know that she is back somewhere. Anita talked about stuff like that all the time, but I didn't pay much attention. I should have." Britney looked at Sebastian, her eyes still wet. The wind kicked up on the spire. "Will I get to meet her? This Marina Abner of Yorkshire?"

"Yes, do we get to meet her?" Halima asked.

"The entanglement of souls brings us face-to-face with friends and enemies alike," Sebastian said. "In unexpected moments and in unexpected ways."

Britney nodded. "I'll take that as a yes."

Something caught Halima's eye. She walked over to the edge of the spire. "Mr. Quinn, who is that woman walking over to Mr. Lawrence?"

Sebastian and Britney joined Halima. They all watched as a woman with long blond hair and dressed in white slowly made her way over some stones toward Lawrence. "I've seen her before," Britney said, continuing to watch her. "She was the woman you spoke to at Salisbury Cathedral when the other people left."

"Who is she?" Halima asked.

"Her name is Razia Ki Rani," Sebastian said.

"She's beautiful," Halima said. "Is she going to stay long?"

"I don't know," Sebastian said. "Her arrival was unexpected."

"Well, she brought a big suitcase with her." Halima pointed to a large brown trunk that had been left on the path near the castle wall.

Two loud horn blasts came from the *Everlasting.*

"It's time!" Halima said.

"Time for what?" Britney asked.

"To set Anita free," Halima replied. "Her ashes are in that blue balloon next to Mr. Lawrence."

The three of them watched as Razia kissed Lawrence on the cheek and exchanged a warm embrace with him. She then made her way back to shore, where she turned and looked at Lawrence with the ocean in front of him.

Sebastian closed his eyes. The wind suddenly calmed. Everything became eerily quiet. The sun had dipped farther into the horizon, and a stunning rose-colored hue filled the sky. "Journey on, Master Anita!" Sebastian shouted, as if calling to the heavens. "May love be your guide and grace your companion."

From down below, Razia's melodic voice could be heard. She repeated the same phrase. Lawrence followed in kind. "Journey on, my daughter. May love be your guide and grace your companion." Lawrence released the balloon, and Bukya let out a series of barks.

Sebastian opened his eyes as the blue balloon rose and floated over the ocean. After a few moments of ascension, a red flare shot up from the deck of the *Everlasting* and streaked into the sky. It struck the balloon, bursting it into flames and allowing Anita's ashes to be carried by the gusty wind, which had suddenly returned. Sebastian whispered the Farewell Axiom of the Guardians again.

Britney wiped more tears from her eyes, deeply touched. "I think I'll go home and ride Biscuit around the glen. There's a tree there that Anita and I liked to climb. I'll bring my PCD with me and wait for that message from the universe," she said, smiling.

Sebastian gave Britney a slight bow. "That sounds like a magnificent idea. But before you depart, I have a little something for you." He walked over to a small table, picked up a leather-bound journal, and held it out to Britney. "This is Anita's story. It is the tale that she told so beautifully in song but struggled to put into words. I know you have often wondered how Anita came to be with us here at Peel Castle." Britney took the book and looked at the opening page, written in Anita's handwriting. "After reading this, that question, and others, will be answered."

"Thank you, Mr. Quinn," Britney said. "Anita so admired all of you. I now see why."

Sebastian bowed again and said, "All I ask is that after you have read it, you bring it back to us here and place it on one of the shelves in the Alexandria Room. Hypatia will ensure that Anita's story will never be forgotten."

"You have my promise," Britney said, and she gave Halima and Sebastian a final hug good-bye, then left through the heavy wooden door.

Sebastian and Halima watched the *Everlasting* make its way back to the dock. They watched the sun set deeper into the horizon.

"What happened to the archer in the story you told Anita and me in the Arcis Chamber?" Halima asked, looking up at Sebastian. "Did his arrow make it? Did he marry the princess and live happily ever after?"

"That is a question only each of us can answer for ourselves," Sebastian replied. "The target above the spinning wheel represents the things we would like to have in our lives. The question is, are we willing to look past all our distractions to attain them? Do you remember what the goal was the day I told you the story?"

"To look into the Jaladarz," Halima said. "We were supposed to lose ourselves in our reflections."

"And did you?"

"No."

"Why?"

"I wanted to hear the end of the story," Halima innocently replied.

Sebastian smiled. "Yes, you wanted to hear the end of the story, whose moral is to get beyond the distractions and stay focused on your task."

Halima looked confused as she tried to understand what Sebastian had just told her. He was about to continue his explanation when Halima's face lit up with realization. "The story is both the lesson and the distraction," she said. "As it is with anything that comes between us and our task."

"Yes," Sebastian said. "To know the deeper essence of anything, everything must be put aside, no matter how enticing, provoking, or distracting that *everything* is. That is singularity of mind—that is singularity of purpose."

Sebastian and Halima looked down from the spire and saw that Lawrence and Razia were each holding one end of the large brown trunk and making their way along the path to the castle.

"Razia does not do things idly," Sebastian said. "Should we go and greet our house guest?"

Halima nodded eagerly.

68

Remember always, you are loved.

—THE CHRONICLES OF SATRAYA

GORNERGRAT, SWITZERLAND, 11:00 A.M. LOCAL TIME, MARCH 30, 2070

Simon sat at his twin pedestal desk and stared intently at the blank page of the last volume of the set of the *Chronicles* that he had taken from Logan. The final volumes of the three other sets also lay open to their last pages in front of him. The curtains behind him had been pulled shut, preventing any light from entering through the tall picture windows. Two lit candles were positioned directly in front of the open books, and the silver box containing the remaining volumes sat on a shelf nearby. Simon was after the final symbol, the symbol Camden had hypothesized would bring immortality to anyone who gazed upon its complete form.

Camden had written in his journal that it had been divided among the four copies of the *Chronicles* for safekeeping. The only way someone would be able to piece together the entire icon was by processing all four books. Simon had been sitting and staring at the page for more than two hours. Any line or shape he glimpsed he would record on a notepad he kept by his right hand.

There was a knock on his door. "Not now," he said loudly. He attempted to regain his focus, but the knocking persisted. "Come," he said, frustrated by the intrusion.

Kashta entered the darkened office. "There is a gentleman here to see you. And I think you're going to want to meet him."

A man stepped around Kashta and entered the room. He was wearing a white winter jacket that fell past his knees and a pair of black snow boots.

"And who might you be?" Simon asked, unable to make out the man's features in the dim light.

"Someone who has never forgotten you," the man said.

While Kashta stood impassively by the door, Simon rose to his feet and pulled open the heavy curtains, allowing sunlight to fill the room. He turned back around and looked at the man again, recognizing him immediately this time.

"Giovanni Rast," Simon said. "Now, why in the world would you have expended so much energy to find me? I suppose that you have come to exact some sort of revenge for what my father did to you?"

"And what do you think he did to me?" Giovanni said, making himself at home by removing his coat and tossing it onto one of the two chairs in front of Simon's desk. A row of seven gold buttons decorated his blue shirt. "Perhaps what you did to me over twelve years in the dungeons of Dugan was far worse than the wrongdoings of your father."

Simon smiled. He walked to the front of his desk and sat against the edge. "I was a stupid teenager back then. Had I been older and wiser, I could have found better ways to make your life with us miserable." Giovanni remained silent, and Simon continued, "My mother never let me have a dog or any other pet, so you were the next best thing. How did you escape, anyway? My father always blamed me for that."

"You may not want to hear the answer to that question," Giovanni said. "There were many people living at Château Dugan who despised your father but gladly accepted his money."

Simon's expression turned serious. "Tell me," he demanded. "Was it Francisco, my parents' driver? How about Cedric or maybe even Floriana? Did one of them set you free out of pity?"

"No."

"Then who?" Simon's voice rose.

Giovanni paused, savoring the moment. "Your mother," he finally said. "It was your mother, Muriel."

Simon clenched his fists. "My mother never went into the dungeons. She was too busy spending my father's money and gallivanting around the world to have cared about what was happening at Dugan."

"Muriel knew more than you thought," Giovanni said, "and she was far wiser than you give her credit for. She came to the dungeons often after she caught wind of a visitor. She is the only reason I survived all those years and the reason I escaped. She told me about the well, and how it led to the dock in the lake, and how the lake could lead to my eventual freedom."

Simon just looked at him. "I should have Kashta kill you where you stand."

"Please, proceed," Giovanni said, raising his arms in surrender. "After you have experienced what I've been through and invited death to arrive into your life as often as I have, all fear of it goes away."

Simon held still a moment. "How did you find me?"

Giovanni lowered his arms and took his PCD out of his pocket. "Everyone always seems to forget the story of the Trojans and the Greeks. You should be wary of the things people give you." Giovanni pointed it around the room. It started to beep. He walked over to the shelf where the silver box containing the *Chronicles* sat. Kashta took a step forward and placed his hand in his coat pocket to ready his weapon. Simon gestured for Kashta to wait. Giovanni pulled one of the books from the metal container and brought it back over to Simon's desk. "This is one of the books you exchanged for Logan's children, isn't it?" Giovanni put his PCD away and started flipping through the pages. "I always loved this line." His eyes moved as if to scan a passage. After he was done, he peeled a thin clear piece of tape off the page and held it up for Simon to see. "This is my company's newest invention; it is called Tracking Tape. If you look closely at it, you can see the transmission circuitry; we are working to make that less visible. Stick this tape on anything, and you can track it anywhere it goes."

"That's better than the Cheater Virus," Kashta said.

"Yes, it is," Giovanni agreed, setting the book down on the desk. Then he went over and took a seat in the chair where his coat lay. "Imagine my surprise when I realized the books had returned to my home country of Switzerland."

"I still don't know why you have come here," Simon said. "Do you need me to invest in your corporation? Have you come to annoy me with stories of my mother? Perhaps you want to kill me or torture me, as I did you?"

"No, Simon. I want none of those things," Giovanni said, shaking his head slowly. "I have come to join forces with you."